THE SECOND
DUCHESS

THE SECOND
DUCHESS

ELIZABETH LOUPAS

NEW AMERICAN LIBRARY

NEW AMERICAN LIBRARY
Published by New American Library, a division of
Penguin Group (USA) Inc., 375 Hudson Street,
New York, New York 10014, USA
Penguin Group (Canada), 90 Eglinton Avenue East, Suite 700, Toronto,
Ontario M4P 2Y3, Canada (a division of Pearson Penguin Canada Inc.)
Penguin Books Ltd., 80 Strand, London WC2R 0RL, England
Penguin Ireland, 25 St. Stephen's Green, Dublin 2,
Ireland (a division of Penguin Books Ltd.)
Penguin Group (Australia), 250 Camberwell Road, Camberwell, Victoria 3124,
Australia (a division of Pearson Australia Group Pty. Ltd.)
Penguin Books India Pvt. Ltd., 11 Community Centre, Panchsheel Park,
New Delhi - 110 017, India
Penguin Group (NZ), 67 Apollo Drive, Rosedale, North Shore 0632,
New Zealand (a division of Pearson New Zealand Ltd.)
Penguin Books (South Africa) (Pty.) Ltd., 24 Sturdee Avenue,
Rosebank, Johannesburg 2196, South Africa

Penguin Books Ltd., Registered Offices:
80 Strand, London WC2R 0RL, England

First published by New American Library,
a division of Penguin Group (USA) Inc.

Copyright © Elizabeth Loupas, 2011
Illustrated map of Ferrara by Don Huff Design and Illustration (donhuff.com)
All rights reserved

 REGISTERED TRADEMARK—MARCA REGISTRADA

ISBN 978-1-61129-466-8

Set in Bembo
Designed by Alissa Amell

Printed in the United States of America

For Jim

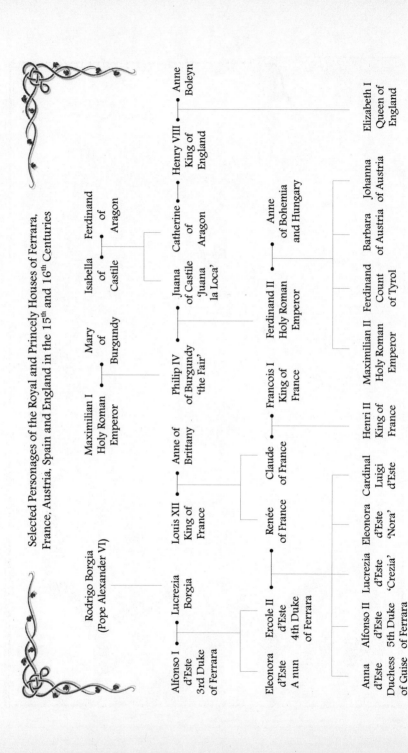

Selected Personages of the Royal and Princely Houses of Ferrara, France, Austria, Spain and England in the 15th and 16th Centuries

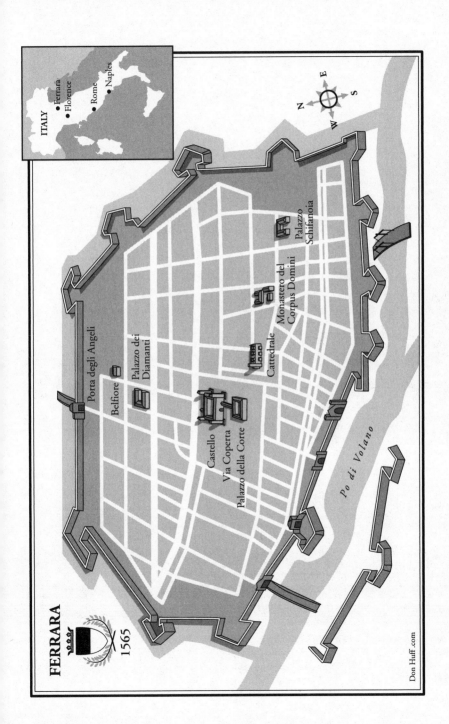

ITALY

• Ferrara
• Florence
• Rome
• Naples

FERRARA

1565

Porta degli Angeli

Belfiore

Palazzo dei
Diamanti

Castello
Via Coperta
Palazzo della Corte

Cattedrale

Monastero del
Corpus Domini

Palazzo
Schifanoia

Po di Volano

Don Huff .com

THE SECOND
DUCHESS

CHAPTER ONE

FERRARA

5 December 1565

"He murdered his first duchess with his own hands, they say," the Ferrarese hairdressing-woman whispered as she braided a string of pearls into my hair. "She was so young, so beautiful."

And I, Barbara of Austria, neither young nor beautiful, would be the duke's second duchess before the pale December sun set. What did the woman expect me to do, shriek and fall down in a faint? Jump up and swear I would not marry the Duke of Ferrara after all, but return straightaway to Innsbruck with my household and dowry and bride-goods down to the last box of silver pins? For all practical purposes I was married already, the contracts signed, the marriage-by-proxy performed. And truth be told, half-a-hundred people had already told me Alfonso d'Este had murdered his first wife.

I looked at my reflection in a hand glass. One loop of the pearls remained unfastened. "You forget yourself, *parruchiera*," I said.

The woman stepped back, a pointed braiding-bodkin gleaming

in her hand, and for one incredulous moment I thought she meant to stab me with it. "Do you think you will be safe here, Principessa, when she was not? The court of Ferrara is like a love-apple, beautiful and rosy-red and alluring to the senses, but poisonous, so poisonous—"

I put the glass down hard. "Enough. You are dismissed."

"The very pearls in your hair might be poisoned," she whispered, sibilant as a serpent. "That posset you have been drinking. Any piece of fruit, any flower you are offered. Your gloves. A flask of perfume. There are a thousand ways to envenom—"

"*Enough.* Madonna Lucrezia, ask the gentlemen-ushers to step onto the barge for a moment, if you please, and take this woman away."

The duke's elder sister raised her hand to the men waiting on the quay; her face was turned away from me and I could not see her expression. The men obeyed her gesture smartly and a scuffle ensued; there were a few cries of surprise and excitement from the ladies crowding the barge, and then the *parruchiera* was gone. My Austrian ladies, my lifelong friends, closed in around me. Lucrezia and Leonora d'Este whispered to each other behind their hands, their eyes glinting with things they knew and I did not. They had assembled my Ferrarese household, or so they told me, at the duke's command. Holy Virgin—had they deliberately chosen a madwoman to arrange my hair, so as to spoil my pleasure in my entrance into their city?

I picked up the glass. Fortunately, it was not broken. I could see them behind me, watching me, waiting to see what I would do.

"Sybille." I spoke to one of my own women with deliberate steadiness. "These pearls are too tightly braided. Would you loosen them, please?"

Sybille von Wittelsbach stepped forward at once. I watched in the glass and felt some of my distress evaporate as the arrangement of the pearls became less severe. Sybille often brushed and dressed my hair at home; her light, familiar touch calmed me further.

"I warned you, Bärbel," she said under her breath. "No foreigner can arrange your hair better than I. Did they think I meant to steal the pearls?"

"Of course not. It was the duke's wish for me to be dressed entirely by Ferrarese women before I entered the city. A symbol, nothing more."

"A fine symbol. I thought she meant to stab you with that bodkin."

As had I, although of course I did not say so. I closed my eyes, breathed deeply, and willed myself to be still. The magnificent ducal barge shifted and creaked beneath me, rocking gently on the waters of the Po di Volano. I could hear the rustle of a cold morning breeze in the imperial standard flying over me, and the faraway cries of cormorants and herons. I could smell the ancient river-scent, weeds and marshes and fish, and the milky sharp-sweet tang of the hot wine posset on the table in front of me.

The posset you have been drinking . . .

"Katharina," I said to another of my Austrian ladies without opening my eyes, "take the posset away, please."

I heard her skirt rustle. The scent of the posset disappeared.

It was my wedding day, and posset or no posset, bodkin or no bodkin, whispers or no whispers, I would marry the Duke of Ferrara. It was my chance to grasp the thing I wanted more than anything else in the world: an establishment of my own away from the Austrian imperial court of my brother Maximilian and my Spanish sister-in-law. It was also my chance to escape the convent at Hall where three of my sisters were already preparing to immure themselves.

Of course I did not delude myself that the Duke of Ferrara wanted me for my personal charms. His great rival, Duke Cosimo de' Medici, had betrothed his eldest son to my youngest sister, and if the Medici were to acquire an imperial bride, well, then, the Este must snap one up as well. That Duke Alfonso's ill-fated first wife had been Duke Cosimo's daughter simply added to the enmity between the two men and the titillation of the gossip. I did not care. With Alfonso d'Este came the magnificent court at Ferrara, the sun, the stars, the court of my own I had coveted for so long.

The court of Ferrara is like a love-apple, beautiful and rosy-red and alluring to the senses, but poisonous, so poisonous—

The ravings of a madwoman, nothing more. I opened my eyes. My hair was finished. Ferrara lay before me, wreathed in icy river mists, my demesne, my dream, my golden city of courtesies and delights. I would embrace it and marry its duke and become its duchess and reign over its court. And I would never look back.

ALL FERRARA MADE merry that day for my entry into the city, with my train of ambassadors and bishops, courtiers and crossbowmen, musicians and ladies and gentlemen from Austria, from Ferrara, and from all over Europe. My first impression, despite the pomp and clarions, was of narrow, twisting streets with buildings of stone and rose-colored brick close enough to touch on either side. The air was dusty and ripe with the smells of ordure and rotting fruit despite the cold. The bells for sext pealed from half-a-dozen directions at once, and the horses' hooves struck hollowly on the ancient, uneven paving stones.

Then, all of a sudden, we crossed into a different quarter, and it was as if we had entered another city entirely. Sunshine. Fresh, crisp air. Broad, straight avenues. Trees, gardens, canals, beautiful open squares in the classical mode—this, then, must be the famous new section of the city. No wonder the duke had wished me to pass through the old city first, so I might properly appreciate the new city's wonders. Crowds of townspeople surged around my litter, cheering and waving. I gestured to my gentlemen to scatter coins and favors. What did I feel? Excitement? Delight? Apprehension? I was not sure—first one, then another, then some unnameable confusion of them all.

I wanted to remember every detail. I imagined myself as if in a great painting: the old city and the new city of Ferrara, the people of Ferrara, and at the center of it all a woman, white-skinned, unveiled in an open litter, wrapped in an ermine mantle and with ripples of reddish-blond hair streaming down her back. It was the fashionable color, and I am sure many of the dark-haired Ferrarese ladies employed cosmetic means to achieve it, but mine was natural, the pure rosy-gold color of fresh apricots in sunlight.

Every eye would be taken by that shining spill of hair, by the pearls gleaming at my forehead and temples, by my scarlet satin gown embroidered and reembroidered with gold and pearls and rubies. Few would notice my long narrow face like a highbred filly's, or the unfortunately prominent lower lip that was the mark of my family. Few would realize I was twenty-six years old.

I could have made myself young and beautiful in my mind's-eye painting. I did not.

A girl-child stepped into the street before us, singing in a high, sweet voice, comparing me to some remarkable amalgam of Saint Barbara, Lavinia the wife of Aeneas, and Vesta the Roman goddess of the hearth. When she finished her song, she came forward, curtsied, and offered me a sheaf of magnificent out-of-season flowers, clearly from the duke's forcing-houses—roses and lilies and lavender and thyme. Their scents were dizzyingly sweet in the clear December air.

Any piece of fruit, any flower you are offered . . .

I took the flowers from the child, gave her back one perfect pink rose, and kissed her on either cheek, much to the delight of the crowd. Neither she nor I fell over dead, thanks be to God. The procession passed on to the heart of the city—the four looming red-brick towers of the Castello di San Michele, the centuries-old fortress of the Este.

TWO MEN AWAITED me on the far side of the Castello's famous moat, each with his own household and retinue. Although they were somewhat alike in looks, it was easy for me to tell them apart, even at a distance. One of them, of course, was the Duke of Ferrara himself, in purple velvet so dark it looked almost black, while the other, shorter man wore the scarlet of a prince of the church. This cardinal had to be Luigi d'Este, the duke's younger brother. With the duke's two unmarried sisters immediately behind me in the procession, I was surrounded by the Este, and the family in Ferrara was complete.

The duke I had met before, in the summer, in Innsbruck. He had courted me—what a mockery! Courted!—in a series of stiff, meaningless meetings, because the contracts were already signed, the dowry agreed upon, the bridal gifts proposed and accepted. The peculiar thing about the whole business was that had I not heard the blood-chilling whispers about the Duke of Ferrara murdering his first wife, I would not have disliked him. He was proud and vainglorious, true, and immoderately attentive to detail; all in all he gave me an uneasy impression of a glittering surface, like a calm sea, with ferocious serpents and dragons swimming in ritualized patterns beneath. But at the same time he was intelligent and cultured, a genuine lover of music and art, athletic, well-dressed, and cleanly in his personal habits. I would have to live with him, and for that matter bed with him; from what I could guess it would not be too unpleasant. He appeared to have much the same reaction to me. If anything, he seemed pleased I was not a lovely, alluring girl of fourteen—but then his first wife, of whom no one spoke, had been a lovely, alluring girl of fourteen. So perhaps I provided a refreshing contrast.

The procession came to a halt at the great gate of the Castello. I felt cold . . . hot . . . light-headed . . . resolute. I put my ermine mantle aside, and my master of horse assisted me to alight from the litter; the duke's sisters and my Austrian ladies formed themselves into ranks of precedence behind me. I stood very straight. The duke stepped forward and bowed with precise formality.

"Welcome to Ferrara, Principessa," he said in his deep, rather cold voice. He had dark eyes, swarthy skin, black hair cut short in the current Italianate fashion, a close-cropped dark beard along the line of his jaw. His height was slightly more than my own; the true shapes of his shoulders and upper body were lost in the padding and slashing and pleating of his skirted coat and furred overgown, but his legs in their tight hose were the fine, sinewy legs of an athlete.

He looked the same, yet he was not the same. Here in his own city, backed by the great fortress of his ancestors, his blood gave him power I had not fathomed in the salons of the Hofburg: the ancient princely blood of the Este, the royal Valois blood of his mother, the ruthless Borgia blood of his grandmother. My own blood responded. I sank into a curtsy, my gemmed scarlet skirts rustling and flowering out over the dust of the paving stones. I made it a point to be careless with them, as if to say, *What is silk, what are jewels, to ones such as you and I?* Then I straightened and placed my gloved hand upon his.

"Thank you, my lord. I bring you my brother the emperor's greetings and goodwill, as well as my own person and the first portion of my dowry, in token of his lasting friendship."

"Let us not speak of dowries or policy today." His face was an unbroken surface that gave no hint of what was concealed beneath. "May I present my own brother, Luigi, the cardinal-deacon of Saint Lucia Septizonio, archbishop of Auch, and bishop emeritus of Ferrara? He will bless our union and offer the Mass."

Undaunted by the weight of his ecclesiastical offices, Luigi d'Este bowed and held out his hand, his ring of office heavy and glowing upon his index finger. His resemblance to his brother was in his bearing more than in his features; he was clean-shaven and his coloring was somewhat fairer, his eyes more hazel, his hair more brown than black.

I withdrew my hand from the duke's and made another curtsy, a fraction less deep but with my head bowed. It caught to a nicety,

I thought, the lesser respect due my husband's younger brother, and at the same time the greater respect due a prince of the church.

"My Lord Cardinal." I touched my lips to his ring.

"My daughter." He seemed to think something was an excellent joke—probably the fact that he was all of one year older than I. "Welcome to Ferrara."

"Thank you, Your Eminence."

He lifted his hand and sketched the sign of the cross over me, then over his brother. The duke bowed his head briefly, then returned his attention to me; his hand was now resting on the hilt of a very fine dagger at his belt. Its design was unusual, but I would not have noticed it in particular if it had not been for the way he stroked his thumb over the damascened pattern, as if it were speaking to him in some way no one but he could discern.

"Your dress and jewels please me," he said. "Crezia and Nora chose your tiring-women well."

Particularly the madwoman they selected to braid pearls into my hair, I thought. Aloud I said, "I am pleased also. Although perhaps I will make one or two changes once I am settled."

"Make what changes you wish. Have a complete inventory made of your costume, if you please, before the end of the day. I desire to have you painted as a bride."

"Yes, my lord."

With great formality he handed me back into my litter for the procession to the cathedral. The duke's sisters took their places again; the cardinal's servants led forward a white mule saddled in scarlet and gold and shod in silver, and placed a gilded stool for the cardinal to mount. The duke needed no such assistance to mount a white Andalusian stallion, trapped in blue and white and embroidered with the eagles and fleurs-de-lis of the Este, and the stylized flame that was his own personal device. He took control of the animal with one hand on the reins; with the other he acknowledged the cheers of his people. We moved forward; behind us a swarm of lackeys in ducal livery began throwing gold and silver coins to all parts of the crowd.

At the cathedral door we were married again, this time without proxies. Afterward we passed under a magnificent bas-relief of the Universal Judgment and into the nave for the nuptial Mass. *Jacta alea est*, Caesar said when he crossed the Rubicon—the die is cast. I also had cast my die, and for good fortune or ill, I was now the second Duchess of Ferrara.

As I stepped into my litter for the procession back to the Castello, Sybille murmured into my ear that the Ferrarese *parruchiera*, with her mad whispers of love-apples and poisons, had escaped from the duke's guards and disappeared into the alleyways of the old city.

I SEE THEM, kneeling at the altar rail, looking chaste as two angels. How dare he? I hate her. I never loved Alfonso, but I hate the emperor's long-faced sister anyway, for taking my place.

My name is Lucrezia de' Medici. I suppose I should say Lucrezia, Duchess of Ferrara, but I'm not the duchess anymore. I'm dead. Mostly. Actually, not all the way dead, but in between—I'm an immobila, *a still one, a watcher. I'm not sure why. Maybe it's because I didn't want to die.*

When I was alive, I was the daughter of Cosimo de' Medici, Duke of Florence. He called me Sodona, "Hard One," because I hated my lessons and ran away from my tutors. He'd laugh and cuff me and swear that in my hardness and stubbornness I took after him. Maybe I did. He had a will of iron, my father, and a ruthless temper when he was crossed.

My mother, on the other hand, was melancholic and full of herself. I learned from her that acting frail was a good way to avoid doing anything I didn't want to do. The more my nurses and tutors scolded, the sicker and weaker I became. How I laughed when I was alone, or with my sister Isabella! I wanted no lessons, no books, no embroidery or dancing. I wanted to run free in the gardens and ride the horses in the stables. I wanted to sleep late every morning and wake up to cream custard with honey and little almond cakes with crisp, shiny sugar on top. Sometimes I managed to slip away and do as I pleased. Other times I was watched too closely.

Alfonso gave out I'd retired to the Monastero del Corpus Domini by my own will, but nothing could be farther from the truth. He had me taken there. Imagine—only two rooms and not even a window, for me, a princess of Florence, the Duchess of Ferrara! And the door was locked. Alfonso knew I couldn't stand being locked in. He did it deliberately, because he knew eventually I'd confess anything just to be free again.

That last night, I never expected to fall asleep, but I drowsed. I didn't hear the door open. All out of nowhere something was pressed down over my face, so hard its softness molded around my eyes and nose and mouth. It terrified me beyond anything I'd ever known. I felt as if my chest was going to collapse in on itself as I scratched and thrashed and struggled for air.

Then in one awful moment I burst free of my flesh. I didn't really, of course, but that's the only way I can describe it. The pain and fear stopped. Life stopped. I felt nothing. I was still there, in the monastery cell; I could see and hear and understand, but I couldn't make any of the living see or hear or understand me. I had become immobila.

I was seventeen, and it was April, and I was only just beginning to live! I can look at my favorite cherry tree now, but I can't breathe the scent of the blossoms, or bite down on the scarlet fruit and feel the sweet-tart juice explode in my mouth.

I want Alfonso to suffer. I want them all to suffer, all of them, damn them. I want them all to suffer for what they did to me.

CHAPTER TWO

*A*fter supper, fireworks, and a magnificent entertainment recounting the life and death of Saint Barbara—a singular choice for a wedding night, considering her gruesome fate, but of course meant as a compliment to me personally—my ladies and I withdrew to the duke's apartments for my wedding-night undressing. By torchlight we passed through a series of small rooms, each opening upon the next, all richly furnished and decorated. Then we entered a covered passageway the Ferrarese ladies called the Via Coperta—in its side rooms I caught glimpses of magnificent art, paintings, and sculptures, the figures appearing to move and breathe in the flickering of the torches. This passageway led to the Palazzo della Corte, another of the great Este palaces, where the duke had furbished up new suites of apartments for each of us; it would allow us to travel back and forth between the Castello and the Palazzo without actually going outdoors. Eventually we reached a door decorated with intricate trompe l'oeil inlay work. Two of the Ferrarese ladies pushed it open, and we went inside.

"I am sure you do not remember our names, Serenissima," said a pretty, dark-eyed woman of about my own age. "I am—"

"Domenica Guarini," I supplied. I remembered her because she was one of the few ladies of the Ferrarese court who had not tried to bleach and dye her dark hair. "You are—let me see, a cousin of the poet Guarini, is that not right?"

She laughed, and I found myself liking her. "I am flattered, Serenissima," she said. "It runs in our Guarini blood, poetry does—perhaps you would permit me to write a madrigal in your honor one day. Please, step through to the bedchamber. There is a fire there, and it will be warmer."

I did as she suggested. The ladies clustered around me, exclaiming in a polyglot of German, French, and Italian upon the richness of my dress and jewels. My head ached and my hands felt cold. My wedding dress, stiffened with jewels and gold laces, had made me something other than myself: *la duchessa*, like a player in a play. Now I had to let them take it off, piece by piece, so I would be only myself again.

Sybille immediately set herself to untwisting the pearls from my hair—she loved any task that allowed her to touch me or be close to me. My lighthearted, sweet-voiced lutenist, Christine von Hessen, rubbed my icy hands between her own, humming a tune we had sung together as children about a forest wedding between a thrush and a blackbird. My wardrobe mistress and closest friend, Katharina Zähringen, began to fuss over the laces of my sleeves.

Most of my Austrian household would be sent home once a month or two had passed, but these three I was prepared to fight for. We-three, they called themselves, the three special ones who remained as other ladies came and went in my household. Even within we-three, however, I was closest to Katharina. She was stubborn, fiercely self-willed, pretty enough, but more forceful than feminine in her ways. Neither husband nor church called to her; instead, she reveled in beautiful fabrics, jewels, and dress patterns, and she devoted her life to them with single-minded passion.

"There are pearls missing," she said. "You have caught the thread against something sharp." Then, under her breath, she added, "Do not trust the Ferrarese, Bärbel. They are all spies."

I nodded slightly, turning to look at the sleeve as a means of disguising the gesture. "I see," I said. "It is unfortunate. Do you have sufficient pearls to mend it?"

"*Ja, Hoheit.*"

"Italian, if you please."

"*Si, Serenissima.*"

The duke, of course, would have informants in my household. Who else? The cardinal? Lucrezia and Leonora, the duke's sisters, who had foisted a madwoman upon me and then embraced me sweetly—too sweetly?—at the wedding supper? The Florentine ambassador, perhaps, puppet of Cosimo de' Medici, the duke's erstwhile father-in-law and bitter rival for the title and precedence of grand duke? I did not know the court of Ferrara well enough to know who would set spies on me, and who would wish me well or ill.

My sleeves were unlaced and folded away. The jeweled scarlet overskirt was next, then the foreparte with its diamonds and pearls, and the silken underskirts. Katharina unfastened my bodices and untied the silken cords of my partlet. One of the Ferrarese ladies unlaced my stiffened corset. Sybille finished untwisting the plaiting around my forehead and temples and turned away to place the strings of fabulous Ferrarese pearls in their boxes. At that moment, much to Sybille's indignation, one of the Ferrarese ladies pushed forward and began to comb out my hair, spiraling it around an amber rod and smoothing it with a silken cloth to make perfect polished ringlets.

"What beautiful hair you have, Serenissima," the girl said. Her own was bleached to a pinkish-blond color, lusterless as dried grass.

She paused, then curled and polished another tress. Then in a different, harder voice she said, "*Her* hair was longer, more golden, the color of sunlight—and what skin she had! What breasts, rosy and firm, like two white peaches bursting with sweet juice."

There was a moment of ghastly silence.

"How dare you!" Katharina cried in German. At the same time, Domenica Guarini burst into a torrent of furious Italian, too quick and colloquial for me to understand completely. The girl stood between them clutching the amber rod, defiant and white as whey. I, on the other hand, felt myself blushing and blushing and blushing until I thought it would never stop, the blaze of the blood under my skin consuming my entire body.

"Enough," I said at last. "You, girl, what is your name?"

"Maddalena Costabili." She did not meet my eyes.

"You forget yourself, Maddalena Costabili—you are dismissed. Katharina, Sybille, my shoes and stockings, please. We do not have time for such foolishness."

"I will never forget the last time I saw her," the girl Maddalena persisted, her voice faint and shaking. "The very day she came sick so suddenly, or so he said when he locked her away at the Monastero del Corpus Domini. She was not sick at all. She was mad, mad with—"

The sharp crack of Domenica's hand across her cheek cut her short. "Stop it at once!" Domenica hissed. "Not one more word. The duke will cut out your tongue if he discovers what you have said here tonight."

Maddalena burst into tears and ran out of the room.

Holy Virgin. Was my household full of madwomen?

"Be silent, all of you." My voice was perhaps sharper than I intended. "My shoes and stockings, if you please."

Katharina and Sybille knelt to remove my shoes, untie my jeweled garters, and roll down my stockings; for all its magnificent marble parquetry, the floor was like ice under my bare feet. Christine and Domenica pulled the shift from my shoulders so it slithered down over my body without disarranging my hair. I had a moment, a single moment, of dizziness. What had I done? Why was I standing here, in a bedchamber in a strange palace, naked, with the Duke of Ferrara with his gentlemen about to come in the door? I was not *Hoheit* anymore, not *Prinzessin*, not *Erzherzogin*; I would be Duchessa or Serenissima now, until the day I died.

I took a breath and touched my hair, rearranging the polished tendrils to lie over my breasts in perfect parallel strands. Yes, I would be Duchessa. I would preside over the court and rule my household and bear my husband sons and daughters. My mother had done the same, and her mother before her. The duke's first duchess was none of my concern.

My skin pebbly with gooseflesh, I stepped to the bed and took my place, propped up against embroidered pillows, with the bed-covers artfully arranged to preserve—barely—my maiden modesty. I felt prickly rosemary sprigs between the fine linen sheets, as well as cool damp flower petals and grains of wheat for fertility. The women extinguished the candles, and when only the light of the fireplace remained, Domenica went to the door and opened it.

The duke and his gentlemen came into the chamber. He looked at me for a moment, and to my bewilderment I saw not pleasure or anticipation but choler in his eyes, black and filled with monsters. The other women saw it, too, because there was a ripple of movement among them as they stepped back.

I could not step back. And I knew if I showed fear now, I would be afraid for the rest of my life.

"Has something disturbed you, my lord?" I asked.

"I would ask you the same question, Madonna."

But of course, either the hapless Maddalena had run straight into him, or some spy had already repeated her words to him. *The duke will cut out your tongue if he discovers what you have said here to-night.* I prayed he had not paused on his way to our marriage bed to perform that bit of impromptu chirurgery.

Aloud I said, "Nothing has disturbed me, my lord."

After what seemed like an endless silence, he lifted one hand.

"Enough," he said. "All of you. There is music in the great salon, and wine and subtleties, and gifts for everyone. The duchess and I will greet you again, come morning."

In haste, without the customary laughter, toasts, and ribald jests, the gentlemen and ladies scuttled out. The door swung shut. We were alone.

I forced down my impulse to speak first, to say anything to fill the silence.

"What did she say?" He came closer to me, close enough to touch me, although he did not. I could feel the heat of—what? Outraged pride? Fury? Madness?—radiating from his flesh. With vicious intensity he said again, *"What did she say?"*

I clenched my fists under the coverlet. "She said your first wife's hair was longer and more golden than mine, and her breasts were like white peaches."

To my surprise he stepped back, and some of the ferocity cleared from his eyes. "What else?"

"That she was mad, your first duchess, the last time the girl saw her."

"That, at least, is the truth. And you, Madonna?" His violence had cooled. His expression was calmer, more appraising. Clearly he had been expecting something else in the girl's gossip—an accusation of murder, perhaps? That would explain his anger. "What did you say to all this?"

"I dismissed the girl, and directed the rest of the ladies to proceed with undressing me."

I saw the tiniest flicker in his eyes, something light in the darkness. Appreciation? Amusement, even? "You keep your composure admirably," he said. "You did the same, in the procession, at the church, at supper."

"I was brought up to do so."

"Indeed. Breeding always tells." He went to the sideboard and poured two glasses of wine, taking his time about it. With his back to me, he said, "We will not speak of this again. You will never mention her, or the whispers about her. Never. Not in my hearing, or out of it. Not if you wish to please me."

I made two pleats in the coverlet, of exactly even size. "Of course I wish to please you."

He brought the wine to the bedside and handed one glass to me. I saw him look at the folds I had made in the coverlet. "Good. Are you hungry? You did not eat at supper."

"No, my lord." I let go of the pleats and they unpleated themselves. "But the wine is welcome."

There was a pause. I did not know what else to say. At last he said, "I have little skill at pretty words. Fighting, yes. Sport. Music, even. But there it ends."

I breathed the scent of the wine for a moment, then took a sip. It was cool and robust, without the honey and spices I had expected.

"Pretty words are unnecessary," I said. "We are husband and wife. The wine is excellent. Is it your custom not to sweeten it?"

"I prefer the flavor of our fine Ferrarese wine itself, and not some motley of sweetness and spice."

The fire crackled and popped suddenly, and I jumped. A few droplets of wine lurched from my glass and spattered the silken coverlet. The half-spheres glittered like rubies for a moment, then sank away into the fabric.

"I look forward to the pleasures of your beautiful city," I said. "Messer Baldassare Castiglione's *Il Libro del Cortegiano* is a favorite book of mine, with its wonderful descriptions of court life in Urbino."

"The court of Urbino is well enough, and the Della Rovere are my allies and friends. Even so, I believe Messer Baldassare's ideal courtier would find himself more at home in Ferrara today, where we enjoy art and music and sport without peer, and manners of unsurpassed elegance."

Unsurpassed pride as well, I thought. "I am sure that is true," I said, to placate him. "I was only ten years old when I first tried to read it, you see, and it was like reading about an imaginary land of perfect shining lords and ladies—I wished so passionately I could be in Urbino and not in Innsbruck."

He drank the last of his wine, put the glass down, and began to unfasten his belt. The damascened dagger glinted in the firelight. "And now you are in Ferrara," he said. "Tell me, Madonna, have you been prepared for this? You are no skittish child, at least, to be wheedled and coaxed."

"No." My own voice sounded strange to me. I took one last sip of my wine and put the glass on the table beside the bed. The spots of wine on the silk coverlet had dried to the color of blood. One was larger than the other, and it made me uneasy. "I am no child, I am not skittish, and I have been quite well-prepared for my wedding night."

He had stripped to his shirt, and the fine white silk looked even whiter against his swarthy skin and dark beard. His shoulders and arms were as well-shaped and athletic as his legs. He turned to face me again. He was not smiling.

"We shall see about that."

I closed my eyes. For a moment nothing happened. Then I felt the coverlet pulled aside and the air of the room against my skin. I could hear the fire, and I could almost feel the patterns of light and dark flickering over my breasts and belly. I breathed—breathed. I suppressed my instinct to cover myself. It was cold in the room, fire or no fire. I knew he was looking at me, and I could not stop myself from remembering what the girl Maddalena had said. *Her breasts were rosy and firm, like two white peaches bursting with sweet juice. . . .*

"I am cold," I said. My voice did not sound like my own.

"You will be warm soon."

His weight made the mattresses sink down on one side. I wanted to show him I was willing, so I turned toward him. He put his fingers through my hair, pulling it from beneath my back and shoulders. Wisps of it crackled and clung to my cheeks; I could imagine it clinging to his hands as well, as if he were taking control of my responses whether I wanted it or not.

"You have beautiful hair. Come closer and put your arms around me."

I obeyed him.

He kissed my mouth. I could taste wine on his lips. He could probably taste wine on mine as well. No honey, no spices. *I prefer the flavor of the wine itself.* I let myself sink farther toward him; the green scent of crushed herbs made me dizzy. He had taken off the shirt. Skin against skin. My husband, my lord. The cathedral. *Jacta alea est.* I would be the duchess, at the center of the court. I would have children.

"Good," he said. He twisted his hands more tightly in my hair. "Open yourself to me."

I opened my mouth and let my full weight press against him. He kissed me again and again, with my hair wrapped around his fists.

"Look at me."

I tried to turn my face aside, but he held me. I could not look at him. I prayed he would not insist.

He did not. He let go of my hair and pushed me back into the center of the bed; then, slowly and possessively, he moved his hands over my throat, my shoulders, my breasts, my arms. I felt ashamed and awkward at first. He calmed me. *I have little skill at pretty words.* A lie, that. Once he had gentled me, all of a sudden he sank his nails lightly into my flesh, and I recoiled at the shock of sensation. He waited until I had stopped trembling, then began the same slow process again. Caresses, murmurs, more caresses, then—not pain, exactly, but intense sensation. This time I half-expected it and only gasped.

He did it over and over. Each time the sensation was more piercing. He began using his mouth as well as his hands. I could not catch my breath. I was sweating all over, everywhere. I could feel herbs and flower petals stuck to my skin. I tried to keep from sobbing but could not stop myself.

Through it all I kept my eyes tight-shut.

"In time you will look at me," he said. "Now. This is the rest of it."

THE EMPEROR'S POOR *ugly sister is sleeping now, and well she should be—Alfonso took his time at the end, and when he finished she cried a little. Alfonso's still awake. I wonder what he's thinking. I wonder if he's thinking of me—of the last time he had me, the last time he saw me.*

I laughed when she said she was no longer a child—at least that's the truth! If I was alive this very night, I'd still be five years younger than she is.

I'm sure she was a virgin. I was, too. I was! Well, in the flesh, at least, I was.

It was my sister Isabella who taught me about men. She was two years older than me and betrothed to the Duke of Bracciano's heir, but she'd been taking lovers since she was twelve. She taught me that noble lovers were dangerous, because they might wake up one morning in a fit of remorse and confess everything to the nearest listening ear. Servants were safest, because a stable boy or a passing soldier wouldn't be believed even if he did tell tales.

We'd go to the chapel, Isabella and I, and pretend we were praying, because then our nurses and tutors would leave us alone. She'd whisper things that made me squirm with excitement, and sometimes she'd draw little sketches with paper and charcoal she kept beneath her kneeling-cushion. We'd burn them later when we went up to light holy candles. Everyone thought we were deeply devout, because we spent so much time in the chapel, looking as pious as the Virgin herself and lighting many, many candles.

It was a lover I wanted, not a husband. Isabella told me husbands expected too much and didn't give enough pleasure in return. I wasn't even supposed to marry Alfonso—he was betrothed to my sister Maria, who was five years older and probably would've been a better wife. Maria died of a fever in a very inconvenient way. Some people said my father stabbed her because he caught her with a lover. Of course it wasn't true. At least, I think it wasn't true. Either way, Maria was dead, and since Isabella was already betrothed and there were no other daughters, that left me.

My father insisted I was too young and delicate for a real nozze. *He wouldn't let Alfonso take me to Ferrara after we were married. Alfonso didn't care—he didn't want to marry me or go back to Ferrara anyway. Three days after the wedding, he galloped off to France, where he'd been living as a great favorite at the court of his cousin, the French king Henri, leaving me Duchess of Ferrara but still a child under my father's thumb, and as much a virgin as I'd ever been.*

I hope Alfonso does cut out Maddalena Costabili's tongue, the bitch. Hair the color of sunlight! Breasts like white peaches! I don't know what she was up to, but someone must have paid her, or coerced her. She never had anything nice to say about me while I was alive, and nothing but gold or fear would make her say such things now, and on the emperor's sister's wedding night at that. Who? Any one of a dozen people who want Alfonso's new marriage to come to nothing, that's who.

She was right when she said I was mad. In those last few days before Alfonso had me locked away, I was mad with a hundred different things. Fury, fear, frustration, passion, joy. Does he remember? Does he remember anything about me at all?

Tonight especially, in bed with his new wife—is he thinking of me?

CHAPTER THREE

*T*he next day at dinner we presided at the high table in the great salon as the Duke and the new Duchess of Ferrara. If one had a penchant for fantasy, we might have been cresting a wave in the midst of the sea, for the room had been transformed, top to bottom, into Neptune's kingdom.

Stylized waves, with sprays of sea-foam and fanciful plants and shells, had been painted on draperies covering the ceiling; branches of candles were upheld by coiled sea-monsters in silver-gilt. The topmost tablecloths were blue-green silk, swirled and gathered to look like the ocean's surface, and the napkins were folded to look like fish, with silver spangles for scales. The high table was set apart inside a sea-reef of papier-mâché, painted in gold and blue.

In contrast to all the blue and green, the duke wore dark mulberry-red velvet set off by pleated white linen, fine as silk and perfumed with sandalwood. In his hat there was a pigeon's-blood ruby the size of a chestnut. I, on the other hand, was a blaze of brilliance in cloth of silver and diamonds. My hair was no longer loose but caught up in a silver headdress embroidered with starfish in pearls and coral, one of the duke's morning gifts. It was both costuming for the celebration and a symbol of my new status as a married woman.

Behind the bright opulence was the hot rosemary-scented darkness of the night. I could not look at him without remembering. Everything reminded me—the tug of the hairpins in my hair, the sound of his voice, the taste of the wine. He was toying with a fine clear glass from Murano, so thin the golden wine appeared to be floating free in the air. I watched his fingers. I remembered what they had done.

I concentrated on my food. I had not been able to eat more than a bite or two of the wedding supper the night before, and prosaic as it might be, I was hungry.

"You eat with good appetite, Madonna," the duke said. "I am pleased. My cooks and vintners have outdone themselves in your honor."

He spoke as if the events of the night before had never happened. I breathed deeply, lifted my head, and made up my mind to do the same.

"They have indeed, my lord. This little tart is delicious, and like nothing I have ever tasted before."

"It is called a *torta di tagliarini*, for the sweet pasta in the filling." He smiled. "It was created for the wedding feast of my grandfather and his second wife, Lucrezia Borgia, in homage to the bride's magnificent golden hair. I suspect you do not eat pasta in Vienna."

When he was in a good humor, when something gratified his pride as his great ancestry did, his smile was pleasant and his mien attractive. I found myself smiling in return. "We have our spätzle, but it is not quite the same."

"You will become accustomed to Ferrarese ways. Crezia and Nora will help you. Is that not so, *mie sorelle*?"

Lucrezia d'Este—Crezia—seated on my right as was her due as the elder of the duke's two sisters, smiled brilliantly. She was already flushed with wine, although her beautiful dark eyes were sharp and cold. Until yesterday, I thought, she was the first lady of the court. Now she was the second. I knew her birth date because I had made it my business to know, and she was four years older than I. I wondered why she had never been married.

"Oh, yes," she said. "Banquets and music, dancing and fashion, loving and loathing—everything is an art in Ferrara." As she said it, her eyes flicked out over the great salon and fused briefly with the eyes of a handsome dark gentleman at one of the lower tables; he leaned forward as if physically drawn by the power of her gaze. So she had a lover. Perhaps that was why she was still unmarried and the *prima donna* of her brother's court. I glanced sideways at the duke to see if he noticed this byplay, but he had turned to his left and was absorbed in conversation with his brother the cardinal.

"You have a task set out for you, *mia Serenissima*," Crezia went on slowly, never looking away from the dark gentleman's face, "to keep up with us all."

With that she laughed. So did her sister, who was seated on her other side. This Leonora—Nora—was the younger of the two, although still two years older than I. Unlike her vibrant sister, she was thin and pale, and her flushed cheeks did not appear to be from the wine but from ill health. As different as their looks were, they seemed at one in their condescension, and I must confess it provoked me.

"I suppose I do," I said. "Of course, there is still some possibility you yourselves may marry and go to live in a strange city, and if you do, it is likely you also will find the ways different from those to which you have been accustomed for such a"—I paused deliberately, to put stress on my next word—"long time."

Crezia's eyes narrowed. Nora paled, then flushed again. That will teach you to patronize me, I thought, then immediately felt ashamed of myself.

"Of course, it is always difficult to leave one's home," I said, meaning to placate them. "Whatever one's age. My sister Johanna, for example, who is only nineteen, will marry Prince Francesco of Florence in a fortnight's time. And many are obliged to leave their homes when they are but thirteen or fourteen—"

I stopped. I wished the words unsaid, but it was too late.

"Yes," Nora said. Her voice was sharp with spite. "Thirteen or fourteen. Take Alfonso's first wife, Lucrezia de' Medici of Florence as you surely know, as your own sister is to marry her brother. She brought her Medici ways to Ferrara, presuming to parade herself as duchess, demanding precedence over Crezia, over me, even over our lady mother, who is of the French royal family and—"

"Enough."

A single word from the duke, softly spoken. Nora pressed her lips together in a resentful line and said nothing more. Crezia pretended to be intent upon a honey-soaked cake in the shape of a scallop shell. I looked down at my tart, surprised by Nora's venom. Obviously to say anything more would only make matters worse.

"Here is a person I wished to present to you, Madonna," the duke went on, as if the awkwardness had never happened. He gestured, and his majordomo approached with a handsome young fellow of twenty or so in tow. The boy's narrow face, aquiline nose, and large dark eyes with the whites glinting all around them gave the impression of a restive, overbred colt; an aura of charm and genius rested like an invisible olive wreath upon his fine brow and curling dark hair. "This is Messer Torquato Tasso, recently come to Ferrara in my brother's service, and the author of a most excellent long poetic epic entitled *Rinaldo*."

The boy bowed with the polished grace of one well-accustomed to courts. "It is my delight to come to your attention, Serenissima." His voice was as flexible and dramatic as a singer's or player's, and he made it sound as if his one aspiration in life up to this moment had been to come to my attention.

"I have heard of you even in Innsbruck, Messer Torquato," I

said. "To find you here at Ferrara is a most pleasant surprise. If it pleases the duke and the cardinal, I would like to hear you read some of your verses to us one day soon."

It was courtesy, nothing more; if anything my intent was to quell his extravagance. I was much taken aback when Nora leaned forward and said with mean-spirited fierceness, "You will have little time for poets, Madonna Barbara. And Messer Torquato is occupied as well, with a new book of sonnets to be dedicated to me."

The boy blushed like a child; it was hard to tell if he was gratified or embarrassed by Nora's possessiveness. Holy Virgin, were both the duke's sisters involved in romantic intrigues? Did anyone else see it, or was it only I, with my eyes so accustomed to my brother's sober imperial court?

"Nora, hold your tongue." The duke's voice was cold and gave the distinct impression he was accustomed to rebuking her; more than ever I wondered what his relationships were with his sisters and why he had not married them off to suitable princes. "The duchess will apportion her time as she chooses, and any sonnets Messer Torquato produces will be dedicated as Luigi or I direct. You are dismissed, sir."

The young poet had recovered his aplomb; with a graceful flourish he bowed first to the duke, then to me and to the cardinal his patron, then to—well, one or the other of the duke's sisters, or perhaps both of them at once—and withdrew. Crezia signaled her server for more wine. Nora sat like a stone, staring straight ahead, although a single knifelike flash of her eyes in my direction told me I had made an enemy. I had no time to mend matters with her, because another gentleman and his lady stepped forward to be presented.

He was of medium height, dark, too thickly made for his rich clothes to fit him with elegance. I suspected he would be more at his ease on a battlefield or in a wine-shop than supping at elegant banquets under the aegis of Neptune. His wife was taller and considerably younger than he, with milky white skin and black eyes; she looked apprehensive, which I put down to nerves at being placed at the center of the court's attention.

"Madonna," said the duke, "I present the Chevalier Alexandre de Bellincé, one of a company of French knights I commanded in the days when I was fighting in Flanders. He pledged his fealty to me at the time, and now that he has made his"—the duke paused, as if considering his words—"his permanent home here in Ferrara, he is called Cavaliere Alessandro Bellinceno and enjoys my greatest favor."

Alessandro Bellinceno bowed like a foot-soldier without saying so much as a word. His wife's smooth cheeks reddened slightly.

"And also his wife, Donna Elisabetta Viviani, daughter of Antonio Viviani, *patrizio* of Ferrara," the duke went on. "Sandro and Donna Elisabetta are also newly wed, having been joined together only since Michaelmas."

Donna Elisabetta curtsied gracefully and correctly, in contrast to her husband's awkwardness—surely she had more than two months of court experience. Perhaps she had been in the household of one of the duke's sisters before being married off to the duke's friend. As she straightened she said, also quite correctly, "I am greatly honored, Serenissima."

"I am pleased to make your acquaintance, Messer Alessandro." I had noticed the *Sandro* and deduced this stocky soldier enjoyed not only the duke's great favor but also his personal friendship. What adventures had they experienced together in their soldiering days? "Donna Elisabetta, I look forward to seeing you about the court."

They made their oddly, almost comically mismatched reverences again and withdrew. The duke then signaled for the gift-giving to begin.

It was an extended process—it seemed as if every city-state in Italy had sent an embassy, and most of the kingdoms of Europe as well; Ferrara's opulent court, its university, its great patronage of art and music and poetry, made it important far beyond its size. The ambassadors were presented, displayed their gifts, received their thanks, then took themselves away to have their offerings inventoried by the duke's secretaries. A representative of Charles IX of France—as the former king Henri II had been the duke's cousin, this young king would be his second cousin—presented an intricate mechanical clock in a gold and rock-crystal case, elaborately chased, engraved, and decorated with fine pearls. The duke was particularly interested in its workings and asked the ambassador to demonstrate each process several times; only reluctantly did he allow it to be taken away.

The envoy from the next embassy to be introduced represented Queen Elizabeth of England, a lady the duke had once wooed with gifts of his own in the days after the death of his first duchess.

"The English ambassador," the duke said to me in an aside, "is Henry Carey, Baron Hunsdon, the queen's own cousin. It is a compliment to us, Madonna, that the English queen would send a member of her own family to wish us well."

"Some say," Crezia whispered on my other side, "that Henry Carey is the queen's half-brother, as well as her cousin, on the Boleyn side of the blanket."

I ignored her, as I did not wish to let her provoke me again. Here I was, after all, Duchess of Ferrara just as I had dreamed, every eye upon me, the envoy of the queen of England awaiting only my word to approach with gifts. The great salon was a tessellation of silks and velvets, with gems and crystals catching the light from the rows of windows, the torchères and fireplaces and the thousands of candles. The famous musicians of Ferrara plucked a delicate melody in the background, harmonies and counterpoints such as I had never heard before. The scents of burning beeswax, of meat cooked with spices, of honey and fruit and perfumes from far away over the sea drifted on the air. The sweetness of wine was on my tongue, and the crisp sugar coating of a tiny almond cake. Oh,

I wanted to stop time, see it all, taste it all. It filled my breast until I felt I might burst with pleasure.

"A compliment indeed." I made my voice soft and sweet. "Approach, Baron. You are most welcome."

He stepped forward, a well-dressed gentleman with fairish hair, large dark eyes, and a pointed chin accentuated by silky whiskers. He was followed by two retainers, one bearing a painted and gilded box draped in Tudor green satin, the other a covered basket.

"Your Grace," Hunsdon said, bowing elegantly to the duke. "Your Grace." This to me, with another bow. "Her Majesty the queen sends her good wishes upon the occasion of your marriage, and directs me to present—"

His pretty speech was interrupted by a shrill baying howl from the basket, followed by yips and scratching sounds. The basket rocked in the retainer's grasp. Then, unforgivably, droplets began to trickle from the basket onto the fellow's gorgeous green silk doublet.

I will not repeat the oath he swore, which was entirely unsuitable for the occasion. He dropped the basket and out popped two parti-colored puppies, hounds from the look of them, with long satiny russet ears and soft dark eyes. A cry of adoration immediately rose up from all the ladies.

"I beg your indulgence, Your Grace," Hunsdon said, shooting a lethal look at the foul-mouthed gentleman with the stain on his doublet. "Her Majesty herself has several of these little hounds— begles, they are called, or beagles, or sometimes *begueules*, after the French. She calls them her pocket beagles because of their size, and carries them with her everywhere. They are primarily for companionship, although like the larger variety, they are keen trackers. These two are littermates of a very fine bloodline, whelped by a pretty bitch in Her Majesty's personal kennel."

The puppies already had their noses down and their tails up and were sniffing for tidbits under the lower tables. I was charmed by them—their sturdy little bodies, their melting eyes, their merry white-flagged tails. I wished I could gather up my silver skirts and jump straightaway down on the floor to play with them, but of course that would be even more shocking than the green-doubleted gentleman's indiscreet oath.

"The duchess and I are delighted Her Majesty would send us such a personal gift," the duke said. "Are we not, Madonna?"

"We are indeed," I said. "And as they are English hounds, they shall have English names."

I paused for a moment. We had all been speaking in French, of course, and my knowledge of English was rudimentary at best. I cast about in my mind for something suitable. Everything I knew about the island nation and its ruling family seemed to be uncomplimentary, and I felt a moment of panic until I remembered an old French book I had read—secretly, of course, as my tutors had not approved of fanciful tales—called *Tristram et Iseult*, and purporting to be a great romance of English legend.

"The male shall be Tristram," I announced. "And the female Iseult."

Hunsdon bowed. "An excellent choice, Your Grace," he said. He made a curt gesture to the fellow with the stained doublet, and that unhappy gentleman went to pick up the puppies and put them back in their basket before they committed any further indelicacies.

"Domenica," I said to Domenica Guarini, the poet's sister, "please take Tristram and Iseult to my apartments, and see they have proper food and water. They will be sick if they continue to eat bits of cake."

Beaming, the Ferrarese woman rose and took the basket of puppies from the gentleman, much to his obvious relief. As everyone turned their attention to the exchange, the duke leaned close to me and said, "Do not forget what I said to you last night, Madonna."

It took me by surprise. I felt my color rise. Last night?

I have little skill at pretty words.

Now. This is the rest of it.

I swallowed and said, "Last night?"

"In your earlier conversation with my sisters, you spoke of the youth of . . . the first duchess . . . when I asked you particularly to avoid the subject."

There had been, of course, no moment for private speech between us at the time, what with the presentations and then the gift-giving. I thought he had forgotten. I myself had certainly forgotten.

The glamour of the moment dimmed. The great salon became—ordinary.

"It was not I who turned the conversation in that direction, my lord," I said.

"That may be so, but you provoked Nora, whether it was your intent or not." His voice was even and cool. "Take more care of your tongue in future."

I felt hot blood surge up into my face. How dare you, I thought, how dare you, how dare you? But he dared because he was now my husband, and his word was law to me.

Stiffly I said, "As you wish, my lord."

"Loose words are a fault in a woman. Maddalena Costabili has learned that, to her sorrow."

The duke will cut out your tongue if he finds out what you have said here tonight.

Maddalena had not been among the Ferrarese ladies who attended me that morning. I felt a moment of sinking fear. Surely he had not done such a thing, or ordered it done. However violent his aversion to any mention of his first wife—*and why is that?* a small voice whispered in my thoughts—surely he would not be so gratuitously cruel to a helpless young woman. I looked down at the tablecloth and drew two lines with my fingernail, exactly parallel.

"You do not ask what happened to her? After she spoke to you as she did?"

"Very well. What happened to her?" I drew another line.

"She has been thrashed like a serving-wench and sent to a convent to meditate on her sins."

"I see." A relief, that was, compared to what I had been imagining.

"Do not think you yourself are above chastisement."

"I do not think so."

With calm triumph he laid his fingers over my hand, obliterating the lines I had drawn. His skin was browned by the hunting-field and tennis-court, in contrast to my own skin, which was pale against the glistening ocean-green of the tablecloth. I felt a chill, which I did my best to conceal. Apparently, I succeeded; the duke did not look at me again, but nodded politely to Lord Hunsdon.

"Continue, my lord," he said.

The gift-giving went on. I smiled and murmured courteous words of gratitude, but all the while I was unnervingly aware of the weight of the duke's hand over mine. I imagined those long fingers grasping a birch-cane. I imagined the cord of a garrote wrapped once, twice around that elegantly jeweled fist—the same fist that had wrapped itself in my hair, the same hands that had possessed themselves of my flesh in the fire-flickered night.

Outwardly I would obey him. I had no choice in that.

But as to my true thoughts—I would teach myself the way of wives everywhere, from princesses to peasants, and keep my true thoughts to myself.

WHAT DID NORA *really have to complain about, or Crezia, or any of them? When Alfonso became the duke, I became the duchess, it was as simple as that, and I had every right to precedence over his hag of a mother and his shriveled-up man-hungry sisters. That man Crezia was staring at? He's Count Ercole Contrari, and she's mad in love with him. And everyone knows Nora's lusted for Tasso from the moment she saw him, no matter that he's seven years younger than she is.*

Sandro Bellinceno? I won't say anything about him or his goggle-eyed wife for now. Although that doesn't mean I have nothing to say.

I just can't think about some things too much. I've learned, being im-mobila, that it doesn't do me any good to be angry. I can't touch the living. I can't make them hear me, no matter how much I scream. At first I tried. Then I learned. I can only watch. I can't even weep.

When I left off my story I was still in Florence, wasn't I? Well, when I turned fifteen, Alfonso's father, Duke Ercole, began to press my father to send me to Ferrara, even though Alfonso himself was still in France acting the fine young gentleman in his cousin's court. It wasn't that Duke Ercole cared whether I was in Florence or Ferrara or at the bottom of the sea—he wanted the rest of my dowry. My father wanted to keep it, of course, so they haggled. They probably would have haggled forever, except Duke Ercole died.

Inheriting the title brought Alfonso home from France in a hurry, you can be sure of that. It was November, and cold, and it turned out I'd played my part as the frail consumptive too well. My mother refused to let me go to Ferrara right away, and it wasn't until Carnival time the following spring I finally made my grand entry into Ferrara as its new duchess.

I was wild with delight that I'd finally be able to enjoy the freedoms and pleasures of a married woman, and even though Alfonso had ignored me for a year and a half, it never occurred to me he'd continue to ignore me once we were actually together. I was young, wasn't I? I was beautiful, wasn't I? Why was he still so cold to me?

When Carnival was over, Alfonso's mother took me in hand. Renata di Francia, that's who she was—Renée de France as she insisted on calling herself, for all the good it did her. She may have been a king's daughter in Paris before she married Duke Ercole, but after he died and Alfonso suc-ceeded, she was only a dowager duchess in Ferrara, and a convicted heretic at that. She was! All through her years in Ferrara she'd invited every ragtag Calvinist in Europe to come to court, giving them refuge and money, and so she was tried by the Inquisition and sentenced to life imprisonment. She recanted, of course, to keep her freedom, but it was a sham—Duke Ercole was hardly cold in his tomb when she embraced Calvinism again. Alfonso wanted to keep on the good side of the old pope, and he didn't particularly like his mother anyway, so within the year she was banished from Ferrara and had slunk off back to France where at least she could speak French as much as she wanted.

I had to put up with her for those first few months, though. She made it clear there'd be no freedoms for me, no matter I was now the duchess and she wasn't. I was to spend my days praying, practicing etiquette, and learning to read and write properly. I played sick again, and pretended I never left my apartments. Then when Madonna Renata wasn't looking—and she was only too happy to put me out of her mind while she quarreled with Alfonso and the pope—I found ways to amuse myself. If Alfonso didn't want me, there were men who did. Isabella had taught me too much about pleasure for me to go without it for long.

As for Crezia and Nora, I hated them and they hated me. They looked down their long Este noses at me and told me Alfonso never wanted to marry me in the first place. He thought the Medici weren't good enough to be servants of the Este. I myself was crude and awkward, they said; my blood wasn't as good as theirs, and I didn't follow all the little details of their etiquette. I didn't care about art or music or books. I dressed like a Florentine and didn't dance correctly. I couldn't read and write elegantly. On and on they went.

Oh, yes, I hated them, and they hated me. And they're alive and I'm immobila.

At least the emperor's ugly sister talks back to them. I laughed so hard when she said one day they might marry and find the customs of a new city strange after being at home for so long, long, long a time. I thought Crezia was going to choke on her cappelletti.

I almost liked her then, the new one.

I wish, oh I wish, someone had given me puppies.

CHAPTER FOUR

*B*y the end of the day I was exhausted; I wanted nothing more than to strip off my tight, heavy costume and sink deep into a feather mattress. I wanted to think, to find a way to fit it all together: the whispers of a *parruchiera* and the magnificence of my entry into the city, the perfumed darkness of the duke's bed and the dazzling brilliance of the gift-giving, the duke's smile as he described pasta named for his grandmother's golden hair and his smile—just the same yet not the same at all—as he detailed Maddalena Costabili's punishments. I wanted to take the puppies, Tristram and Iseult, into the bed with me for comfort and do nothing but think about it all.

That, of course, was out of the question; the duke had commanded me to attend him in his private apartments for the night. I was not feeling sanguine toward him after his threat—and threat it was, however much he might cloak it in courtesy—at the gift-giving. Still, it would be worse if he ignored me, for then the gossip would begin. *He does not like her. . . . She is too old, too ugly. . . . His first duchess was younger and more beautiful. . . .*

My new presence chamber was quite astonishing to me—
emperor's daughter or no, I had been accustomed to much more
austere surroundings in Innsbruck. Here in Ferrara, it seemed, I
would live among rich furnishings, paintings, and sculptures; this
room's marble floor was spread with patterned carpets from the
Orient, and its high, high ceiling was frescoed with figures of Jupiter and Juno. In one corner, on a heap of blue and scarlet cushions,
Tristram and Iseult were fast asleep, curled close together.

I smiled and put one finger to my lips. Tiptoeing like children, my
ladies and I passed through the presence chamber, a well-appointed
study with an oratory in a niche to one side, a breakfast-room and
a wardrobe-room, until at last we reached the privy chamber, and
just behind it, the bedchamber. There I saw, to my astonishment, a
tiny wizened woman who looked none too clean, standing by the
bed with a bottle and cup in her hands and a mad gleam in her eye.

Domenica Guarini burst into a torrent of Italian, too fast for
me to follow. The old woman gave back as good as she got, in what
I assumed was a much less refined vernacular. This did not seem
helpful, and so I took matters in hand.

"Stop at once, both of you."

My Habsburg blood may have given me a long horselike face
and a prominent lower lip, but in compensation it had also given
me the ability to command a room if the need should arise. Both
women broke off midsentence and looked at me, Domenica guilt-
ily, the old woman with an openly calculating expression.

"What is this about?" I demanded. "You. Old woman. What
are you doing here?"

"Aren't you the high and mighty one," the wretched creature
retorted. "I go where I want in the duke's palaces, and never'll
come the day when the likes of you will stop me."

"It is the duke's old nursemaid and foster-mother," Domenica
said. "Maria Granmammelli, she is called. It is true, Serenissima,

she was the duke's wet-nurse. He gives her license to go where she wishes, and he will hear no word against her."

I did know enough Italian to grasp that the old woman's sobriquet meant "Big Breasts." Perhaps once she had lived up to the name, but it would have been years ago. If she was expecting me to blush and stammer at the reference, she was in for a disappointment.

"Well, Maria Granmammelli," I said, "what do you want in my private bedchamber?"

A spark of respect flickered in her piercing black eyes. "It don't look private to me," she said. "With all these fine ladies flocking about. Make it private in truth, *Austriaca*, just me and you, and I'll tell you a thing or two you might like to hear."

I hesitated for a moment. Once already this day—and only my first full day as a wife!—I had incurred my husband's displeasure for an unseemly conversation. Did I wish to risk it again? On the other hand, if he valued the old woman and gave her license to come and go as she pleased, he could hardly blame me for making an effort to be pleasant to her.

"Very well," I said. "Ladies, you may withdraw. I will call you when I need you."

They whispered, but they complied. The old crone and I were left to ourselves.

"Red clover, red clover," she crooned. "Motherwort and lady's mantle." She held out the bottle and the cup. "And other things, *erbe segretissima*. You're here to breed, you are, though you're not good enough for him, not good enough by half, despite your brother calling himself an emperor and all. You can prove your worth, though, with a babe in ten moons. Drink."

The very pearls in your hair might be poisoned. That posset you have been drinking. Any piece of fruit, any flower you are offered . . .

"If you think I am going to drink that concoction," I said, "motherwort or no, you are madder than you look."

"'Tis good for you, *Austriaca*. Drink it up and go to the duke, and you'll be with child by Lady Day."

"Or dead by morning."

She laughed, showing her toothless gums. "Nay, not you. You're safe enough. The other one, now, that's a different tale."

I stared at her, not quite sure I had heard her correctly. "What other one?"

"The Costabili wench, o' course. She'd best take care what she eats and drinks, off in the cloister where they've sent her to kneel on stone floors for her sins."

"That is ridiculous. A thrashing, perhaps. Banishment from the court. But poison? For nothing more than a few impertinent words?"

"I'd poison her myself, for disturbing the duke's peace. Sure as bark on tree she was bribed or threatened—I hear she's deep in debt for card-playing."

"Then the person who coerced her should suffer."

The old witch cackled. "Easy to say. Could have been anyone, wanted your wedding night spoiled and the duke angered. Everyone knows he hates any mention of that little Medici slut and her—"

"Enough. I do not wish to hear it."

"Delicate imperial ears!" she jeered. "Confess it, *Austriaca*, you're thirsting to know more about the duke's first wife."

"I am not."

"Liar. No better than she should have been, that one. Duke Ercole was mad as a bag of loons to make that marriage, and sully the blood of the Este with pawnbrokers' *palle*."

I had seen the arms of the Medici embroidered all over my sister Johanna's bride-goods: a shield with seven mysterious circles, the *palle*, said by some to be coins representing the family's origin as bankers and pawnbrokers, and by others to be pills characterizing their background as physickers. Rich and powerful the Medici may have become, but the old woman was right: in blood they were far inferior to the Este, who had been feudal lords since the tenth century and were much intermarried with French and Spanish royalty.

Was this, then, how the duke's first wife had died, by means of an old nurse's potions? Or had the old nurse herself—

"No better than she should have been," the old woman was saying. "*Stupida!* Laughed and asked me for love potions instead of my good *infusione* of motherwort."

"Love potions!" That took me aback, and I could not help myself. "But she was young, beautiful! Surely she did not need love potions to excite the duke's interest."

Maria Granmammelli gave me a sly look. "Wild teasel and mandrake, ginger and cinnamon. It made her hot, and as for who she lusted for and what came later, that's another tale. Mayhap I'll tell you another time. Drink my potion first, if you want to loosen my tongue."

I did not want her witch's brew, but how could I help but wonder who Lucrezia de' Medici had lusted for and what had come later? The duke, manlike, thought forbidding me to speak of his first wife would eliminate her from my thoughts; the result, of course, had been exactly the opposite.

Red clover, motherwort, and lady's mantle. Harmless enough, if that was really all that was in it. I deliberated for a moment and then I said, "Give it to me."

She yanked the stopper from the bottle with her teeth—or perhaps her toothless gums, who knew? The less thought about that the better—and poured the potion into the cup. It was clear and greenish, with flecks of red and green. Clover petals and motherwort leaves? One could only hope. I took the cup from her and sniffed it; a sharp, cold scent made my eyes water. The old witch had infused her herbs in aqua vitae, then. Diluted, I hoped.

Mentally I crossed myself, and drank it down.

Holy Virgin! It was enough to make a goat gag. I gulped and

coughed; my eyes watered and my head swam. It was not diluted, not diluted at all. I could feel bits of herb in my mouth and the numbing burn of pure spirits.

"Katharina!" My voice was little more than a whisper. "Sybille! Christine! To me! Water!"

All of them burst in with exclamations of surprise and concern. Sharp little barks and then the characteristic baying howls indicated Tristram and Iseult—already shortened to Tristo and Isa—were hot on the scent to my rescue as well. There was chaos for a moment as water was fetched, the puppies were recaptured, and recriminations were exchanged between the Austrian ladies and the Ferrarese. In the course of it all, Maria Granmammelli slipped away.

"Enough, enough," I managed to gasp, as Sybille, Christine, and Domenica all pressed cups of water on me at once, and Katharina scolded me—although I knew it was her way of expressing her concern—over water-spots on the silk of my skirts. "I am well enough. I am not poisoned, I promise you all."

"You cannot know that for sure, not yet." Sybille pushed Domenica Guarini aside and pressed her cup of water upon me again. "Drink some more of this. Send the rest of them away, Bärbel— we-three, Katrine and Christine and I, we are all you need."

The collective name they had always called themselves, from the days when we were children together, gave me a pang of loss so bitter it brought tears to my eyes. I could not send the Ferrarese ladies away. The duke would be displeased. The days of we-three were gone forever.

"I will take the puppies outside to the garden," Domenica Guarini said. She had not mastered the court trick of hiding her emotions behind a smiling mask; her hurt feelings were clear in her eyes, but her voice was steady. "Paolina, come with me. I will need your help. We must manage leashes and cloaks and pattens—it is quite cold. By your leave, of course, Serenissima."

The other Ferrarese girl was reluctant, but Domenica picked

Tristo up off the floor and thrust him into her arms before she could protest. Then Domenica herself collected Isa, and with puppy-laden curtsies the two young women left the bedchamber.

How good of her to give me a few minutes more of my dear we-three, despite her own disappointment! I promised myself I would remember.

"I have your night-gown warming here by the fire," Katharina said. "We will just get you out of that dress. I can remove the water-spots, I think. You must have slippers, too, Bärbel. These floors are horribly cold."

"Don't cry." Christine gave me a hug, something she did only in private—princesses and duchesses were far above hugs, or for that matter, touches of any kind, according to imperial etiquette. "Some of the Ferrarese ladies seem good and kind, and as long as we-three can stay with you here in Ferrara, we can manage having them about as well."

"You perhaps," Sybille said. "Not I. That old witch tried to poison Bärbel."

"I am not poisoned," I said. "Although I do feel strange—I am a little dizzy, and my lips feel numb."

"There, you see?" Sybille began taking down my hair, freeing it from its braidings, twistings, and jewels. Holy Virgin, it felt good to have it loose. She combed her fingers through it and then rubbed my scalp, as only she could do. "Stay here tonight," she whispered. "We will send word to the duke that you are indisposed."

"I wish I could, my Sybille, but you know I cannot. Just run a comb through my hair, and help me out of my dress—he will be wondering what has become of me."

Even I was surprised at the matter-of-factness of my words. Just last night I had been apprehensive at being put to bed with the Duke of Ferrara. Today, during the gift-giving, I had hated and feared him. Now, all of a sudden, I felt nothing but a strange combination of light-headedness and bravado.

They undressed me. Katharina folded the pieces of the dress away, smoothing the creases, putting the laces and gems in their boxes, while Sybille wrapped me up in the warmed night-gown and Christine tied fur-lined slippers on my feet.

The slippers were hardly necessary; I went to the duke's private apartments as if I were treading a hand's span above the marble of the floors. I had never drunk pure spirits before, and so it was only the next morning, when I awoke with a thundering headache, that I realized how much of my dreamlike boldness had been due to Maria Granmammelli's potion.

I CAN SEE in the dark. Inside the bed-curtains, even, I can see.

The skin on Alfonso's back is shiny with sweat, and the thick muscles in his shoulders and arms are bunched up and standing out. He's strong, I'll give him that—he should be, with all his hunting and fighting and tennis matches. This way, when I can't see his face, I can almost admire him, the shape of his buttocks and the power of his thighs like those old Greek statues he collects and marvels at.

What can I see of her? Mostly just her hair—much as I hate to admit it, Maddalena Costabili was lying when she said my hair was more beautiful than the Austriaca's. Hers is so bright it almost glows in the dark, and it's spread over the pillows like spilled apricot brandy. Her arms—she's not embracing him, because he has twisted her arms back against the bed. One leg is drawn up, ghostly white, jolting each time he thrusts into her. She's drunk—that's what she is—after swallowing that old witch's potion all in a gulp like she did. Even I knew better than that.

I always knew Maria Granmammelli hated me, and I poured her potions into my chamber-pot whenever I could. I should have been sweeter, because in the end I needed her herb-lore. I sent Tommasina to ask her for the potion, pretending she wanted it herself, but Maria Granmammelli knew it was a lie and ran straight to Alfonso. I denied everything, but he locked me away anyway.

Tommasina finally came to my aid, just as she'd always done. She was my parruchiera, my hair-dresser, and she was my friend, too, the only real friend I had in Ferrara. Her father was my father's favorite alchemist, Messer Tommaso Vasari, and she had been given her place in my Ferrarese household as a favor after her father created a secret formula for my father. One story said it was a poison even better than the famous cantarella of the Borgias, quick, sure, and undetectable. I always thought it was probably an aphrodisiac.

Because of her father's position, Tommasina was brought up around the court and she could read and write easily, which was more than I could. She read my father's letters to me—he was always writing, telling me what to do and how to act, even though he knew perfectly well I couldn't read more than two words in ten. When Tommasina read the letters, she read them in my father's voice, and she could mimic him perfectly. I had fits of laughter listening to Tommasina read my father's letters.

We laughed, too, when she finally brought me the potion stupid Maria Big-Breasts refused to give me, and we imagined what Alfonso would do when he was forced to admit his suspicions had been wrong. I was so happy that night in the Monastero del Corpus Domini, preparing myself for what I was going to do, thinking of how Alfonso would wait, and see nothing, and eventually be forced to admit his mistake and set me free.

The next morning I was dead. Within a week my flesh was entombed and everybody forgot about me. Alfonso dangled after queens for a while—he fancied himself as king of England or king of Scotland—and once both ladies rejected his suits, he turned to the emperor's sisters. It was as if I had never existed at all.

I think I'll call the Austriaca la Cavalla, because she has a face like a horse. Poor la Cavalla. She'll never have any lovers. At least she'd better not.

Not if she wants to live longer than I did.

CHAPTER FIVE

"*I* wish to have Frà Pandolf paint your portrait, to mark the occasion of our marriage," the duke said. "He is wonderfully talented, and has a knack of breathing the very appearance of life into his subjects."

The evening had begun with the performance of a comedy by Messer Ludovico Ariosto, whose name was known even in Vienna. Afterward, we all withdrew from the great salon so tables could be set out for supper. In one corner of the anteroom, the duke's consort of viols played softly, entertaining us and at the same time masking our words from those around us. The air was warm and heavy with the scents of fire and perfumed flesh.

"Of course, my lord," I said. "I had an inventory made of my bridal costume, as you directed. But Frà Pandolf? I have not heard the name before."

"He is a Franciscan friar, loosely attached to a monastery under my patronage," the duke said. "A proud and worldly fellow for a

Franciscan, and often too familiar for my taste, but a remarkable artist nevertheless. I will make the arrangements."

I toyed with a comfit of candied angelica. "He will have his work cut out for him," I said. "I cannot pretend to be a promising subject."

"Nonsense. You are the Duchess of Ferrara, Madonna, and an archduchess of Austria by birth, and as such you will be an adornment to any canvas. Be certain, when you dress yourself to be painted, that your hair is loose, as it was when you entered the city."

I could not keep myself from being shocked. "With my hair loose?" I repeated. "That is for children and courtesans, my lord."

"Of course with your hair loose." From the darkening of his expression it was clear he disliked having his wishes questioned, even in such a small matter as a portrait. "This is Ferrara, Madonna, and here the considerations of art and beauty outweigh the petty scruples of etiquette. Your hair is remarkable, and I wish it commemorated, not only for my own pleasure but for the appreciation of future generations as well."

I stood there speechless. I had known, of course, that Alfonso d'Este was a patron of the arts and a lover of beauty. I had just never thought that he would apply his artistic eye to me.

Me. Ugly me. Painted all in my hair for future generations to goggle at.

"As you wish, my lord," I said stiffly.

"Then there is no need to discuss it further. Good evening, Luigi. Good evening, *mio zio*."

Luigi Cardinal d'Este and the duke's uncle, the Marquis of Montecchio—another Alfonso—greeted us pleasantly. Already I had heard whispers of the cardinal's illicit connection with Lucrezia Bendidio—and another Lucrezia! How was I ever going to keep them all straight?—a pretty young countess in my sister-in-law Nora's household; the whispers hinted that young Messer Torquato Tasso, the poet, made passionate advances to this same young woman whenever he could escape Nora's attentions. The Marquis of Montecchio, by way of contrast, was a somber widower. His own legitimacy was doubtful—he was the late-in-life son of Alfonso I, the current duke's grandfather, and a beautiful young mistress named Laura Dianti. Some said the first Alfonso had married la Dianti on his deathbed, but the old pope had not recognized the union—the papacy was feudal overlord to the Este for Ferrara, and every potential heir it could disinherit brought it one step closer to taking over Ferrara completely as a papal fief. Thus, in theory, the marquis's two young sons were barred from succeeding to the ducal throne. In practice, however, the older boy was the heir-apparent for sheer lack of any other candidate.

Unless the cardinal renounced his vows, took a wife, and fathered legitimate sons. Such things were not unheard of, and Luigi d'Este did not seem to take his holy orders too seriously.

Or unless, of course, the present duke, my husband, produced an heir of his own. He had certainly kept his promise to instruct me in further details of the relations between a husband and a wife; I had begun to take a certain amount of pleasure in his caresses, and that in its turn pleased him a great deal. Delightful as it was, he informed me the pleasure was not an end in itself; his physicians and the *professore* of medicine at the famous University of Ferrara had assured him it made the woman more likely to conceive. If that was true, it seemed I would have little need of further potions from Maria Granmammelli.

Such thoughts, and while in conversation with a prince of the church!

"Good evening, Your Eminence," I said. "Good evening, Marquis. I hope the comedy was to your taste?"

"Enchanting, my daughter," the cardinal said. There was a gleam of humor in his eyes. From the comedy, perhaps? Or from sheer mischievous mockery? "And the more so that it was in honor of so charming a lady."

"No feasts are so pleasant as wedding feasts," the marquis said.

"Baptisms, perhaps." The cardinal smiled. "Soon, I pray, we will be celebrating the birth of an heir."

Was he a wizard, that he knew my thoughts? Aloud I said, "I pray to the Blessed Virgin and Saint Anne that such news will be forthcoming soon." For good measure I made the sign of the cross.

All three gentlemen crossed themselves as well. "My own two sons are a great comfort to me," the marquis said. "Cesare, of course, is almost a man—he has turned thirteen. Little Alfonso is five. I shall have them brought from Montecchio one day, Serenissima, so you may make their acquaintance."

"I shall look forward to it." That, at least, was not a lie. Although I intended to foil the marquis's ambitions with a son of my own as quickly as possible, I still enjoyed the company of little boys. The imperial court had been teeming with them; Maximilian had seven sons and my second brother, Ferdinand, had two. One of the greatest pleasures of my rare visits from Innsbruck to Vienna had been the opportunity to play with the children. "Tell me, what are your views on the subject of—"

"Enough," the duke said. There was a flick of the whip in his voice; after all, what man wants to hear of little boys when he himself is childless? "Let us go in to supper."

He offered his hand, and I put my own hand upon his wrist. The cardinal murmured a sardonic blessing and turned away. The marquis fell in behind us. We had taken only a few steps when we were compelled to halt by the expansiveness of one gentleman's bow, which placed his extended leg and deeply swept feathered cap directly in our path.

"Serenissimo." He straightened. "A word, if you will allow me."

"Messer Bernardo." The duke sounded—what? Annoyed, surprised, wary? Perhaps something of each. "We did not know you had returned."

"Only this morning, Serenissimo. I bear letters from Duke Cosimo, and gifts for you and your new duchess. I pray you will

forgive my importunity, that I was in such haste to be presented
to her."

So at last I would be introduced to the ambassador from Cosimo
de' Medici of Florence, the duke's former father-in-law and my sister
Johanna's father-in-law-to-be. My first thought was to wonder how
Duke Cosimo could send letters and gifts to the man people said
had murdered his daughter. But with my next breath I knew the
prickly relations of the two dukes, the two cities, would continue
with little more than a ripple as each man pursued his ambition. For
more than a hundred years, the Este and the Medici had been con-
tending for supreme power and prestige in the courts of Europe and
the papal conclaves of Rome—the Este with their ancient blood and
the Medici with their upstart riches. The marriage of the duke to
Lucrezia de' Medici had provided only a brief lull in the Precedenza,
as the rivalry was called; with her death, contention had flared anew.

"You could have chosen a more suitable moment," the duke
said. "Madonna, may I present to you Messer Bernardo Canigiani,
the Florentine ambassador."

"Serenissima." The ambassador swept another bow. "My pleasure is unbounded."

I inclined my head without speaking or smiling, granting the
barest acknowledgment. The ambassador's effusions were too ex-
travagant, and I found them distasteful.

This seemed to please the duke, because he smiled. It was not
one of his pleasant smiles. "You have had your wish, Messer Bernardo," he said. "Now begone. And next time, apply for an audience in the customary manner."

The ambassador bowed deeply for a third time, and we passed
on. The duke turned his head to speak to another courtier. From
the corner of my eye I saw Messer Bernardo's expression as he
straightened, and it was utterly different than it had been a moment
before. It was narrow-eyed, calculating—and chilling.

What did he know about the duke? What did Duke Cosimo know?

What schemes were they brewing?

It had all seemed so straightforward back in Innsbruck: I would marry the duke and take my place as Duchess of Ferrara, protected by my family's imperial power. I would grasp the dazzling fruits of my newly married state and keep both eyes tightly closed to the truth about the death of my husband's first wife. Now that I was in Ferrara, however, now that I was actually married to the duke and there was no turning back, it did not seem so straightforward anymore.

Some of my Ferrarese ladies were paid spies. Or were they?

My sisters-in-law had disliked my predecessor. But did they like me any better?

My husband's mad old nursemaid pressed potions upon me. Were they always—had they always been—as harmless as they seemed?

And the Florentine ambassador looked at the duke, and at me—me? Why me?—with eyes as cold as the deepest circle of Messer Dante's hell.

What had I done when I had agreed to this marriage?

Holy Virgin—what had I done?

"TURN YOUR HEAD to the right just a bit, Serenissima," Frà Pandolf said. "Then the light will limn the line of your cheek with gold, and add heavenly fire to your hair as it falls over your shoulder."

I turned my head, although I did not care for the fellow's obsequious manner. Limn the line of my cheek with gold, indeed. Flatterer.

"Yes!" he cried. He painted away, his foxy face intent, his brush flourishing. He was only of medium height but strongly made and with an animal energy about him. He wore a short reddish-brown beard, glossy and bristling with vigor; his round dark eyes and pointed nose reinforced the impression of a fox's slyness. Not at all what one would expect in a Franciscan friar, for all his coarse and paint-stained brown habit. Could the jackanapes really be as talented a painter as the duke said he was?

"Tell me, Frà Pandolf," I said. "How long have you enjoyed the duke's patronage?"

"For almost six years now, Serenissima. I came to Ferrara just after he became the duke, because even in France he was known for his artistic taste. He is generous. and such discernment! He understands the heart of the artist—that everything, everything, must give way to the art."

Including religious vows, I thought, although of course I did not say it. Instead I asked, "And what other works have you executed?"

"Two portraits of the duke himself, Serenissima." He continued to paint as he talked. "Two of Principessa Lucrezia, one of Principessa Leonora, one of the cardinal, and of course many classical and pastoral—"

"But *mio frà*, you have neglected to mention your greatest triumph," the Ferrarese lady-in-waiting Paolina said, in a teasing, I-know-a-secret voice. Her full name was Paolina Tassoni, and she was related in some way to the duke's majordomo; that was all I knew about her so far. She clearly knew rather more about Frà Pandolf. From the tone of her voice I wondered whether she and the painter— But no. That would be unthinkable.

"I've neglected nothing," Frà Pandolf said. His self-satisfied smile had disappeared, and his vulpine eyes had narrowed. Even so he continued to paint.

"No?" Paolina laughed and shook herself free of Domenica, who was trying to silence her. "What of the portrait of Serenissima Lucrezia? I know it is hidden away and meant to be a secret, but everyone knows, do they not? Should not the new duchess have an opportunity to gaze upon the face of her predecessor?"

Holy Virgin. How many of my ladies' tongues was the duke going to have to cut out?

"You and your secrets," Domenica said. She sounded as if she was trying to make light of it all. "You think you know everything."

"Perhaps I do know everything. I know there are whispers the duke shows the portrait privately to those he chooses, and boasts of his—"

"Ladies."

I did not raise my voice, but the girl stopped midsentence. I let the silence hang in the room for a moment, and then said, "If a thing is meant to be secret, it should remain secret. Will you chatter so blithely of my own private matters, the moment my back is turned?"

Paolina had the grace to look down. "*Chiedo perdono, Serenissima*," she murmured. Then she spoiled the effect of her pretty pardon-begging by adding, "But you will never truly appreciate Frà Pandolf's genius unless—"

"Enough. If the duke chooses to hide this portrait away, I am sure he has reason. Perhaps he believes it is not a good likeness."

Frà Pandolf stopped painting. "It's a perfect likeness!" he cried. "Go and look for yourself, Serenissima. It's at the top of the stairs past the bronze statue of Neptune, in the old gallery the duke has partitioned for his library. There's a hanging in front of it, so most people don't realize it's there."

"It is the duke's express order that no eyes but his gaze upon it," Domenica said.

The voice of reason. Naturally it did nothing but further inflame my desire to see the thing. How could I help but wish to gaze upon her face, the girl whose death had made a place for me here?

"Thank you, Domenica," I said. *Say nothing more, Domenica. I have heard your warning and I will pretend to heed it, but of course you and I both know I will see that painting, one way or another.* "Frà Pandolf, we will not speak of this matter further. In any case, if I were to leave you now, you would lose your light. Just as it—limns—my cheek."

He did not even blush. "Just so," he said. "Ah, Serenissima, paint must never hope to reproduce the living gleam of your hair, just as the sun strikes it."

I did not respond. The Franciscan continued to paint, his expression once again fixed in a self-satisfied smile as if he were already anticipating the praise and gold he would receive for his efforts. Or as if he knew he had planted a poisoned dart of curiosity in my breast. Probably both. I held my pose and thought of the duke's first duchess, and watched as little by little the squares of sunlight and shadow crept across the floor.

AT THE END of the day I looked at the friar's work, and even I must confess, it took my breath away.

How had he done it? My face and the spill of my hair floated ghostlike on the canvas, with only the barest sketch of the rest of the figure; he would finish the costume and the background with one of my ladies to wear the red dress and sit for him rather than I myself. But in what he had done so far, he had caught me to the life: my eyes, my mouth, the shape of my face, my hair, light and shadow and luminous color, each touch of the brush vividly revealing. He seemed so slapdash as he worked, yet he had produced a portrait that looked more like the real me than I myself.

A tall, slender woman, not young, sat next to a window with the sun streaming in upon her, limning—and yes, even I must confess that was the perfect term for the effect—the long but well-bred line of her cheek and jaw with light. Her hair was combed back from her high forehead with nothing but a narrow jeweled band to confine it, and it seemed to shimmer with lifelike color. Yes, her lower lip thrust out a bit, but in the painting it was sensual, soft, not a defect to be jeered at as the "Habsburg lip." And her eyes! The color of cloves, clear and steady and full of secrets.

"It is you, Serenissima," Frà Pandolf said, leaning over my

shoulder as I looked at it, close enough that I could feel the heat of his breath against my cheek and smell the scents of paint and turpentine and animal male upon his habit. I drew away. A genius the fellow might be, but as the duke had remarked, he was unpleasantly familiar in his manner.

"It is very good," I said coldly. "But it is for the duke to decide. You will wait upon him, Frà Pandolf, when it is finished."

"Yes, Serenissima," he said. "Who could help but admire it, when it shows your very soul, your inner beauty, so clearly?"

"You forget yourself," I said, in an even more icy voice. God knows if it really had any effect on the fellow, but at least he stepped back from me and looked away.

"Domenica," I said. "Sybille. Paolina. Attend me. Gather up the puppies, if you please, and let us go."

I COULD TELL la Cavalla a thing or two about Frà Pandolf. Now there's one who has no business in a friar's robes! I expected him to be a virgin, but I couldn't have been more wrong. He told me afterward he'd had dozens and dozens of women, peasants and ladies, merchants' wives and craftsmen's daughters, even holy nuns—he'd had plenty of opportunity, because he came from a sunny island somewhere to the south where oranges and lemons grew year-round, and had wandered to Rome and other cities I'd never heard of before coming to Ferrara in hopes of catching Alfonso's eye.

He was nobody, a foundling, he said, but he always wanted to paint pictures. He laughed when I asked him why he became a friar. Visions? Callings? Prayers? Not Frà Pandolf. He took Franciscan orders because they gave him standing without requiring him to be confined to a monastery. Under the pretense of preaching—preaching!—he could travel anywhere, ask for charity from anyone, paint when it pleased him, and find ever richer and nobler patrons. He liked to fottere the women he painted, he said—it made his paintings better. When he was painting a great lady, he imagined himself in bed with her. I wonder what his imaginings were about la Cavalla.

He didn't have to depend on imaginings with me. Who seduced who? I'm not sure. I just know he made me look beautiful, so beautiful, with his paints and brushes. He said I was the most beautiful of all the women he'd painted, and I believed him. Oh, I could've lain in his bed forever with nothing but air on my skin and the smell of paints and turpentine sharp in the room.

When he had his fill of painting me, though, he didn't want me anymore. He began to paint a girl in the kitchen instead. Never mind how I found out. Was she more beautiful? He said it was just a way to get special food, special wine. I told him gluttony was a sin. He laughed. I laughed, too, but only because I didn't want him to know he'd hurt me.

Someday I'll tell you more about him, and about all of them. Yes, I had lovers, so many that sometimes I lost count. Once you have one, it's easy to move on to another, and then another, and one morning you wake up and realize there have been ten or twenty or more.

At first I had to be careful—Alfonso would go weeks without touching me, and everyone was watching, and it would've been a disaster if I'd found myself with child when it couldn't have been Alfonso's. But Isabella had taught me ways to play with a man without the risk of catching a child. Oh, I had a lovely time, all that first year. I pretended to be sick, and I succeeded so well, my father sent his chief physician from Florence, and what awful purges and cuppings I had to endure! But it was worth it. Alfonso left me alone more and more, and for a while, at least, I was free to do as I pleased.

I was shocked when I found out half the court had been whispering in Alfonso's ear about my avventurini *with other men. They were looking for favor, assuming he'd find out everything anyway and falling all over each other to be the first to tell him. I swear, there was a line of people from one end of the Castello to the other, waiting to tell Alfonso all my sins.*

It didn't matter. I was young, I was beautiful, and I thought I would live forever.

I was wrong.

And Frà Pandolf, for one, could tell you: I was not ready to die.

CHAPTER SIX

*B*efore I could go in search of the painting, I had to escape my ladies.

That is one of the disadvantages of rank: a highly placed person is almost never alone. Emperors even have grooms of the close-stool to attend them while they perform their most intimate bodily functions, as I was in a particular position to know, having had an emperor for both a father and a brother. Fortunately, my own rank was not quite that high.

Even so, it was a delicate matter to escape my attendants. First, I sent Domenica to the garden with the puppies, telling her they appeared to be in need of some time outdoors. Then I pretended to realize I had an appetite for my favorite angelica comfits, and sent Sybille to fetch them. Lastly, I feigned a sudden headache and sent Paolina running for lavender oil and an infusion of valerian.

And lo, there I stood, alone. It gave me an eerie feeling, as if I were being watched by hidden eyes. Gossip, of course, honey-combed Italian palaces—all palaces, for that matter—with hidden

passageways peopled with secretaries and spies, eyes pressed to
peepholes. But surely the duke would not have set his lackeys to
watch me on an afternoon when I was occupied with something
as innocuous as having my portrait painted at his own command?

It did not matter. One of them—or all of them—would report
the conversation with Frà Pandolf, and the duke would be angry
anyway. I would be subjected to another humiliating reproof and
probably more threats as well, whether I went in search of the portrait or not. So why not satisfy my curiosity, once and for all?

*It's at the top of the stairs past the bronze statue of Neptune, in the old
gallery the duke has partitioned for his library.* The statue of Neptune I
remembered, as it was a piece by Claus of Innsbruck, a celebrated
countryman of mine. I gathered up my jeweled scarlet skirts and
hurried through to the next room, took a turn, passed through another room. Yes, there was Neptune with his half-tamed sea-horse.
I ran up the stairs, and just a few steps farther on a portion of the
wall was indeed covered by a hanging. It was in an alcove with two
gilded chairs placed in front of it, all so cleverly arranged no one
would ever guess a painting was concealed there.

No time, no time to stop and think about it, and probably just
as well. I reached out and drew the curtain.

And there she was. The duke's last duchess.

She was beautiful. She was a hundred, a thousand times more
beautiful than I could ever have imagined. Frà Pandolf's unmistakable style had caught her so vividly, it was as if she were standing
there between one breath and the next, ready to step down from
the wall.

Beautiful. And young, with charmingly childlike freckles like
a dusting of cinnamon over her nose and forehead. Her eyes were
golden, alive with adolescent willfulness, high spirits, and the careless selfishness of childhood; her hair was gleaming russet, braided
and bound up with jewels. Her cheeks were luminous with a flush
of pleasure that died out delicately along the line of her throat. In

the curve of her lips I read secrets and sensuality. She held a spray of cherry blossoms, white as snow, with the palest of pink at their hearts.

I tried to imagine her sick and mad. I tried to imagine her dead. After what Maria Granmammelli had told me, I could not keep myself from wondering—was she poisoned? Poisoned twice, perhaps, first to make her appear mad, and then, when she was safely hidden away, a medicinal posset or sleeping draught to kill her? How horrible, to sink trustingly into sleep and be sucked down into death, unready and unshriven.

I was so caught up in my thoughts, I did not hear so much as the sound of a step behind me. I had no idea he was there until he reached out and drew the curtain closed.

My heart stopped. My hands went cold. I jerked around guilt-ily before I could stop myself.

"What is this, Madonna?" the duke said. There was anger such as I had never heard before in his voice. "Your woman tells me you have a headache, yet I do not find you where she left you, waiting for her potion."

Paolina, I thought. It was Paolina I sent for the headache po-tion. She, then, is the duke's spy. That is one way she learns the secrets she loves so much. But she did not know I was coming to look at the painting. How did he know where to find me?

"You are watched," he said, as if he had heard my thought. His voice had an icy intensity. "You are the Duchess of Ferrara, Madonna, and *per Dio* you do not take a step that someone does not know it."

Holy Virgin. I had been right, then, about the spies and the secret passageways.

"I must beg your forgiveness, my lord." My voice shook; I put my hands behind my back and began to count the rubies in the chain around my waist, like the beads of a rosary. *One, two, three* . . . "One of my ladies spoke of this painting as a masterwork, and Frà Pandolf himself told me where to find it. My woman's curiosity got the better of me."

He was not disarmed. "Curiosity does not become you," he said. "Woman or no. You will oblige me, Madonna, by resisting it in future."

I inclined my head in acknowledgment. He was unaccompanied by his usual train of gentlemen and secretaries, which was uncharacteristic and must have been deliberate; we were alone in the gallery but for whatever secret watchers he might have set. If he were to do me harm, they would hardly rush to my aid.

"I will do so," I said. "Again, I ask your pardon."

He stepped closer, and although I had intended to take my leave with what few shreds of dignity remained to me, I was left with no way to escape unless I pushed against him. That, I must confess, I was afraid to do. He was so close, I felt the heat of his flesh and smelled the scents of sandalwood and amber that always clung about his clothes.

. . . *seven, eight, nine* . . .

"That is not enough," he said. "I am sure you have been told, Madonna, and more than once, what is said to have become of my last duchess whose likeness so aroused your curiosity."

"I should like to go," I said, a shaming quaver in my voice.

"No. You will listen to me. It displeases me that you lend your countenance to such gossip. And as for Frà Pandolf, he is a remarkable painter but in anything but his art he is utterly beneath your notice. I thought better of you, Madonna, than that you would plot petty schemes with him."

I was becoming more and more afraid. Never before had I met a man who was not conciliated by submissiveness and contrition. Would boldness serve me better?

"It was not a petty scheme," I countered. Of course, it had been—my own rather petty scheme to look at the painting of the first duchess while I had the opportunity. But the very fact that I was lying gave me spurious strength. "And I did not plot. I would remind you, my lord, that I am——"

He grasped my arm with hard fingers.

"You are my wife," he said. "And I will teach you, Madonna, that it is not my wife's place to defy me."

HE DRAGGED ME to my apartments like a prisoner, all in my scarlet wedding finery and long loose hair. No one interfered. One of his secretaries and two gentlemen-of-honor fell in behind us without so much as a word. Those we passed, whether courtiers or servants, turned their faces away and feigned not to notice us. Humiliation made my blood burn like fire under my skin, and fear made me sick and dizzy. I could only think—is this what happened before? Did he kill her in plain sight of his whole court, and did they all look away and pretend to see nothing?

When we entered the Jupiter chamber, Sybille was there with two serving-maids. She stepped forward, surprised, and began to say something about angelica comfits; the duke told her shortly to make off with herself, the maids, and anyone else who might disturb us. I had only a moment to glimpse her outraged expression— she is a Wittelsbach, after all, and proud as Niobe—before he propelled me into the inner chamber. I breathed a prayer of thanks that Sybille, at least, would know what was happening.

Inside the bedchamber the duke let go of my arm and pushed me toward the bed. I caught hold of one of the carved bedposts and turned to face him. My tangled hair fell across my face and caught in the jeweled clasps of my mantle.

"What do you intend to do, my lord?" I found my voice at last. "Surely we can——"

"Be silent," he said. "I am not accustomed to having my wishes flouted, Madonna, and this time I intend to make certain it does not happen again."

I stared at him, breathing hard. I wanted to shout, *And what is it exactly, my lord duke, about your first duchess's life and death that you are so resolute to conceal?* But frightened and angry as I was, I did not dare. It would be foolish—dangerous, even—to anger him further.

"I have warned you twice," he said. The deadly choler in his voice was terrifying. "And even so, you have defied me. She had the excuse of being fifteen years old and a pawnbroker's daughter. You, a woman grown, an emperor's daughter, an emperor's sister, should know better than to sink so low."

Holy Virgin, was he reading my mind? In desperation I made my voice soft and pleading. "It was conversation for courtesy's sake, no more. I am sorry I disobeyed you. I will not do it again. Please, my lord, you are frightening me."

He did not reply. He stepped over to the hearth, where a bundle or two of poplar withes lay awaiting the *domestica* who would light a fire in my room later on. With short, angry movements he pulled first one stick, then another from the bundle, until finally he found one about as long as his arm, about as thick as his finger. He cut through the air with it twice and then turned back to me.

I stared at him in horror.

I had been beaten as a child, of course. My father had been brought up at the strict Spanish court and brooked no disorder or disobedience in his sons and daughters. I had been switched by my nurses for clumsiness, for insolence, for dirtying my clothes; caned across my palms by my tutors for wrongly conjugated Latin verbs and errors in history lessons. But that was when I was a child, and now I was a woman and married. It was not unheard-of for husbands to beat their wives, but despite the duke's threats and the fate of poor Maddalena Costabili, I had never seriously believed it could happen to me.

To me! An archduchess of Austria! And with a commonplace stick from the hearth!

"You would not dare—"

Before I could finish the sentence, he caught me by the arms and threw me down across the bed. Holy Virgin, he was strong. I jerked back, and it was as if I were struggling against steel or stone. He pinned me flat on my face with his hand between my shoulder blades.

"I will be master in my household," he said. "Never forget it."

He jerked my skirts up over my back and struck me across my legs with the switch. Through my thin taffeta stockings the blows were hard and sharp and stinging. He struck me again, this time over the fine embroidered linen of my drawers, and then again. I clenched my teeth and twisted under his hand and refused to cry out at first. Then I did cry out. After that I could not help myself, and I screamed. When I screamed, he stopped.

I heard him break the stick and throw it aside. I pushed myself up on my hands and turned my head. I could feel tear-wet strands of my hair stuck to my cheek and the heavy strings of pearls and rubies swinging loose against my shoulder. My brave scarlet bridal silk was rucked and crumpled around me. The stripes on my flesh burned and throbbed.

"If you think," I said, my voice sick and shaking. "If you think—"

I could not go on. I swallowed and closed my eyes and struggled to breathe.

He stood there quite calmly, one hand on the latch of the door. His eyes were cold and his clothing was hardly disarranged. The storm had passed, and hardly a ripple remained to mar his dark, glittering surface. Underneath the monsters intertwined: the fifteenth-century Este lord who had beheaded his young wife and his own son for incest; the vicious and rapacious Cesare Borgia, his great-uncle; the mad Valois princes of his mother's blood.

"If I think what, Madonna?"

From his expression he might have done nothing more than correct a mastiff for disobeying a command, or dismiss a singer for a C in *alt* that was slightly flat. I wanted to kill him. I wanted to scream my suspicions, the world's suspicions, at him, just to provoke some response. I sank my nails into the silk of the coverlet, trembling with fear and hurt and fury.

"If you think you will beat me into mindlessness, you are mistaken."

He looked at me until I could bear it no longer. I capitulated. I looked away.

"If I had wished to beat you into mindlessness," he said, "I would have done so."

He turned and left the room.

I heard the puppies begin to bark in the outer chamber. Had Domenica returned? Had Sybille clung to her post despite his dismissal? Then I heard his voice, cool and emotionless, and Paolina Tassoni's voice replying. I wondered what he was saying. I wondered what she was telling him.

Spy, spy, spy. I would have her out of my household. I would have her out of the court entirely, if it were ever in my power. If I ever had power again.

I jerked the dangling string of pearls from my hair; the thread broke and the perfectly matched spheres scattered over the bed and the marble floor. I remembered what the Ferrarese tiring-woman had whispered when she braided them into my hair on my wedding day. I remembered being careless with my jeweled bridal skirts as I was formally presented to the duke in the forecourt of the Castello. *What are silks, what are jewels, to ones such as you and I?*

I threw myself down on the bed again and gave myself up to my tears.

FIFTEEN YEARS OLD and a pawnbroker's daughter! By the Baptist, I want to kill him. It drives me mad sometimes that I'm immobila, *that I can only watch and not touch the living.*

I expected him to fottere her when he finished thrashing her. That's how it would've ended if he'd thrashed me. I never would've let him walk away like that—there's nothing like a touch of the whip to make the pota cry out for the cazzo. La Cavalla didn't look aroused, though. She looked angry and frightened. Well, it's about time she learned what Alfonso is really like.

He never beat me. He would accuse me of some misbehavior, oh, yes, and it would make him angry when I would face him down sweetly and swear to my innocence and protest that I had been sick that day, so sick. I could see the scorn in his eyes, in the way his whole face would stop moving. He never raised his voice, though, or lost his temper, or struck me, and I think that's why I kept doing it. I wanted him to show anger. I wanted him to show something. I wanted him to admit that I was his wife. Why is he different with la Cavalla? Is it because he admires her and values her, and never cared a fig for—

Enough, enough, enough. I can't think about such things. The painting. I'll think about the painting.

How wonderful to see it again. Isn't it beautiful? And such a tale there is about it.

I loved it from the moment Frà Pandolf presented it to Alfonso. What a furor it created! All the court was there to see the unveiling, and everyone gasped—even Alfonso, and he isn't easily surprised. The room buzzed so, I was reminded of the time Isabella and I stole honey from the bee-man's hives. Everyone who looked at it exclaimed about how much it looked like me.

But then— It was never displayed. I never saw it again. I badgered Alfonso over and over, but he ignored me. He called in another painter, who painted another portrait; that's the one in the main gallery. Frà Pandolf's portrait of me vanished. I always believed Alfonso destroyed it, just because it made me so beautiful. He wanted to think of me as a lowborn merchant's daughter and didn't want to see me painted as a beautiful young duchess.

But he didn't. He hid it away. I wonder why.

Chi lo sa! I'm just glad it wasn't destroyed. Someday poets will sing praises to me, all on account of that portrait. La Cavalla looked like she'd swallowed a frog when she saw it. I wish she could see the other one, too, but it's hidden away where no one will ever find it.

She's stopped crying now. I wonder what she's thinking. I wonder if she's sorry she didn't fight back. I know if Alfonso had beaten me like that, duke or no duke, he never would've walked away without a few bites and scratches to show for it.

CHAPTER SEVEN

$\mathcal{I}$ did not go down to supper, and the duke did not send a message requiring my presence. After my first tears, I lay awake on the bed, dry-eyed, staring at nothing, thinking of nothing. I collected the loose pearls on the bedcover and counted them over and over, dividing them into even piles; when I realized what I was doing, I struck the pearls aside with a cry of despair.

It terrified me when I became aware of myself doing such things, counting, pleating, rearranging. I'd had the habit as long as I could remember, and my nurse in Innsbruck had slapped my fingers over and over and threatened me with tales of madness in my blood, tales of my grandmother Johanna of Castile, who was called Juana la Loca, Johanna the Mad, and locked up in a castle in Spain for fifty years because of it. Such tales they told of poor Juana and her single-minded obsession with her handsome husband; my nurse had been a young waiting-lady in Juana's household and had never forgotten her mistress's passionate tempers and furies. Madness like that began, she would hiss at me, with little habits like counting candied almonds into piles or arranging the skirts of my dress in perfect pleats. It was a known thing that madness some-times skipped from one generation to another in noble families, and I struggled to quell my singularities. I did not always succeed. How often did I set things straight, count things, make creases and pleats, when I myself did not know I was doing it?

My head ached fiercely. I was cold. When the soft silver dusk began to press in at the windows, I knew I would have to call my ladies to undress me. I could not sleep in my bridal scarlet with its jewels and wide skirts and stiffened bodice, and I was sewn into it; it would be impossible to cut the stitches and unfasten all the hooks and clasps and unlace my corset by myself.

This was yet another of the disadvantages of rank and fashion. A third: they had all been, I was sure, avidly listening at the door. Appearing as the chastised wife before my beloved we-three, who knew me so intimately, would be bad enough; I hated the thought of facing the Ferrarese ladies, who were relative strangers.

Holy Virgin, I hurt all over. The thought that my disgrace would be whispered from one end of the Castello to the other did not help matters. I tried to sit up, and quickly changed my mind. I rolled to my side and slid off the bed.

"Sybille," I called. My throat was sore with crying. Please, I thought, let her have waited in the outer chamber. "Katharina. Christine. Please come in, my we-three. I want you."

Sybille, Katharina, and—not Christine but Paolina—came in with suspicious promptness. Tristo and Isa gamboled among their skirts, sniffing the floor for treats, their little white-tipped tails whipping back and forth with delight.

"Paolina, you may go." I was hardly going to have the duke's spy undressing me and goggling at the marks of the duke's displea-sure on my flesh. To my surprise, the girl's eyes filled with tears, but she whispered a husky, "*Si, Serenissima,*" and fled.

"Where is Christine?" Even as I said it, I knew I sounded like a fretful child, but I could not help myself. "I want all three of you together."

"She is off somewhere with Messer Luzzasco, the organist," Katharina said. "She and those Bendidio sisters, the ones who sing. You know Christine—if she hears a little music, she is lost for hours."

This lightened my misery a bit—Christine's delight in music always gave me pleasure. "Perhaps she will come back with some new songs to play for us. Will you undress me, please, the two of you, and bring my night-smock and coif? I will have a cup of wine and go straight to bed."

Katharina took up the silver-gilt scissors that hung on a chain at her waist and began to clip the stitches in my bodice. "Your dress is ruined," she said. "And you have broken the string of the Este pearls—they are everywhere."

Little Isa, in fact, was about to eat one of them. I gathered her up just in time and put her in the middle of my bed.

"Pick them up, then." Perhaps I was too brusque with her, but I did not want to think about the loose pearls, and in any case it was certainly not my doing the scarlet dress was spoiled. In a more temperate voice I said, "Ask the duke's wardrobe master to tell you how many there were, and be careful you have them all."

She did as I directed, grumbling to herself in German. Sybille, always so loving, her hands always so gentle and warm, unhooked the clasps to free me from my mantle. She stroked my disheveled hair as she unlaced my corset, but said nothing. It was a huge relief to be dressed again, at last, in the loose cambric night-smock.

"Would you like some bread sopped in your wine, Bärbel?" Katharina had gathered the pearls in a handkerchief and looked— well, not contrite exactly, but a little less prickly. "You have had no supper."

"No, I think not, but thank you. What entertainments are arranged for tomorrow?"

"A hunt in the morning after Mass, and a performance of the duke's consort of singers after supper."

"I shall not hunt." It was, of course, ludicrous to imagine myself in the saddle, and mercifully both of them managed to keep straight faces at my pronouncement. "Sybille, go at once and tell the duke I shall not see him until supper tomorrow."

"Yes, Serenissima."

She curtsied and went out. Katharina prepared my wine in a long-handled copper warming-pot over the fire. In deliberate defiance of the duke's preference for unspiced, unsweetened wines, I directed her to stir in generous pinches of cinnamon and cloves and a good deal of grated white sugar. While I drank it, she gathered up the pieces of the scarlet wedding dress, bodice, sleeves, skirts, and mantle, smoothing their wrinkles and creases and folding them with the tender care of a mother.

"Would you like a lotion, Bärbel?" she asked me at last. "I will make it myself, with bayberry oil and marjoram and honey, and you may do as you wish with it in private."

I put the wine-cup down. My eyes felt dry and hot. "Thank you, Katrine," I said. "Yes, please. I would like the—marks—to disappear as quickly as possible."

She nodded. "And this," she said, tilting her head to the heap of heavy scarlet silk in her arms. "I will repair it, so it is just as it was. No one will ever know."

I could not help but laugh. "Do your best," I said. "But I assure you, everyone knows already."

EVEN AFTER KATHARINA had made up the lotion, even after Sybille had returned and banked the fire and reposed herself on the pallet at the foot of my bed, I could not sleep. At first I was afraid the duke would send for me, and if he had, God alone knows what I might have done. Fortunately, he did not. I rolled over, curled up, rolled over again, trying to find a comfortable position. It was cold in the room, even with the banked fire. I heard bells somewhere out in the city, bells from convents and monasteries in every direction ringing the hours. I counted them. Finally when they rang the third vigil of matins, I whispered a prayer to Saint Monica, the patroness of unhappy wives, promising her a novena if my pains and fears might be eased. After that I slept at last.

I awoke late, heavy-eyed and aching. Domenica Guarini and my dear Christine fussed over me until I wanted to scream, pressing bread and wine upon me to break my fast, sponging me with warm water, massaging my flesh with more of Katharina's lotion, dressing me like a child's poppet. The lotion had achieved its end, or perhaps the duke's strokes had not been so cruel as they seemed in the heat of the moment—there were a few faint red marks on my buttocks and thighs, but no bruising or broken skin.

"Has the hunt begun?" I asked Christine as she brushed out my hair.

"Yes, Serenissima, they left an hour ago, directly after Mass."

"And you are certain the duke was among the hunters?"

"I saw him myself, all in black and gold like the devil he is. May he burn in hell."

"Shush. He will only be further angered if he hears you have said such a thing." I glanced sidelong at Domenica. Christine was quite clever enough to take my meaning; she said no more, but pressed her soft lips together and bent her attention to braiding my hair with a chain of amethysts.

"You need not fear I will repeat what you say, Serenissima." Domenica sounded sincerely hurt. "No, nor what Christine says, nor anyone in your household. There may be spies around every corner in Ferrara, but I swear to you—" She looked around, and her dark eyes alighted on Tristo, who was sniffing and circling in the corner the way all puppies do when they need a walk in the garden. "By the little dog of San Domenico himself, I am not one of them."

"There is no need for such vows," I said. Her earnestness touched me even through my fog of humiliation and misery. "Now fetch the dogs' leashes, if you please, and my mantle. We will take some air in the orange garden, and then we will go to the chapel. I have promised a novena to Saint Monica, and I wish to begin it at once."

THE ORANGE GARDEN was not, as one might think, in a courtyard on the ground level with the other gardens and orchards of the Castello; it was a hanging garden, a square rooftop terrace jutting out from the great Lions' Tower, landscaped with small paths and flower-beds with soil in boxes. The orange and lemon and citron trees in their wooden tubs were carried upstairs and downstairs as needed, and in cold weather such as this they were tended indoors like the petted aristocrats from the south they were. Surrounding the garden were parapets over which one could gaze out upon the city with its ancient walls, its marshes, its fields, and the silver branches of the Po, as if floating above it all.

The duke's younger sister Nora happened to be there when we arrived, with her ladies and gentlemen—including the poet Tasso, handsome, long-legged, and elegantly dressed as ever but looking restless and moody—and her tame astrologer. The astrologer was discoursing upon the absent orange trees' subjection to the sun and the value of the fruits' juice in dissolving malignant planetary influences. Naturally, the fellow broke off when I approached, and abased himself; Nora and her ladies curtsied; the gentlemen bowed. Next to young Messer Torquato I recognized the Florentine ambassador, Messer Bernardo Canigiani, by the ostentatious sweep of his hat. I acknowledged the salutes and spoke politely to Nora. The puppies wagged their tails furiously and jumped up for petting, and then I passed on, not wishing to interrupt Nora and her little court any further.

Behind me I heard whispers and a woman's half-stifled laughter. Laughter.

How dare they? How *dare* they? Not only were they laughing in the presence of the astrologer, a lowborn fellow and a failed priest from the look of him, but in Messer Bernardo's presence, too; now he would write to his master in Florence not only that the duke had beaten me, but that the duke's own sister was laughing behind my back. For a single scalding moment tears blurred my vision; furiously I blinked them away. Domenica began chirruping to the puppies as if trying to cover the humiliating sounds behind us.

We stood at the walls for a while, but I saw nothing of the much-vaunted city view. I ran my fingers over the lines of mortar between the bricks, tracing their symmetrical pattern. At last I could bear it no longer, and without a word we made our way back inside the Castello and across the corridor to the chapel. I was hardly in any state of mind to humble myself, but I managed to say three Paters, three Aves, and three Glorias, and at least begin my petition to Saint Monica, on my knees on the cold marble floor with its polychrome inlay-work. The familiar cadence of the Latin calmed me a little.

The chapel was beautiful, small but with elegant geometric lines and a vaulted ceiling frescoed with images of the four Evangelists attended by their traditional symbols—Saint Matthew's angel, Saint Mark's lion, Saint Luke's eagle, and Saint John's bull—as well as by the proud white eagles of the Este. There were two or three niches along the walls, with statuary in the classical style. Each piece was beautiful but not to my personal taste—one could hardly tell if they were Christian saints or pagan goddesses. At last I signaled for Christine to fetch me a chair so I might save my knees and think awhile. Saint Monica might indeed intercede for me, but in the meantime it was only practical to assess my situation and decide for myself upon a course of action.

Clearly the duke's desire to ingratiate himself into my brother's imperial good graces did not extend to his private dealings with me. And I knew Maximilian well enough to know it would do me little good to write him an outraged letter; he was unlikely to cast aside the duke's promises of Ferrarese troops against the encroaching Ottoman Empire simply because a husband had corrected his wife. I was married now, he would write back, the duke was my master, and that was the end of it.

Except I was not willing for that to be the end of it.

I could close my ears to whispers about the duke and his first wife. I could even swallow the humiliation of a thrashing, if it had remained a private thing between the duke and me. Although of course that was impossible; of course it would be talked of. Nora had done more than talk. She had laughed, and that meant the whole court was laughing. I could almost hear the scratching of a hundred pens eager to spread the story all over Europe.

I would not be publicly humiliated. I would not accept it. I—

"I hope, Serenissima, you are finding comfort in your prayers?"

I looked up, surprised anyone would dare interrupt me. It was Messer Bernardo Canigiani, the Florentine ambassador; his mobile face was arranged in an expression of sympathy so artless that for a breath or two I was taken in. Then I remembered who and what he was.

"I always find comfort in prayer," I said. "And I would prefer to do so alone."

With bland disregard for my rudeness, he made a gesture and a servant appeared beside him with another chair. He settled himself, arranged the folds of his gown, and waved the man away. I could see Domenica and Christine just outside the door, and two or three fellows wearing the red, blue, and gold livery of the Medici. Messer Bernardo and I were not exactly alone, but there in the center of the chapel, with no hiding places for listeners, we were surprisingly well-placed for low-voiced private conversation.

Which was obviously his intent. I wondered why, and rather than call my own waiting-gentlemen to eject him from the chapel, I allowed him to remain.

"How difficult it must be," he said at last. His mask-face changed from its expression of sympathy to one of sympathy tinged with outrage. "Listening to them laugh."

That bit of effrontery left me speechless, which was not an easy thing to do. He apparently took this as encouragement, for he leaned closer and lowered his voice even more. "Perhaps you would welcome an opportunity to escape from Ferrara, from the monster who mistreats you so?"

I said nothing.

"Your sister and Prince Francesco were married two days ago. She would welcome you with delight, if you chose to make a congratulatory visit to Florence."

My first thought was this: *I will throw myself into the Po di Volano before I slink off to Florence with all my dreams in shatters.* My second thought followed hard upon it: *I need not slink. I could travel in state, my train hand-picked so there would be no one to laugh.*

It did not matter how many thoughts I had, of course. The duke would never allow me to leave the city alone, so soon after our marriage.

"That is impossible," I said.

He leaned closer still. "Perhaps. Perhaps not. Imagine his humiliation. Would it not make a magnificent revenge?"

I would like to leave out what happened next, because I am ashamed of it. But what is the point of telling a story, if one is not completely truthful about one's own thoughts and actions? There in the cold marble chapel, my flesh still tender from the duke's chastisement and my anger still smoldering from his sister's laughter, I heard the word *revenge* and felt a rush of response. *Yes!* my Habsburg blood cried, pulsing in my veins. *Yes!* cried my wounded pride and my lacerated dignity, amid the ruins of the

Cloud-Cuckoo-Land I had created in my imagination, in which I presided over the court at Ferrara like the perfect and queenly Duchess Elisabetta Gonzaga—not the real woman, of course, who died before I was ever born, but the heroine of *Il Libro del Cortegiano*, the guide-book and lodestar to all my dreams.

Would it not make a magnificent revenge?

"Magnificent, indeed," I said carefully. "But you understand, one such as I cannot simply ride off to another city."

His mien changed, like a fisherman who had, somewhat unexpectedly, hooked a fish. I knew instantly I had been a fool, a hundred kinds of a fool, to encourage him even for the space of a single sentence.

"Naturally not," he said, his voice unctuous as clotted cream. "But such a matter could be arranged discreetly. It would be like a tale from Boccaccio—you could easily be one of the illustrious ladies of whom he wrote so delightfully. Imagine the joy of sister greeting sister! Imagine the fetes and entertainments! Imagine the abandoned husband gnashing his teeth, repudiated by his imperial bride."

Repudiated? Holy Virgin. That was taking the fantasy too far.

"I do not care for that story," I said.

"Imagine further," he went on, as if I had not spoken, "the newly freed lady seizing the opportunity and speaking publicly, writing letters—oh, let us say, about an evil deed her husband did, before their marriage. Before she escaped she had every reason to be curious, after all. Every right to come and go in her husband's private chambers, every right to speak with his retainers, look at his papers—"

"For the love of God," I said through my teeth. "Are you mad, Messer Bernardo? That is treason."

He leaned back in his chair, his face inscrutable. "Treason? You mistake me, Serenissima. It is nothing but a tale, a work of imagination after the model of Boccaccio. I was told you looked forward to the discussion of literary works here in Ferrara."

"I do not wish to hear such tales as that." I could feel my heart thudding and a sweat of fear breaking out under my fine gown. In what net of conspiracy was this man attempting to entangle me? "Nor would the duke."

He shrugged. "It would make conversation for a cold winter's night, that is all. Perhaps each person could conceive a different version of the tale, and we could judge one against another."

He seemed so sanguine that for a moment I myself was not sure I had heard what I had heard. I stared at him in wordless revulsion. He rose from his chair, smiling, and bowed with his characteristic sweeping effulgence.

"I will leave you to your prayers," he said. "Good day to you, Serenissima. I look forward to further literary discourse with so learned a lady."

He gestured to his servant to come and take his chair, and they went out. I could hear him speaking to Domenica and Christine in that silky voice of his. I felt dizzy, and I rubbed my icy palms against the prickly gold-embroidered brocade of my skirts. There were sequins sewn in the loops and curves of the design. I touched each one, following the lines of the pattern.

Be calm. Be calm. Think.

Imagine further the newly freed lady seizing the opportunity and speaking publicly, writing letters—oh, let us say, about an evil deed her husband did, before their marriage. . . .

So the Florentines had not forgotten the death of Lucrezia de' Medici, despite the gifts and good wishes Cosimo de' Medici had heaped upon us. Political expediency had not, after all, eclipsed a father's natural desire for revenge.

My first impulse was to go to the duke and recount the entire conversation. But Messer Bernardo would give his own version, with a tolerant laugh at the foolish fancies of women. A different expression, a different emphasis on a word here or there, and the whole thing indeed became little more than a bit of elegant literary amusement. And once again, I would appear to be taking an un-suitable interest in my husband's first wife.

Or—

What if there was no plot to avenge Duchess Lucrezia at all, and Messer Bernardo's whole intent was that I run to the duke with my suspicions, so as to further inflame his anger against me? It would be in Duke Cosimo's interest for my marriage into Ferrara to founder—he and the city of Florence would then surpass Duke Alfonso and Ferrara in my brother Maximilian's imperial favor. This in turn would put Duke Cosimo closer to winning the grand ducal title and precedence both he and my husband coveted.

Or—

What if my reception in Florence would consist not of fetes and entertainments and the joy of sister greeting sister, but of im-prisonment, luxurious imprisonment, of course, but imprisonment nevertheless? And what if then the Florentines began sending let-ters in my name, letters I myself would never see or sign? Forgery was an Italian art. They could say what they wished and attribute it to me.

Or—

Or what?

A hundred plots branched off from Messer Bernardo's curious words, like the stalks of a noxious weed. Each stalk sprouted leaves and tendrils of menace. How could I know the right thing to do?

Do nothing, I told myself. Say nothing. Watch and wait.

She has had every reason to be curious, after all. Every right to come and go in her husband's private chambers, every right to speak with his retainers, look at his papers—

Messer Bernardo had been right about that, at least. I was par-ticularly suited to penetrate the duke's secrets, simply because I was his wife, with a legitimate place in his most intimate house-hold. And I was a woman. Gossip, questions, secrets—they were women's prerogatives, women's amusements, women's weapons. I would have to be careful, because I wanted no more thrashings and no more laughter at my expense. But if I could find out the truth about Lucrezia de' Medici's death, I could hold it over the duke's arrogant dark head and make certain there would be no more thrashings, ever.

No more thrashings. No more laughter.

My pulse quickened. I stopped counting the sequins and crushed handfuls of the brocade in my fists.

I could do it. I would have to be very careful, but I could do it. I could, for instance, go to the Monastero del Corpus Domini where the girl Maddalena Costabili claimed Lucrezia de' Medici had died. It was Advent, after all, and not even Alfonso d'Este could quarrel with his devout new wife's impulse to retreat to a religious house for a day, to pray for a son. And if she happened to choose the Monastero del Corpus Domini—well, that could be explained easily enough, a suggestion from one of the Ferrarese ladies, perhaps—

"Serenissima?"

I started guiltily, as if I had been caught voicing my dangerous thoughts aloud. Domenica did not seem to notice anything amiss; her pleasant, open face showed only her hesitation to interrupt me at my prayers.

"Forgive me, Serenissima, but it will be suppertime soon. The duke will expect you."

I crossed myself. I would finish my prayers to Saint Monica another day; she would understand. She herself had been burdened with a husband of violent temper and dissolute habits, and surely she would guard me as I pursued my inquiries.

"I am coming," I said. "Naturally I would not wish to keep the duke waiting."

LA CAVALLA HAD best take care in her dealings with Messer Bernardo Canigiani. He's deep in my father's counsels, and most of what he does, *he does at my father's command. He pretends to be Alfonso's friend, but he isn't. He's the one who paid Maddalena Costabili's gambling debts, by the way, in exchange for her outbursts on la Cavalla's wedding night, and look at Maddalena now.*

I don't understand what he was hinting at with that silly business of telling a story like Boccaccio—and even I know about Boccaccio, with his one hundred bawdy tales, because Tommasina used to read them to me, or at least pretend to read them while she made up new versions of her own, with people of the court as characters. Anyway, whatever it was Messer Bernardo was getting at, la Cavalla had better take care. Messer Bernardo is plotting, as usual, and if he draws la Cavalla into his web, she'll be sorry.

He wants her to go to Florence. He's probably plotting to have brigands attack her train and kill her along the way. That'd be a fine revenge. I'd like to think my father will someday take a real revenge on Alfonso.

But Florence. Oh, Florence.

Imagine traveling to Florence, all in state, with wagons and wagons of dresses and jewels and white horses trapped with gold. We would enter the city from the north, riding toward the Duomo, pushed up over the city like a breast in a tight bodice. I can see myself gazing at the bell tower of the Old Palace, which hasn't had a bell since some old uncle or cousin of mine stole it and melted it down to keep anyone from ringing it out against him. Then we would go clip-clopping over the Ponte Vecchio, smelling the muddy, sweet stink of the Arno, and at last pass through the arches of the Pitti Palace, which my mother bought with the gold she brought from Naples. Oh, Florence. Oh, home.

I wish I could go. I wish I weren't trapped here where I died.

I didn't know, when I came to Ferrara, I'd never see my home again.

CHAPTER EIGHT

$\mathcal{T}$he Monastero del Corpus Domini was in the old part of the city, occupying almost an entire city block in a section of narrow cobblestoned streets with names like Via Campofranco, Via Praisolo, and Via Pergolato. There were, however, no fields in sight, no meadows, and certainly no trellised arbors; the rose-colored brick walls of the church were almost flush with the pavement, with only the narrowest of paved walks to keep one's feet out of the gutters. Connected to this building, however, was a much more elegant and patrician house where visitors were welcomed; Domenica whispered to me it had once been the home of a Messer Giovanni Romei, who in the previous century had married an Este princess and left the house to the Clarissas of Corpus Domini upon his death. The dukes of Ferrara had been the monastery's patrons for generations, she went on to say, and many of the Este were entombed there.

It was icy cold and the air was silvery with mist from the river; I was well wrapped up in marten-fur and a heavy woolen mantle. The bell for terce was just ringing as I directed my Austrian gentleman-at-arms to go up and knock. Nothing happened at first, and he knocked more vigorously. At last, a wicket inset into the wall beside the door was drawn back and a face appeared, framed in a wimple and veil.

"Her Grace the Duchess of Ferrara desires entrance," he said.

His tone was too peremptory for my taste; I gathered my skirts, stepped down from my litter, and approached the door myself.

The nun was young, probably a postulant or at best a novice. Fright, or wonderment at such fine visitors, appeared to have struck her dumb. I gestured to my gentleman to step back, and I said more gently, "Good day to you, holy sister. I am the Duchess of Ferrara, newly wed as you may know, and I beg permission to enter and pray I may give the duke a son."

This was perfectly true, as far as it went. In fact, I intended to pray quite fervently, because even with my scheme to use the duke's sins against him, another most excellent way to ensure my own well-being was to have the heir to Ferrara in my womb.

"I will fetch Sister Orsola," the girl stammered. She was so nervous she ran off without shutting the wicket, and thus I was able to occupy myself with an inspection of the house's courtyard while I waited. A loggia of graceful arches surrounded a neatly manicured garden; on one wall there was a large and graceful monogram of Christ in terra-cotta surrounded by brickwork angels. Even the stacks of new bricks and the pile of sand in one corner had been swept and tidied. Clearly the monastery was in the midst of some new building. Idly I wondered if secular workmen were allowed inside the enclosure.

After a few minutes a tall, thickset professed nun, distinguishable by her black veil, came striding to the doorway.

"*Deus vobiscum*," she greeted me.

"*Et cum spirito tuo*," I replied, quite properly. "Sister, I am—"

"I know who you are." She was rude for a nun. "You can

come in, but not your attendants. They can come back for you at vespers."

I hesitated. It would indeed be simpler to ask the questions I wanted to ask without any long-eared Ferrarese ladies dogging my every step. Yet at the same time a tiny voice whispered, *Lucrezia de' Medici was in this very monastery when she died in whatever mysterious way she died. . . .*

"Very well," I said, putting aside the cowardly voice of doubt. I turned to my waiting attendants. "All of you may go. Please be so kind as to return for me at vespers, so I shall have time to dress for the Festival delle Stelle tonight."

None of them looked happy about this dismissal, but the monastery was under the duke's own patronage, so they could hardly object. Ungracefully they departed and left me standing on the paved walk. After a moment's pause, probably with the thought she was teaching me humility, Sister Orsola opened the door and I went inside.

The private parlor where the abbess received her guests was on the first floor. To my surprise, there were carpets on the floor and tapestries on the wall—one of Saint Francis, bearing the stigmata, preaching to fanciful birds and beasts; the other of Saint Clare, robed and veiled and brandishing a monstrance to quell a mob of equally fanciful attackers. The carved chairs were padded with silken cushions, and on the table were silver cups set with cabochon amethysts and a jeweled rock-crystal flagon full of wine. The abbess herself was seated in a chair by the window, with the warm terra-cotta-tinged light of the courtyard casting a glow over her face.

It was difficult to tell her age; her skin was smooth as a girl's, although she must have been forty and more. Her strikingly pale tawny-colored eyes were those of an aloof and ruthless lioness. My own eyes must have widened noticeably, because she laughed and beckoned me closer. There was no grille in her parlor, as I had

expected in a monastery of the Clarissas; she might have been receiving me in an Este palazzo.

"I enjoy it so much when people come to see me," she said. I
bent down and she kissed me on both cheeks, habit and wimple
and veil notwithstanding, for all the world as if she were a lady of
the court. There was wine on her breath. "I am Mother Eleonora,
and I am your aunt. Or at least, your aunt by marriage. Duke Ercole, *requiescat in pace*"—she crossed herself—"was my brother. You
did know that, my dear?"

"No, Mother Abbess." My mind lurched in a dozen different
directions. If she was Duke Ercole's sister, she was Lucrezia Borgia's
daughter. When my Lucrezia—and so I was beginning to think of
her, my Lucrezia, by her Christian name alone as if she were my
younger cousin, perhaps, or even my younger sister—had come
here, how easily this woman, the duke's own aunt, with Borgia
blood strong in her veins and a monastery full of nuns at her beck
and call, could have obliged her nephew by ordering a powder or
potion dropped into a medicine cup.

"I knew the monastery was under the patronage of the duke,"
I said, "but that is all."

Mother Eleonora signaled to a white-veiled novice, who hastened to pour me a cup of wine. She refilled her superior's cup as
well, put a fresh plate of sliced cake on the table, and departed in
silence.

"Sit down," Mother Eleonora said. "Have some wine and a
slice of *pampepato*. Yes, the monastery has been under the patronage
of our family since the days of my grandfather, the first Ercole. Are
you all right, my dear?"

I had seated myself stiffly on the edge of the chair. The cushions may not have been strictly monastic, but I was glad for them.

"Oh, yes." I took a sip of the wine and smiled. "I am quite all
right."

She nodded, put a whole slice of cake into her mouth, and

wiped her fingers daintily on a napkin. Abbess or no, clearly she did not practice austerities of the flesh. "Sister Orsola tells me you have asked to make a retreat," she said, once the cake had been chewed and swallowed. "Already you wish to escape Alfonso?"

How foolish I had been to think gossip would not penetrate monastery walls.

"For the day only, Mother Abbess." I sipped the wine again. "To pray for a son."

"Ah, I see," Mother Eleonora said. "What do you think of the wine? It is from our own vineyards at Eliceo."

It has hard to tell if she meant vineyards belonging to the monastery, or an Este family property. I sipped the wine again; it was as good as anything on the duke's tables. At the same time I cast about for a way to bring Lucrezia de' Medici into the conversation. Perhaps if I just encouraged Mother Eleonora to talk of the family of Este in general? That certainly did not seem as if it would be an impossible task.

"It is delicious," I said. "And I am sure you do not enjoy such a luxury every day, as you might have done in the world." In truth I was not sure of that at all, but it led me to what I really wanted to ask. "How did you come to enter the religious life, Mother Abbess? As an Este princess, you could have made a brilliant marriage, taken a place of importance in the world."

"A brilliant marriage!" There was an edge to her laughter. "Oh, yes, a prince or duke for a husband, to put me in childbed every year, to accuse me unfairly of taking lovers, and then after my death to consort openly with mistresses. I am happier as I am, and as for luxuries, I have many noble visitors and in charity I must receive them with a few small comforts."

Wine from Eliceo, cakes of fine-milled white flour stuffed with almonds and citron and spicy with pepper. Small comforts. Mentally I crossed myself and promised to do penance for my uncharitable thought. I had certainly seen worldly nuns before; my own sisters, I suspected, might well end in similar circumstances. But there was something odd, something at the same time scornful of the world and avid for its fleshliness, about Eleonora d'Este. Who could know what she might have seen, growing up in the Ferrara of the first Alfonso and his golden-haired Borgia duchess?

"There is something in what you say," I said. "And I am sure you offer great spiritual comfort to all those who visit you." More penance for me, alas. "One day I would like to make a more extended retreat. Is that what you are building, perhaps? A place for ladies from the court to spend time away from the world?"

"Building?" she said. "Ah, of course, you would have seen the bricks in the courtyard. No, not a new visitors' house, simply an addition to our cellarium. It is almost finished after years of disruption and dust, thanks be to God."

Room for more wine from Eliceo, I thought. My penances were accumulating rapidly. "Thanks be to God," I repeated after her.

"We have ample space for visitors now." Her smile was all courtly pleasantness; I was reminded of the duke's ability to present a polished, smiling surface whatever the darkness beneath. "You are welcome to visit, my dear, whenever you wish. I can offer you accommodation quite suitable to your station. Or a plain cell with bread and water, if you feel a need to do penance."

Her expression remained bland and her tawny eyes were unmoving, but even so I could feel her eagerness to know every succulent detail of my experience at my husband's hands so she could serve it up hot and fresh to her next visitor. I hesitated. Surely she would not recount her gossipings in detail to the duke himself. Surely she knew as well as I such whispers made him dangerously angry. Surely—

I took a deep breath.

"I am told," I said, keeping my expression one of anxious innocence, "the duke's first wife did penance here. Some even say her mortifications contributed to her death." No one had said any such thing, of course, but I hoped my supposedly innocent misstatement would pry out fresh information.

It was spectacularly successful.

"Chè bugia!" Mother Eleonora put her wine-cup down with a thoroughly nonreligious crack of indignation. Drops of the wine spilled over onto the embroidered tablecloth. "Who has been telling you such untruths? The young duchess practiced no mortifications at all, and in fact was provided with every comfort. She came here upon Messer Girolamo Brasavola's recommendation, and Messer Girolamo is the best of Alfonso's physicians, a doctor of our university, and a great scholar. She was to have rest and quiet and good nursing care and that is what she received. She died of a sudden imbalance of humors, something not even our infirmarians could have anticipated."

I did my best to look abashed. "One hears such tales," I said. "Everyone has been whispering to me, and I cannot remember exactly who has said what."

"Such whispers are for fools. I tell you plainly, my dear, if you listen to gossip about Alfonso and his first wife, you will find yourself very unhappy in Ferrara."

I was taken aback by her vehemence, and by the hint of a threat in her words. What was this strange half-monastic, half-worldly woman concealing, that made her so quick to attack me? I hung my head as if I had taken her scolding to heart, but even as I did it, I was thinking perhaps one of the infirmarians she spoke of would be looser-tongued and less zealous to defend the duke.

"It is difficult to be a second wife, Mother Abbess." To my surprise and everlasting shame, my throat thickened with genuine tears. "It is difficult—difficult to hear people speak openly of one's husband's beautiful first wife."

"You will make it more difficult if you give credence to every bit of tittle-tattle you hear."

I kept my head bowed meekly, although I did not believe a word of her protestations. Blood called to blood, and the duke's aunt could hardly do anything but defend him. Her very fervor told me there was something she was concealing.

"You are right, of course, Mother Abbess."

"Excellent," she said briskly. "Now come, you are here to pray for an heir to Ferrara, and rightly so. I will set two sisters to pray with you, so your own prayers may be strengthened."

She picked up a silver filigree bell and rang it vigorously. I did not care for the idea of two sisters watching my every move, as I had hoped to slip away from the chapel to search for the infirmary. Well, if I wanted to get myself to the infirmary, I would have to take a more direct approach.

"Oh, dear," I said. I put one hand over my mouth. "Oh. All of a sudden I feel unwell."

Mother Eleonora frowned and rang her bell harder. "Sister Caterina!" she called. "To me! Fetch Sister Orsola at once!"

The pretty novice rushed into the parlor. I did my best to look wan and allowed her to fan me with the hem of her veil. "I am going to be sick," I whispered. I had no intention of going to such lengths, of course, but it was an effective threat. Mother Eleonora called for water, towels, and a basin, clearly fearing for her luxurious carpets, and poor Sister Caterina fetched them at once. Then she went out of the room, and came back a few minutes later with Sister Orsola, the nun who had admitted me.

"Sister Orsola is our infirmarian," Mother Eleonora said, patting my hand. "She will take you to the infirmary, where you may rest until the sickness passes. May God and Our Lady bless you, my dear."

"Thank you, Mother Abbess." So the rude Sister Orsola was the infirmarian! I resolved to make it quite some time until my sickness passed, so I would have a chance for a good long talk with Sister Orsola.

★   ★   ★

MOTHER ELEONORA'S A *fine one to be calling people liars! Everything she said was a lie.*

First, I wasn't in the monastery for nursing care, and Girolamo Brasavola did nothing but give me a draught meant to calm hysterics. It calmed them, all right—it left me so befuddled, I didn't resist when Alfonso took me to the monastery. If I'd had my wits about me, I'd have forced him to drag me through the streets screaming and clawing.

I was in the monastery as a prisoner, and Mother Eleonora knows it. The door to my cell was locked, and she had the only key. When the infirmarians, old Sister Addolorata and her assistants, Sister Benedicta and Sister Orsola, wanted to open the door, they had to beg on their knees for the key from Mother Eleonora. I know, because Sister Addolorata was arthritic and complained she was too old and stiff to be kneeling to anyone but God, Our Lord, and the Blessed Virgin.

I hated being locked in. Mother Eleonora knew it, too, because that first night I lost my head and cried and begged the nuns to let me out. They were afraid I'd hurt myself, I think, and they called her from her bed. I found out later she never got up in the night, even for the Holy Office, but that night she got up and came to my cell, just to gloat.

We'd hated each other from the day I came to Ferrara. She was like a brown-and-white Franciscan spider, sitting in her parlor swilling wine and cakes and whispering, whispering, whispering with the ladies of the court, who came to visit her just so they could learn the gossip about each other. She gossiped about me, too, and one day I told her to her face she was a Borgia whore's daughter and a dried-up old arpia who'd never been to bed with a man. After that she hated me, and we never spoke again.

Until that night.

She opened the door and I flung myself in her arms, gabbling out all the stories about how my old nonna would lock me in a wardrobe when I was bad and tell me devils would come out of the walls to pluck out my eyes for my sins. Mother Eleonora just looked at me with those eerie weasel-colored

*eyes of hers, and then she smiled, turned around, and went away, locking
the door again behind her. I'll never forget her smile. I screamed the rest of
the night. None of them cared. They thought I was making it up, just to
be free.*

But I wasn't.

*Mother Eleonora was right about one thing—I didn't practice morti-
fications. But to say I was given every comfort? Yes, I had some chests of
things Alfonso sent, once he had me safely locked away. Clothes and cups
and plates, lotions and towels,* giocattoli *to play with to while away the
time. I had fruit and comfits and wine Tommasina smuggled in without
Alfonso's knowledge. Seeing Tommasina again, unpacking her baskets, was
something to do in the long dreary days with no one to talk to, no musicians
to play lively tunes, and no handsome young men to laugh and dance with.*

I would have gone mad, I think, if I hadn't been murdered first.

*And that's the biggest lie of all. An imbalance of humors! Mother El-
eonora knows perfectly well I didn't die a natural death, and Sister Addolorata and Sister Benedicta knew, and Sister Orsola knows. Mother Eleonora
will never tell the truth. Sister Addolorata is dead. Sister Benedicta isn't
in the monastery anymore. Sister Orsola—now that's another story. Sister
Orsola is crafty, and has some secrets of her own.*

*It's too soon for la Cavalla to be with child, so she's only pretending
to be sick. Why? It's very odd, now that I think of it, that out of all the
churches and chapels and convents and monasteries in Ferrara, she chose to
come to the Monastero del Corpus Domini.*

CHAPTER NINE

"I should give you a good strong purge and see how you like it," Sister Orsola said once she had loosened my clothing and settled me on a narrow cot in the infirmary. It was a plain whitewashed room with a stone floor, nothing like the abbess's parlor. "You're no more sick than I am."

Clearly she did not believe in beating about the bush. Did I dare be similarly frank? Lucrezia de' Medici had died in this very monastery, perhaps in this very room. Was there a way to buy Sister Orsola's complicity? Did she have a taste for the same luxuries the abbess flaunted? Apprehension made my palms cold and clammy. My heart seemed to have expanded in my breast, and the wine quivered in my belly.

"Perhaps I am, and perhaps I am not." Deliberately I played with a ring on my right middle finger, a fine dark ruby set in a gold band engraved with pomegranates. I had not worn it in Ferrara until this day, so even if one day it came to light, the duke would not recognize it.

"I wonder," I went on, pulling the ring off and on and off my finger, "if it would be possible to speak frankly. To ask a question or two, without a sister detailing the conversation to her confessor, or to the abbess, or to anyone else."

Sister Orsola stared at the ring and flexed her own ringless fingers. Her hands were chapped and hardened, although they bore some evidence of care—her fingernails were as neatly trimmed as my own, and had even been rubbed to some vestige of a luster. I wondered what Mother Eleonora thought of that bit of vanity.

"I don't tell my confessor everything." She raised her eyes to mine, and I saw greed and something like concupiscence in them. "Not by half I don't, and I can hold my tongue when I've got a reason to."

I slipped off the ring, as if by accident, and let it drop to the pallet. She snatched it up and thrust it under her apron. Holy Virgin, I prayed silently, blessed Saint Monica, let her truly be as venal as she seems. An odd prayer to pray about a nun in a convent. I asked her, "Did you tend my husband's first wife?"

"So that's your game." She sat back, looking smug. "I thought so. Seems even fine ladies want to know about the other women their man's had."

"Did you know her?" I persisted. "What was she like?"

"She was a brazen one, that one. And she wasn't sick, either. She was here because he put her here."

"Put her here? What do you mean?"

"Oh, they pretended she was sick, but she wasn't, no more than you are at this moment. She'd been playing fast and loose with some of the gentlemen of the court, and the duke had her shut up here to put a stop to it. She was never sick for so much as a day."

My stomach turned over, and for a moment I feared I might be as sick as I had pretended to be. Was it really going to be this easy? "But she died of an imbalance of humors. The duke himself attests to it, and so does Mother Abbess. What of that?"

"She was healthy as you or me when I saw her last. It's none of my affair what tales the duke or the abbess tells."

"How did she come to die, then?"

"Don't you go trying to blame anything on me." The infirmarian's coarse-skinned cheeks had gone red and her voice was truculent. "She was well that evening at compline and dead in her cell by lauds the next morning."

It had been poison, then. What else would kill a perfectly healthy young girl in her sleep?

"What did she eat for her supper?" I asked. "Perhaps the meat was bad."

"Meat! She didn't get meat that night, good or bad. It was a fast day, and she had bread and water. That's all any of us had."

"Tainted water, then."

"She had her water from the same jug I drank from, *Serenissima*, and her bread was sliced from the same loaf as mine. There was nothing tainted in the food I gave her that night, no, nor any other night."

It occurred to me that Sister Orsola remembered the young duchess's last meal surprisingly well, considering it had been three and a half years ago and more. Perhaps she had simply told the story too many times. Or perhaps she had been bribed or frightened into remembering one particular tale.

"She had nothing else to eat or drink? You are sure?"

Her eyes slid away from mine. "Sure as I am that you're making believe you're sick when you're not. I've seen people die of poison, and it's a hard death. The young duchess died in her sleep, quiet as a babe and without a mark on her."

"Could she have been smothered? That might leave no obvious mark."

"She would've had to smother herself," she said, "as there was no one else in the room. Locked in, she was, and guarded."

"So if she was not poisoned, not smothered, not sick, and there were no marks on her body, of what did she die?"

"Shame," the infirmarian said, readily if implausibly. Again it was as if others had asked her the same question, and she had the answer at the tip of her tongue. "And well she should have, after coming face-to-face with the duke again."

I leaned forward. "The duke was here? That very day?"

"He came an hour after nones, and you should have heard the screaming and shrieking she did! He was here the next morning, too, after I gave the alarm, because Sister Addolorata called Mother Eleonora and Mother Eleonora sent for him, quick as a stoat. He claimed she was still alive, and he called for his fine university physician and a priest and made a great commotion about giving her the unction. But I know what I saw, and what I saw when I looked over Sister Addolorata's shoulder was a dead woman."

"The duke acted as if she were still alive, when she was dead? Why?"

"I've said enough. You're his wife—ask him, if you dare."

I could coax no more out of her, nor could I be certain everything she had told me was the truth. At last I gave up and said, "Remember your promise, Sister Orsola. If you tell anyone what I have asked you, the story will come back to me, I promise, and I will swear you stole that ring from me while I was sleeping."

A fine threat; I did not know if I would have the heartlessness to carry it out. Fortunately the threat alone seemed to be enough.

"Didn't I tell you I can hold my tongue when it suits me? Your secret is safe, Serenissima."

"Good. Now, I find that I feel much better. Please tell the abbess I am recovered enough to go about my prayers as I had planned."

FOR MY PRAYERS I was allowed to enter one of the stalls of the choir, a concession to my rank most visitors to the church would not enjoy. Not far from where I knelt were the tombs of the Este: the

first Alfonso and the notorious Lucrezia Borgia, Ercole II the present duke's father, and a number of others. With them lay Lucrezia
de' Medici, entombed not quite four years previously.

My petitions to the Blessed Virgin that I might conceive a son
by the duke as quickly as possible were perfectly sincere. The two
sisters assigned to pray with me were silent, stolid black-veiled professed nuns without a word to say for themselves between them, so
I was not distracted. When the bell for vespers had rung and I was
putting my rosary away, I saw a small thin woman come into the
church. She was not dressed in the habit of the Clarissas but in lay
clothing, all in black, and veiled. Something about her struck me
as familiar—the way she moved? The shape of her hands? A trick
of the fading light, perhaps. As I watched, she prostrated herself at
Lucrezia de' Medici's tomb and began to pray.

"Who is that?" I asked the elder of the two sisters who had
been praying with me.

"She is a *terziaria*, Serenissima. A tertiary, you understand, a lay
person, but one who lives close by the monastery and runs errands
when such things are needed."

"She seems to be praying for Serenissima Lucrezia, who died
here some time ago."

The sister looked at the black-clad figure and shrugged. "I
hadn't entered the community when the Serenissima was here,"
she said. "But I see the *terziaria* often. Usually at vespers, as now.
She does not talk much, that one, and unless we are dispensed from
our rule as I am now, we keep the silence, too."

I said nothing more; somehow I would have to investigate the
mysterious tertiary further, although at the moment I was not sure
how I would do so. As I left the chapel, something else caught my
attention: the Stations of the Cross were marked by small paintings
that seemed familiar as well. At first I did not understand why—I
had never been in the Monastero del Corpus Domini before. Then

I realized they were executed in the realistic, evocative color-and-light-and-shadow style of Frà Pandolf. It was absolutely unique; there was no mistaking it.

He is a Franciscan friar, the duke had said, *loosely attached to a monastery under my patronage.* The Clarissas were the second order of Saint Francis; they often took spiritual direction from Franciscan friars, as St. Clare had done from St. Francis himself. Offhand, I thought as I made my way out of the chapel and into the sunlit courtyard, I could not imagine anyone less suited to direct a nun's spiritual life than the sensual, obsequious painter-friar with his bristling reddish-brown beard and vulpine eyes. But the presence of his paintings in the chapel told me Frà Pandolf, beholden as he was to the duke's patronage, was *persona grata* at the Monastero del Corpus Domini.

FOR THE NIGHT'S entertainment, entitled La Festival delle Stelle, I was to wear a foreparte, sleeves, gown, and mantle of midnight blue satin, embroidered all over with jeweled representations of Taurus, my personal astrological sign. A matching headdress, silver and pearls, was fashioned in the shape of the crescent moon. Each of the guests was to follow the same conceit, and there had been much whispering and secrecy among the ladies. As my women dressed me, I wondered what stars had attended the duke's birth.

Suddenly there was a hubbub in the Jupiter chamber, accompanied by the unmistakable beagle howls of Tristo and Isa. After a moment, Sybille came into my dressing-room, her cheeks flushed and her expression unusually discomposed.

"The duke is here, Serenissima," she said, "and requires to speak with you."

It was not at all usual for great noblemen to descend upon their wives—or anyone else, for that matter—unannounced. Brief as our married life had been, I knew the duke was both a thorough purist when it came to protocol, and an active participant in the preparations

for his elaborate entertainments. Why was he here, only half an hour
before the first performance was to begin, wishing to speak to me?

There was little I could do but receive him. I had expected
to see him again only when there were courtiers around us, so I
would be able to take refuge in formality. How could I face him
for the first time alone, not two rooms away from the bedchamber
where he had switched me like an errant child? Even more disturbing, how could I face him with Sister Orsola's words whispering
at my ear: *I know what I saw, and what I saw when I looked over Sister
Addolorata's shoulder was a dead woman. . . .*

"Invite him to step in, Sybille," I said, keeping my voice cool
and steady. "Domenica, Paolina, Katharina, you may go."

They all left.

He came in.

He was wearing a long surcoat of heavy black brocade, jeweled
and furred and embroidered all over in gold with the sign of Scorpio. His shirt, hose, and shoes were blood-red. In his hat he wore
a brooch in the form of a scorpion, worked in gold and diamonds
and with a magnificent ruby set in its sting. At his belt, as always,
hung the damascened dagger in its jeweled sheath.

"Madonna," he said.

I curtsied formally. "My lord."

There was a silence. Finally he said, in a different, colder voice,
"Look at me."

I kept my eyes down as long as I dared, for the satisfaction of
rebelling against him in one small way. At last I looked up.

We stared at each other for a moment. My knees shook.

"What is this I hear," he said at last, "of your going to Corpus
Domini today? Of your being sick there? This disturbs me deeply,
Madonna. Is there not a chapel here in the Castello where you can
make your devotions?"

I could see nothing different in his dark eyes. His glittering surface was undisturbed, the coiling dark creatures of his temper and

his arrogance deep-hidden. Was disciplining his wife with a stick from the fireplace such an unimportant thing to him, then? I knew I myself was flushing, probably unattractively, under his gaze.

At least he said nothing of my questions about Lucrezia de' Medici. So Sister Orsola had kept her word and held her tongue. So Mother Eleonora had the wit to keep her webs of tale-telling to herself.

"I experienced only a moment of dizziness, my lord," I said. My voice quavered, and to my shame I realized I was trying to placate him because I feared him. That was probably exactly what he wanted me to feel. I hated the fear, hated my own weakness.

"The chapel here at the Castello is beautiful," I went on as steadily as I could, "but the statues and decorations are very much in the classical mode. They distract me—I fear I am accustomed to plainer chapels and more saintlike saints. I chose a monastery church so I could ask the good sisters to add their prayers to mine, that I might bear you a son within the year."

There, I thought. Thrash me for that.

"I see." He looked thoughtful, and I hoped I had not offended him further by my distaste for the ducal chapel, which was quite genuine. Apparently I had not, for after a moment he said in a more temperate voice, "It pleases me you would make such a petition. It is my prayer as well."

I said nothing.

"In future, however, I wish you to inform me if you desire to travel into the city or the countryside. I will make arrangements more fitting for your state than a single litter and a handful of at-tendants. I will also arrange for a physician to accompany you."

I turned away. I would have been unable to hide the rush of my fury otherwise. What did he think I was planning to do, slip out of the Castello to tryst with some lover? For something to do, I stepped over to the table where my cosmetics and perfumes were strewn about. Carefully I rearranged them so they were neatly patterned and aligned with the edges of the table itself. Finally I picked up a heavy rock-crystal perfume-bottle. How I would have loved to have thrown it at him, all in his black and scarlet and his emblems of Scorpio.

"Very well," I said, without looking at him. "I trust such arrangements will be forthcoming without undue delay."

"If you have suitable reason for going out, Madonna, they will."

His hands came to rest quite lightly on my shoulders. Once again I had not heard him step up behind me. I jumped, and my heart seemed to stop.

"I am sure you chose Corpus Domini because you were told it is under our patronage," he said, his voice very soft in my ear. He moved his hands slightly, so they lay curved around my neck. "Or perhaps someone told you my aunt is abbess there. Not for any other reason, eh, Madonna?"

I thought my heart was going to burst out of my chest. Suddenly I was so frightened of him, my belly melted and my legs went weak.

"I do not know what you mean, my lord. It was close by, and my Ferrarese ladies directed me."

"Good." He took his hands away. "I will leave you to complete your preparations. The opening chorale will begin in half an hour, and I expect you to walk in the procession with me."

I said nothing. I could not have spoken if I had wanted to.

"Your costume pleases me. The dark blue color sets off the whiteness of your skin quite beautifully. I would like to see a bit more of your hair, at your forehead and temples—ask your woman to rearrange your headdress."

I nodded, still not turning to look at him.

He went away. I clung to the edge of my dressing table, shaking with terror.

Courage, I exhorted myself. You cannot pursue this scheme of investigation if you become a quivering coward at the slightest check. You knew he would question you when you chose that particular monastery. You had your explanation prepared. He accepted it. Anything else exists only in your imagination.

After a moment, I felt stronger.

In half an hour I would be called upon to process into the Castello's Salone dei Giochi and convince a hundred gentlemen and ladies I was a happy, sweetly satisfied new wife. I would have to convince him as well, because tonight he would likely require me in his apartments again, acting the submissive bride to her imperious bridegroom. At least I hoped it would be nothing more than an imperious bridegroom I would encounter there.

The dark blue color sets off the whiteness of your skin quite beautifully.

Did he think compliments would sweeten me? After thrashing me like a servant? After ordering me confined as a virtual prisoner? Angry—I wanted to be angry. I was angry. I was afraid. But it would be a lie to claim I felt nothing but anger and fear. Compliments, after all, were a new thing to me, and they were sweet—frighteningly sweet.

I clasped my shaking hands together. "Holy Virgin," I whispered, in the moment of rare solitude before my ladies returned. "Blessed Saint Monica. Let me learn the truth so I can use it as a shield. Let me get with child, and quickly."

Only then would I be truly safe.

SAFE. *HA! LA* Cavalla *will never be safe now that she's put herself in Sister Orsola's power. I don't tell my confessor everything. I can hold my tongue when I've got a reason to. Fine words, but I could tell la Cavalla, give Sister Orsola a taste of jewels or secrets—or a man—and she always wants more.*

Let me tell you about Sister Orsola, the holy Clarissa, the lustful she-cat. Oh, yes, she told me all about herself while I was shut up at Corpus Domini—the afternoons were long and dull for both of us. She's the daughter of a common baker in Copparo, one of nine brats—six girls and three boys. Providing for three sons left nothing much to pay dowries for the girls, of course, and although Orsola claimed she fought tooth and nail against being shut away as a nun, she was lucky to end up at Corpus Domini and not a draggle-tailed doxy on the streets like the others. Although who knows? Maybe she would have been happier that way.

Her mother and father spent their lives making ciupèta *bread for the court, and that's probably why Sister Orsola is so lustful. Have you ever seen* ciupèta? *It doesn't taste like much, but it's got a special shape the Ferrarese love—at first it looks like four devil horns with two seashells in the middle, and then you realize it's actually two* potas *in the middle and four* cazzi *sticking out proudly to the four winds. Can you imagine what it must have been like for a girl to spend her childhood making* potas *and* cazzi *out of bread dough? No wonder she turned out the way she did.*

Somebody must have liked her father's ciupèta *well enough to put in a good word at Corpus Domini, because Orsola entered the monastery when she was twelve, with one dress, two aprons, and a few bags of flour for her dowry. For years she was not much more than a scullery maid, but finally she learned she had to stop crying, pretend to be holy, and toady to the abbess and the inner circle of professed nuns if she wanted any privileges at all. That's how she got to take vows and be named assistant to old Sister Addolorata, the infirmarian. Now she's the infirmarian herself.*

I can see her—she's in the choir for vespers, with all the other nuns, but she doesn't look very holy to me. Look at her hands. Tucked inside her sleeves, she has them, and what's she rubbing and stroking with her eyes all closed with ecstasy, while the other nuns chant psalms and prayers? La Cavalla's ring. She's turning it over and over and feeling the polished slickness of the ruby, caressing the carvings on the gold, and hefting its weight. Rich things to her are almost as good as a man—not quite, but almost.

I wonder how long it'll take for her to decide she wants more. And I wonder what Alfonso will do when he finds out his precious new imperial wife has been trading jewels for silence with a nun in the monastery where his first wife died.

CHAPTER TEN

The Salone dei Giochi was draped in black velvet spangled with thousands of stars made of gold and glittering crystals. Spaced at equal intervals around the room were intricate mechanical devices representing the houses of the zodiac—a charging ram with ivory horns, a pair of sinuous swimming fish with opalescent scales, a golden lion with a mane of real silk that tossed and swayed—each blazing with countless candles. At each sign a beautiful young girl in white classical drapery tended a fountain cascading with wine and a table of crystal dishes piled high with sweetmeats.

In one corner a silver-painted sphere was suspended, a blaze of torchères behind it reflecting on the polished surface and lighting the salon with an unearthly glow. The chains holding the moonsphere were blackened so as to give the appearance it rode magically against the velvet sky; inside, dressed all in silver cloth and with their hair and faces painted silver to represent men in the moon, the duke's consort of viols played softly.

The duke and I processed in without a word to each other. After the chorale, we mounted a crescent-shaped dais representing the planet Venus, studded with beryls, chrysolites, and green jasper, wreathed with maidenhair ferns, valerian, and thyme. Turtledoves in silver cages cooed and fluttered. The scents of the herbs and the wines, the burning candles, and the perfumes of the courtiers were enough to make my eyes water.

Eight lavish courses of food and wine ensued. At the first course, the guests were presented with silver-gilt wine-cups, each engraved with its recipient's star-sign and device; the duke and I shared a single cup, solid gold, filigreed with bulls and scorpions and the arms of Ferrara and Austria impaled, picked out in jewels. After the subtleties were presented, there were songs and dances by the duke's players, representing the signs of the zodiac and the planets. When at last the general dancing began, the duke led me to the center of the salon for a pavane.

He was an excellent dancer, with his passion for music and his athletic physique. After the first figure, other couples joined us: Crezia with the duke's uncle, the Marquis of Montecchio—the one whose boys were the heirs apparent—and the duke's French friend Sandro Bellinceno with his tall young wife. I looked particularly for the duke's younger sister Nora but did not see her anywhere.

Was it a dream or was I truly dancing in this fantastical setting with the man who had taken a switch to me for disobedience two nights before? I could not help but wonder what Messer Baldassare might have written about the duke's anger and my terror, and about our dancing as if none of it had ever happened. Such things had apparently never occurred in the perfect world of *Il Libro del Cortegiano*.

After the pavane and the galliard that followed it, the duke and I parted. He turned to dance with Elisabetta Bellinceno; Crezia exchanged the Marquis of Montecchio for a handsome, sensual-looking gentleman wearing the sign of the Virgin—the same one, I was certain, with whom she had exchanged such a smoldering look at the Neptune banquet. I found myself, to my surprise, matched with Luigi d'Este, cardinal-deacon, archbishop, and bishop.

He laughed at my shocked expression. "Of course, *mia cognata*, I dance," he said. "Do not the Psalms enjoin us to praise God's name in the dance? And does not Ecclesiasticus tell us there is a time to dance as well as a time to mourn?"

He placed his hands around my waist and lifted me easily as the violists played the first bars of music; considering he was no more than my own height, his strength took me by surprise. He swung me around and put me lightly on my feet again so we were both facing the same direction, then took two steps away from me, did a double-step in *tempo di piva*, and three more single steps.

I recognized the dance as *Amoroso*. My first thought—although of course I kept it to myself—was that *Amoroso* was probably not quite what the psalmist and the prophet had in mind. I hastened to follow his lead, performing exactly the same steps, my heavy indigo velvet skirts swishing and the bull symbols catching the moon-sphere's silver light.

"Well done," the cardinal said when we stood side by side again. "You and my brother have long faces tonight. Does marriage not agree with you after all?"

He moved away in a new figure of the dance, light-footed as a cat. He was richly dressed in secular clothing; his doublet and coat were of deep purplish-red brocade scented with ambergris, the bows and arrows of Sagittarius embroidered in gold upon his sleeves. He was more attractive than his older brother; it was not so much that his features were more regular or his person more manly, but that there was life and amusement and sensuality in his expression, while the duke's face showed nothing of his thoughts.

I performed the figure and stood next to him again. "Marriage agrees with us both very well," I said. A lie, of course, but what did he expect me to say? To strike back at him I added, "What a shame it is, My Lord Cardinal, that the delights of the nuptial state are forbidden to you."

He laughed and clutched his heart, as if I had run him through with a rapier. "A ready wit and a sharp tongue," he said. "There are delights enough for me outside the nuptial state, I assure you. Tell me—have you any news as yet, with which to gratify the court?"

He stepped to the left, perfectly in time with the music, and then half-turned to face me. With one hand over his breast he performed a *reverenza*, exquisitely elegant, a placement of the feet, a bend of the knees, a straightening, rather as if one were making a deep and languid genuflection. I did my own *reverenza* in return, wishing it were possible to smack a prince of the church. The duke and I had been married less than a month, and surely it was premature to begin asking for news of an heir.

I said, "You must apply to the duke, My Lord Cardinal, for the answer to your question."

"The answer is no, then." He smiled. "Well, I will hold hope in my heart. I must be off to Rome tomorrow—the old pope has died and a conclave has been called. Perhaps when I return, your news will be better."

"You do not seem overcome with sorrow that the Holy Father is dead."

He smiled. "Remember, a time to mourn, a time to dance. Tonight is for dancing."

In the next figure the lady led the way; I measured out the two steps, the *piva* double, and the subsequent three steps, feeling the weight of my skirts rippling with my movement, leaving him behind me. It annoyed me that he was so cavalier. I looked at him over my shoulder and said, "You dally like a courtier, Your Eminence. Did you do the same with your brother's first duchess?"

That took him aback, as I had intended it would. He recovered himself so nimbly, however, that he did not miss even a step of the dance.

"But of course. This is Ferrara, *mia cognata*, and everyone dallies with everyone."

"And no one takes any of it with any seriousness?"

"Seriousness? What is that?"

He laughed. I laughed. Once again we performed our paired *reverenzi*, signaling the end of the dance. As I sank down, I saw Messer Bernardo Canigiani, standing by the sign of Gemini, watching me.

Watching me.

I straightened, too abruptly. The cardinal caught my hand to steady me.

"Is something wrong, *mia cognata*?"

"Oh, no." I looked away from the Florentine ambassador's gaze. "No, I am perfectly well, Your Eminence. I have simply not yet had sufficient practice in the—dances—of Ferrara."

AFTER HALF-A-DOZEN DANCES I retired to our Cytherian haven to rest and watch for a while, and to drink some of the golden *frizzante* wine from my own sign of Taurus. Among the sweetmeats offered with the wine was a dish of delicately candied angelica root. It was a compliment to my personal taste and I could not refuse it, although for once I had little taste for sweets. I accepted it with a smile and a word of thanks, but when I returned to the dais, I set it aside.

The duke continued to dance, first with one, then with another of the ladies of his court. After the first figure, Crezia danced with no one but her Virgo gentleman; by imperial court standards it was most unsuitable for her to single him out so pointedly. Idly I looked about for Nora again but still did not see her. On the other hand, I did see Tasso, the graceful young poet, his dark eyes burning with sensuous emotion as he gazed at the singer Lucrezia Bendidio, so wherever Nora was, it was not with her *inamorato*. Sandro Bellin-

ceno seemed to be a popular partner, despite his lack of grace; perhaps the refined court ladies were titillated by his rough battlefield
manners. Katharina Zähringen, not on duty that evening and so
free to dance and enjoy herself as she pleased, was apparently one
who was not. I had to laugh ruefully to see her refuse him and send
him on his way with a smart slap for his pains.

My dear Christine was at my side, humming along with the
music. She and Paolina Tassoni were formally in attendance upon
me, with a newly appointed Ferrarese lady named Nicoletta Rangoni who had joined my household to replace poor Maddalena
Costabili. Paolina looked sad and tired and would not meet my
eyes. My anger with her sneakings and spyings had faded; she was
no more than a pawn in the hands of the duke and her father, just
as I was a pawn in the hands of the duke and my brother. In fact, I
thought, putting my wine-glass aside, there might be advantages in
a rapprochement with her.

"Paolina," I said softly.

Instantly she came closer and sank into a curtsy. Her popingay-
green dress was embroidered with capering bulls much like my
own, intricately entwined. "Serenissima?"

"Let us be frank. You are in the duke's service as well as my
own, are you not?"

She colored. So faintly that I could hardly hear her over the
music, she said, "Yes, Serenissima."

"I shall not ask you why. I understand these things are not always of one's own choice. I intended to ask the duke to remove you
from my household—"

"Oh, no! Please, Serenissima, I beg you." She clasped her
hands, and to my horror a tear spilled down her cheek. "My father
will be so angry if you send me away. Have mercy."

"Hush. Stop crying and allow me to finish my sentence, if you
please. I intended to ask the duke to remove you from my household, but upon further thought I realized he would only replace

you with another to serve him in the same capacity. Perhaps you and I, on the other hand, can come to a private arrangement."

"Oh, yes!" She looked up at me, her eyes suddenly alight. "I must always have something to tell the duke, but I need not tell him everything. Only let me stay, Serenissima, and I shall be more discreet. I swear it."

"And the secrets you learn, which you love so much. You will tell me alone. You will tell me everything."

"I will. I swear it."

"Very well. Now, when did you last eat or sleep?"

"I have not been able to rest, Serenissima. I have not eaten since you sent me away."

"Drink a little wine; it will put color in your cheeks. Where is your cup?"

She looked around distractedly. There were several silver-gilt cups on the table; from the array of lions, sea-goats, and water-bearers, she picked out her own bull with the Tassoni badger on a blue-and-gold shield. Obediently she took a swallow of the wine.

"Thank you, Serenissima," she said.

"And eat a bit of the sweet—angelica warms and comforts a cold stomach. I shall—"

"Are you sulking?"

I started. The duke's sister Crezia had come up unnoticed, flushed with wine and dancing. She was wearing silver satin embroidered with fanciful black and white centaurs wielding curved bows embroidered in diamonds and jet. Her beautiful dark eyes were scornful, and for a moment I saw myself as she might have seen me, the new bride sitting alone with her ladies while her husband danced with others.

"I am resting," I said, "after a vigorous *Tesara*. That will be all, Paolina."

The girl curtsied and stepped back. Crezia sat down and held out her cup to be refilled. "Such tales I hear of my new sister Barbara," she said, with one of the expressive gestures the Ferrarese used so often. "Married barely a month and already at odds with your husband?"

This was becoming rather tedious.

"Hardly at odds," I said. "All new-wed couples find things to disagree about."

"How tactful you are. You need not mince words with me, you know."

I said nothing.

"Alfonso is difficult enough as a brother—he is proud and inflexible and will not even discuss matters once he has made up his mind. I cannot imagine what he would be like as a husband, even for a sensible woman such as you."

The music covered our words, and our ladies had tactfully withdrawn a bit. Crezia herself was being indiscreet enough; she could hardly run to the duke with a tale of our conversation. I said cautiously, "At least I am not a child of fifteen."

"Nor are you an illiterate fool. Nor do you fling yourself indiscriminately at every male about the court, from the page boys to the dotards. One can hardly blame Alfonso—"

She broke off and drank some of her wine. I waited, but she said nothing more. I thought of the Virgo gentleman, and wondered if the beautiful young duchess had cast her eye upon him. Crezia seemed to combine hot blood and cool calculation in equal measures, and she had clearly disliked her young sister-in-law intensely. Jealousy? Like her aunt the abbess, she could well have been a compliant tool in her brother's hands.

"How awkward it must have been," I said at last. "Yes, I have heard strange tales about the duke's last duchess."

"And you will hear more, I am sure." She took another swallow of her wine. "Perhaps the married state is not such a desirable thing, after all, whatever one's age."

So that was it. She was still smarting from my remark at the Neptune banquet.

"Perhaps not," I agreed.

"Ferrara is my home. My father never pressed me to marry—it pleased him to make me first lady of the court after my mother . . . after she withdrew to the Palazzo di San Francesco."

How coolly she spoke of her father's imprisoning her mother for heresy.

"Now, I have my own *palazzi*, my own income, my own household. Alfonso knows better than to try to force a marriage upon me—I am a match for him and quite happy as I am."

"Anyone would be happy in Ferrara." I could not help but wonder if she would indeed be a match for the duke if he chose to arrange a marriage for her, but the last thing I wanted now was more conflict. I wanted to keep her talking and somehow direct her conversation back to Lucrezia de' Medici, so I signaled to Nicoletta to bring more wine. "I suppose I must simply wait and hope the duke will begin to understand I am a very different woman." The unsaid words—*than she was*—hung between us.

"I think he already understands quite well. Why did he beat you, Barbara? Do tell me. There are a dozen different tales being whispered."

Obviously she was in no mood to be led, and I was in no mood to tell her the lurid details of the duke's anger. "Crezia," I said. One Christian name deserved another. "I beg you. Do not give credence to gossip. The duke would be very angry if he knew people were whispering of his affairs."

"Then he should not have beaten you. If he ever does try to marry me off, I shall defy him, even if he beats me a hundred times."

I thought again of Mother Eleonora, this time of her diatribe against marriage. Apparently independence ran in the blood of the Este women.

"You certainly enjoy every luxury and pleasure here in Ferrara," I conceded. "There is nothing a husband could give you that you do not have already."

It was my way of giving her the victory. She understood exactly what I had done, and she laughed. Perhaps her satisfaction would make her less wary and more likely to speak of Lucrezia de' Medici another day. We each took a sip of our wine, the truce called and the provisional treaty of friendship signed.

"Now, please," I said. "Say nothing more of beatings. Assure everyone the tale has been vastly overblown."

"That is easy enough," she said. "It is much out of character for Alfonso, anyway. If he were to take a switch to anyone, it should have been to that little *sgualdrina* from Florence, and yet he never laid a finger on her."

I was surprised, and of course I could not help being curious. If it was out of character for the duke to employ physical chastisement, what had driven him to such an extremity? I took another sip of wine and said in my most careless tone, "It is very strange."

"You must understand, he did not treat the Medici girl as a wife at all, but as an unwanted encumbrance. I do not think he cared if she disobeyed him. You, on the other hand—he has made no secret of an imperial wife's being a great prize to him. If you flouted his will in some way, when he had put you on such a pedestal for all the court to see—it touched his honor, I think. Who will ever understand men?"

I did not like to think of myself as nothing more than an object the duke prized, however greatly. "Yes, indeed," I said. "Who will ever understand—?"

And it was just at that moment Paolina Tassoni collapsed and began to convulse, amid spilled wine and screams and the shattered remains of a dish of candied angelica.

AND I THOUGHT *the court would be dull, with la Cavalla as duchess! Even I never poisoned one of my own ladies, in full view of everyone.*

That's only a jest—of course la Cavalla didn't do it herself, although

Paolina Tassoni carried tales about her to Alfonso and so she had cause. And was it the wine or the angelica? Anyone could have dropped a powder in Paolina's wine-cup—it was easy to pick out from the rest, covered with bulls and the Rangoni arms. Did she learn some secret she shouldn't have? That wouldn't surprise me. On the other hand, if it was the angelica— well, the angelica wasn't even meant for Paolina, now, was it?

I wish I could be there with them, plotting and scheming, drinking wine and eating sweets and dancing. When la Cavalla was performing that pavane with Alfonso, they might have been two mechanical figures like the zodiac signs, perfect but lifeless. When she danced with Luigi, she came to life. But then I came to life when I danced with him, too.

Luigi. It's not very respectful to call a prince of the church by his Christian name, is it? Let me tell you the truth about His Lordship-Eminence-high-and-mightiness Luigi Cardinal d'Este. He was the closest of them all to my own age, just six years older—Alfonso was eleven years older and might as well have been a hundred and eleven. I knew Luigi for what he was the moment I saw him, and he knew me, too, the mascalzone. *We were alike, craving pleasure and luxury, laughter and excitement, and most of all freedom to do as we pleased. If I'd been married to Luigi, I think we both would have been happier. But poor Luigi was the second son, and so of course he was made a bishop when he was fifteen. What a waste.*

I remember the marvelous torneo *that was held to celebrate his election as cardinal—Il Castello di Gorgoferusa it was called, and afterward it became famous all over Europe. When the music and mock battles were done, we danced together, Luigi and I, and it was wonderful. When I watched la Cavalla dancing with him tonight, I imagined myself in her place, wearing cloth-of-gold with motifs of Gemini brocaded in silver, and diamonds and moonstones in my hair.*

He dallied with me, just as he dallied with poor la Cavalla, but that's as far as it ever went, more's the pity. I had a wonderful dream about him after the torneo—*in it we danced out into the gardens under the stars. I lured him with my eyes and my lips and my body until we were under the cherry tree, my favorite place. It was foaming with white-and-pink blossoms* and heavy with ripe red cherries all at the same time—I know that can't really be, but this was a dream and the cherry tree was enchanted. I pulled him down into sweet spring grass—the white petals floated around us like perfumed snow, and the sweet cherries were crushed into blood-red juice under the weight of our bodies. And we enjoyed each other, brother and sister, cardinal and duchess, so sweet and so forbidden.

It would've been the greatest revenge I could've taken against Alfonso, for ignoring me as he did. But it was only a dream. And only a few weeks later I was taken away.

I wish I could have come home from Corpus Domini and somehow made the dream real and got with child by Luigi, just so I could have thrown it in Alfonso's teeth. How I would have loved to see his face then. How I would have loved to look straight into his ice-cold black Este eyes and laugh when he realized, once and forever, it would not be a son of his own to follow him as Duke of Ferrara.

CHAPTER ELEVEN

"She has been taken to the Saint Catherine Tower." The duke spoke softly, so the people around us could not hear. "One of my physicians is attending her."

The duke's majordomo—Count Niccolò Tassoni, who was Paolina's own grandfather, although from his icy demeanor one never would have known it—had stepped in so quickly most of the people in the salon never realized what had happened. A gesture from Count Niccolò to the duke, a nod from the duke to the musicians, and the music was louder and gayer. Paolina was whisked away. Servitors appeared as if by magic to tidy every trace of disarray. Those who had seen her swoon were assured it was nothing; too much wine perhaps, poor lady. All she needed was a quiet place to recover herself.

"I wish to go to her, my lord," I said as forcefully as I could while keeping my voice to a whisper. "You know it was not just wine that affected her so terribly. She was—"

"Stop." His expression was impenetrable. "We will not discuss it now. It is impossible for you to leave the Festival so early—it would only create further talk."

I looked around the salon. At the house of Taurus, a life-sized gilded bull pawed the ground with a diamond-shod hoof; his head moved up and down, wisps of smoke erupted from his nostrils, and his horns were wreathed in jeweled flowers. The same pretty dark-haired girl in her white dryad's robes continued to offer wine and confections, just as she had offered the dish of angelica to me.

I could not stop thinking about that dish of candied angelica.

What might she be able to tell me?

If I could take action, any action, I would not feel so helpless.

"May we walk, then, my lord?" I said. "I am intrigued by the mechanical devices, and I would like to examine them more closely."

He looked surprised, and then, not unexpectedly, pleased. Anything to do with complex mechanisms and clockwork always interested him. "Of course, Madonna."

I put my hand upon his wrist and we made our way about the room, leaving a swathe of bows and curtsies in our wake. I wanted to go straight to the house of Taurus, but I held my tongue and admired each sign in its turn. At the house of Aquarius the duke stopped. The device consisted of a charming gilded statue of Ganymede with a silver water-pitcher in his arms; the figure would lift the pitcher, pour out a stream of water, then turn its head from side to side as a breeze—Aquarius, despite its name, was one of the air signs—from a hidden source made its golden hair and silken draperies flutter. The mechanism controlling the flow of water through the device had apparently ceased to function properly, and a puddle was beginning to spread on the polished marble floor.

"Fetch Messer Lorenzino at once," the duke said to one of his gentlemen. Then to me he said, "I wish to see this made right, Madonna. Go on, if you will, and I will rejoin you when I have consulted with Messer Lorenzino."

"Yes, my lord," I said, sweeping a curtsy and breathing a prayer of gratitude that the duke was such an admirer of anything mechanical. With my own ladies and several of the duke's gentlemen attending me, I continued my progress around the room until I reached Taurus.

"*Bentornata, Serenissima,*" the attendant said. She had a soft, musical voice. "May I have the great privilege of offering you wine once again? A pastry or a candied fig, perhaps?"

"Have you no more of the angelica?" I said. "It is my favorite."

"I am desolated, Serenissima, but no, there was only the one dish."

I picked up a sugared almond and nibbled it. "That is odd," I said. "There is so much of everything else. Are you certain?"

"Oh, yes, Serenissima. The angelica was not part of the original arrangement—angelica is an herb of the sun in Leo and has nothing to do with Taurus. But before the entertainment began, a kitchen girl brought it—she said I was to keep it aside and give it to you alone."

"A kitchen girl," I repeated. "Did you know her?"

"No, Serenissima."

"Why did you take the angelica from her, then?"

She looked puzzled. "She wore the duke's badge, the flaming fire and the *Ardet Aeternum.* She told me it was a special *delicatezza.*"

I cannot describe how I felt just at that moment. Overwarm of a sudden, then chilled, then dizzy as if I had drunk too much wine. I knew what she was going to say next before she said it.

"For you and no one else." The girl's dark eyes were clear and earnest. "From the duke himself."

I DO NOT know how long I stood there, transfixed as if I had looked into the eyes of Medusa. It must have seemed longer than it was, because no one appeared to find anything amiss. Finally, with great effort, I thanked the girl, gestured to Christine to fill another cup of wine for me, and made my way back to the grotto of Venus.

There common sense reasserted itself. Of course the mysterious kitchen girl had worn the duke's badge; such a thing could be stolen or fabricated. Of course she said the dish of angelica was from the duke; it was the obvious way to disarm suspicion. There was simply no reason for the duke to wish to poison me. Even if I angered him, I was useful: with his marriage to me came my brother Maximilian's favor, and although he held Ferrara as a papal fief, he was duke in Modena and Reggio as an imperial vassal. For those cities it was Maximilian alone who could grant him the title of grand duke and the precedence that accompanied it. More than that, I was the potential mother of a half-imperial heir.

Ridiculous—I would not even think of it.

I had no desire to dance again, nor to look at any more of the duke's marvels. All I wanted was to see Paolina, reassure myself she would recover, and then undress and curl up in my bed with Tristo and Isa. The music, the heat of the torchères, the rippling colors of the dancers' costumes, the thick scents of honey and herbs and wine, exotic perfumes and dance-warmed sweat, were becoming almost too much to bear.

At last the duke returned. "I beg your pardon for abandoning you, Madonna," he said. "Have you seen the rest of the devices?"

"I have, my lord, and it has tired me. I have no more stomach for dancing and celebration—may I retire?"

"We shall both retire." He lifted one hand and the music stopped. The dancers stumbled on a step or two in the silence, then stopped as well. All eyes sought the dais.

"We wish you a good night." The duke did not raise his voice, but I was sure every person in the salon heard him. He held out his hand to me; I put my own hand upon his wrist, and we left the Salone dei Giochi. I heard the music begin again behind us, picking up the same bar with which it had left off.

"It would please me," he said as we walked, "if you would come to my apartments tonight."

His voice was calm and pleasant, as if he had never threatened me, never beaten me, never forbidden me to leave the palace without his consent. As if one of my ladies-of-honor had not collapsed in convulsions an hour before, after eating a confection meant for me. I wondered what he would say if I refused, although of course I did not dare.

"The pleasure is mine, my lord," I said, making my voice as serene as his. "Allow me a little time, if you please, to undress and prepare myself."

We reached the door to the Jupiter chamber. He stopped. Christine and Nicoletta stepped forward and pushed the door open.

"I shall expect you shortly," he said.

I SLIPPED OUT of my apartments again as soon as the duke's party had gone, with only Christine to attend me. I found Paolina in the Saint Catherine Tower, in a room less than half the size of my own bedchamber, with four narrow pallets and a single high shuttered window. A lamp flickered on a chest behind the far pallet, throwing misshapen shadows around the figure crouched beside it. The ghastly smells of sickness were unmistakable.

"You there," I said, "are you the physician?"

The figure turned its head, and to my surprise I recognized Maria Granmammelli, the duke's old nurse. She straightened, casting even more sinister shadows in the tiny room. "That I am not, *Austriaca*, though this poor child would've been better served if her grandfather had called me first instead of that fool of a physicker."

I crossed myself. "She is not dead?"

"Not yet, though no thanks to the physician. Nor to that grandfather of hers, who poked his head in just long enough to call for a priest."

I pushed between the chests and coffers, careless of my rich costume, and knelt beside the pallet. Paolina's face was ghostly pale in the wavering light, her eyes sunken in their sockets; the gleam of holy oil was visible on her forehead, eyelids, and lips. I laid one hand on her cheek and found it cold.

"She's not regained her wits," Maria Granmammelli said, "so she couldn't repent her sins properly, poor poppet. But the priest anointed her and said the prayers, and that'll have to do."

I crossed myself again and murmured a prayer of my own.

"She needed plain warm oil right away," the old woman said. "Lots of it, boiled up with mulberry bark and mixed with water, so she could cast up what she'd taken while she still had the strength. What she got was bleedings and powdered unicorn's horn in wine and a string of amethyst stones on her belly. Physicians! Useless, the lot of them."

"I should have come sooner." I stroked Paolina's hair; it felt rough and dry under my fingers. My throat felt tight and my eyes blurred. I whispered, more to myself than to Maria Granmammelli, "She is in my household. I should have come no matter what she did. No matter what the duke said."

The old woman squinted at me. "Candied angelica it was, or so I hear. 'Twouldn't surprise me if 'twas meant for you, *Austriaca*, not her."

That was what I was trying not to think of. I felt shocked, shocked to the bone, and sad, and angry, and frightened, but if I were to be honest with myself, what I felt most of all was relief— guilty relief. *Not me, not this time, please God, thank you Holy Virgin, I am still alive and warm and breathing, seeing and feeling and touching. . . .*

"It could have been an accident," I whispered. "Perhaps the angelica itself was tainted, or something noxious was introduced by chance. Or perhaps it was not the angelica at all. She was drinking wine as well."

"You may be a fool, *Austriaca*, but you're not that much a fool."

Who?

Don't think. Don't think.

I stroked Paolina's hair again, then straightened. "I will return in the morning. Stay with her, do everything you can do for her, and tomorrow you will have five silver *diamanti*."

Her little eyes glistened. "Even if she dies?"

"Do your best for her. But yes, even if she dies."

"A bargain, *Austriaca*," the old woman said. "And if I was you, I'd have my food tasted from now on."

"An excellent suggestion," I said. "Good night, Maria Granmammelli."

so it was the angelica. Poor Paolina, off she goes to purgatory in la Cavalla's place. But who would want to poison la Cavalla, when she's been in Ferrara only a few weeks?

I wonder if it has something to do with la Cavalla's visit to the Monastero del Corpus Domini. Having la Cavalla poking around had to have frightened Mother Eleonora half to death—can't you just imagine what a papal inquisitor would say if he could see her sitting there with her tapestries and carpets, drinking wine and eating sweet cakes and gossiping all day with ladies from the court? One of her friends at court could have prepared that angelica for la Cavalla, oh, so easily.

Crezia could have done it, too. She was the first lady of the court as long as there was no duchess. Then Alfonso gets married again, and suddenly she has to bow and scrape to the emperor's sister. No, Crezia hasn't liked that at all, and she's liked it even less since la Cavalla said she was too old to be unmarried. She certainly came up to la Cavalla at just the right moment, Crezia did, dripping honey for no particular reason. Maybe she wanted to watch. Maybe she's oh-so-disappointed now that la Cavalla evaded her venom.

And then there's Messer Bernardo, with his hints and plots. La Cavalla refused to let him entangle her, and this could easily be his revenge. On the other hand, he could have tried to poison la Cavalla for no other reason than to make trouble for Alfonso. Or even—do you think my father ordered it, to revenge himself on Alfonso for my death? That would only be fair, and it'd be like my father to play a waiting game.

Who else could have done it?

Well, there's the Marquis of Montecchio. He'd poison a dozen duchesses if he thought it would put one of his weedy little boys on the throne.

Whoever it was, he—or she—had a friend in the kitchen. He—or she—knew enough to make or steal a badge with Alfonso's flame device. Alfonso told me once what it meant, something about burning forever. I thought it meant burning with passion. I was wrong. He burns with pride and ambition—cold fires.

I hope he burns forever in hell.

It would almost be worth going to hell myself, just to see Alfonso burning forever in the flames beside me.

CHAPTER TWELVE

$\mathcal{I}$ had myself undressed quickly to make up for the time in the Saint Catherine Tower. Nicoletta helped me don a sable-lined night-gown, combed out my hair, and held long, pointed slippers of gold brocade for me to step into. I half-wished I had asked Maria Granmammelli for one of her potions, to calm my thoughts of poisoners and give me courage. Sybille offered me a posset of hot spiced wine, and I felt a moment of uncertainty; then I chided myself that this was Sybille, after all, my beloved Sybille, and I drank it down in one draught. They followed me to the duke's apartments and left me there.

"Sit for a moment," the duke said. He was lounging at his ease in his *studiolo*, his favorite room, filled with magnificent paintings and classical sculptures. He had also put aside his Festival costume; he was wearing a loose gown of mulberry-colored velvet furred with marten and was sipping red wine from one of his Murano glasses. The damascened dagger in its sheath lay on the table beside him.

I curtsied formally before him—as formally as I could, at least, while wearing nothing but a night-gown—and seated myself on the gilded, velvet-cushioned *sgabello* next to his chair. He leaned forward, tipped my face up with two fingers under my chin, and to my utter astonishment kissed my mouth.

"You have been drinking wine," he said.

"A p-posset, my lord." I was so taken aback I stumbled over the word.

He gestured toward the wine decanter on the table. There was a second, empty glass beside it. "Would you like another?"

I would have welcomed another, or for that matter two or three, but I needed to keep my wits about me. "Thank you, but no."

He leaned back in his cushioned chair. "How does the Tassoni girl?"

So much for my thought I had slipped away to the Saint Catherine Tower unnoticed.

"Her grandfather fears for her life, so she has been given the unction," I said. "Maria Granmammelli is with her."

He frowned but said nothing.

"It is unfortunate," I went on, turning my head away but watching his face from the corners of my eyes, "that such an accident marred the Festival. Your confectioners should be reproved, my lord, for their carelessness."

"Indeed they should."

I looked down at my hands. Too quick, that facile agreement; he did not believe for a moment it was an accident and he was humoring me like a child. Well, let him think he had succeeded. If I told him I believed it was a deliberate attempt to poison me, he would either take more care the next time—if he was behind it all—or demand to know why I believed someone wished to poison me. That was a question I did not wish to answer.

After a moment he said, "You were praying for a son today, at Corpus Domini. Tell me, Madonna, what else were you praying for?"

My heartbeat quickened. "Nothing else, my lord."

He put the wine-glass down on the table and picked up the dagger; thoughtfully he ran his thumb over the pommel, which was oddly fashioned with two round gold medallions like wings. For the first time I was close enough to recognize the engraved designs, and to discern among them the famous capital *H* and intertwined double crescents of Henri II of France. Had the dagger once belonged to his older cousin, whose death in a joust had shocked the world? Clearly it held some unusual significance for the duke.

"Not a single Pater," he said, "that I might be punished for my sins?"

"What—what sins are those, my lord?"

"Wrath, perhaps. Or pride. Or even lust. Three of the seven deadly sins."

I felt color flood up into my face, and I looked away. "My own sins were quite enough to occupy me."

"Indeed. The besetting female sin of curiosity, for one. Your brother told me you were disquisitive and difficult, and would require firm handling."

"My *brother* told you that?"

"That and other things. What is it, Madonna? You look surprised."

"I would have thought Maximilian had more important things to do than to write you a list of my shortcomings."

"Maximilian? Not at all. It was Archduke Ferdinand who warned me about you. And it was not in writing—we spoke at length when he was here in Ferrara."

"Ferdinand was here?" I realized I was shivering, and not with cold. "When?"

"You did not know? He acted as Maximilian's emissary to arrange the preliminary details of the marriage. He came to Ferrara incognito, as an envoy of the Count of Tyrol."

"But Ferdinand is the Count of Tyrol. I mean, it is one of his titles."

The duke smiled. "Exactly. It was a jest between us. Naturally I would not negotiate such a serious matter with one who was not my equal in rank."

"Naturally."

"He was frank about rumors he had heard. I was similarly frank about my first wife and the circumstances of her death. It was later, as we were going downstairs to rejoin the court, that he described your nature to me. It appears he was right."

I pulled my night-gown more closely around my body and moved one foot so it was placed more exactly in the center of a motif on the carpet. What had the duke told my brother? Had he confessed to the murder of his young wife? Had both Ferdinand and Maximilian known the truth all along, and arranged my marriage into Ferrara regardless?

"You are shivering. Are you cold?"

"No, my lord."

"Very well. Stand up, if you please."

I remained seated. What would he do if he knew I was shivering with—I was not sure, excitement, terror, determination, breathlessness—at my own disquisitive and difficult presumption in plotting to gain power over him?

"What do you intend to do?"

"Stand up."

I stood up slowly.

He began to unfasten the gold-corded knots on the front of my night-gown. I flinched away at first, but he caught hold of the brocade and pulled me back. Rather than humiliate myself by struggling, I stood quietly as he finished opening the gown and pushing it back from my shoulders. It fell with a rustle of silk and fur. I was naked beneath it but for my hair.

"You have such lovely hair," he said. "Golden-rose, like apricots. I should like you to obtain an apricot-scented perfume to enhance the impression. Turn around."

I turned. I felt him rest one hand on the curve of my hip. The touch was firm and surprisingly calming. I closed my eyes. I thought of him jerking my skirts over my head and thrashing me with the stick from the fireplace, and I hated him.

"A faint mark or two left," he said. "By tomorrow, they will be gone. Obey me in future, Madonna, and there will be no more."

I began to shiver again, all through my body. It was cold in the *camerino*. It was December in Ferrara, after all, and I was naked. I wanted to walk away, but I did not. Where would I go? Duchess I might be, but he was the duke and my master. I thought of the day when I would have proof he had killed his first wife, and could walk away if I chose.

"Let us go to bed," he said. "The sheets have been warmed."

I gathered up my night-gown and wrapped it around me; I could not quite bring myself to walk through into the bedchamber naked. He followed me. The bedsheets were indeed warm and scented with his favorite sandalwood. I put the night-gown aside again and climbed into the bed's silken softness, my hair crackling and clinging to my skin like gossamer.

"So you were praying for a son and nothing more," he said. "Let us do our part, then, Madonna, to bring that particular prayer to fruition."

He put off his robe. I turned my face into the pillow—yes, he had taught me all sorts of things about men and women and what they could do together, but gazing openly at his naked body was something I could not yet quite manage. He said nothing, but lay on the bed beside me and put his arms around me. I stiffened. I still felt cold. Holy Virgin, I could not forget the pressure of his hand between my shoulder blades, holding me down while he thrashed me with a poplar switch. How could any man expect any woman to forget that?

"You are not yourself," he said. He ran his hand over my shoulder.

"Did you expect I would not be changed by what you did?"

He ran his hand over my shoulder again, then slowly down my arm. His palm was warm and firm and more insistent. After a moment he said, "The only change I expect from you is a greater desire to please me."

I no longer felt chilled. Was it the luxurious coverlets and the heat of the duke's body next to mine, or was it the fire of resentment simmering in my heart and slowly pulsing out through my flesh to the very tips of my fingers and toes? Bide your time, I exhorted myself. You will have your chance for revenge, after you have found the truth and can use it to protect yourself. Bide your time.

"Very well, my lord." I tried to make my voice soft and humble. "I will do my best."

The movement of his hand along my arm stopped. To my surprise he laughed again, very softly. "I am not such a fool as to be taken in by a pretty voice and lowered eyes," he said. He took hold of my wrist and pinned it against the pillow. "Be angry if you must. A sweet is always improved by the addition of a little spice."

HE'S GETTING MORE *spice than he bargained for, Alfonso is—who would've thought la Cavalla had such fire in her? I remember thinking if he'd thrashed me, I wouldn't have let him off without a few slaps and scratches. I guess it took la Cavalla a few days to work up her courage, or a few glasses of wine—or both.*

I remember when Alfonso showed my portrait to the archduke from Austria, the one who thought he was so clever by posing as his own servant. Just look at that spot of joy on her cheek, Alfonso said. 'Twasn't only for me she blushed, but for everyone who said a kind word to her. Smirk smirk. Wink wink. Che mucchio di merda! *He might as well have said straight out I'd played the whore with half the men of the court. Too soon made glad, he said. Well, maybe I was. But did he ever think it was because he never made any effort to make me glad himself?*

The archduke nodded and smiled. They fawned on each other, the two of them. All the archduke cared about was getting Ferrarese soldiers to swell the emperor's armies. He said so, after they walked away down the stairs. And then he laughed and started telling Alfonso how he'd have to do a bit of taming when Madonna Barbara arrived. I suppose it was the statue of Neptune and the sea-horse that put the thought in his mind.

Well, she's tamed, or at least Alfonso thinks she is. It drives me wild to see them together, and to know I'll never feel that pleasure again. I try to get it back by imagining I'm watching myself. Not with Alfonso—he never gave me much pleasure—but with one of my lovers. What gives it spice for me is to think of the ones who would've made Alfonso the angriest. Like Sandro.

Yes, he was one of them, Alfonso's French friend, Sandro Bellin-ceno—oh, he was passionately in love with me, and sent me notes, even poems sometimes. I had a book called I Modi, full of pictures of men and women in bed with each other. Such a wonderful book it was, condemned by the pope himself. I stole it from Alfonso—I'm sure he had it just because it was rare and had poetry as well as the pictures. He was furious when he found it was missing, but he never suspected me because he knew I couldn't read. He couldn't search for it openly because it was a forbidden book and he shouldn't have had it in the first place.

Sandro loved it, and we tried to duplicate all the positions. I think I liked the eighth one best. I coaxed him to write his own poetry in it, beside the printed poems, and in the heat of lust he did. Later he was sorry, because I threatened to tell Alfonso he stole the book himself, and to use his writings in it for proof. But that's another story.

Yes, Alfonso thinks he's tamed his fine imperial wife. He doesn't know she went questioning Mother Eleonora and Sister Orsola behind his back. I wonder what he'll do when he realizes she hasn't been tamed at all.

CHAPTER THIRTEEN

*T*he next morning my ladies goggled avidly at my flesh as they helped me to dress. There were no fresh marks to titillate them, thank God, but when Katharina held a mirror for me, I could see the marks of the duke's pleasure in the faint violet shadows under my eyes, and in the way my lips were swollen and reddened enough I had no need for lip-paint. Would everyone else see as well, and whisper behind their hands? Better that, at least, than the titters and whispers after the duke had beaten me—or the cardinal's insinuations that our marriage was an unhappy one.

I gestured the mirror aside. I had left my own marks on the duke's chest and arms—bruises, or so I hoped, scratches, and a bite-mark or two. *A sweet is always improved by the addition of a little spice.* Spice he had been given, in generous measure, and I had found it eased a bit of my own resentment to strike back physically for the way he had treated me. Perhaps that had been his intention all along. Perhaps—

"Serenissima." It was Nicoletta Rangoni, who had been left on duty in the Jupiter chamber. "Forgive me, Serenissima, but there is a lady here to see you."

"Who is it?"

She shrugged, one of the surpassingly expressive gestures of the Ferrarese. "She would not say, Serenissima. She is masked and wrapped up in a cloak and hood, and speaking in such a way as to disguise her true voice—but from the quality of her silks and furs, she is a lady of the court."

I did not think to be afraid, not here in the heart of the Palazzo del Corte; I was only torn between annoyance and curiosity. "Very well," I said. "Katharina, you may go. Nicoletta, tell your mysterious visitor I will see her. Then go to the Saint Catherine Tower and fetch news of Paolina."

They went out, and after a moment a woman came in, dressed all in black, masked and heavily veiled, with a hooded cloak wrapped about her. It was almost too much, as if she were affecting some sort of theatrical costume. Nicoletta was right about the quality of her garments—the black gown was silk, the black veil silk as well, and the black velvet cloak was lined with gleaming sable. She was a lady of the court, and a highly placed one at that.

"What is this mummery?" I said.

She put back the veil and removed the mask. To my astonishment, it was the duke's younger sister.

"Madonna Nora! What—"

"Hush!" She cut me off crossly. "Why do you think I am wrapped up in mask and cloak and veils as I am? I do not want anyone to know I am here. Particularly Alfonso."

"But you are always perfectly welcome to come here openly, and I cannot imagine why the duke would object."

Her dark eyes narrowed; she had used belladonna, I was certain, to make them look larger and more brilliant. She needed no vermillion on her cheeks, as her natural color gave her an unhealthy flush. "Alfonso objects to everything I do. And in any case, if I came here in the ordinary way, I would have half-a-dozen ladies with me, and your ladies would be crowding around as well, listening to every word. I want to speak with you privately."

I could not help but think her dramatic entrance swathed in black was more likely to create whispers than an ordinary visit, ladies or no. She was playing some game, and I wondered what it was. "Of course you are welcome. Please, seat yourself, be comfortable. I suppose you do not wish me to call for refreshments?"

She threw off the fur-lined cloak and like a sulky child left it lying on the floor. "No, nothing."

"Very well." I seated myself in one of the two gilded leather chairs arranged in front of the window and gestured encouragingly for her to take the other. "Now tell me your secret."

She did not sit, but began to pace about the room. Her flesh and clothing must have been drenched in her perfume of orange blossoms, roses, and musk, because the scent was chokingly strong each time she came close to me. "I suppose you noticed I was not present for the Festival delle Stelle."

More and more mystifying. "I did. I hope you were not ill?"

"Ill!" she burst out. "No, I was not ill. I was locked up at Villa Belvedere, and it was Alfonso who arranged it, and I hate him. I would kill him if I could."

Holy Virgin. Even sisters were not wise to say such things about reigning dukes, and I knew to my sorrow there were secret passages and silent listeners everywhere. "Madonna Nora, guard your tongue, I beg you. Sister or no, if you say things like that where anyone else can hear, you will find yourself locked up for good, and in much less comfortable circumstances than the Villa Belvedere."

"Why do you think I am saying it only to you? He wants to keep me away from Tasso. He told me a few days of solitary fasting and prayer would tame my flesh. Do you know why he has not arranged a proper marriage for me? He thinks I am too frail, too often ill, to be a proper wife. And then he dares say to me my flesh must be tamed."

I remembered her whispers and laughter, that morning in the orange garden. "Perhaps," I said, with an unseemly but irresistible sense of satisfaction, "he only feared there would be talk. Laughter, perhaps, behind your back."

I might have saved myself my sin of vengefulness, because she did not even hear me. "And then!" she went on. "And then he told me he could not trust me to act with decorum at the Festival delle Stelle. And meanwhile Tasso is spending all his time with that little slut Lucrezia Bendidio. Oh, I *hate* him."

It wasn't entirely clear whether she hated the duke, the poet, or both—probably both. I said cautiously, "I understand you are distressed, Madonna Nora. What I do not understand is why you have come to me."

She threw herself in the chair beside me and grasped my wrist. I flinched back, but she held on, her fingers bony and cold as a merlin's claws. "To hurt him in return," she said. "Emperor's daughter! Emperor's sister! He dared to marry you, and it is nothing but a mockery. Do you know what they whisper about him?"

He murdered his first duchess with his own hands, they say. She was so young, so beautiful. . . .

"Madonna Nora, repeating gossip to me will not harm him." I struggled to free my wrist, panicked and at the same time feeling a sort of sick eagerness to hear what she was going to say. "It will give you no revenge, only—"

"He is not a whole man, they say. He will never father a child."

I stared at her. I was not sure I had heard her correctly.

"The great Duke of Ferrara!" she went on scornfully. "Soldier and horseman and athlete! Has he managed to consummate his splendid imperial marriage, Serenissima? Some even whisper he is incapable, ever since—"

"Be silent at once." I found my voice at last, and my strength as well; with one violent twist I wrenched my wrist from her grasp and rose to my feet. "How dare you, Madonna Nora? The duke is your brother and the reigning prince of Ferrara. No matter what he has done to antagonize you, it is treason and lèse-majesté for you to impugn him in such a despicable way. I will hear no more of it, Madonna—you may go."

She smiled like a satisfied cat and stood up, stretching slowly and sinuously. "Reigning prince," she mocked me. "Lèse-majesté. Fine words. Just tell me, my proud new Habsburg sister—is your marriage a complete one?"

Is your marriage a complete one?

A sweet is always improved by the addition of a little spice. . . .

"I will not dignify that question with an answer," I said. "I have asked you to leave."

"He had a bad fall, jousting in Blois," she said. She lingered over every word, savoring each one. "It was spring, April, oh, perhaps ten years ago when he was a young man. He was galloping in the lists before a tournament, and his horse fell with him—fell full upon him and crushed him. The king of France himself rushed to his aid, they say. You know the king of France is our cousin."

I was so angry, my hands were shaking. "One would think a king's cousin would not lower herself to such contemptible innuendos," I said. "And—"

"Alfonso wrote to my lady mother at once and claimed it was nothing," she continued. It was as if she were part of a ghastly dream from which I could not make myself awaken. "But it was one of those injuries men never speak of, except in whispers. And even knowing he cannot breed an heir, he has dared to marry, not once but twice! You will be a childless wife, Serenissima, and I tell you now—the fault will not be yours."

"I do not believe you."

"Ask him."

"Are you mad? I will say to you one more time, Madonna Nora—be silent and go. If you do not, I will call my ladies and my guards, and all your secrecy and disguisings will have gone for naught."

She laughed—and why not? She had achieved her purpose of revenge upon her brother by casting an unthinkable slur upon him. She had not dared to do it publicly, but was it not almost as good for her to plant the poison of doubt in his wife's breast? For one endless moment I hated her so much, the air shimmered before my eyes and my hand came up, as if— But no. I would not strike her. That would be lowering myself. And I would not hate her. I would pity her. Tasso would never love her, and even if he did, the duke would never permit her to take the poet as her lover.

And my marriage was a complete one. Were the marks of the duke's passion not clearly visible to her upon my face, in my heavy eyes and reddened lips? I longed to say as much to her, but stooping to defend the duke's capability would only give substance to her claim.

"Go," I said. There was nothing else to say.

Quite casually she gathered up her fur-lined cloak from the floor and replaced her mask and veil. "I want you to hate him, you see," she said. "Who is he to think he has the right to love, when he denies it to me?"

"You are a fool to listen to those who whisper against your brother, Madonna Nora." Even as I said it, the irony of my words did not escape me. Was I not listening to every whisper I could find about the duke and his first duchess? "And I assure you, nothing you say will make me hate my husband."

"We will see." She went to the doorway with much rustling of silk and another overpowering waft of musky perfume. "In a year or two, when you are still childless and he throws it in your teeth that the fault is yours, remember what I have told you. Ask him then about the tournament at Blois."

★   ★   ★

MY LADIES WERE abuzz with curiosity, of course, but I forestalled their questions as they dressed me. I went to Mass, where the duke greeted me publicly with his customary chill courtesy. I felt awkward at first, remembering what had passed between us in the night and Nora's bitter accusation, but the duke's unruffled calm helped me summon up my own self-possession. This, then, was something else I would be required to learn as a wife—the separation of the night from the day, secrets from public things, darknesses from daylight.

After dinner, we collected our perpetual train of courtiers and made our way to the portrait gallery—not the hidden niche where the glowing portrait of Lucrezia de' Medici dreamed away the days behind its velvet curtains, but a long gallery in the upper level of the Castello. We found Frà Pandolf there already, with two boys in the habits of Franciscan novices holding a canvas. It was covered. How like the fellow to arrange a dramatic unveiling.

"Good day, Frà Pandolf," the duke said. He took his seat in one of the two chairs provided, and gestured to me to take the other. Our households remained standing, clustered behind us: two of the duke's secretaries, several gentlemen, my ladies Sybille and Domenica, and Christine with Tristo and Isa on scarlet leather leashes.

The Franciscan did not look at me but bowed like a dandy to the duke. "Good day, Serenissimo, and I thank you for the privilege of waiting upon you. Such a pleasure it was to execute your commission—the hours flew by."

"I am sure they did," the duke said. "Your conversation with the duchess on the subject of your previous commissions must have particularly sped the time."

I sat still, looking straight ahead. Frà Pandolf, sycophant that he was, only laughed. "Oh, yes, so it did," he said. "I am honored—"

"Enough." The duke held up his hand. "You could paint as well as ever, I think, if your tongue were to be cut out. Show me your portrait of the duchess."

Frà Pandolf appeared to take the duke's threat as a fine jest. Perhaps he thought his genius gave him license. Perhaps he and the duke had sparred in such a way before. In any case, he laughed again and gestured to the boys holding the canvas. They lifted it higher, and he drew away the covering with a flourish.

"Ecco la duchessa!"

He had finished it perfectly, every detail and jewel of my wedding dress faithfully represented. Katharina had worked for hours repairing the damage it had suffered. I felt humiliation burning in my cheeks; the duke did not move or say anything, and when I looked at him sidelong, his dark face was expressionless. The ladies all gasped and whispered with excitement, and even the gentlemen murmured among themselves. Tristo and Isa, catching the excitement in the air, began to bark.

"Quiet the dogs." The duke's voice was cool but not unkind, considering he had just threatened to cut out Frà Pandolf's tongue. I took Isa up into my lap, and gestured for Christine to take Tristo.

"Step back," Frà Pandolf said to the boys. "Allow the Serenissimo to take in the long view."

"No." The duke rose and stepped closer to the painting. I watched him, trying to calm myself with stroking Isa's velvety russet ears, measuring their length one against the other. What would he see in the face of the woman painted there? Would he see the secrets in her eyes, the calculation behind the soft convexity of her lower lip? Would he denounce me instantly for daring to pursue the truth?

"You have caught the color of her hair precisely," he said. He moved to one side and looked at the canvas from another angle. "The composition is excellent. The light appears to shine through the paint, and the tones of her skin are perfect."

There was much murmuring in agreement. My anxiety receded, but in its place I felt an odd sensation—as if I were no longer present in the room. "Barbara, Duchess of Ferrara" had become the iconlike figure captured in Frà Pandolf's paint for the duke to possess and the court to admire. The duke stepped very close and examined the brushwork; the ladies and gentlemen made flattering remarks about the lifelike presence of the figure, the subtlety of the eyes, the dignity of the expression. I petted Isa's ears again and again, and I felt her squirm with pleasure against my whalebone-stiffened stomacher. At least she knew I was still there.

"And you, Madonna?" the duke said at last. "What do you think?"

I jumped, lost as I was in my strange thoughts. "I think—it is remarkable."

"As do I. Very well, Frà Pandolf, I accept the portrait. Please deliver it to Messer Giovanni Pigna and apply to him for your fee."

The Franciscan bowed. He had not looked at me once or acknowledged my presence in any way. I wondered if flesh and blood became meaningless to him once he had transferred their essence to canvas. But no, he had painted the duke, and the duke as his patron was still very much alive to him. Perhaps just my flesh and blood—female flesh and blood. It was a disturbing thought, and one that made the painter even more distasteful to me.

"Thank you, Serenissimo," he said. "My brushes and colors are at your service forever."

"In fact," the duke said, "I do have another commission for you. I desire you to create a series of panels illustrating the life of the Holy Virgin, to be placed in the chapel here in the Castello. The duchess finds its present classical style of decoration not to her taste."

The Franciscan rubbed his hands together; his foxy red-bearded face lighted up with an artist's pleasure at the thought of new creations. "A wonderful idea, Serenissimo. God will reward you for your piety. I can see them now, the Blessed Virgin at the knee of Saint Anne, and then the Annunciation—"

"Sculptures as well. Bronzes, I think, of the Virgin, Saint Anne, and Saint Elizabeth. Both the duchess and I admire the work of Claus of Innsbruck, although you are to make it clear to him that the statues are to be done in an ecclesiastical and not a classical style. Draw up a list and submit it to Messer Giovanni with your account for the duchess's portrait." The duke's tone was one of clear dismissal. "Madonna?"

I put Isa down and handed her leash to Christine, then rose and put my hand on my husband's wrist. Frà Pandolf bowed yet again, then straightened and gestured to the boys to draw the cover over the painting.

"He has captured you to the life," the duke said to me as he led me out of the gallery. The courtiers followed at a distance. "As much as I dislike his manner, the fellow is a genius."

"He certainly has an unusual talent."

"There is something about the eyes. I had not truly grasped it until I saw it set down in paint. I believe you have depths, Madonna, you have not shared with me."

I kept my steps even and my hand steady. "Depths, my lord? We have been married barely a month, and I suspect you also have depths you have not shared with me."

To myself I damned the toadying Franciscan's acuteness, and the duke's discernment as well. I could feel my hand beginning to tremble, so I stopped, pretending I wished to take the puppies' leashes from Christine.

"It is an illusion of the paint, my lord," I said, taking great care with the looping of the scarlet leathers around my wrist—two loops for each, no more, no less. "That is all."

"Perhaps," he said. "But I do not care to think my wife is deceiving me."

My knees went weak and my chest tightened. I remembered

my conversation with Messer Bernardo Canigiani in the very chapel to be decorated with the work of Frà Pandolf for my sake. I
remembered my determination to pursue the truth of Lucrezia de'
Medici's death, so as to use it against my husband. I remembered
my conversations with Mother Eleonora and Sister Orsola. I remembered the exchange with Nora. *Ask him then about the tournament at Blois. . . .*

A litany of deceptions. What was one more?

"I am not deceiving you," I said.

The duke did not look at me—a fortunate thing, because if he
had, I might have lost my courage and confessed everything. "Oh,
not in the common manner," he said. "I grant you that. You have
hardly had the chance, and in any case, you have a sense of your
position and a decent dignity before the court. But there is something disturbing in that painting."

We walked on in silence for a minute or two. I could hear the
gentlemen and the ladies whispering behind us. Tristo tugged on
his leash, his little claws clicking and scratching against the marble
parquetry. "I assure you, my lord," I said, half-expecting the devil
to rise up and snatch my tongue away, "that I shall always make
every effort to be completely straightforward with you."

"Every effort?" His voice was cool, and something about it
reminded me uneasily that he had secrets of his own. "Somehow,
Madonna, I doubt that."

Just then, Nicoletta Rangoni came running from the Saint
Catherine Tower, and without so much as a curtsy or a proper address to either one of us, blurted out that Paolina Tassoni was dead.

*"YOU HAVE CAUGHT the color of her hair precisely! The tones of her skin are
perfect!" How dare he? Her portrait isn't half as beautiful as mine.*

*I remember them all exclaiming over my portrait, too, saying they could
almost hear me laugh, could almost smell and touch the cherry blossoms in*

my hand. I didn't sit by blushing like la Cavalla did today—I laughed and preened and urged them on to give me even more compliments. By the end of the day, even I was sated—well, almost sated—with admiration.

Almost, because Alfonso was as cold as ever.

Paolina Tassoni was wrong when she hinted to la Cavalla that Alfonso shows the portrait to people, complaining of my light-mindedness and boasting of how he stopped my smiles forever. Oh, yes, people say he does—they've been whispering that since the day he sent me off to Corpus Domini. But it's not true. The only time Alfonso ever showed the portrait to anyone was the time he showed it to the archduke.

As if that wasn't enough, with all the bad things he said about me.

I wonder if Nora's somehow got hold of the truth, and there's no life in his seed. He can wield his cazzo strongly enough, that's for certain, but now that I think of it, he's got no bastards. Don't all great princes have bastards? If Alfonso does, he's kept them so secret no one's ever heard of them. And no one can ever keep bastards that secret.

What a bitch Nora is, though, to take revenge on Alfonso for his keeping her away from Tasso, by repeating that story to la Cavalla. The high and mighty Principessa Leonora d'Este! Ever since Tasso arrived in Ferrara, she's been following him around like a weasel in heat. She even dabbles in witchcraft—she's always drinking potions to give herself powers or make herself irresistible, and I know she's got a new one she's taking just to make Tasso love her. No wonder she's sick all the time.

I'm sure it's not true about Alfonso and the tournament at Blois. At least, not the part about it making him less than a man.

Alfonso himself must not believe it, or he wouldn't keep getting married. He wouldn't be so hot to get the Precedenza for himself, if he didn't think he'd have a son to come after him.

But if it is true—if it is! If it is, oh, that would be the most satisfying revenge of all.

CHAPTER FOURTEEN

*T*he celebrations marking my wedding to the duke fused seamlessly into the festivities of Christmastide. I tried to enter into the spirit of the holiday, but could not throw off my grief and melancholy over Paolina Tassoni's unexpected death or my fear that I myself could easily die in the same sudden, meaningless way. She had been entombed—too hastily? To me it seemed so—and once her funeral Mass was over, she might never have existed at all. A girl named Vittoria Beltrame, some sort of cousin of the Tassonis, was added to my household to replace her. She was openly the duke's informer. I did not like her, but I had no choice in the matter.

Paolina had been so pleased over our small secret pact to deceive the duke. *Only let me stay, Serenissima, and I shall be more discreet. I swear it.* I could not forget the light in her eyes at that moment, or the dry texture of her hair as she lay dying, barely two hours later, on her pallet in the Saint Catherine Tower. Nor could I forget Maria Granmammelli's warning. I struggled to eat the rich

Christmas delicacies, the artistic marvels of the duke's chefs and bakers; I did not always succeed. Katharina, Sybille, and Christine vied with one another to taste every morsel of food before I did. We took care to make it seem accidental so the duke would not see and question.

On Christmas Eve we fasted: we ate no meat, but our supper was made up of dozens of different fish dishes, rice with nuts and spices, sweet pastas, fruits, and a fabulous subtlety in the form of Saint George's dragon breathing fire, the delicate curling melted-sugar flames painted with cinnamon and saffron and gilt. On Christmas Day we went to Mass; the rest of the day was given up to the performance of a magnificent chivalric fete entitled Il Tempio d'Amore, which featured even more elaborate machinery than the Festival delle Stelle, as well as dazzling verse, music and dancing, and an astonishing pyrotechnical conclusion.

The second day of Christmastide, Saint Stephen's Day, there were tennis matches—the duke was one of the best tennis-players in Europe, and even in the winter sometimes arranged matches in the large courtyard of the Castello. After supper we gathered to hear Torquato Tasso recite excerpts from his romantical work *Rinaldo*. Crezia was everywhere, whispering with everyone, dancing with her handsome lover, and celebrating the season with a fine goodwill. Nora was present as well, as she had been for all the Christmastide events; apparently she was back in her brother's favor for the moment at least. She seemed subdued, and she made it a point to avoid me; I wondered if she regretted her visit to me. I did not see her exchange so much as a word with Tasso. Had they quarreled? Tasso was the center of attention, his fine long-legged figure clad in amethyst satin, the color of poets; once again I was struck by the almost visible aura of brilliance and magnetism that surrounded him.

So many secrets. So many shifting loyalties. That night I was dressed in pale blue satin and silver lace, set off by a magnificent necklace of diamonds and sapphires. I seemed to be one with the richly dressed company, but in truth I felt outside it all. The duke, on my left, paid me no attention. On my right, Crezia leaned close, her lily-and-musk perfume so intense it made my head swim.

"See there?" she whispered. "That is Sandro Bellinceno, a great friend of Alfonso's from his days in France, with his new wife. I can tell you tales about him."

"He was presented to me at the Neptune banquet," I said. "But I know little about him, other than the fact that he and his wife are newly wed."

"He first came to Ferrara when Alfonso returned from France as duke, six years ago," Crezia went on. "He and Alfonso had been battlefield comrades, and much was made of Messer Sandro transferring his allegiance from France to Ferrara and making his home here. But in less than a year he ran back to France."

She paused. Clearly she expected me to coax her for details. I was not particularly interested in Sandro Bellinceno, but to please Crezia I said, "And why did Messer Sandro go back to France?"

She took a sip of her wine. "Because he was fool enough to bed with that little strumpet from Florence."

That caught my attention. The terms she actually used were unfamiliar to me, as my tutors had not thought to acquaint me with the Italian vernacular of the gutter. From the general context, though, I had no difficulty getting the gist of her accusation. I assumed a shocked look and whispered, "No!"

"Oh, yes." Crezia drank more wine. "He was besotted with her. She was only toying with him, as she toyed with all the men."

"Does the duke know? If so, I am surprised Messer Sandro dared show his face again."

"I was surprised as well when he returned. Alfonso welcomed him like a lost brother, however, providing him with another place here at court and even marrying him to a rich wife so he could pay his debts. She was in Lucrezia de' Medici's household, the wife—

she was so desperate to come back to court, she would have married a goat."

"The duke could not have known," I said. "Men will forgive many things, but cuckoldry is not one of them."

"I am not so sure. Sometimes I think the men Alfonso soldiered with and jousted with in France were more family to him than we are. What is a wife, particularly a wife for whom one feels nothing but disgust, between men who have fought and killed together?"

Holy Virgin. And I was sitting next to the man, wearing the gems of his ancient family while smiling and listening to poetry. I looked at him sidelong. He was also dressed in blue, although a very deep blue, almost black, and at his belt was the damascened dagger with the arms of Henri II. Perhaps Crezia was right. He certainly seemed to treat Sandro Bellinceno more as a brother than he treated his own brother the cardinal. But then, the cardinal, with his innuendos and flirtations, did not seem to act as one might expect a brother to act.

The duke's face was expressionless, as aloof as the face of one of the classical statues he so admired, as he listened to the verses glorifying stalwart young Rinaldo. Romance did not seem to move him. Perhaps it was only the technical brilliance of Tasso's verse he appreciated.

How different he was in the hot, herb-scented darkness of his curtained bed. Perhaps his lust was only for getting an heir as soon as possible—and whatever Nora whispered, the duke himself was intent on an heir. Then again, perhaps his desire was only to break me to his will and silence my questions once and for all. Whatever it was, his original prediction had come frighteningly true. I had, indeed, come to like some of the things he had taught me.

"Messer Sandro was not her only lover," Crezia hissed in my ear, persistent as the serpent who tempted Eve. "You would be surprised at how many, and who. And not all of them remain in

Ferrara to tell the tale. Alfonso may pretend not to notice, but certain men just"—she made a sweeping-away gesture with one hand—"disappeared. Messer Sandro may vanish one day as well."

The conversation was veering into deep and dangerous waters. "To accept a different employment, perhaps." I made my voice as severe as I could while whispering behind my hand. "Or take service in another city."

Crezia looked at me strangely for a moment. "Oh, yes," she said at last. "To take service in another city, to be sure."

"WHAT WERE YOU and Crezia whispering about during the *Rinaldo?*" the duke said to me, in the interval between the recitation and the mummers' performance. "You surely know, Madonna, that I do not care for gossip."

"She is your own sister, my lord."

"That does not prevent her from having a poisonous tongue. Befriend her if you like, but keep your conversations to subjects that do not require whispering."

I inclined my head, the model of wifely submissiveness. "Yes, my lord," I murmured.

As I said it, I swore to myself I would find a chance to have a reasonably private conversation with Sandro Bellinceno, whispered or no. Little do you know, I thought as I sat there so gracefully and pleasantly beside the duke, little do you know what your sisters are saying about you. Nora dares to whisper against your very manhood, and Crezia hints you have conspired in the murder of your first wife's lovers. *Certain men just disappeared. . . .*

And a charming but faithless young wife disappeared as well, into a tomb at the Monastero del Corpus Domini, to make room for an older, uglier, better-born and more obedient duchess. Outwardly obedient, at least. Inwardly seething.

"You are angry," he said unexpectedly. "It pleases me, Madonna, that you have the self-restraint to act as the Duchess of Fer-rara should act, anger or no."

What could I say to that? I was torn between an even hot-ter anger and a disconcerting sense of being gratified. Fortunately I was not called upon to respond, as Messer Bernardo Canigiani chose that moment to approach us.

"Good evening to you, Serenissimo, Serenissima," he said. The Florentine ambassador's bow was, as always, overdone. I had begun to wonder if he did it deliberately, as a subtle form of mock-ery. "A fine entertainment. I understand young Tasso has begun a new work, centered upon the siege of Jerusalem."

"I do not ask Messer Torquato about his unfinished works," the duke said. His voice was cold and formal. "I find such discus-sions hinder the artistic spirit."

"There are those who say just the opposite. I myself have found the boy charmingly forthcoming. Even Duke Cosimo is aware of his brilliance and would be delighted to lure him from your broth-er's household to the court of Florence."

I felt the duke's arm stiffen. It seemed he was also to be given the opportunity to act with self-restraint, anger or no.

"I believe he is happy here in Ferrara."

"He is certainly a great favorite with the ladies of the court." Messer Bernardo smiled, showing his teeth. "But I will take no more of your time this evening. I thank you for your generous at-tention, Serenissimo, Serenissima."

He went away. The duke said something under his breath I did not understand. It was probably just as well.

"I do not care for that man," I said.

"Nor do I."

"It is unfortunate the necessities of politics require us to be cordial to such an unpleasant fellow."

"So it is. I had not thought you would take such an interest in politics."

"I take more of an interest than you may think, my lord. One reason, I believe, why Messer Bernardo is so interested in Tasso is that stealing him away from Ferrara would be a great triumph for Duke Cosimo in the matter of the Precedenza, and a loss for your brother and you."

The duke sat back. I had surprised him. "So you understand the Precedenza," he said.

"I am neither blind nor deaf. In Innsbruck this past summer, there were many arguments between the Medici ambassadors and your own, as my marriage and my sister's were being arranged—precedence and prestige were at the bottom of them all. So far my brother has been clever enough to balance Ferrara and Florence, one against the other. But it would be much in the best interests of the Medici for my marriage—our marriage—to fail, so Ferrara would lose my brother's favor and Florence would gain what Ferrara has lost."

"Perhaps I shall ask you for your advice, when next I am faced with a knotty problem concerning the emperor and the Medici."

I could not tell if he was mocking me or not. I said, rather tartly I fear, "You could do worse, my lord."

"I am certain I could. Now, oblige me by mingling with our guests during the intermission. I wish to speak privately with the Venetian ambassador."

So he had been mocking me. I rose, with much rustling of my satin skirts. "Yes, my lord," I said.

And I quite intended to obey him. Who better to mingle with, after all, than Messer Sandro Bellinceno, one of his own great friends from his days in France?

"GOOD EVENING, MESSER Sandro," I said. "Tasso is a talented young fellow, is he not?"

There are advantages as well as disadvantages of rank, and one of the advantages is that one can simply walk up to anyone and initiate a conversation. The other person, if he is lower in rank, has no choice but to stop whatever he might be doing and respond as if he were delighted to be interrupted.

Messer Sandro, most unfashionably, had been speaking tête-à-tête with his tall young wife. He gave her a quelling look and then turned to me with one of his graceless bows and a polite smile.

"Talented indeed, Serenissima," he said. His Italian was markedly French-accented. "You have of course already become acquainted with my wife."

"Indeed I have. Good evening to you, Donna Elisabetta."

She sank into a deep curtsy. As she straightened she said, "It is my pleasure to speak with you again, Serenissima. The court is brightened by your presence."

It was a meaningless remark, of course, but an excellent opportunity for me. I said, "Ah, yes, there has been no duchess for what? Almost four years? Since the death of Lucrezia de' Medici."

I said her name deliberately, just to see what Sandro Bellinceno would do. I suppose I was expecting a look of sorrow or shame or sly treacherousness or even remembered lust. To my surprise, his face lost all expression and his eyes turned dark and flat.

"I pray your pardon, Serenissima," he said. "I feel an urgent need to withdraw."

He bowed again, so curtly the gesture was barely acceptable by court standards, and left the room. I was taken aback, and I suppose my shock showed on my face because his wife hastened to repair her husband's breach of courtesy.

"He has been ill, Serenissima," she said. "The doctors have cast his horoscope over and over, given him purges and vermifuges to regularize his humors, applied poultices of—"

"Enough," I said, having no desire to hear about Messer Sandro's almost certainly fictional ills and medicaments. "Very well, we shall agree for purposes of courtesy your husband is unwell.

Now tell me why he truly turned his back upon me and walked away in such an offensive fashion."

The soft music of the intermission and the hum of many voices made our conversation almost as private as it might have been in a separate withdrawing-room. Messer Sandro's pretty wife looked at me with dark beseeching eyes.

"I beg of you, Serenissima, leave the matter where it lies. My husband is not himself whenever . . ." She stopped.

"Whenever what? Surely, Madonna, you do not wish me to complain to the duke of your husband's rudeness?"

I would never have done it, but it was an effective threat. Poor Donna Elisabetta's eyes grew even larger and darker and took on a hunted look.

"Whenever someone speaks of . . . *her*," she said.

At last I was getting somewhere, although I felt ashamed of myself for my browbeating methods. I would have to find a way to make it up to her.

"Of Serenissima Lucrezia?" I feigned surprise. "But why would a mention of the duchess's name distress Messer Sandro so profoundly?"

She lowered her voice, so I had to lean forward to hear her. In a strangled whisper she said, "He loved her, Serenissima. I was in her household, and I saw it all. She boasted of it, in private. But I did not know all the terrible things she forced him to do, not until we were married and he confessed them."

I stared at her. The young duchess, sixteen, seventeen perhaps, forcing a brutish-looking fellow like Sandro Bellinceno to do terrible things? To do anything? Donna Elisabetta's anguished expression made it clear she was telling what she thought was the truth, but I wondered if Messer Sandro himself had been completely forthcoming with his wife.

This had gone beyond anything we could speak of safely in the great salon of the Castello, no matter what music or conversation

there was to disguise our words. In any case, people were returning to their places; the mummers' play was about to begin. I did
not want the duke to look for me and see me in conversation alone
with Donna Elisabetta.

"I wish to speak to you further," I said. "Come to my apartment tomorrow, before dinner, and tell your husband only that I
have invited you to speak of—oh, fashions, or dogs, or some such
ordinary thing."

She looked at me in white-faced terror. I felt more guilty than
ever.

"Calm yourself, Donna Elisabetta," I said as gently as I could.
"I have no evil designs on you or your husband. Say nothing of
what we have spoken of, and reassure him I believed your tale of
his illness. Tell him I have no intention of mentioning any of this
to the duke."

That at least was true enough. Some of the color came back
into her cheeks, and she nodded wordlessly.

"Tomorrow, then," I said, loudly enough for those around
us to hear. "I wish to know where you found that beautiful silk,
Donna Elisabetta, and how your needlewomen achieved such an
elegant drape alongside the foreparte."

"Yes, Serenissima," she said. She curtsied, and I acknowledged
her with a smile and an inclination of my head, the gesture a bit
more pronounced than the strictest court protocol called for. Word
would instantly ripple through the court that Elisabetta, wife of
Sandro Bellinceno, had gained my favor. I hoped it would make up
for the way I had frightened the truth out of her.

I went back to my place. Upon the dais, the duke had already
taken his seat, and the Venetian ambassador had withdrawn. "You
found some agreeable persons with whom to pass the intermission, Madonna?" he murmured as the mummers came out onto
the stage.

"Oh, yes." I made it sound trivial, and of course said nothing of

my arrangement to speak privately with Sandro Bellinceno's wife
in the morning. "Most agreeable."

*SANDRO BELLINCENO CAN'T even hear my name without getting gripes
in his belly! It serves him right. I'm sure he's also afraid the book, the one
called* I Modi *I stole from Alfonso, will come to light. Sandro would be
in as much trouble as Alfonso if the pope ever got his hands on that book.*

*Where is it? I put it in my treasure box with some letters and things
Tommasina had written for me, and the very morning I was taken away to
the monastery Tommasina hid it. She picked the most obvious place in the
world, but men are stupid, and neither Alfonso nor Sandro ever found it. I
wish I could tell la Cavalla where it is. It would be so funny if I could just
whisper a word or two in la Cavalla's ear.*

*On the other hand, I wanted to scratch out stupid horse-face's eyes when
she sat there and said, "No!" to Crezia so innocently, as if she didn't believe
Crezia's tale that I seduced Sandro. She believed it straight off, and she just
wanted Crezia to tell her more. And the look on her face when Crezia said I
was a* puttana *who had* fottuto *Sandro Bellinceno! I suppose the emperor's
sister is too genteel to know such words. She probably doesn't use the privy,
either, but just wafts her* merda *up to heaven in clouds of perfume.*

*Stupid Crezia fell straight into la Cavalla's trap, of course, and gibble-
gabbled on, retelling all the lies people tell about me. I wonder if she knows
about Niccolò in the stable. He had a lovely long thick* cazzo *and he was
clever with it—he could've written his own book, and better than* I Modi,
too, if he'd been able to write.

*The trouble was, he fell in love with me. I only wanted him to pleasure
me sometimes and other times leave me alone, but he kept bleating about
wanting me to run away with him. A word to Sandro was all that was
necessary, a hint I had Alfonso's* I Modi *hidden away, and Niccolò was
gone from Ferrara. Sandro found him a place in France, in the queen's own
household. I hope he's happy there. Well, maybe not too happy. I hope he
still loves me.*

It's funny. Niccolò wanted me to run away with him, and I didn't want to. But with one man it was just the opposite. For that one man I'd've thrown Alfonso and Ferrara and my father to the four winds, my rank and clothes and jewels and everything. Well, maybe not my clothes and jewels. But I would've followed him to the ends of the earth. He was the one who didn't want to run away. He could have had me for his own and he didn't want me.

What a fool I was to love him so.

If only I could live, and taste and smell and touch and speak, even for a day! I'd cram my mouth with cherries and let the juice run down my chin. I'd steal those beautiful puppies from la Cavalla and stroke their ears, which look so satin-soft. I'd throw Alfonso's moldy old I Modi back in his face and shout the name of my murderer for everyone to hear, and laugh and laugh when the whole court recoiled in shock.

I'd find Niccolò in France's royal stables and fottere *him one last time right there in the straw, until we both screamed with pleasure. Then I think I could go into the dark and sleep peacefully, and let go of the things of the world, and be* immobila *no longer.*

CHAPTER FIFTEEN

*T*he duke did not summon me to his bed that night; it was just as well, for I woke the next morning with incontrovertible proof I was not with child. If I had been alone I would have wept with frustration and fear—was Nora right? Could she possibly be right?—but I did not have a single private moment. Katharina and Domenica were already awake and dressed and bustling about the chamber. Christine was sent for water and clean linen and the humiliating necessities of an unfruitful bride, and to my further mortification she returned with Maria Granmammelli close behind her. Poor Christine! She looked so apologetic, but I did not blame her for being waylaid. The old witch could count days on her fingers as well as anyone, and she had probably been lurking in the shadows waiting for her opportunity.

"Your potion failed," I said at once, hoping to gain the advantage by striking the first blow. "I shall not—"

"'Twas you who failed, *Austriaca*," Maria Granmammelli retorted. "You were born under the sign of the bull, you were, and that makes you cold and dry, too cold and dry for one potion to help you make a babe."

"How did you know—" I began, and then I remembered the Festival delle Stelle and my dress embroidered all over with my astrological sign.

"I know all kinds of things," the old woman said, with a crow-like cackle of laughter. "And I've made you a new potion, with extra spices to heat you—cinnamon and cloves and ginger, red pepper seeds, and the juices of sweet plums and strawberries to make you soft and moist inside."

It did not sound as bad as the last potion. She had spoken of ginger and cinnamon as ingredients in the love potions she made for Lucrezia de' Medici. *That's another tale*, she had said tauntingly. *Mayhap I'll tell you another time.*

Well, I had drunk her potion, for all the good it did me, and it was time for the old witch to keep her part of the bargain.

"Leave me," I said to my ladies. "I would speak privately with Maria Granmammelli."

They looked at each other meaningfully—*already grasping at straws, poor lady, but then, she's old for a first babe*—and went off to the outer rooms. I turned to the old woman and said, "Very well, Maria Granmammelli, I will take your new potion, but only if you tell me more of the love potions you gave Serenissima Lucrezia, and who it was she wished to ensnare with them."

"What do you care what she did?" the old woman said. "She's dead and gone, she is, and her misbegotten babe with her."

"Her *what*?"

"Why else would the pawnbroker's daughter send her *par-ruchiera* to ask for a potion of pennyroyal and vervain, trying to pretend she wanted it for herself? Little Serenissima Lucrezia was with child by one of her lovers, I daresay, and didn't want it. Thought it would spoil her slender waist and pretty little *tetti*."

I stared at her.

She laughed and pushed the flask into my hand. "Drink this, *Austriaca*, and pray to Saint Elizabeth. She was eighty and eight years old when she bore the blessed Baptist, so she should hear you with sympathy."

"I am not that old," I protested. I still could not quite take in what she had said. The words seemed to whisper over and over, all around us: . . . *with child by one of her lovers, with child by one of her lovers* . . .

"You're old enough. Drink a swallow every morning, and hie yourself to the duke's bed every night, and next month at this time the news may be better."

She turned to go.

"Wait!" I cried. "You cannot be serious! Just because her hairdressing-woman asked you for a potion—who knows what she wanted it for? Perhaps she was telling the truth. Or if the young duchess was with child, how did you know it was not the duke's own?"

"And if it was? What of it?"

"What *of* it? It would have been the heir to Ferrara, that is what of it. Did you give the hairdressing-woman the potion or did you not?"

"I didn't give her what she asked for, I'll tell you that much. And as for Serenissima Lucrezia's babe being the heir to Ferrara, well, I'm betraying no secret, *Austriaca*, when I say the duke wanted no half-Medici cuckoos in his nest."

I stood there stunned.

The old witch laughed. "You're a fool, *Austriaca*. 'Tis no concern of yours what became of the pawnbroker's daughter or why, and if you have half the wits I think you have, you'll leave off with your questions before you go the same way she did."

My stomach lurched. "How dare you threaten me!" I whispered. "Get out. Get out of my apartments and do not come back. I do not care what the duke says about the matter."

I cast the flask to the floor at her feet, and it shattered in a spray of crimson liquid. She looked at it, then looked up at me again.

"You'll be sorry for that fit of spite, my girl."

"Get out!" I cried. "Katharina! Domenica! Bring the dogs!"

It was ludicrous to expect Tristo and Isa to snap at the wretched crone's heels, or for that matter expect the old witch to care. The puppies bounded in anyway, tails wagging, eyes bright with mischief; they ignored their supposed quarry and went straight to lick the sweet fruit juices of the spilled potion. I snatched them up, frightened about what else the damnable liquid might have contained. They struggled and whined. My ladies clustered about me, tut-tutting over the puppies and the broken flask.

When I looked up again, Maria Granmammelli was gone.

I HAD A good deal to think about as my ladies bathed and dressed me. Had Lucrezia de' Medici really been with child? Had Maria Granmammelli given her an abortifacient potion or not? And most terrifying of all, did the old witch's hints mean the duke had poisoned his young wife when she got with child, because he felt her blood was not noble enough to mingle with his? Was that the heart of the whole business—Lucrezia's family, and not Lucrezia's infidelities at all?

I could not stop my thoughts, even as Katharina and Domenica laced me into my gown. The duke had not yet succeeded to the title when he married her—the marriage had been forced upon him by an arrangement between his father and Duke Cosimo. There were odd tales I had heard, since I had been in Ferrara—the duke's leaving his young wife in Florence and galloping off to France three days after the wedding; the duke's returning to Ferrara in great pomp and triumph after the death of his father and his own accession to the title, yet allowing his young wife to join him only months later, and then reluctantly. Had it all been because he did not wish to acknowledge her, the pawnbroker's wayward daughter?

One thing was clear. Maria Granmammelli would do anything for her cherished nursling. And how easy it would have been for the duke's old nursemaid to gain entrance to the Monastero del Corpus Domini, to give Lucrezia poison in the guise of the potion she had asked for. Sister Orsola had sworn Lucrezia had nothing to eat or drink that the nuns themselves did not have, but was she telling the truth? She had certainly taken my own bribe readily enough.

I had no time to work out all the possibilities, because Elisabetta Bellinceno arrived just as Katharina was clasping a string of citrines over my braided hair. I went out into the presence chamber and greeted her as calmly as I could.

"Good morning, Donna Elisabetta. You are well, I hope?"

She curtsied formally, her back so stiff and straight you could have turned it sidewise and laid out a game of *tarocchino* upon it. "Very well, Serenissima, I thank you."

I gestured to Domenica. "Bring two glasses of the orange cordial, Domenica, if you please," I said. "Katharina, Tristo and Isa require a walk in the garden. Christine, play for us."

My motives were twofold in all this: to get rid of my ladies, and to soften Donna Elisabetta's stiffness. The cordial would take some time to prepare, as it was a combination of good white wine, sweet syrup, cinnamon, cloves and anise, mixed with preserved oranges from the Castello's own orange trees. Domenica would be occupied for a while with its preparation; Katharina would be strolling in the garden where she would not hear our conversation. I could not send them all away, not after what had happened the last time; but Christine could be depended upon to get lost in her lute and her songs.

I seated myself in one of the gilded chairs and gestured to Sandro Bellinceno's wife. "Please, Donna Elisabetta, draw the other chair close and sit comfortably."

This was another mark of special favor, as she would not ordinarily be considered of high enough rank to sit in my presence. She hesitated for a moment, then did as I asked, her back not touching the back of the chair. "Thank you, Serenissima."

"Now, I swear I mean you and your husband no harm."

"I told him you said as much last night, Serenissima, but he was not convinced."

"Men!" I said with a shrug and a smile. "Obstinate as mules, all of them." I leaned forward and spoke more softly. "Do you understand I wish you to speak with complete openness? I will deny this conversation took place if any other person should ever ask me, but if you tell me what I wish to know, in complete confidence as one woman to another, it will be to your advantage, I promise you."

She looked at me warily. "I understand, Serenissima."

"Very well, then. I wish to know more about your husband's dealings with Serenissima Lucrezia, because I have heard disturbing whispers since I came to Ferrara, whispers about the duke and his first wife."

"The duke, Serenissima?" she repeated cautiously.

I clicked my tongue impatiently. "Let us not fence with each other. The rumors are that Serenissima Lucrezia was poisoned, and that the duke had a hand in the matter."

Elisabetta Bellinceno turned white, and for a moment I thought she would faint. She clutched the lions' heads carved on the arms of her chair and whispered, "*Santa Maria.* Someone will hear you."

I could not help remembering my own horror at Nora's reckless attacks on her brother, in this very room. Since then I had examined the walls and doors with great care, taking we-three into my confidence to help me, and we had concluded that my bedchamber and private presence chamber, at least, were safe.

"No one will hear," I said. "Tell me."

"I swear to you, I do not know the truth about how Serenissima Lucrezia died. I know only what my husband told me—if she had not died, he would never have come back to Ferrara."

"Why not?"

"He loved her, Sandro did. He thought he had seduced her, but I knew her, Serenissima, I knew her down to her heart and soul, and I was there in her household when it happened. She beguiled him with her beauty and took her pleasure from him and then discarded him. He loved her and he was bitter she treated him so, and all the more bitter when she threatened to betray him to the duke if he did not do what she asked."

She stopped for breath, tears glimmering in her eyes. I waited, saying nothing.

"She had another lover," she said at last. "A handsome boy in the stables. He was importuning her, and she wished to be free of him. She asked Sandro to see to it for her."

"What is so bitter about a beating for an upstart groom?"

She swallowed. A tear slipped down, leaving a glistening streak on her cheek. "It was more than a beating. Sandro cut the fellow's throat like a hired assassin, and he has regretted it ever since—that he was slave enough to passion to sink so low, and take a mortal sin upon his soul."

I crossed myself. Killing a man in battle or in the hot blood of a quarrel was one thing; murder by stealth, even of a groom who had dared lay a hand upon a duchess, was something else altogether.

"Could not Messer Sandro have turned the tables upon her?" I asked. "Gone to the duke himself, denied it all? From everything I have seen, he is one of the duke's most trusted friends, as close to him as a brother."

"She had a book," Elisabetta said. "A forbidden book of lustful sonnets and engravings, with love-notes Sandro wrote to her on its pages. She had stolen it from the duke's library, and she threatened to spin a tale that Sandro had been the thief, and used the book to seduce her. He was convinced he would have been damned utterly in the duke's eyes, and that is why he fled."

She broke off with a sob. My heart went out to her, and for the first time I found myself feeling animosity toward Lucrezia de' Medici.

"You were in her household, then," I said at last, to distract her from her distress. "You knew her well."

"Yes." She gulped and swallowed her tears. "I waited upon her from the beginning, when she came to Ferrara during the Carnival. I never thought she meant any harm, not at first, but the duke scorned her for her Medici blood and her lack of learning. She might as well not have been his wife at all, for all the attention he paid her, and it made her resentful and foolish. She might have loved him, I think, if he had given her any warmth at all, but he did not. So she hated him. And then he began to hate her as well."

She had lost herself in her memories. I said nothing, praying Domenica would not come in with the orange cordial and break the spell.

"We were all terrified when she was taken away, afraid we would lose our places or even be arrested ourselves for keeping silence about her wrongdoings. But after she had been in the Monastero del Corpus Domini for a few weeks, she died suddenly. Her household was broken up, and we were all sent away. The duke did not want to see any of us about, because we would remind him of her. The last thing we did, the saddest thing, was to divide up her possessions—what would be returned to her family in Florence, what would be stored away, and what would be given to the poor for charity's sake."

. . . *what would be stored away* . . .

Lightly, as if it meant nothing to me, I said, "Are there some of *Serenissima* Lucrezia's possessions stored away here in Ferrara then, even after all this time?"

She nodded. "Nothing valuable, of course—the jewels and plate and fine clothes were returned to Florence to repay part of her dowry. What remains in the coffers are only the things not good enough to send back, but not suitable to be given away. They are hidden in a locked room somewhere in the Castello, or so the tale is told, and at least one of the coffers is supposed to have come from the monastery where she died. The duke keeps the key to the room very close, and no one but he sets foot inside."

I felt a frisson of . . . what? Fear? Recognition? It took me a moment to realize why Donna Elisabetta's words sounded so familiar and so chilling to me.

Domenica's voice, the voice of reason, when I learned of Frà Pandolf's portrait of Lucrezia de' Medici: *It is the duke's express order no eyes but his gaze upon it. . . .*

Was it guilt driving him to hide all traces of his crime? Was it possessiveness, that he alone could look upon the radiant face of his victim, that he alone could see and touch what remained of her possessions? Was it pride, a wish to expunge her from the Este, wipe out her beauty and folly and all traces of her Medici blood, and at the same time keep her portrait and her possessions so he could gloat over his victory? Or was any of it true at all, and had the ever-whispering tongues of the court created and embroidered the tales?

"I am surprised you wished to come back to court," I said. I wanted to lead her away from thoughts of the hidden coffers. "Surprised you agreed to marry Sandro Bellinceno, knowing what you knew about him."

"I would have done anything," she said simply. "Married anyone. You have lived at courts all your life, Serenissima, and you cannot imagine the tedium and meaninglessness of country life. I thanked God on my knees for the duke's arrangement."

So she and I were kindred souls, more than she knew. I wondered if she had read *Il Libro del Cortegiano,* with its vivid and delightful exchanges on the manners and entertainments of court life. "You might be surprised at how well I can imagine your country life," I said. "In Innsbruck I—"

Just then Domenica came in with the cordial. Elisabetta Bellinceno and I turned our attention to the drink, well-sweetened and cooled with snow. She seemed relieved to have shared her secrets; as she relaxed, I saw how pretty she was and how sweet her expression could be. Perhaps one day I could persuade the duke to give her a place in my own household. Perhaps she and Domenica could be the first two of a Ferrarese we-three.

I sipped my cordial, spoke lightly about dressmakers, and thought about two things. First, how it was becoming increasingly clear that the duke was not the only one with reason to wish Lucrezia de' Medici dead. And second, how I might manage to discover where the duke kept the key to that secret room.

HE KILLED HIM? He killed him? Oh, no! I didn't want that! I didn't ask him for that!

I only wanted him to send Niccolò away, or scare him, so he wouldn't bother me anymore. Not kill him! Never kill him! When Sandro told me Niccolò had gone away to France, I believed him.

I was a fool.

I can't cry. It's so strange. I'd like to cry, but I can't. It was easy when I was alive. Now I have no tears.

I can't think about it. I won't think about it.

Instead I'll watch the terrific broil going on between Sandro and stupid Elisabetta Bellinceno. She's right that Alfonso didn't treat me as a husband should treat a wife, but how dare she say I was resentful and foolish? How dare she, a nobody, say I would have loved Alfonso if he'd given me the chance? She's even more of a fool than I was, and she deserves to be married to a murderer.

He's shouting at her, and she's shouting right back. I didn't know! How could I have known? Now he's drawing back his hand as if he's going to slap her, and . . . she has thrown one of his own boots at his head! She gives as good as she gets, does tall, skinny Donna Elisabetta, however much a fool she may be.

And what's it all about? The I Modi! How funny! Sandro thinks it's hidden in those coffers in that secret room, and he's full of choler at his wife because she told la Cavalla about it. He's afraid la Cavalla will find the book and give it back to Alfonso. What a jest! As if Tommasina would have hidden the book in such a stupid place. Poor Donna Elisabetta is getting all her husband's hard words for nothing, because whatever's hidden away in those coffers, it isn't I Modi.

I can see by the sly look on la Cavalla's face—and yes, I can see her, too, though she's in her apartments in the Palazzo della Corte, and Sandro and his wife are in their tiny rooms in the Castello—she can't wait to get her prying fingers into my coffers and chests. Elisabetta Bellinceno seems to think Alfonso's in and out of his secret store-room in the Lions' Tower every day, but the truth is he's never been in the room once since my things were locked away. I myself don't remember everything that's there. If I were alive again, I'd steal the key and go look. I wonder if la Cavalla will have the courage to do it.

I might as well confess—yes, I was with child, and no, it wasn't Alfonso's. Whose was it? It wasn't Sandro's, I'll tell you that much, and thank the blessed Baptist for it, the filthy murdering swine. No wonder he became so long-faced and prickly, refused to have anything more to do with me and ran away to France again like a cowardly dog. And he'd been killing enemy soldiers on the battlefield all his life. I'll never understand men.

Sometimes we immobili *see one another, drifting, just shapes like wisps of smoke. I wonder if Niccolò is* immobilo, *like me, or if he went straight to purgatory. He wouldn't have gone to heaven, not after all the sinful things we did together, but he was funny and kind, and surely he didn't go to hell.*

Maybe he's immobilo *because he was murdered. I hope so. I can't bear the thought of Niccolò suffering for his sins because of me.*

I wish I could cry.

I wish I could do something good, something to balance against my sins so I don't go to hell. Do you know what I'd do, if I could do a good thing?

I'd whisper the truth in la Cavalla's ear: it was not Alfonso who murdered me.

CHAPTER SIXTEEN

*T*he duke said nothing to me about my conversation with Elisabetta Bellinceno, so it seemed she had kept her promise of silence. Nor did he mention my confrontation with Maria Granmammelli. He expressed his regret formally when I told him I was not yet with child. I suppose the news was hardly a surprise to him; Maria Big-Breasts would have run and told him long before I had the opportunity. I could not help but wonder what his initial reaction had been.

The whole business left me feeling—I was not sure. Empty? Disheartened? Frightened? I had not been able to shake off the slow poison of Nora's rumor-mongering, however much I struggled to convince myself that false stories were always told about the great. Oh, please, Saint Monica, I prayed, let them not be true. Deceiving the duke about my investigations was beginning to exhaust me, and the simplest and safest way to protect myself was to become the mother of his son.

Next month, perhaps. Next month.

Christmastide continued, the celebrations and entertainments coming to a magnificent climax with the feast of the Epiphany on the sixth of January. The weather turned fine, unusually so for the time of year, and so a few days later we removed to a small palazzo called Belfiore, just to the north of the ancient city walls but inside the imposing newer walls built by the first Ercole, the duke's great-grandfather. It was called a *delizia*, a delight, because it was meant for nothing but pleasure; this particular *delizia* was surrounded by fishponds and gardens, and by passing through the great gate called the Porta degli Angeli one reached the ducal hunting preserve known as the Barco, filled with game both natural and stocked. Here, the duke told me, the court would hunt, and in the evenings repose ourselves in richly painted rooms, where fires would warm us and more music and dancing would entertain us.

"In the duke's *studiolo* here at Belfiore there are paintings of the Muses, all of them a hundred years old and more," Domenica said as she braided my hair for our day of hunting. "Just wait until you see Urania—she might step down from the wall and tell your stars. And Erato! She is enough to make any maiden look about for the nearest gentleman. I wrote a sonnet to her last year, and one day I will read it to you."

I still could not help liking Domenica. She was the one Ferrarese lady, barring perhaps Elisabetta Bellinceno, I had come to trust. Nicoletta Rangoni remained a mystery to me, aloof and silent as she was; she showed some small emotion only when she was brushing or walking or playing with the puppies. I continued to dislike Vittoria Beltrame for her perverse delight in others' misfortunes, but she was openly the duke's spy, and I preferred to know who was spying on me.

"Will you take your little hounds on the hunt, Bärbel?" Christine asked.

I smiled at the thought of the two tiny beagles in their embroidered scarlet collars among the greyhounds, the spaniels, the running hounds, and the huge alaunts that made up the duke's hunting pack. Isa was asleep, curled nose-to-tail in an impossibly tight circle in the middle of the embroidered bedcover; Tristo was sitting next to her, watching me attentively, his dark eyes bright with intelligence, his head tilted, his russet ears perked wide.

"They are only babies yet," I said. "And they are bred from the queen of England's companion dogs, so they are not strong enough for the roughness and danger of the hunt."

Nicoletta went over and lifted Tristo into her arms. "It is in their blood," she said, kissing his nose. "You should see this one tracking rabbits and mice in the garden. His sister likes to chase little birds, and she will jump up at the tree branches when they fly away from her."

When I was dressed in my hunting-habit of bracken-green wool, its bodice and sleeves slashed over gold-colored silk and the hem of its skirt heavily embroidered in gold thread, we went through Belfiore's colonnaded loggias to the central courtyard. Katharina and Sybille, in hunting-habits of their own, accompanied me. One of my Austrian grooms was waiting with a beautiful Iberian mare named Tänzerin, Dancer in my own language, a wedding gift to me from my brother Maximilian's court stud at Kladrub. She was silver-gray, almost white, with dapples over her shoulders and hindquarters like water-spots on silk. I had been offered the pick of the ducal stables, but until I was more settled I preferred to keep to the horses I knew, which had come with my train of household goods from Austria.

"She is ready to run, Prinzessin," the groom said in German. "I have been exercising her myself to keep her fresh."

I stepped up on the mounting block and settled myself into the gilded and cushioned saddle, made with two pommels in the modern style of the French queen Catherine de' Medici. How I had loved my few opportunities to hunt at home, and how I was looking forward to more riding in the open air in Ferrara! The saddle had been another of the French wedding gifts, and I was eager to try it.

"Thank you, Conradt," I said as I tucked my left foot into the leather-covered slipper stirrup. I gathered up the reins; Tänzerin shook her head and danced at the touch of the bit against her mouth. Jewels glittered on her headstall and cheek straps. "You look pale. Are you well?"

"Yes, Prinzessin, perfectly well, thank you."

I nodded. "You may go, then. I can manage her."

The courtyard was brilliant with color and pungent with horses and straw, the ancient river-water smell of the Po di Volano, and the spice of costly perfumes. In my ears rang the sounds of iron-shod hooves against stone, voices and laughter, jingling bits, and creaking leather. There were people everywhere: the huntsman and master of hounds and their underlings, grooms and stable boys, two prelates in rich robes arriving in state and, by way of contrast, a Franciscan friar in a brown hooded habit taking his leave. The sixteen white-painted brick columns supporting the loggia gleamed in the morning sun. Kitchen workers were loading baskets and hampers and firewood on mules, so we would have our dinner in the open air even if we did not make a kill.

The ladies—and the gentlemen, too, for that matter—were as richly and impractically dressed as I: Crezia in the Este colors of blue and white, Nora in the purple called *amaranto*, the Marquis of Montecchio in dazzling marigold satin slashed with peach. At one side of the courtyard I caught a glimpse of Elisabetta Bellinceno in blue-gray, looking like a frightened—why frightened?—long-legged heron beside her dour husband in peacock chevrons of gold, blue, and green. He stared at me, to my surprise, with open hatred.

"Good morning, Madonna."

I turned. The duke wore russet leather and velvet, faced with black and with diamond clasps; there was a hawking glove on his left hand. He was mounted on a long-tailed bay Andalusian stallion with a wicked rolling eye.

"Good morning, my lord," I said.

There were two lines like knife-cuts between his dark brows, and his mouth was set; yet his eyes showed a spark of interest when I responded to his greeting. I was struck afresh by the complexity of his expressions and the impossibility of reading them easily. His pride was like a polished shield, deflecting understanding, hiding the thoughts and feelings and human things—or inhuman things—that lived beneath it.

"All is in readiness," he said. "When we have killed, we will— Ah, good morning, Messer Bernardo."

"Good morning, Serenissimo." The Florentine ambassador was dressed in scarlet, with a jaunty feathered cap. "Good morning, Serenissima. It is my great pleasure to see you again."

His courtesy was feigned; I could see wariness and dislike in his eyes. I nodded to him politely.

"The day is fine for January," he went on blandly, "and I think we will see excellent sport. Do you not agree, Serenissimo?"

They immediately fell into talk of hunting, as men will do even when they are enemies. Katharina and Sybille guided their horses close to mine; Katharina stared at Messer Bernardo with such open dislike that I felt it necessary to make a sign to her to mitigate her rudeness. She did, albeit with poor grace. We waited while the duke's bow was brought, and the Florentine hawkmaster took his place. Tänzerin danced impatiently, tossing her head like a petulant lady, her mane rippling silver silk.

"Let us go," the duke said at last.

He touched his spurs to the stallion. I reined Tänzerin around to pace beside him, and we led the procession out into the paved street, to all appearances in perfect accord. A few people had gathered to cheer us, muffled in brown and gray mantles, hoping for largesse. I obliged them, having made sure beforehand I was well supplied with the small copper-alloy *sesini* and *quattrini* the Este minted in Ferrara.

We said nothing to each other as we passed out of the city through the Porta degli Angeli and into the hunting preserve. Here we were closer to the river, and mist drifted along the ground; the cypress and cedar trees bore some green, but the great oaks, hornbeams, and poplars were stark and bare against the sky. The grass was patchy with brown and green on either side of the path.

Once the trees had thickened into something resembling a forest—I could well imagine it being lush and green in the summer—we met the huntsmen who had brought out the dogs, the huge, noble alaunts, the yapping spaniels, and the bell-voiced running hounds. Excitement began to crackle through the crowd of courtiers; in the center of a fawning cadre of young men I saw Crezia and Nora, laughing and coquetting outrageously. As I stared at them—and I must confess I was looking for young Messer Torquato Tasso and Crezia's Virgo gentleman, whose name, I had learned, was Count Ercole Contrari—Nora turned and looked me in the eyes. She had regained her spirit, it seemed, after her subdued demeanor the night Tasso read from his *Rinaldo*. Even from a distance I could see the open scorn in her smile.

Suddenly Tänzerin laid back her ears, and I felt her kick as another horse lurched against her. It was Sandro Bellinceno in his peacock colors, his black Friesian stallion more suited to a battlefield than to a day's amusement.

"Good day to you, Messer Sandro," I said evenly. "Take care with your black, if you please."

I expected a courteous, meaningless answer. I did not receive one.

"I have forbidden my wife to speak to you outside my presence," he said, addressing me as rudely as he might have spoken to a camp follower. "See you respect my wishes."

"How dare you." I must have gripped my reins too tightly,

because Tänzerin backed and tossed her head. "This is not an army's camp, Messer Sandro, and I must insist on decent courtesy if
not—"

He jerked the Friesian's reins and turned away before I could
finish. One or two people next to me saw what he had done, and
they began to murmur behind their hands. Just at that moment the
master of the hawks came forward to ceremoniously offer the duke
a magnificent rock falcon, hooded and jessed in blue and silver.
There was little I could do but swallow my outrage and attend to
the presentation.

"A fine bird, my lord," I managed to say.

"Indeed," he said. The falcon stepped from side to side res-
tively, and he stroked it with a feather to calm it. Then he turned
and looked at me, and I could not help but think that when the
falcon's hood was removed, its eyes would have the same intensity.
Very softly he said, "I commend your self-control, Madonna. I
will speak to Sandro Bellinceno after the hunt. He is my particular
friend and ally, as you know, and once in Flanders he was gravely
wounded when he deflected an arquebus-ball meant for me. But
even so, I assure you he will regret his discourtesy."

I felt a rush of hot satisfaction that my husband would take my
side, and then immediately surprise that the feeling was so fierce.
Did I really care so much? His reaction was nothing but pride, of
course—his self-importance had been stung by his friend's open
contempt for the Duchess of Ferrara, and at the same time he had
been gratified by that lady's dignified response. The humiliation
of Barbara, a living and breathing woman, his wife, was nothing
to him.

"Thank you, my lord," I said steadily. "I value your care for
my position."

The falcon suddenly lifted its wings and made its harsh kack-
kack-kack cry, as if disturbed; he stroked it into submission again.

His face was turned away from me. "Indeed," he said, after a moment.

"I assure you, there is no need to call Messer Sandro to account."

"Then no more need be said of it." He handed the falcon back to the master of the hunt, took his bow and quiver, and reined his stallion around. After a moment, I tapped Tänzerin with my whip and followed, off the path and into the forest. The rest of the court came after us, more or less in order of precedence. We trotted through the trees, fanning out as the beaters worked ahead of us, driving the carefully husbanded deer from their hiding places.

At last one of the hounds gave tongue, and the others joined in; amid the exhilarating clamor I leaned forward and urged Tänzerin to a canter, my ladies behind me. On my left, a little ahead of me, the duke raised his bow. On my right I saw flashes of marigold and scarlet and peacock blue.

Suddenly there was a flicker of brown among the hornbeams and poplars, the size of a fine young stag. Arrows made whispering sounds all around me as horses crashed among the brush and the dogs' baying reached a fevered pitch. That is the last I remember clearly. I think Tänzerin shied, whether at some small animal or a straying hound or the streak of an arrow against her hide, I will never know. I felt her jump, and I thought quite calmly I was keeping my seat despite it all. Then there was an explosion of light, and nothing more.

ALFONSO DIDN'T SEE *her fall. It was one of her Austrian ladies who screamed, and then they all started shrieking and weeping. You should have heard them! Even I was shocked at first, but when I realized her heart was still beating, I knew she was still alive and they were screaming for nothing.*

The girth of her saddle snapped—I saw it clearly. It had been cut almost all the way through. Alfonso will have that Austrian groom's head for it, I'll wager, because he should've checked the saddle more carefully.

Anyway, the girth snapped when the horse shied, and la Cavalla went flying off, sitting up in her saddle with her foot in the stirrup as pretty as you please, straight into a tree. When Alfonso got to her, she must have looked like I looked that morning they called him to the monastery and told him they had found me dead.

A shock for him—at least I hope it was. I hope he really thought she was dead, for a moment at least. It would serve him right.

The odd thing is, he did the same thing he did when he first saw me, even though I was already dead, and had been dead long enough there could hardly be any mistake about it—he sent for that physician of his, Messer Girolamo Brasavola.

Now I could tell some stories about Messer Girolamo that would chill your bones. He keeps notes, secret notes, on every patient he attends, and some patients he doesn't attend but just observes about the court. There are many ladies who think they've rid themselves of a bastard in secret, but Messer Girolamo knows. He looks at their skin and hair and waist and nails, and smells their breath, and I don't know what all, and somehow he knows. And he writes it down, too. I've seen—

There, la Cavalla's coming back to herself. Her ladies are rubbing her temples and wrists with aqua vitae, and Alfonso is in a black rage about it all. It's not just choler. It's indignation that such a thing could happen to his precious imperial duchess. Fear, too, when he saw her lying white and still. And even—well, I don't know what to call it. What he was feeling when she said he was only taking care for her position, and he looked away to calm the falcon. I could see his face then, when she couldn't, and what I saw there was something I never saw when I was alive, not for me or for anyone else. Even the falcon felt the intensity of it. He was taking care for more than her position, although she didn't see it.

Someone tried to kill her. The dish of angelica could have been a mistake, or somehow meant for Paolina Tassoni all along. But the girth of la Cavalla's own saddle cut clean and neat, that's unmistakable.

Someone wants Alfonso's second duchess to stop asking so many questions. Someone wants her dead.

CHAPTER SEVENTEEN

I heard the duke's voice say, "Bring the groom." Then I heard hoofbeats and the crackling of brush, growing fainter as the riders went off. Something cold and wet was pressed to my forehead and wrists, which annoyed me because I feared it would stain my favorite hunting-habit.

Holy Virgin, my head hurt.

I opened my eyes.

"Leave her alone," the duke said. The wet dabbing stopped. My sense of smell rushed back all of a sudden, and I coughed at the fumes of aqua vitae that enveloped me. For a moment I thought I had been poisoned by one of Maria Granmammelli's potions. Then I realized I was in the hunting preserve outside Belfiore. We had been hunting on horseback. I remembered dressing in my green riding-dress. Mounting Tänzerin, with Conradt at her head. The courtyard. Sandro Bellinceno insulting me, and the duke with his falcon. Riding out through the great gate in the walls.

I frowned. There was nothing after that.

"You have had a bad fall," the duke said. His black-and-russet velvet was smudged with mud, and one of the diamond clasps was torn away. Never before in the daytime had I seen him with his clothing less than perfectly arranged. "Do not try to get up. Can you move your arms and legs?"

I lifted my right hand, then my left, and flexed my knees. There were no new pains, just the incessant throbbing in my head. "It does not hurt to move," I said. "I have hit my head, I think."

"You have indeed," the duke said. "There is some bleeding, and a bruise coming up already. What of your vision? Can you see clearly?"

"Yes."

"Good. Try to sit up, then. Slowly."

"What happened? I do not remember falling. Is Tänzerin hurt?"

"Your saddle-girth had been cut almost through, and when that mare of yours shied, it parted. She is perfectly well, with not so much as a scratch. I have sent for your groom, and we will get to the bottom of this quickly enough."

"Cut through?" I sat up abruptly and paid for it with a violent throb of my aching head. "Cut through deliberately?"

"Yes." The duke looked at me steadily. "Someone wanted you to be hurt, even killed, Madonna."

"Not Conradt," I said. "Never Conradt. He has been one of my grooms from the time I was a little girl."

"He could have been bribed. Try to stand."

With his help I managed to get to my feet. I felt a little dizziness, but I suppose that was to be expected. There was a murmur of approbation, and I realized the courtiers were packed in a ring around us. I saw Crezia's blue-and-white, Nora's *amaranto*. Sandro Bellinceno's green-and-gold, with Donna Elisabetta's heron-gray beside him. I saw Messer Bernardo's scarlet feathered hat and the Marquis of Montecchio's marigold and peach, slashings fluttering.

"I am quite all right." I tried to make my voice sound steady and strong. "Please, my lord, do not cut short your hunt. I shall return—"

"The hunt is already cut short. And you will go nowhere until a physician has examined you. Be seated, Madonna, if you please."

He gestured. I turned my head cautiously, and to my amazement two carved walnut chairs with blue-and-white striped cushions had been placed under a spreading bay tree, with a fire crackling in front of them. Then I remembered we had planned to dine in the woods, on fresh-killed meat cooked over open fires; of course arrangements would have been made for every comfort and luxury.

"Thank you, my lord," I said. "I am quite—"

I broke off when I heard hoofbeats again, and more crackling of brush. Two men-at-arms in Este livery trotted into the clearing, with my Austrian groom Conradt on a horse tied with a leading rein between them. His hands were roped behind his back, his face was bruised, and his shirt was torn.

"Prinzessin!" he cried in German. "Help me, I beg you. I don't understand—I've done nothing wrong."

For a moment I was too surprised and angry to speak. One of the men pushed Conradt from the horse and he fell headlong to the ground, unable to catch himself with his hands bound behind him. I stepped forward, the forest reeling around me as pain throbbed again in my head.

"Untie that man at once," I said. "My lord, I protest this outrage. Question Conradt if you must, but he is a member of my personal household and I vouch for him without reserve."

The duke made a gesture to the two soldiers; they dismounted and helped Conradt to his feet. One of them cut his bonds, and the other made a half-hearted effort to brush the grass and mud from his shirt.

"Now," I said. "Conradt. No one will accuse you unjustly,

so do not be afraid. Tell us what you know about this business of my saddle-girth being cut, and speak in Italian, please, so all may understand you."

"It was not cut when I saddled Tänzerin, *Prinzessin*," Conradt said. "By the millstone of Saint Florian I swear it. The girth was whole and strong."

"Then it was cut after the mare was saddled," the duke said. "Was she out of your sight, from the moment you saddled her until the moment the duchess mounted?"

"No!" he said. Then color mottled his cheeks and he said, "For a moment only. She was standing so beautifully, and I had gripes in my belly so bad I feared I'd shame myself. I tied her to the ring and left her only for a moment."

"That moment could have meant the duchess's death," the duke said coldly. "When you returned, did you see anyone close by, or anyone who looked suspicious?"

"No, Serenissimo," Conradt said. "But I did not think—I did not look."

"Go back to the Castello, collect your things, and go," the duke said. "You are dismissed from your place, and you have one day only to be out of the city."

"My lord!" I protested. "Conradt was ill. It was not his fault. He has cared for my horses since I was riding fat ponies in the gardens of the Hofburg."

"He shall do so no longer," the duke said. "Do not oppose me in this, Madonna."

"I will not oppose you. But give me time to arrange for Conradt's salary to be paid, at least. I will give him letters to my brother in Prague—Ferdinand is particularly interested in horses and will find a place for him."

"Very well, so long as I do not set eyes upon him again. You, groom. Go."

Conradt fled. I said nothing more, fearing further pleas would only make matters worse. Conradt would be provided for; I would make certain of that. My dizziness had passed off, but my head was throbbing and my whole body ached. The duke had seated himself in one of the waiting chairs, and gratefully I took advantage of the other.

"So, Madonna," he said. He took off his gloves. A gentleman-in-waiting handed him an orange and he began to peel it, strip by strip. "What do you think is the meaning of this?"

"Someone wished me to fall," I said. How stupid I sounded. I realized I was counting the strips of orange peel as they fell to the grass, and that only distressed me the more.

"Someone wished you dead, I think. I wonder why."

"I do not know."

It was a lie, of course, because there were any number of people who could very well want me dead or injured. Messer Bernardo was one of them, if he was regretting his insinuations and fearing I might still report them to the duke. Mother Eleonora was another, if she feared my questions might draw the attention of those who could deny her the luxuries she loved with such a worldly passion. Nora, obviously, for spite's sake. The Marquis of Montecchio, ambitious for his sons. Sandro Bellinceno, despite the friendship the duke bore him, although I did not quite understand why he suddenly hated me so much. Even Maria Granmammelli had threatened me.

And of course there was the duke himself.

I said again, "I do not know."

He leaned close and spoke very softly. "You do know," he said. "Do you think you can deceive me so easily?"

"No." I was starting to feel dizzy and sick again. "I am not—I do not know. I am not deceiving you."

He sat back and continued peeling the orange. The strips of peel were as perfectly spaced as a geometrical drawing from Euclid's *Elements*. I watched him, fascinated.

"We will not discuss it here," he said. "But by the lance of Saint George, when someone tries to kill the Duchess of Ferrara, unmistakably and before my very eyes, I will get to the truth of the matter. You will tell me the truth, even if I must force it out of you."

I swallowed back a fresh surge of sickness and said, not as firmly as I would have liked, "I do not respond well to force, my lord, as you may have gathered."

"We shall see about that."

I ENDED WITH bruises and a few aches and twinges, nothing more, may the Holy Virgin be thanked. The duke must have called for Maria Granmammelli, because she popped up at Belfiore like a mushroom after a rainstorm; the noxious poultices she insisted on applying and reapplying to my forehead, my shoulder, and my ribs were much more unpleasant than the bruises themselves. At the same time Messer Girolamo Brasavola, the duke's physician, plied me with *tormentilla*, fried parsley, and leeches to draw the pain and the black melancholic humors. Who knows which one was the more successful? They each vowed it was their treatment alone that cured me.

After two days, I had myself bathed and dressed, intending to go to Belfiore's tiny chapel and offer thanks for my deliverance. It was an unpleasant surprise to discover guards at my outer doorway, and that by the duke's command I was confined within my apartments. My first reaction was blistering anger. My second reaction was horror.

. . . even if I must force it out of you . . .

Vittoria Beltrame and Nicoletta Rangoni, who were attending me, would not meet my eyes. The guards themselves, two halbardiers wearing the duke's personal badge, were outwardly deferential but unrelenting. There was no point in making a scene in front of them. I acted as if I had not really wanted to go to the chapel at all, and went back into my apartments.

"Vittoria," I said. "I wish to write the duke a letter, and you will deliver it for me. You, I am sure, are not restricted in your movements."

"No, Serenissima."

I seated myself at a little writing-table of carved and inlaid walnut, neatly supplied with papers and pens, ink, sand, and sealing wax. I prepared a quill, smoothed out a half-sheet of paper, and wrote:

> *My Lord Duke,*
>   *I find I am confined to my apartments, at your command. I beg you will wait upon me at your earliest opportunity, to explain yourself in this matter.*

I did not sign it. I folded it, then took a seal from the velvet pouch at my waist—not the seal of a Duchess of Ferrara but my personal imperial seal with the double-headed eagle of the Habsburgs. Nicoletta lit a stick of red wax at the fire and brought it back to the writing-table. I dripped the wax upon the folds of the letter until it had made a satisfactory wafer, then pressed the imperial seal into it, deep and hard.

"Vittoria," I said again.

She took the note, curtsied, and went out.

I waited at my writing-table. I heard the bells for terce ring, from the south where the Castello and the city lay. Vittoria did not return; Domenica arrived to take her place. She whispered with Nicoletta. I lifted little Isa onto my knees and stroked her silken ears. She would not lie quietly, exactly in the center of my lap. I shifted her position. She moved again. My head throbbed and my back ached. Tristo dozed in front of the fire, his white paws twitching as he dreamed.

At last I heard a hum of talk, a rustle of soft-soled shoes on marble floors, and the ring of the guards' halberds as they straightened and presented their arms. The door opened and the duke came in, unattended. He gestured to my ladies without a word, and they went out. The door closed behind them.

I lifted Isa to the floor, got to my feet, and plunged straight to the heart of the matter. "I should like you to tell me, if you please, my lord, why I am not permitted to leave these apartments."

"I will be happy to tell you." His voice was quiet and at the same time utterly terrifying. "Someone attempted to assassinate you. First, I will not put you in the way of another such attempt. Second, I wish to know what exactly you have done to cause someone to wish to kill you. Until you can satisfy me as to that matter, you will remain exactly as you are."

"I have done nothing wrong." My stomach lurched and my knees turned to water. "How dare you confine me against my will?"

His eyes darkened. His voice grew softer and deceptively gentle. "My mother lived under confinement for years, Madonna, at the will of my father, and she is the daughter of a king of France. Do not deceive yourself that you cannot be treated in the same way, for all your imperial eagles."

He took my note from his sleeve and threw it down on the writing-table before me. Involuntarily, I reached out to pick it up, and only at the last moment stopped myself.

"I have done nothing wrong," I said again. "I believe—I believe—I believe the attempt upon my life was—"

Was the work of the Florentine ambassador, or of your aunt the abbess, or of one of your most favored friends, or of the person who murdered your first wife, who may or may not be you yourself—

Was to silence my questions, those awkward questions about your first wife I have been asking without your knowledge and contrary to your express wishes, so I might learn the truth of her death and use it as a weapon to keep you from ever humiliating me again—

I could not form the words. I leaned against my writing-table to hold myself up, shaking with fury and terror and indecision.

He waited for a minute or so. Neither one of us spoke, but I could feel the force of his will pressing against mine. I resisted with all my strength. "Very well," he said at last. "Remain as you are. I will speak with you again tomorrow."

And with that he went out. I heard the sound of the guards' boots and the ring of their halbards against the marble, as they took their places in front of my door again.

I looked down at my writing-table. My own letter lay there, the red wax seal with my Austrian double-headed eagle mocking me with its pride. With a cry of despair I swept it aside, sending pens and papers and sticks of sealing wax, the silver box of sand and the bottle of ink, flying in all directions. The heavy crystal bottle cracked against the tiled floor but did not break. Tristo jumped, cocked his russet ears forward, and looked at me with an anxious expression.

"Holy Virgin," I whispered. Tears made a stone in my throat. "What shall I do?"

Tristo put his head down again, but he did not close his eyes. Isa sat next to him, watching me uneasily.

Domenica came back into the room. Vittoria Beltrame, the duke's known spy, was with her in place of Nicoletta, who loved the puppies so. I took a deep breath and struggled to calm myself.

"Did something break, Serenissima?" Domenica asked cautiously.

"Some things—fell off my writing-table. Will you gather them up, please? I fear the ink may stain the tile if it is not mopped up immediately."

Silently they complied.

"Shall I bring you dinner, Serenissima?" Domenica said gently, when all was as it should be again. "You can eat, and drink some wine, and then we shall play at *tarocchino*, perhaps. Or have some music."

"Very well." I bent down and picked up the puppies. "Where

is Katharina? Where are Sybille and Christine? If we are to have music, I want Christine to play."

There was an uncomfortable silence. Finally Domenica said, "They are at the Palazzo dei Diamanti, Serenissima, not too far from here, with the rest of your Austrian ladies and gentlemen, preparing to leave for Vienna at the duke's pleasure. All but—"

She stopped. I waited, and then I said, "All but?"

"All but Katharina. She—did not go quietly with the gentleman-usher who attempted to—escort her. It was nothing but a slap, a scratch or two as I understand it, but she used some very hard words against him, and he has accused her of—of witchcraft and immorality."

"Witchcraft? Immorality? Katharina? That is ridiculous."

"I agree, Serenissima. The gentleman's pride was touched, and it is his way of striking back. But she is confined separately, in the Castello, because of his accusation."

"Some say," Vittoria put in, her eyes shining with excitement, "the duke means to sentence her to *la scopa*."

"Holy Virgin. What is that?"

"A punishment for women of low character and morals. The prisoner is stripped naked and forced to run through the city streets while onlookers throw garbage and filth. It is very exciting, and even the greatest of the nobles laugh from a safe vantage while their servants throw slops and night-soil."

I would not cry. I would not cry. Oh, Katrine, Katrine, my childhood playmate, my dearest most fastidious friend, have I brought you to Ferrara for this?

"I see," I said at last. "When is this sentence to be carried out?"

"No one knows," Domenica said. She was pale, and the look she directed at Vittoria Beltrame would have curdled new milk. "It is only a rumor, and no one knows what the duke will do."

"But Katharina is confined separately? She has been accused? These are known things?"

"Yes."

Check and mate, then, to the duke, before the game had even fairly begun. Clearly he had sent the hateful Vittoria Beltrame because he knew she would tell me of Katrine's plight in all its ghastly detail. Would he carry out such an injustice simply to compel my submission? I did not know, but I could not take the chance my beloved prickly Katrine would be abused so outrageously when it was in my power to prevent it.

I said, "Very well. I will speak to the duke again in the morning. I want no dinner, no card-playing, no music. You may go, all of you."

Even Domenica did not press me, although she looked hurt and sad. They went out.

Just in time.

I put my face down against the puppies' warm fur to muffle the sound—because my ladies would be listening, always listening—and stopped struggling to hold back my tears.

IF LA CAVALLA really has the courage to tell Alfonso everything she's done, well, she's braver than anyone else in Ferrara. Or Florence. Or the world. I wonder what he'll do. Oh, I can't wait.

I'm glad he locked her up. I'm glad he sent her Austrian ladies away. He sent my Florentine ladies away, too, all but Tommasina Vasari, who was faithful to the end. She stayed behind in secret, living here and there and scraping out a living dressing the hair of rich merchants' wives, all for love of me. Because she could read and write, I could send and receive letters with her help, without Alfonso knowing. He never looked at servants, so he didn't recognize her.

She'd come into the Castello, or the Palazzo del Corte, or the Palazzo dei Diamanti, or any one of our palaces, supposedly selling fruit or flowers, and pass right in front of Alfonso's face. He'd look straight through her as he always did, and lo! Inside a hollowed-out pomegranate rind or a tightly furled leaf would be my love-note. She'd read it to me, making faces and adding her own comments. Then I'd tell her what to write in return, and she'd write it. How we laughed!

I was happy then. It was so short, the time I was happy.

I'm afraid of going to hell. I have Niccolò's death on my conscience, and that's a mortal sin. I didn't love him, but I liked him and he loved me and I never meant for him to die. Holy God, blessed Baptist, San Luca my patron, please keep me immobila. *Please don't let me dissolve away into only a soul and be sucked down to eternal torments and damnation.*

CHAPTER EIGHTEEN

In the morning I arose with my head aching, my eyes swollen, and my purpose fixed.

For Katharina's freedom I would tell the duke everything—my resolution to ignore the gossip when the marriage was arranged, my fury when he thrashed me, my humiliation when I heard Nora's laughter. I would tell him of Messer Bernardo's sinister suggestions and how they had flowered into my own secret determination to find the truth and use it as a weapon to protect myself. I would tell him what I had learned at the Monastero del Corpus Domini and what Elisabetta Bellinceno had revealed to me.

I would ask him only one more question, face-to-face, without reservations and without pretty words: *Did you murder your first wife?* When that was asked and answered truthfully, whatever that truth might be, I would swear to him I would meddle no more in the matter, and I would mean it.

For Katharina's freedom.

And because I myself could lie no more.

Was it determination or terror that made my stomach roil and my knees shake as I stood for Domenica and Nicoletta to wash me and dress me and do up my hair with sapphires? Would I lose my courage? Would I end the day locked away in the Palazzo di San Francesco like Renée of France? Even more terrifying, would Katharina suffer the agony and humiliation of *la scopa* even if I did submit?

I could not eat. My headache had gone, but my back was aching fiercely. While I was waiting for the duke to come to my apartments as he had promised, I paced from the antechamber through the presence chamber to the bedchamber, forward and back and back again. I tried not to think of the guards on the other side of the door. I prayed to the Holy Virgin and to my patron, Saint Barbara, for every ounce of courage and humility I could muster. *Help me, Holy Mother. Help me, Saint Barbara, my patroness, protector of prisoners. I cannot live my life in fear and uncertainty and confinement. . . .*

Finally I could bear the delay no longer. I ordered Nicoletta Rangoni to stop brushing and playing with the puppies she adored so much, and I sent her off to the duke with a message, asking him to come and speak with me at once. To my surprise I had a message in return within a quarter of an hour, assuring me he would wait upon me immediately after dinner. Had he been waiting for me to break? Perhaps. I did not care. All I could think of now was escaping the rooms that seemed to be enclosing me more and more tightly, until I could hardly breathe.

I could not stop thinking of her. No, not Renée of France. Lucrezia de' Medici now. How long, exactly, had she been imprisoned in the Monastero del Corpus Domini? Had her prison been a single room, or two, or three? Had there been a window? What had she done all day to amuse herself? Somehow I could not imagine her reading, or sewing quietly, or praying. And then somehow Lucrezia de' Medici changed as well and became Juana la Loca, my grandmother, locked up in her tower at Tordesillas for fifty years.

My nurse said she would not eat or sleep or change her clothes. She said she talked to people who were not there.

When the duke arrived, it was all I could do to keep from flinging myself at him and begging him to allow me a breath, just a breath, of some air outside my own apartments. Fortunately I was able to control myself. I took the time to breathe deeply and say a *De profundis*; it was important to address him with dignity. Dignity was the one thing that seemed to touch him.

"So, Madonna," he said. His bearing was sanguine; in his expression I could see nothing of the monsters gliding and curling under his polished surface. Clearly Nicoletta had described my distress to him, and he was unsurprised by my surrender. "Have you reconsidered your silence?"

I did not answer his question directly. Instead I said, "There is a condition."

"And that is?"

"You know what it is, my lord. The freedom of my lady and friend, Katharina Zähringen."

He inclined his head slightly—not quite a nod. He did not smile; I will give him that. He said, "Tell me everything, Madonna, as you should have done from the beginning, and your woman will come to no harm."

"She must be completely exonerated. And I would like her to remain with me here in Ferrara, she and Sybille von Wittelsbach and Christine von Hessen as well. You may send the others away, but I beg you to allow me to keep those three."

"Do not think to bargain with me. If I am satisfied by your confession, perhaps I will choose to grant your wishes. Whatever my choice is, you will accede to it."

Breathe, I thought. Breathe. "Very well," I said. "Please, my lord, I have had no fresh air for three days. May we walk in the gardens as we speak?"

"Of course." He gestured to Nicoletta and Domenica. "You, accompany us, but at a distance, if you please."

They sank into obedient curtsies. He led me from the room as if it were the most ordinary thing in the world, and the halbardiers stood aside as if they had never stepped forward and prevented me from passing.

The die was cast. *Jacta alea est*. I remembered thinking that on the day I was married, and I could not help laughing at myself now. How fatuous and smug I had been, thinking I could arrange my own life so easily, do what I wished even in the face of the duke's displeasure. Well, at least I was out of my prison. I had the means to protect Katharina within my power. Now all I had to fear was the duke's reaction to my confession.

He was dressed simply, in a black damask surcoat with hanging sleeves, black breeches and hose, a white linen shirt, and a black velvet cap with an onyx brooch and a small curling scarlet feather. The golden clasps of his coat were worked in the shape of flames, his personal device. We walked in silence, with my ladies, his secretary Messer Giovanni Pigna, and two of his gentlemen-ushers following us. Shortly we came out into what was called the Giardino delle Stagioni, the Garden of the Seasons.

A pergola of vines divided this garden into four sections, and hedges of thick yew surrounded it. Each quarter was devoted to a season of the year, with flower-beds mimicking the patterns of the exquisite mosaic pavement. The duke led me to Primavera, the spring quarter; when the duke and the court were in residence at Belfiore, it was filled and re-filled from the forcing-houses each morning, so it would always delight the court with spring blossoms. Please, please, I thought, let this be a spring, a rebirth, for me and my life here in Ferrara.

My ladies, Messer Giovanni, and the gentlemen-ushers occupied themselves in Autunno, on the other side of the garden. The duke seated me upon a carved marble bench and took his own seat on another bench situated at a right angle to it.

"Now, Madonna," he said. "Let us get to the bottom of this attempted assassination, once and for all."

How to begin? I took a breath, mentally crossed myself, and plunged forward. "I will tell you everything, my lord, I swear it, but first I would ask you a question."

He looked at the flowers. He seemed to be focusing on a line of pale violet pasqueflowers with hearts of sunny gold. "Ask, then," he said.

Silence. Agonizing silence. I could not make my tongue work.

"Ask." It was no longer an invitation, but a command.

"Did you—" I began. My voice failed me. I took a breath, closed my eyes, and finally said all in a rush, "Did you murder your first duchess? Or did you order it done?"

Silence again. I held my breath.

"No," he said, quite calmly.

Belatedly I realized he had probably been expecting exactly that question from me, and so had his answer prepared. I felt as if I were going to faint.

"I did not murder her, nor did I order it done, nor do I believe she was murdered at all. Does that satisfy you?"

My first impulse was to believe him. Alfonso d'Este, scion of six hundred years of feudal lords, grandson and great-grandson and cousin of kings, was too arrogant in his blood and bone to lie. So for the space of a few heartbeats I believed him. Then I did not. Then I did again. Then my thoughts became paralyzed between the two, and I did not know if he had killed her or not.

I did not know what to say, either, and so I said nothing. *Nor do I believe she was murdered at all.* Was he reiterating his public tale that the young duchess had died suddenly of a wasting imbalance of humors? Or was there something else he had not made public? The vaulting pride of the Este—it would not be out of character for the duke to have a defense and yet to refuse to stoop to defend himself in the face of gossip from one end of Europe to the other.

"Look at me."

I looked up slowly. His eyes were narrowed, his lips pressed together in reticence or wariness or anger, or perhaps all of those and more. I did not know his expressions. I was married to him, I had shared his bed, I was at his mercy, and I did not know him at all.

"You do not believe me."

"I do not disbelieve you." My voice wavered. I swallowed and said more strongly, "I have the rest to tell you, and that may make it clearer why I cannot make myself certain, one way or the other."

He looked at me for a long time. "You are fortunate, Madonna, that I choose to put my alliance with the emperor above my personal displeasure," he said. "I have answered your question. It is your turn to speak. Who wishes to kill you, and why?"

I looked down at my lap and made a neat little pleat in the russet-colored silk of my overskirt. "There are those, I think, who may wish to silence—some questions I have been asking. And there are also those who—who whispered to me of conspiracies and old sins, and who may now regret their words."

"By the bloody lance of Saint George," he said, his voice so quiet and cold I almost expected the flowers around us to blacken and wither. "You had best tell me exactly what questions you have been asking, Madonna, and what conspiracies you have dared to listen to, and I warn you to leave off any women's lies or dissimulations."

I had thought I knew what fear felt like. When I was five or six, I had lost my way in a garden-maze at dusk, in Innsbruck. As a young girl, perhaps thirteen, I had skated too far from the edge of a frozen lake in Vienna, crashed through into the water, and for a few heart-stopping moments flailed against the underside of the ice. Only recently I had stood before the painting of Lucrezia de' Medici, lost in my thoughts, while the duke came up silently behind me to jerk the curtain closed.

Those moments, it seemed, had been nothing. Now—now I was truly afraid.

But it was too late to turn back. I made another pleat in my skirt.

"I have been asking questions about your first duchess's death," I said, speaking slowly, one word at a time in the hope it would keep my voice from failing. "The conspiracy—I am not even sure it is a conspiracy. The Florentine ambassador said some unnerving things to me, under the guise of a literary conversation, and afterward claimed they meant nothing."

I could not look at him as I said it. I thought I heard a single quick intake of breath, but my pulse was thudding so violently in my own ears I was not sure. I closed my eyes and crushed the silk of my skirt with both my hands, obliterating my careful pleats. Juana la Loca had been locked up, locked up mad and raving for fifty years. Her blood ran in my veins—would I go mad as well, if I were confined?

He was silent for a long time. I don't think I breathed at all, not once.

"I see," he said at last. There was no expression in his voice—he might have been acknowledging a secretary's explanation of some small miscalculation in his accounts.

I took a shuddering breath and swallowed hard. Tears stung hotly in my eyes, but I would not, would not, would not acknowledge them by lifting my hand to brush them away. They blurred my vision and spilled over without a sound, hot on my fingers and making dark patches on my rich brocade.

Finally, in the same expressionless voice, he said, "I made it clear to you, I believe, that I did not wish you to ask further questions about my first duchess. And even so you pursued the matter?"

"Yes," I managed to choke out. "I did it because—because you made it clear to me. Because of the way you made it clear to me."

I had to stop. I had to regain my self-control. I closed my eyes tightly and concentrated on breathing slowly and deeply. I smoothed out the creases in my skirt and began to make another series of perfect pleats in the fabric. After a moment I felt calmer.

"I am waiting," the duke said.

"After you—thrashed me," I said, "I was humiliated, angry, frightened, just as I am sure you intended me to be. By the next morning, the tale had been whispered from one end of the Castello to the other."

He said nothing.

"I went out to walk in the orange garden. Nora laughed at me behind my back. In front of all her little court, she laughed. In front of her lowborn astrologer and Messer Bernardo Canigiani, she laughed."

Still he said nothing.

"From there I went to the chapel. While I was attempting to collect myself, Messer Bernardo approached me. He presented it very delicately, my lord, in the guise of a conversation about literature. But I believe he thought to use my humiliation and my anger to tempt me into a plot he was devising."

"I see. And what sort of plot was this?"

"First, he invited me—pressed me—to leave Ferrara and travel to Florence, ostensibly to visit with my sister. It soon became clear his true design was to make it appear I had repudiated our marriage and fled to my sister's protection."

The duke said nothing.

"He then suggested I use my position here to gather evidence against you in the death of Serenissima Lucrezia. That I should convey that evidence, whatever it might be, to Florence, and put it into the hands of Cosimo de' Medici."

I stopped. I could hardly put it more baldly than that.

"And did it not occur to you," the duke said after another long pause, "to tell me of this conversation immediately?"

I swallowed. "I might have imagined Messer Bernardo's meaning. It might have been a deliberate attempt to create disharmony between us. You had just beaten me for expressing an interest in Lucrezia de' Medici. If I had come to you with a tale of some Florentine plot to avenge her death, a tale Messer Bernardo would surely deny, I feared you would—"

I broke off. We both knew what I might have said. *I feared you would beat me again. I feared you would murder me as well.*

He said nothing.

There was no longer any hope of concealing my tears. "There is another reason I did not tell you. What Messer Bernardo said led me to think. If there was indeed proof you had—" I hesitated. I still could not quite believe I was speaking the words. "Proof you had participated in the death of your first wife, and if the Florentines could plot to use that proof against you—then I could do the same. I could find the proof first, keep it from the Florentines, and at the same time use it privately against you to protect myself against further mistreatments."

Neither of us said anything then, for a long time. I looked at the blue hyacinths on the other side of the pathway. Despite the sun, they were already drooping.

"You are the Duchess of Ferrara," he said slowly. "As such you are my subject. For you to attempt to prove a charge of murder against me, privately or publicly, is treason."

He gave the last word no particular emphasis, but still it felt as if he had struck me across the face. I had no defense, because what he said was true. But neither did he have a defense against the accusations of murder, other than his unsupported word.

I lifted my head. The duke was looking at me as if he were trying to decide which palace would be my prison while he petitioned the pope for an annulment of our marriage. Or which monastery— But I did not dare think of that.

"My lord, I cannot defend myself against your accusation, because it is true," I said, as steadily as I could. "I can only give myself up to your mercy. I swear I will ask no more questions, meddle no further, and pattern myself to be exactly what you wish me to be, now and always. I ask only that you allow me my freedom and exonerate Katharina Zähringen from the unjust charges against her."

There. It was said.

There was a long silence.

"Do you take me for a fool?" the duke said at last. "You will never be a silent, subservient wife. And as I told you only a short time ago, I am not a man to be bargained with like a shopkeeper."

Jacta alea est.

I had cast the die, then, and I had lost. I felt as if I had turned to stone. Even my tears froze in my eyes, unshed. Katharina would be subjected to *la scopa*. And I would go mad. Locked up, I would slowly and quietly go mad. I would make pleats in my skirts and count the stones in my prison-walls forever.

He put one hand over mine and held my fingers still. "You do that when you are distressed," he said. "Make folds in your skirts, put things straight. Do not think I have not noticed."

That was the final humiliation. I found myself shivering with the effort it took to keep my hands still.

"Now," he said.

Now . . .

"You are my wife. That cannot be easily undone, and in any case it is important for me to get an heir for Ferrara. It is also to my advantage to maintain good relations with your brother."

I blinked. My tears were liquid again and blurred my sight.

"Therefore we will keep up the appearance of an amicable marriage. You will not be confined in any obvious way, although you will have at least two Ferrarese ladies with you at all times and you will not go outside the Castello or the Palazzo della Corte without a suitable escort, whom I will choose. This is for your own protection, you understand, until I can be sure there will be no more assassination attempts."

"Yes, my lord," I whispered. It was all I could do to speak at all.

"You will tell me everything you have done so far, and every-one to whom you have spoken, in this mad scheme of yours to collect information about my first duchess's death." He made it sound as if I had been collecting night-soil in the street.

"I swear it, my lord."

"You will say nothing to your women about this, nor to anyone else. I will not have your foolishness become a byword about the court."

I felt hot color flood up into my face, but I also felt a spark of anger. It stiffened my spine, which was, I must confess, sadly in need of stiffening. I said, in a steady voice, "I will say nothing, my lord."

"You will be absolutely truthful with me, in everything, from this moment forward."

"Yes, my lord."

To my amazement he smiled. Though wintry as the midday air, it was still a smile. "I am sure you think you mean that," he said, "but I do not believe it. Nor do I believe for a moment you will ask no more questions. Oh, you will refrain for a fortnight or two, but then that disquisitive nature of yours—and it was your brother who called it that, you will recall, not I—will overcome you. You will tell yourself one or two questions will do no harm. You will tell yourself, 'The duke will never know.' Am I correct?"

As much as I wished to imagine myself keeping my word faithfully down through the years like the patient Griselda of Messer Giovanni Boccaccio's famous tale, he was probably correct. I said nothing.

"Therefore the investigation will be continued, but at my direction and under my command. I will allow you to ask whatever questions you wish, of whomever you wish, but it will be in my presence."

Holy Virgin. Was he serious? "And if you do not like the answers you hear?"

He stopped smiling. His voice was like ice burning against naked skin. I looked at the clasps of his surcoat, golden flames, and for the first time I truly understood his choice of the device.

"I will hide nothing from you," he said. "May God and Saint George be my witnesses, Madonna, whether I like the answers to your questions or not, I will satisfy you once and for all as to what became of my first duchess."

I WONDER WHAT he thinks he's going to prove to her. After all, he doesn't really know how I died. Nobody knows but me and my murderer. Does Alfonso think he knows? That would be just like him, to think he knows everything even when he doesn't.

It didn't take la Cavalla long to break, did it? I would never have submitted so quickly just to save one of my women from la scopa. But of course, she had a choice. She could tell Alfonso the truth and he'd set her free. I didn't have a choice. I could've screamed the truth from the rooftop of the Lions' Tower, and it only would've made Alfonso angrier and more determined to keep me walled up forever.

That's what he told me that last afternoon. That's what made me scream filthy names at him, and try to claw his eyes out, and swear I'd kill myself and it'd be his fault. He was going to keep me confined in the monastery indefinitely. I could swear all I wanted I wasn't with child, but if he kept me locked up, the truth would come out. I knew what he wanted—he wanted to send me home in disgrace with my bastard in my arms for all to see. My father would have killed me. Oh, well, probably not really, but he'd have shut me up in another convent somewhere forever, and that would've been worse than death.

At first I was happy to be with child, because it made me more beautiful and that new glow brought my lover back to me. I dreamed we'd run away and I'd be happy forever and he'd gain the great ambitions he desired and Alfonso would be sorry at last. I let myself get with child because I thought it'd make these things happen. I found out I was wrong soon enough. After a fortnight or so of fresh lust, he told me he didn't want me or the baby. He had more important things to think about.

Can you blame me if I wanted to rid myself of the baby and go back to my old life? Yes, that's what the potion was, the one Tommasina brought me even though Maria Big-Breasts refused to help her. An abortifacient. She wouldn't tell me where she got it, but I can guess—her father, after all, was a court alchemist in Florence. She swore it was absolutely safe, made of the very finest ingredients. It was sealed in a jeweled flask, after all, so that must have meant it was the best. Maria Big-Breasts isn't the only one who can make fine potions.

I drank it. It was the only way for me to be free again, and I didn't even think about the baby really being a baby. I was angry at it. It was ruining everything. And I was so angry at its father. I just wanted to be free and back at court and a duchess again.

I was murdered before the potion could take effect. So did I kill my baby or didn't I? I don't know. If I did, I'm sorry. I'm sorry, sorry, sorry. Not that it matters now. It's too late for me to be sorry or do penance or be forgiven. I'm an adulteress and I caused Niccolò's murder and I may have murdered my own baby.

I wonder what's become of my baby's soul. It had a soul, didn't it, even if it wasn't born? There's supposed to be a special limbo for unbaptized babies. When I was six or seven, my mother had a stillbirth, and she told me the baby would be safe and happy there forever. She bought perpetual prayers for its soul from the nuns of the Convent of San Onofrio. So maybe my baby is in limbo, too. There's no one to pray for it, but maybe it's there.

Or maybe it's in hell because it's a bastard.

I'm afraid of hell. I'm so afraid. Tommasina prays for me, but it isn't enough.

God, God, I was murdered myself! Can't that be my penance? Isn't that enough to win me one tiny little corner in purgatory, forever?

CHAPTER NINETEEN

*W*e were to return to the Palazzo della Corte for supper, and the duke's presence was required for matters of state in the meantime, so he sent me back to my apartments—with two of his gentlemen-ushers at my heels, looking rather mystified—to rest and make my own arrangements for the move. We would continue our conversation, he said, once we were back in the Palazzo and I had collected myself. I was not sure if he was deliberately drawing out the agony of my complete confession so as to take further vengeance on me for my deceptions, or if he was genuinely showing mercy upon my distress.

In the duchess's apartments at Belfiore—and as beautiful as they were, I would never feel at ease in them again—I changed out of the creased and tear-spotted russet brocade and into a dress of serviceable blue camlet. Nicoletta Rangoni and my kindly Domenica Guarini asked no questions, and I hoped they would not spread the tale of my mysterious tears. The russet dress would be sent off to the wardrobe-women once we were back at the Palazzo;

my face could not be so easily exchanged for another. I touched up my swollen eyes and reddened nose as best I could with a little tinted ceruse and some powder.

"I will take charge of the puppies for our ride back to the Palazzo della Corte," Nicoletta said. She had Tristo under one arm and Isa on her scarlet leather leash at her feet, and as always seemed happiest in their company. "They can ride in their basket, strapped to my saddle where they will be safe."

"Everything else is packed, Serenissima," Domenica said. "Would you rather rest here, and perhaps have some wine and cakes, or would you prefer to go straight back to the Palazzo now and rest in your own apartments there?"

"Let us go now," I said. "I wish to be home."

I said the word without thinking. Was it only in contrast to the shock, fear, and humiliation of Belfiore that the Palazzo della Corte suddenly seemed like home to me? I was well into my second month of marriage, and both the simplicity of Innsbruck and the rigid ceremony of Vienna seemed far away, in time as well as distance. In any case, I wanted to be away from Belfiore, and the sooner the better.

With Domenica, Nicoletta and the puppies, and the duke's gentlemen-ushers making a motley train in my wake, I went through the loggia and into the courtyard, where our horses were waiting. Not my beautiful Tänzerin; she had not been blamed for my fall, as horses sometimes were, but with her Arab and Iberian blood she was not an animal to be ridden through city streets. Not Conradt, either—a Ferrarese groom I had never seen before stood holding a placid white mule equipped with an old-fashioned side-saddle, looking like nothing so much as a green velvet padded chair with a footrest towering disproportionately over the animal's back. I mounted sedately—there was no need to gather up the reins because there were no reins for me, only for the groom who would lead the animal—wondering if I would ever again be allowed to ride in the hunt as I loved to do.

It was a sunny afternoon and late enough in the day that the perpetual winter fog of Ferrara had burned off. As we clopped along through the spacious and geometrical new city of the duke's great-grandfather Ercole I, we came upon a building entirely faced with white marble blocks, veined with rosy pink, set and carved in pointed pyramid shapes. I had never seen such stonework before; it gave the whole building a strange granulated aspect.

"It is the Palazzo dei Diamanti, Serenissima," Domenica said, guiding her own mule up beside mine. She was allowed reins of her own. "See, the stones are carved in the shape of diamonds—the diamond was one of the first Ercole's devices, and he was even called Il Diamante, some say for his hardness."

However she might chatter to distract me, I remembered the name.

"This is where my Austrian ladies and gentlemen are being kept, is it not?"

"Yes, Serenissima, all but Donna Katharina."

"And you say she is at the Castello?"

"Yes, Serenissima."

"Domenica?"

"Yes, Serenissima?"

"I wish you to call me by my Christian name in private, as Katharina and Sybille and Christine do. I hope—I pray—the duke will allow them to stay, but in the meantime there is no one to call me by my name, and I miss the sound of it."

She looked surprised and uneasy. My practice of calling my ladies by their Christian names, and allowing some of them to address me in the same way in return, was generally considered a breach of etiquette; in Austria it drove my protocol-conscious brother and sister-in-law mad with exasperation. The duke had made no comment. But of course as he had told me scornfully in the matter of Frà Pandolf's portrait, manners were freer and more modern here in Ferrara.

"I am not sure—what of the others, Serenissima? Will they be affronted?"

"If they are, I will speak to them. Please, Domenica."

"Very well, Serenissima. Barbara." She smiled warmly. "You give me a great privilege, and I swear to you I will value it with all my heart."

I smiled in return. It was good to hear someone say my name; it gave me back some sense of myself as an individual and not solely the Duchess of Ferrara. "You will be my personal court poet," I said. "The cardinal may have young Messer Torquato Tasso, and the duke may have his singers, but I shall have you."

She laughed and blushed. My heart lightened a bit. But as the Palazzo dei Diamanti was left behind us, I did not forget we-three. Sybille and Christine would be safe enough for the moment. Once I was back at the Palazzo della Corte—once I was home—I would go straight through the covered walkway to the Castello and at least satisfy myself that my dear Katrine was being held in comfortable circumstances, as befitted her rank.

AS IT TURNED out, I did not have the opportunity. I had barely arrived in my apartments at the Palazzo when one of the duke's gentlemen appeared with a message.

I wish to speak with you before supper, the duke had written. His hand was even and clear, in a cultivated italic style without flourishes. Again the polished and effortless surface, the intricacies hidden from the eye. There was no further explanation and no signature, not even an initial.

I refolded the note, taking my time about it to give myself a few moments to think.

"Tell the duke I shall wait upon him in half an hour's time," I told the gentleman. "First I wish to walk in the garden with the puppies. Nicoletta, Domenica, accompany me, if you please."

They did, as did the duke's guards. I whispered to Domenica, and she ran off through the Via Coperta to the Castello; within the half-hour she was back with news that she had seen Katharina and all was well, or at least as well as it could be. My true objective achieved, we returned to my apartments and settled the puppies with their doting Nicoletta to mind them. Only then did I make my way to the duke's *studiolo*, the guards still trailing silently behind me. An equerry admitted me.

"Good afternoon, Madonna," the duke said. "Come and sit down." He dismissed the guards and gestured to the gilded armchair next to his own.

I crossed the room with its exquisitely inlaid walls, its magnificent painted and coffered ceiling, its polished cabinets displaying leather-bound and gilded books as if they were objets d'art. In one corner a harpsichord was situated at an angle, its case beautifully carved and the inner surface of its lid painted with a scene of Orpheus and Eurydice. The light was partly slanting late-afternoon daylight from the windows, partly the gleam of candles scented with amber. The equerry poured wine into two Murano glasses, presented them with two formal bows, and left the room.

"So you went to walk with those little hounds of yours before coming to me as I requested," the duke said. "I would have expected you to be more eager to obey me."

I took a deep breath. "Is that what you wish, my lord? That I fear you, and creep to your feet in trepidation at your slightest word?"

He took a sip of his wine. "You have courage," he said. "I will grant you that."

"Is that not what you want, in your duchess and the mother of your sons?"

He gave no sign he doubted I would ultimately be the mother of his sons. His hand was absolutely steady as he put his glass on the inlaid table between us. I could not say the same for mine.

"Courage, yes," he said. "Foolhardiness, no. Do not think to push me too far."

I sipped the wine, swallowed, waited for a moment. Then I said, "I understand."

"Good. Now, let us discuss your investigations to date. Begin with your—retreat—at Corpus Domini. I suspected at the time there was more to it than prayers for a son."

I took another sip of my wine. "I spoke with Mother Eleonora, my lord, and with Sister Orsola, the infirmarian. I learned of your visit to the young duchess the afternoon before she died. I learned she was not ill, as was put about officially, but imprisoned at your command."

"Go on."

"Earlier I had learned from Maria Granmammelli that Duchess Lucrezia asked her for love potions, and later one of her women asked for another potion, which the old woman described as an abortifacient. Thus I deduced the young duchess had lovers, that she was with child and did not wish to bear it. When I put this together with Sister Orsola's information, it seemed obvious why you imprisoned her at the monastery."

"Indeed. Go on."

"Your sister Crezia also spoke of her lovers—"

"*Vipera*," he said, cutting me off. "She has always fancied herself as *prima donna* of Ferrara, and would be happiest if there were no duchess at all so she could reign undisputed. I suspected she had nothing good to say when I saw the two of you whispering behind your hands at the entertainments."

I looked at him steadily. "It gets worse, my lord," I said. "Do you wish me to continue?"

His eyes narrowed. "Continue."

"I spoke at length with—a lady, both that evening and the next morning. Her husband was also Duchess Lucrezia's lover, and it seems she coerced him—"

"You will tell me this husband's name, if you please."

I had hoped to protect poor Donna Elisabetta from her husband's sins. I also hesitated to mention the name of the duke's great friend. Would he believe me? Crezia had seemed to think the duke knew of his friend's betrayal, but I was not so sure. I smoothed the blue camlet of my skirt and made a pleat. Then I remembered the garden at Belfiore, the duke's hand coming down hard over my fingers, and I stopped.

"His name, Madonna."

There was nothing to do but tell the truth. "It was Messer Sandro Bellinceno, my lord. Donna Elisabetta told me Duchess Lucrezia had some sort of forbidden book she had stolen from your library, and had enticed him to write in his own hand on its pages. With that the young duchess coerced him to rid her of—yet another lover. He cut the fellow's throat in secret and has been tortured by the memory of it ever since."

I am not sure what I expected—an explosion of rage? A vow of vengeance? Neither came to pass. The duke frowned briefly when I said the words *forbidden book*, but then continued to sip his wine without expression. "It distressed you to tell me that," he said thoughtfully, looking at my hands, "because you know Sandro Bellinceno and I are close as brothers? Be comforted—I have known for some time that Lucrezia de' Medici seduced my friend, although I did not know about the book. I did not blame him for it then, nor do I now. It was her work, not his."

That absurd pronouncement angered me. Why did men always blame the woman? Although of course men had been blaming women for their sins since the fall of Adam. "He is a man grown," I said, keeping my voice even. "Surely he must bear some of the responsibility."

"Oh, he was a fool to be taken in by her, I will grant you that. Now, you are certain Donna Elisabetta described a forbidden book in the duchess's possession? Can you tell me more about it?"

"Yes, I am sure. She said it had sonnets and engravings of a lascivious nature."

"I see," he said. "Well, if this business of your investigations leads to the recovery of that book, Madonna, it will have had some value to me after all."

"I do not understand."

"Perhaps one day I will tell you. Go on with your story."

"There is really nothing more. Donna Elisabetta told me some of Duchess Lucrezia's possessions were stored away in a secret room, and I hoped to find a way to examine them. That is as far as my investigations have proceeded, my lord, I swear to you."

"Very well. Sum up for me, if you please, the conclusions you have drawn."

"I initially concluded that you—you poisoned her, my lord, perhaps with the connivance of Maria Granmammelli or Mother Eleonora or both. And with some—provocation. But—"

I stopped. He waited.

"But over the past fortnight or so," I said slowly, "I have come to see other possibilities."

"Such as?"

"She was with child. She attempted to obtain an abortifacient potion from Maria Granmammelli, and such potions are always dangerous. If the old woman ultimately relented and gave her the potion, or if she found some other herb-woman to give her what she wanted, she may have dosed herself excessively and died by accident."

"That is one possibility."

"On the other hand, Sister Orsola claims to believe the young duchess took her own life. Public shame stared her in the face, and she had made few friends and many enemies in Ferrara. One argument against this theory of self-murder is that she is buried in the Monastero del Corpus Domini, in holy ground."

"I shall have more to say about that in a moment. Continue."

"You understand, my lord, I am speaking completely frankly, just as the thoughts occur to me."

"I understand."

"Crezia and Nora loathed the young duchess and were jealous of her youth, her beauty, and her precedence."

The duke laughed. There was a cold, bitter sound to it. "And so they are repaid for their gossiping. Go on."

"The cardinal and the Marquis of Montecchio each have claims to Ferrara, if you remain childless. If they heard whispers she was with child—"

"The marquis, perhaps," he said. "My brother, no. I will not bring him into this business. It is true we are often at odds, and true as well that Luigi is little suited for the church. But throw his scarlet hat over the wall to usurp my position? Murder a woman and child? I think not. His ambitions center on Rome, not Ferrara."

"Maria Granmammelli, then," I said. "She hated the young duchess because her blood was not blue enough for the Este."

He looked thoughtful. "A possibility. Although I have reason to doubt it, which I will expand upon in a moment. Go on."

"The Medici themselves, through intermediaries. If you intended to openly repudiate Lucrezia de' Medici and her child, it would have been a scandal. Daughter or no, Duke Cosimo might have thought her death the lesser evil."

"I could believe it easily."

"There were whispers about the elder daughter. He is said to have stabbed her in a passion of fury, when he discovered her with a lover."

"I have heard those stories. What else?"

"Any one of Duchess Lucrezia's lovers, through jealousy of the others, and particularly Messer Sandro, who had already committed one murder on her account."

"The monastery is enclosed, and the duchess was kept straitly without gifts or visitors from outside. How do you propose this procession of potential murderers obtained the opportunity to poison her?"

"It would have been Mother Eleonora, would it not, who kept the keys to her cell? She is quite accustomed to—unusual comforts. Silken cushions and fine wines. Perhaps she was bribed."

"And so you suspect even my aunt, locked away in her monastery."

"She has many friends about the court. She could easily have arranged for the slashed girth, my lord. Or for that matter, the poison that killed Paolina Tassoni. She was disturbed by my questions."

"That is ridiculous."

"Perhaps. Perhaps not. I am sure there are others who should be suspected as well, persons I am forgetting, or whom I have not yet encountered or thought to suspect."

"You have a remarkable imagination, Madonna," he said. "I trust you have not spoken these thoughts to anyone else?"

I felt a little chill of apprehension. "No, I have not."

"Good," he said. "Now I will tell you what really happened."

I finished my wine and put the glass down on the table. "Please do, my lord."

"My first duchess," he said with calm precision, "took her own life. She was indeed with child by one of her lovers, although she herself denied it to the end. I myself had not approached her for some time, and yet Maria Granmammelli believed it, and in such matters I trust her shrewdness."

So far, I thought, the ring of truth.

"I did not intend to allow the Duchess of Ferrara to make a scandal of herself. That is why I gave commands for her retirement to Corpus Domini. In time, once her child was born, she would have been—convinced—to return to Florence, take vows herself, and petition the pope for an annulment of our marriage."

And you, I thought, would have drafted that petition for her.

"I wished to know the names of the men who had dishonored her. I questioned her several times, and she refused to speak—she continued to swear she was not with child at all. That last afternoon at Corpus Domini, I questioned her again. She responded with wild importunities, curses, and threats to make away with herself."

"And you left her there? Alone and in such a state of mind?"

His eyes narrowed briefly, but his voice remained steady. "The infirmarian was with her, and there were two other sisters keeping watch as well. I particularly charged them not to leave the duchess alone. Even so, sometime in the night the duchess took poison, and was found dead the next morning."

I looked at him for a moment. He met my gaze steadily. It would have been easy, so easy, to simply accept what he said and say nothing more. The duke himself seemed to believe it. Perhaps he was right. And yet—

I thought of the portrait, that flushed, joyous face, so spirited, so alive, with the branch of cherry blossoms in her hand. Would that girl have taken her own life, even on impulse, even in an extremity of fear or fury?

"My lord, forgive me." My voice shook, however much I strove to control it. I looked at my wine-glass on the table and adjusted its position slightly so it was equally distant from either side of the table's corner. "But have you some proof the duchess took her own life? How, for instance, did she obtain the poison?"

He leaned back in his chair and sipped his wine. "You do not believe me?"

"It is not that. The Medici are using this matter to blacken your name. Unless there is proof that you are innocent, tangible proof in your hands alone, you will never achieve the Precedenza or the title of grand duke."

He did not say anything for a long time. I sat very still, looking at my empty wine-glass placed so precisely on the corner of the table.

"Consider the facts," he said at last. "The Clarissas are enclosed. The monastery is locked securely, day and night. The duchess threatened to kill herself in my presence and the presence of two holy sisters, as well as the half-dozen more who were probably listening at the door. The next morning, she was dead in her locked cell, lying as if asleep without a wound or mark on her body and with an empty flask on the table beside her bed."

"An empty flask!"

"Yes."

"But nothing has been said about a flask! Where did it come from? What became of it?"

He held up one hand. "Perhaps I should tell the story of that morning from the beginning, Madonna. And then you will tell me exactly what Sister Orsola has told you about the matter."

I nodded in agreement.

"I received a message just after lauds." He spoke slowly, choosing his words. "When I arrived at Corpus Domini, Mother Eleonora told me the duchess was dead. She swore to me the room had been closed and the door locked again the moment the infirmarian gave the alarm, and nothing had been touched."

Was Mother Eleonora telling the truth? I wondered, but said nothing.

"I was admitted to the enclosure, given my position as patron of the monastery and the extremity of the circumstance. I unlocked the door myself. When I went in, the flask was on the table beside her bed. There was no sign of any struggle or sickness. She lay there quite peacefully, as if asleep. I called for Messer Girolamo, my physician, as a matter of form, and of course for a priest as well, but it was clear she had been dead for several hours."

He paused and took a sip of his wine, his face expressionless. When he did not go on, I asked, "Why did you put it about she had died of an imbalance of humors? Why not simply tell the truth?"

He looked at me, and for a moment I feared I had gone too far. Evenly he said, "Self-murder is a mortal sin, Madonna, and in taking her own life she had taken the life of her unborn child as well. Bastard or no, it was an innocent soul. I thought to protect her name, and the name of Este, from those stains."

Pride is a mortal sin as well, I thought, although of course I did not dare say it aloud.

"You are thinking I was more concerned with my own pride than with the truth," he said, reading my thoughts with uncanny accuracy as he sometimes did. "Perhaps you are right. I can say only that there was gossip enough about the duchess as it was, and I did not wish to encourage chattering tongues by making it public she had taken her own life."

"Did Mother Eleonora and Sister Orsola see the flask? Did they realize its import?"

"I do not know. I have always thought not, as I put the flask away immediately with the duchess's other things, and had the coffers removed to the Castello that very day."

"Sister Orsola was uneasy when I questioned her, too ingratiating one moment, too belligerent the next. Could she have given the duchess the flask?"

"Given its value, I think not. Even if she had, would it have been filled with poison?"

I said nothing.

"I believe it was among the duchess's belongings from the beginning. I assure you I did not send her to the monastery in sackcloth and ashes, Madonna. She was supplied with two of her own coffers, clothes, household goods, and such personal possessions as she valued. I did not look inside the coffers before sending them."

"I would like to look at them, please."

He finished his wine and put the glass down. His expression had darkened again. "Since I suspect nothing else will satisfy you, I will take you to your so-called secret room, and stand by as you unpack the coffers with your own hands."

I had not expected to win the skirmish so easily. "Thank you, my lord," I said. "Perhaps we will find the missing book packed away as well."

"I examined the coffers before they were placed in the storage room. The book is not there."

"A secret compartment, perhaps? Such things are not unheard-of, and the young duchess's coffers would have been manufactured by Medici workmen, to Medici designs."

He looked thoughtful for a moment. "That is something I did not look for," he said. "And I should have. You are devious, Madonna, as well as disquisitive. Tell me, have you secret compartments in your own bridal coffers?"

He rose. I rose as well. I said, "You are quite welcome to examine them, my lord, at your leisure. Now, however, I would like to go to the secret room, as you have promised."

SECRET COMPARTMENTS! EVEN *if there had been secret compartments in my coffers, I wouldn't have put the book in one of them—far too easy to find. Better to hide things in separate boxes no one knows about, well-locked and well-hidden. It's strange, though, to hear Alfonso admit he didn't look for them. He's never been a man to admit his mistakes to anyone.*

It's strange, too, to listen to Alfonso tell la Cavalla about how he found my body. I was still there, of course, when he came into the monastery cell that morning. I was separated from my flesh but not entirely free of it— it takes a long time, when one becomes immobila, *to let go of the flesh. Death isn't such a sudden thing as the living imagine. It's slow, slow—the flesh cools little by little, and all the things that make us alive, our hearts and brains and muscles and tripes, don't stop working instantly. I was there, oh, yes, frightened and furious, trying to fit myself back into that familiar, comforting flesh, even as it stiffened and became more and more not-me.*

Mother Eleonora was there, too, and Sister Orsola and old Sister Addolorata, who were looking guilty because they'd gone off to sleep. Alfonso held a broken piece of my own mirror to my lips—well, to my body's lips, at least. He noticed the flask at once, I think, but didn't say anything. Just imagine how surprised I was when he said, "The duchess is alive, but barely. Call a priest. And send a messenger to Messer Girolamo Brasavola."

Alive! I was not alive, and he knew it. He lied so I would have the holy unction and be buried in holy ground, all for the sake of his own pride. And of course he wanted to prevent any gossip about how I died. How I've laughed, through the years, as the same gossip he tried to stop has buzzed around his pompous head.

Other than that, he's been more or less telling the truth so far. One thing he didn't tell her, because he doesn't know it himself, is that the monastery wasn't all that securely locked, day and night. Sister Orsola used to steal the keys, both the key to the back door and the key to my cell. That's how Tommasina got in, to bring me a few delicacies and playthings. She's a sly one, Sister Orsola is, and she does love jewelry and sweets, which makes her easy to bribe. La Cavalla found that out for herself.

The other thing he didn't tell her was that he wants to find the book of lascivious poems and engravings because it's forbidden by the church. Sandro told me about it. The old pope threw the man who did the engravings in prison and had all the copies of the book burned—twice, because it was printed a second time—and pronounced that anyone caught with a copy of the book would be committing a mortal sin. Can you just see what would happen to Alfonso, who's the pope's vassal for Ferrara, if that book came to light, with his device and name embroidered on the covering, and even worse, another man's love-poems written in the margins? He'd be the laughing-stock of Italy, and never gain the Precedenza he wants so badly.

I hope my father does get the Precedenza for himself. La Cavalla goes too far when she suspects him of having a hand in my murder. I loved my father. He loved me. I was surprised when he believed Alfonso's tales so easily. I expected him to do more than just spin one of his political webs around it all. I expected him to march to Ferrara with soldiers and raze the city to the ground in his rage.

Well, perhaps not. But I expected him to be angry. He's angry, I'm certain. He's just waiting for the right moment to ruin Alfonso forever.

I'm certain.

I think.

CHAPTER TWENTY

"This is the Torre dei Leonis', the Lion's Tower, the oldest part of the Castello," the duke said as we came out onto an open gallery with a white marble balustrade. "The lower levels of the tower are three hundred years old. This gallery and the balustrade were added more recently. If you look down, you will see the orange garden on the terrace."

I looked down and felt a wave of vertigo. The duke was standing close enough to touch me; I was without any attendant ladies, and he had forbidden both my guards and his own secretaries to follow us. The garden seemed dizzyingly far below, and the balustrade was only breast-high. He was close enough to lift me and—

But no, I could not allow myself to think such things anymore. My dizziness cleared; whether he noticed it or not I did not know. He led me to a low door opening off the gallery. From his purse he extracted a fine golden chain with several keys strung upon it, one large and the rest small; using the large key, he opened the door.

The room was tiny and undecorated, clearly meant for nothing but storage. There was no window; the only light was from the open door, and dust motes glittered in the shaft of late-afternoon sunshine. Behind the veil of dust, along one of the side walls, there were four—no, five wooden chests. The fifth was smaller, perfectly plain, with none of the carving or gilding or faded paint that covered the larger chests. Other than that, the room was empty.

"The four large *cassoni* were hers," the duke said. "Two of them were brought back from the monastery, where I closed them and locked them with my own hands. The other two contain the things left here in Ferrara, after most of her personal possessions were returned to Florence or distributed to the poor."

I walked over to the wall and put my hand on the largest of the coffers. It was carved with intricate fruit and flowers, symbols of fecundity; the heads of virginal unicorns peeped out among the foliage. A cipher of an *A* and an *L* intertwined was painted in the center of the lid. Alfonso. Lucrezia. I wondered if she had ever addressed the duke by his Christian name, a liberty I had not yet dared to take.

I wiped the dust from my hand against my skirt.

"What of the fifth coffer, the small one? It is not like the others."

"The Clarissas provided it, and I used it to gather up the items lying about in the cell where the duchess died. Here, I will show you why I believe she took poison."

He picked up the small chest and put it on top of one of the larger ones, then unlocked it with one of the smaller keys upon his golden chain. He put back the lid and gestured to me to examine the contents.

The first things I saw were white linen fabric, an ivory comb, and some small gilt boxes such as I myself used for cosmetics and comfits. The boxes were cracked and dented. Underneath, there were the broken shards of a mirror and pieces of brightly flowered majolica, which had probably once been a cup and a plate.

Deeper still, at the very bottom, I found a crudely carved wooden cup-and-ball toy, a bundle of painted jackstraws, a basket with a few shriveled cherries, and a small rock-crystal flask banded with gold and heavily studded with jewels. It was long-necked, round-bodied, with a golden stopper attached by delicate chains. A beautiful thing, no doubt, yet at the same time faintly malevolent, like some many-eyed creature out of a myth.

The duke picked up the flask and turned it so the slanting sunlight flashed off its cabochon emeralds and topazes and rubies. Through the carved crystal I could see a small amount of dry silvery residue in the bottom.

"It is Florentine work, probably from the workshop of Cellini, if not from the master's own hand," he said. His voice had changed, taken on the rapt, musing note of the collector. "Unmistakable. Notice the delicacy of the gold-work, the repoussé technique, the way the stones are polished and set."

"It is certainly not something one would ordinarily find in a monastery." I had expected a plain glass or earthenware container, not such a valuable piece. I could not help but think of Mother Eleonora's luxurious room, the hangings, the carpets, the jeweled cups for fine wine.

He put the flask down and frowned, as if he were deliberately wresting himself free of its spell. "I agree. I do not remember seeing it among the duchess's possessions, but it is definitely Florentine work, and I was not familiar with all the things she owned." Here an edge of contempt crept into his voice. "Nor with the ways in which she obtained them."

"But, my lord, if you are correct and the flask was filled with poison, why would she have such a thing among her possessions?"

"She was a Medici, and they are hardly known for niceties when it comes to poisons. Perhaps at one time she intended to rid herself of some rival, or an importunate lover like the one she persuaded Sandro Bellinceno to assassinate for her. I think the poison was there, for whatever reason, and in her fit of uncontrolled passion she drank it down for sensation's sake."

"You are very frank, my lord," I said slowly. It still disturbed me that he seemed to hold his friend entirely innocent despite his crimes of adultery and murder.

"I would never say such a thing publicly, of course. But we were to be honest with each other from now on, were we not? I did not kill my first duchess, but I did not marry her willingly, nor did I feel any affection for her, nor did I care for her merchants' breeding and her whore's morals."

He spoke quite softly, but even so I flinched at the brutality of his assessment. "She was hardly more than a child. Surely you could have molded her."

"Molded her? Her childhood name was 'Sodona,' and for good reason."

"Sodona?"

"It means 'hard one.' She had no desire to be lessoned, and she set her wits plainly against me when I attempted to teach her— lies, excuses, trickeries. I did not choose to stoop to such children's games."

I looked down at the coffer again, the cup-and-ball and the jackstraws. There was no half-finished needlework, no musical instrument, no books, nothing an adult woman might have used to while away hours of captivity.

"Even so, my lord, she did not deserve to die for her childishness. Nor for her breeding, which was certainly none of her own fault. You said when you went into the locked cell, she was already dead, and lay peacefully, as if asleep. Could she have died naturally? She was with child, after all, and her humors could have been disordered."

"She was perfectly healthy only a few hours earlier."

"Could she have been smothered? That would leave no mark."

"The cell was locked and guarded by the Clarissas. She was

alone. The flask was beside her pallet, with its stopper unstopped. If she died by any other means, what was in it?"

I reached down and touched the jeweled crystal phial, turning it slightly so the bit of silvery residue inside was more visible. As I did so, one corner of the white cloth underneath turned back as well, revealing a coiled silken tape. I stared at it for a moment, trying to think why it looked familiar. Then I realized I had seen just such cloths myself here in Ferrara, and not so long ago.

"I think I know what was in the flask, my lord."

He said something between his teeth, an oath in Italian I did not understand. "Speak plainly, Madonna," he said in a hard voice.

I lifted one of the cloths. It was a narrowish strip of white linen made with several layers quilted together; at each of the corners there was sewn a silken tape. "If you found this"—I laid the cloth down and removed the toys and the pieces of majolica to uncover others—"and all of these, unpacked and lying ready in the duchess's cell, then I assure you she did not take poison. And I further assure you she had every intention of living to see the morning."

I doubt the duke had ever actually seen such a cloth before; they had been the private business of women since the beginning of time. But he was no fool, and he divined its purpose at once. "You think the flask contained an abortifacient potion, not a poison, and the duchess had prepared herself for its effects."

I nodded. "Does it not make sense, my lord? It was the one thing that could save her. Maria Granmammelli refused her, but somehow, from someone, she procured the potion she desired. That night she drank it and prepared herself for her deliverance."

"Perhaps she took too much. You yourself pointed out that such accidents are not unknown."

"If so, would there not have been evidence? You said when she was discovered, she was composed, unmarked, without any sign of blood or agitation."

He nodded slowly. "That is true."

I replaced the cloths in the coffer and picked up the flask again. "So she procured her potion," I said thoughtfully. "But from whom? And why in such a valuable flask? Perhaps it was among her things, filled with perfume or a sleeping draught—it is the sort of thing a Florentine person of wealth and position would own. Perhaps she made a bargain with one of the infirmarians—refill the flask with a suitable potion, and when it had achieved its purpose, the flask itself would be payment."

I could not help remembering my own bargain with Sister Orsola. Had Lucrezia de' Medici found her as easy to bribe as I had?

"An ingenious speculation," the duke said. "However, if the potion was not, after all, a poison, it brings us back to the question of how she died."

"You are certain she could not have died of natural causes?"

"As certain as it is possible to be. When she was first taken to Corpus Domini, I instructed Messer Girolamo to examine her, will she or nill she. He found no evidence of any disease, and there were no reports from the infirmarian of any ill health."

"It is all very mysterious." I put the flask back in the coffer. Its jewels glittered like a hundred basilisk eyes. "The flask was empty, which argues she drank whatever was in it. She laid out the cloths, which argues it was an abortifacient, not a poison. And yet she showed no signs of the potion ever taking effect, and died quietly in her sleep."

"Perhaps she only thought it was an abortifacient," he said. "She had enemies aplenty. She may have been given the flask and been deliberately misled about its contents."

"That is another possibility. My lord, if we are to learn the truth, we must—"

A howl interrupted me. A moment later Tristo bounded into the room, eyes bright with joy, white-flagged tail high. Isa was just behind him, her baying higher and shriller than her brother's. They flung themselves at me and almost bowled me over in their excitement.

"What is this?" The duke sounded surprised and angry, and at the same time amused in spite of himself. "What are your little hounds about, Madonna, running unleashed?"

Nicoletta came panting in just at that moment. A wisp or two of her hair had come loose. She had the scarlet leather leashes in her hand.

"Forgive me, forgive me, Serenissima," she gasped, too much beside herself at first to realize I was not alone in the little room. When she saw the duke, she sucked in her breath and attempted to curtsy, which was less than successful in the tiny room. "I beg your indulgence, Serenissimo, but they escaped me. They seemed determined to track their mistress, and before I knew it they had followed her scent, first to your apartments, then here."

The little beagles were delighted with their accomplishment, and not at all cowed by my half-hearted scoldings. I stroked Tristo's russet head and hugged his warm, sturdy little body as I reproved him, which I suspect diminished the effect. Then I handed him back to Nicoletta and did the same with Isa.

"It is what they have been bred to do, so they can hardly be blamed," the duke said. "Next time take more care to keep them leashed. Now carry them back to the duchess's apartments, and she shall follow shortly."

When Nicoletta and the puppies had departed, the duke and I looked at each other.

"If we are to learn the truth," I said, picking up the thread of the thought I had begun just as the puppies interrupted us, "we must try to find out how it was she truly came to die. My lord, I suggest we interview your physician. And I also believe Sister Orsola must be questioned again."

"I agree."

I straightened and brushed the dust from my skirts; as I did I felt a sharp twinge in my lower back and a throe of exhaustion such as I had never felt before. "I would like to rest now," I said. "And with your leave I shall not come down for supper. Later I would like to come here again and examine the large coffers."

"You are welcome to come when you like." I must have looked surprised and dubious, because his expression darkened. "You do not believe me? I assure you I am quite sincere. I will even leave it to you to search for hidden compartments, and perhaps find the missing book."

And to my astonishment, he took the golden chain with its keys out of his pouch again and dropped it into my lap.

MERCHANTS' BREEDING! WHORE'S morals! How dare he? I was starting to feel like I hated him less, but now I hate him more than ever.

The Medici may have been merchants—actually we were bankers, I think—but it was hundreds of years ago, and anyway, we made so much money we became the most powerful family in Florence, and what's wrong with money and power? The Este won their power by swinging their swords and killing Guelfs—or was it Ghibellines? Or Longobards? I can never remember. They may have been lords of Ferrara for longer than the Medici have been lords of Florence, but their blood's gone pretty thin over the years.

So. About the flask.

I myself was surprised when Tommasina brought it, because she was only a poor parruchiera and it was covered all over with gold and jewels. I asked her where she got it, and she told me a long story about it being a present from a rich merchant's wife who seduced her lover with the beautiful hair-coloring Tommasina had concocted for her. Any fool could tell it was all a lie.

I think she begged the potion from her father in Florence and he made her promise not to tell, because of course he could get in trouble with the church for making such a thing. I didn't really care where she got it. Bringing it to me proved she loved me. And the valuable flask was practical—la Cavalla was right about that much. Tommasina told me to pry out the jewels, after the potion had done its work, and use them to bribe the nuns to whisk

*away the worst of the bloodied cloths, leaving only enough to make it appear
as if I'd started my courses normally. We laughed, Tommasina and I, at the
thought of Alfonso never knowing, and ending up having to admit he'd been
wrong when in truth he'd been right all along.*

*I never finished telling the story of how they found me dead, so I'll tell
the rest now. Alfonso called for a priest. The one who came was young and
looked frightened at being rousted out of bed; he was even more flustered
when he realized it was the duke he'd been brought to, and the supposedly
not-quite-dead body of the duchess. It turned out later he was an itinerant
Franciscan who was only spending the night at the monastery, which was
lucky for Alfonso—what would he have done, I wonder, if Mother Eleonora
had turned up with Frà Pandolf? How would I have felt, I wonder, to have
that* figlio di puttana *touching my flesh again, to give me the holy rites?*

*The priest gave my body the unction, which of course did me no good at
all. Then Messer Girolamo, the physician, arrived and examined my poor
body yet again, and said I was dead. Mother Eleonora and Sister Orsola
and all the gawking nuns outside the door crossed themselves. Fools—I'd
been dead and damned for hours. Surely Sister Addolorata knew that. But
they were all too frightened of Alfonso to speak up against him. They were
also too frightened to notice he'd picked up the flask and put it in his sleeve.*

*He then demanded a coffer, and with his own hands gathered up every-
thing I'd left strewn around the cell. You'd think he'd have walked out and
left such menial tasks to the nuns. Maybe he wanted to give the impression
he was distraught by grief. Maybe he suspected, even then, and didn't want
to leave any evidence for anyone else to see.*

*La Cavalla was sad when she touched my unused cloths. Seeing them
again tore my heart. I'd been so happy, so excited Tommasina had managed
to bribe her way into the monastery one last time and bring me the potion.
I'd been looking forward to the weeks and months to come, even if I did have
to stay in that dark little cell, while Alfonso watched me and my waist stayed
willow-slim. What a triumph it would've been.*

*If I had tears, I would've wept when I saw la Cavalla lift up those clean
white cloths.*

She's clever. I'm beginning to think she may find out who murdered me after all. I'd like that, I think. I'd like to have my revenge, and have it soon, because no matter how hard I try to stay in the world, I can feel myself slipping away. Even hating Alfonso isn't enough. Even wanting revenge isn't enough. Hell is yawning beneath me, calling me, and I won't be im-mobila much longer.

CHAPTER TWENTY-ONE

$\mathcal{I}$ was in Innsbruck, in one of the small plain chambers in the Hofburg I shared with my sisters, stitching silken tapes on hundreds of pure white cloths. They were to go in my bride-chests. The chests themselves stood before us, carved and gilded, painted with birds and animals, fruit and flowers and foliage; the center of each lid was embellished with the letters *A* and *B* intertwined. To my astonishment, the top of the largest one suddenly swung open and Lucrezia de' Medici emerged, holding a gilded leather-bound book in one hand and with her other arm around the neck of a milk-white unicorn.

"You must never speak his Christian name," she said. Her voice was prickly and glittering, like the points of pins. "If you do, he will shut you away from everything living and beautiful." She put the book into a painted box—where had it come from? It had not been there before—and took out a basket of crimson cherries, the fruit glossy-ripe and tempting. She ate one, and laughed, and handed one to me. I put it in my mouth and bit down, and it dissolved into a silver liquid as bitter as death.

"You may go."

It was the duke's voice. For a moment I was frightened. What was he doing in Innsbruck? What would he do if he knew his first wife was still alive? Then I realized I was not in Innsbruck at all, but in Ferrara, in my bedchamber in the Palazzo della Corte, in my bed. It was dark. Morning? Night?

"Yes, my lord. I wish you a good night, my lord."

A polished, subservient male voice. In the background, ladies' voices as well, whispering.

Night, then. I sat up. Holy Virgin, I was thirsty. Hungry, too. I still could not remember why I was here, what had happened before. Standing beside my bed was the duke in the flesh, wearing a night-gown of black velvet corded and frogged with gold. Something did not seem right about him, and after a moment I realized he was not wearing the damascened dagger. But of course he would not be. He was in his night-gown.

"What hour is it?" I asked.

He lifted his eyebrows. "Past compline. In the tower you said you were tired and did not wish to come down to supper."

The tower. The tiny secret room. The bride-chests, the white cloths, the jeweled flask. Before that—the hunt, the fall, confinement at Belfiore, terror for Katharina and capitulation. Confession in the icy Primavera garden. I knew it all had happened, but it was jumbled together and I could not quite put it in the proper order. I remembered exhaustion crashing down upon me as a golden chain of keys had fallen in my lap. Yes, now I remembered my plea to be excused from supper and the evening entertainments. I had come here to my apartments instead, I had refused food and drink, I had kept myself on my feet barely long enough for my ladies to undress me before I collapsed into the bed.

"I am thirsty," I said. "May I have some wine?"

"Of course."

He went to the table and poured wine into two glasses. I had a brief, vivid flash of my wedding night, and I thought, that is why he is here. He has come to bed with me. Too many things had happened, too many things had changed, and he meant to reassert his power over me. The thought frightened me, and at the same time gave me a feeling of—what was it? Expectation? Eagerness, and at the same time a sort of liquid languor? Whatever it was, I had never felt anything quite like it before.

He handed me one of the glasses of wine and drew a chair to the side of the bed for himself. Again, it was a strange mirroring of the events of my wedding night. He sipped his wine. I drank mine in deep swallows. I remembered wishing, on my first night as his wife, I had drunk more than a sip or two of wine. This time I intended to remedy that omission.

"I was dreaming," I said. "I thought I was back in Innsbruck."

I expected him to disregard my words. Instead, to my amazement, he took another sip of his wine and said calmly, "I am interested in your life in Innsbruck, before you came here. It made you what you are. Tell me about it."

"I—I do not know how to begin," I said. His interest made me uneasy. Had that scalding half-hour of honesty between us in the garden at Belfiore changed everything in some unexpected way? "It was very different from your life here. My sisters and I lived apart from the court most of the time, very quietly. We were taught prayer was more important than amusement."

"Your devotion is obvious. I would like you to instruct our own children in a similar fashion—I wish to improve my relations with the Holy See now that there is a new pope, and as part of that effort I want no more heresy in Ferrara."

I crossed myself. "God forbid," I said automatically. A question about the tournament at Blois rose to my lips—*I would like you to instruct our own children*—but I did not have the courage to ask it.

"And yet even with your pious life, you were educated," the duke said. "You are literate, and you have an appreciation of music and art."

"We were taught languages and history and a little mathematics, along with music and dancing and riding and other courtly accomplishments. My father always intended me for marriage and not the cloister—several matches were discussed over the years."

And came to nothing. I did not say that aloud. The ugly archduchess Barbara of Austria was refused or jilted, a half-dozen times and more. How else did she come to be twenty-six, ten years past what little bloom she had, when you at last selected her as a weapon in your battle with Cosimo de' Medici for the Precedenza? And why are you asking me these questions now? Is it yet another way to possess me, to make my childhood self your own as well as the woman who is now your duchess?

"I was not always happy," I said. It was not entirely a lie. "I told you that as a young girl I was much struck by Messer Baldassare Castiglione's book, *Il Libro del Cortegiano*."

"You did."

"My language tutor gave me the book when I was ten, to help me learn Italian—my older sister Katharina had just married the Duke of Mantua, and there was some talk of making a match for me with the duke's brother."

I paused and took another sip of the wine. He said nothing, but drank his own wine and waited for me to continue.

"I had to puzzle my way through the book at first, but as I became more fluent in Italian and read it over and over, my heart was fired with desire to be like the courtiers of Urbino, particularly Duchess Elisabetta. She was so gracious, so witty, had such a refined and cultivated circle of friends. I was only ten, you remember—I was filled with dreams, and the book made the dreams more real."

"Books will do that."

"The Mantuan match came to nothing—Katharina's husband

died within the year, and his brother chose to marry my sister Eleonora rather than me. After that, I must confess I hid my precious copy of Messer Baldassare's work in my prayer-book and read bits of it in the chapel where no one could see."

He laughed. "I would never have guessed you would do something so deceitful."

I took another swallow of wine.

"I would like to know about your life as well," I said. My voice shook a little. I was not sure why turning the subject frightened me, but it did. Perhaps it was because I was not really sure whether I wanted to know too much about him.

"That will have to wait for another time," he said. "Are you more yourself now?"

"Yes. Thank you." I drank the last of the wine.

"Good. Loose your hair."

A pang halfway between pleasure and pain stabbed me low in my belly. I handed him the empty glass and reached up to take off my night-coif. I said, "I have been using the apricot scent you suggested."

"So I have noticed. It is difficult to assess the full effect unless your hair is loose."

I put the coif aside and began to pull out the braiding. My hands had begun to tremble. Anticipation? Passion? Fear? I could not separate the one from the other.

Silken, sleep-warmed, braid-crimped, scented with apricots. I pulled a strand or two of my hair forward, over my breasts. Then I looked up at him.

He tossed the glasses aside, and I heard them shatter on the tile. The work of an artist, the value of a *scudo d'oro* at least, carelessly reduced to fragments. Then he half-knelt on the bed and without gentleness or ceremony jerked the night-smock down over my shoulders.

"Do not think to toy with me," he said. "However gentle I

may seem, I am permitting you to continue this—investigation—
into the death of my first duchess because I choose to do so. If I
choose to put an end to it, an end there will be."

I could feel the silky weight of my hair against my naked skin.
The abrupt change in his manner exhilarated me, but frightened
me, too. Everything was different. He was possessing me, but in
some strange way I had gained power over him as well. We were at
the edge of a precipice. Would we fall? Would only one of us fall?
Would I be the one?

I whispered, "I understand, my lord."

*You must never speak his Christian name. If you do, he will shut you
away from everything living and beautiful.*

I did not have the courage to speak it.

"This time you will open your eyes. No, do not turn your face
away. *Per Dio*, you will look at me."

He had thrown off his own night-gown. I had never looked
at him naked without immediately looking away; now I looked
steadily and saw a man's body, a man's hardened skin and muscu-
lature, patches and lines of dark hair where before I had seen only
silks and velvets. He bore scars, one on his arm, one over his ribs on
the left side, an ugly one from hip to inner thigh on the right side,
which at first surprised me—*Holy Virgin, the tournament at Blois*—
but of course for all his courtier's cultivation, he had known battle-
fields and tilt-yards in Italy, France, and Flanders.

"I am looking at you," I said.

His fingers were brown from the sun, calloused from bow and
reins, lute-strings and tennis-racquets. He twined them in my hair
and spread it out over the pillows, leaving me as naked to him as he
was to me. "My difficult wife," he said. "My disobedient, obstinate
wife."

My blood and nerves rose to his touch, and my skin quivered. I put my arms around his neck. Neither of us spoke again.

He had not come into my bedchamber, after all, for the sake of conversation.

I SLEPT THROUGH the morning bells, through Mass and breakfast and the call of the horns as the court rode out to hunt. I never knew when the duke left me. I slept and slept and slept, stuporous with exhaustion and excess. When I woke at last, I found myself stiff, bruised, hungry, and restive as a mare shut up in the stable too long.

"Bring me bread and wine, please," I said to Nicoletta Rangoni, who was attending me. "Quickly, no ceremony. Then hot water to wash, and the blue gown and the dark green surcoat, the one lined with fox fur."

"Are you going out, Serenissima? The duke ordered us to call the captain of his guard if you wished to go out, so you would have a proper escort."

"A proper escort!" I laughed. Even that could not discourage me. "Proper spies, you mean. No, do not look like that, it does not matter. I am only going to the Lions' Tower, and it is cold out on the galleries. I think you and Vittoria and the puppies will be escort enough."

"Yes, Serenissima. The duke also suggested, Serenissima, you go and look at the work that has been done on the chapel. Two of the new panels have been completed, and the duke wishes to know your opinion of them."

"Very well, we shall stop at the chapel for a moment. Now, the golden chain, the one with the keys? I brought it here yesterday, and I am not sure what I did with it. Look for it, please, while I am eating. Oh, and collect a lamp, and some oil. And the puppies' leashes."

I sopped the bread in the wine and ate it with relish. I refused jewels and braiding in my hair and bundled it all—*silken, sleep-*

warmed, braid-crimped, scented with apricots, twisted around the duke's fists—into a plain silver net. Within half an hour we were ready, Nicoletta and Vittoria, Tristo and Isa and I.

"Good day to you, Frà Pandolf," I said as I stepped inside the chapel. I was surprised to see scaffolding, the walls broken through in places and the removed blocks of stone stacked amid dust, broken shards, piles of bricks, and buckets of sand and water. I was suddenly reminded of the bricks and building materials I had seen at the Monastero del Corpus Domini. How long had the building of the new cellarium been in progress? Years of disruption and dust, Mother Eleonora had said. How many years? And were secular workmen allowed inside the enclosure?

"The duke suggested I come and assess your progress," I said to Frà Pandolf, who had been greeting me almost as effusively as Messer Bernardo Canigiani might have done. Apparently he had decided to acknowledge my existence again. "He did not tell me the renovations were so extensive."

"Yes, Serenissima, the duke informed me he wished you to look at the work I have done so far. As you can see, in addition to the new wall-paintings, there will be niches where suitable bronze figures will be placed, the Blessed Virgin, of course"—he crossed himself; we all followed suit like startled birds taking wing, making a sudden colorful flutter of motion in the little chapel—"and Saint Anne her mother, and Saint Elizabeth the mother of the Baptist. It was the duke's suggestion. He has already commissioned Claus of Innsbruck to cast the bronzes, and specified that they are to be in a very simple and monastic style. They will come all the way from Austria, in your honor, of course."

"Of course." I was taken aback that my glib excuse for my visit to the Monastero del Corpus Domini had borne such extensive fruit. "From the size of the niches, the figures will be life-sized."

Tristo and Isa were tugging at their leashes, exploring the great gaps excavated in the wall opposite the windows. Their little black noses, always sniffing, had become comically smudged with white dust from the broken stone.

"Yes, Serenissima. In the late morning, the sun will illuminate them like the very light of heaven. Will you come and look at the paintings? I have finished two of them, and there will be four more."

I gestured to Nicoletta to gather up the puppies before they hurt themselves on the sharp fragments of broken stone. "Yes, of course, I would be pleased to look at them." A lie, of course, because I wanted nothing more than to get away and go to the tower room while there was still time for a thorough, leisurely search of the wedding chests.

"This one shows the Blessed Virgin as a pure child, at the knee of her mother, Saint Anne," Frà Pandolf said. "Move closer to the window, Serenissima, to gain the full effect." He came up very close to me and actually dared to touch my arm, presumably to guide my attention. I stiffened and withdrew, although in the throes of his encomium to himself, I did not believe he noticed.

"Look at the way the light illuminates her! Look at the folds of Saint Anne's mantle, and the individual perfection of the pages of the book that—"

"Yes, yes," I said, stepping back even farther. There was something about the painting, for all its virtuosity, that made me uneasy. The face of the Virgin, the half-closed eyelids, the parted lips—it was like the portrait of Lucrezia de' Medici and yet unlike. Surely unlike—surely I was seeing a resemblance that was not there.

"It is beautiful," I said. "I am sure the chapel will be magnificent when your work is completed. Nicoletta, Vittoria, come, let us go."

AND SO AT last I was on my way to the Lions' Tower, to search through Lucrezia de' Medici's wedding chests for further evidence, to look for hidden compartments, and to collect the jeweled crystal flask. If I found anything useful in the chests, particularly the mysterious missing book, I would give it to the duke; the flask I would give to Maria Granmammelli. I would even let her dose me with further potions if she would examine the sediment and make an attempt to identify it.

At the top of the tower, I unlocked the door to the storage-room. Nicoletta lit the lamp and gave it to me; I went inside alone and closed the door behind me. The small coffer from the monastery was just as the duke and I had left it, and we had already examined it quite thoroughly. It was the four large coffers I was interested in. Two of them, I remembered, had been used to transport the duchess's clothing and possessions to the monastery. The other two held what remained of her property, left behind when her valuables were returned to Florence in repayment of her dowry.

The ones taken to the monastery, I reasoned, would have been unpacked and repacked at the time, their contents examined and reexamined. But the other two would have been hurriedly filled with the detritus of the young duchess's life. Who knew what they might contain?

I chose the largest first, the one with painted fruits and flowers and unicorns wreathing the initials *A* and *L*. It took two tries to find the right key, but when I did, it clicked satisfyingly in the lock. Slowly, with a sense of—what, awe? fear? anticipation?—I lifted the lid.

What first met my eye could not have been more prosaic: piles of smocks, headdresses, kerchiefs, and night-coifs with the remains of embroidery that had been picked away, probably for gold and silver thread and small jewels. I rummaged deeper and found a few gauze partlets and veils, leather gloves also stripped of their orna-mentation, and several pairs of slippers. At the very bottom there were a heavy woolen cloak, spotted by rain, and two pairs of worn wooden chopines.

I went through the chest again, then unlocked and searched

the second chest, then even the third and fourth. Still I was frustrated: all four chests were filled with nothing but clothes of the less valuable sort, dishes and candlesticks and wine-cups that had been chipped or scratched, half-used cosmetics and pomades, and other equally meaningless bits and pieces of a young girl's life. There were no papers, no letters, no trace of the book the duke had described. But perhaps there were secret compartments.

I crouched down in front of the largest chest and ran my finger over the painted carvings. Here again, on the side, there were flowers rioting and lush fruits, pomegranates and peaches and berries, the color fading and flaking. Here again was the cipher combining the A and the L. I traced the letters with my forefinger. Each loop and swirl seemed to end by curling back upon itself. Perfect hiding places for hidden latches. But there was nothing.

I moved the lamp closer and examined the outer surfaces of each chest carefully, all the carvings, all four sides, tops and bottoms. Then I looked at the interiors, felt for joinings or rough edges, and compared the apparent size and depth of each chest with the actual measurements.

Nothing was out of order. The chests were ordinary wedding chests, with no hidden spaces.

So if there were no secret compartments, and the book was not here, there was another hiding place. There had to be.

I sat back on my heels in front of the largest chest and ran my finger one more time over the painted carvings, the flowers and fruits and unicorns, the cipher combining the A and the L. I remembered my dream. I traced the A with my forefinger, and said aloud to the dusty air, "Alfonso." It sounded strange to me. I wondered if I would ever call him such, to his face. There was something else about my dream—but as dreams will do, it flickered in and out of my understanding, and I could not quite catch hold of it.

I locked the large chest securely, and then opened the small coffer, intending only to take the flask. Everything was as it had been—the clothes, the broken majolica, the toys. Suddenly I looked at the toys more closely. They were not the gilded and jeweled playthings of a duke's daughter, a duke's wife. They were plain wood, crudely painted. I could not imagine Lucrezia de' Medici owning them; yet here they were, among the other objects from her monastery cell.

Someone had given them to her, to help her while away the time.

Sister Orsola? Would a Clarissa, vowed to poverty, have painted toys, however cheap and crude they were? She had grasped my ring quickly enough, but that was an adult acquisitiveness; I could not see her playing with a child's toys.

Where had they come from, then? Who had brought them to the Monastero del Corpus Domini, and who had given them to the young duchess? Had the doors of the monastery been less firmly locked and barred than the duke presumed?

I took the crystal flask from the depths of the chest. Its jewels glittered balefully at me in the flickering flame of my lamp. I tucked it into my sleeve, straightened up, and brushed the dust from my skirts.

At suppertime I would tell the duke what I had done, and pose to him my question about the toys. But before that, I would speak to Maria Granmammelli and persuade her to employ her best arts to discover what had been in the crystal flask.

I COULD TELL la Cavalla what was in the flask. It was an infusion of pennyroyal, tansy, and rue, with a bit of a special magical powder made from certain kernels of rye. Tommasina told me it was absolute proof against failure. I remember lifting that beautiful flask, and how heavy it was for its size. I remember removing the seal and the stopper, and how the stopper swung loose on a thin gold chain. The potion tasted awful—bitter and sour. But what was a moment of bitterness, when by morning I would be free?

Except I wasn't. I was dead, and Alfonso was free instead.

Will Maria Big-Breasts be able to identify the potion? If she does, will she tell Alfonso and la Cavalla the truth about it? It was so bitter I would think she could still taste it, even after four years. I know I never tasted anything else like it.

I died with that bitterness in my mouth.

After I was dead and gone, you'd think Tommasina would've gone back to Florence, but she didn't. She stayed in Ferrara. She may have been afraid to go back, because she knew if my father ever learned what she'd tried to do for me he'd kill her, and probably kill me all over again if I hadn't been dead already. So she was safer in Ferrara. It would be nice to think she stayed because she loved me and wanted to devote her life to praying for my soul.

She does pray for me, you know. Do you remember the day la Cavalla first visited the Monastero del Corpus Domini? The day she pretended to be sick, and then went to pray in the choir of the church with two nuns? That afternoon la Cavalla saw a woman come in, veiled and dressed in black, and the nuns told her the woman was a tertiary, a member of the third order who helped the nuns with errands in the world. La Cavalla wondered about it at the time, but so many things have happened, I think she's forgotten.

The tertiary is Tommasina.

Yes, Tommasina Vasari, the one person who loved me, is the mysterious black-clad woman la Cavalla saw praying over my grave in the choir.

CHAPTER TWENTY-TWO

*T*he ache in my back had become more pronounced by the time I reached my apartments, and I was not such a fool I did not know what it portended—another unfruitful month for the Austrian duchess, another disappointment for the duke. The hard fall in the forest might well be to blame, although that seemed as if it had happened in another life entirely. There would have been no slashed girth and no fall if I had not—

But no. Done was done. I could not go back and start my life in Ferrara over from the beginning, however much I might want to. But I could start it over from the garden at Belfiore.

We went into the Jupiter chamber and set the dogs free from their leashes. The door to my receiving-room was closed, which was unusual. I could hear whispering, and behind me Nicoletta and Vittoria giggled. More and more mysterious. I drew breath to ask them sharply what was afoot, but before I could speak the door opened.

Domenica came in first. Behind her were my cherished Austrian ladies, Christine von Hesse and Sybille von Wittelsbach, and a few steps farther behind, as if she had waited to make a grand entrance, came Katharina Zähringen.

"Katrine!" I cried. "Christine! Sybille! Oh, my dears, I am so very glad to see you all! Katrine, are you well? Have you been entirely exonerated from those ridiculous charges? Are all of you to remain in Ferrara after all?"

They came forward and embraced me, laughing and crying all at once. "Sybille and I were not really confined," Christine said in her sweet, musical voice. "Just—invited—to remain at the Palazzo dei Diamanti. But after dinner today, pfft! Suddenly, we are invited no longer. Naturally we came straight to you."

"And you, Katrine?" I held her at arm's length from me and looked into her eyes. "You have not been harmed? How could you have been mad enough to slap and scratch the duke's gentleman, and call him such names he perjured himself in revenge?"

She laughed. I could have shaken her. I did shake her, just a little. "You do not know what I had to do to save you. The duke threatened to sentence you to *la scopa*."

All the Ferrarese ladies sucked in their breaths, shocked. Katharina only looked puzzled. "I do not know what that is," she said. "I was frightened, I grant you that, but I thought the worst they could do was send me back to Innsbruck."

"That was not the worst. No, Domenica, do not explain. It is better we all forget."

Katharina folded her lips together; it was her stubborn expression, and I knew she would pry the truth out of one of the Ferrarese ladies. "I did not know," she said. "Oh, Bärbel, I did not realize—I am sorry if I caused you unpleasantness. Whatever you did, I will be grateful to you forever."

I embraced her again. "It was nothing, now I see you are safe and free. What about the rest of my household?"

"Some have already gone," Sybille said. She hugged me in her turn, clearly anxious to have me all to herself for a few moments at least. "Some are still at the Palazzo dei Diamanti. Most did not intend to stay in Ferrara in the first place. But what of this 'nothing' you speak of? We heard strange tales, frightening tales, that you had been imprisoned as well."

"Only tales," I said, not quite truthfully. "Nothing more. And I have missed you terribly. Come, tell me everything, and help me dress. There is something I want to do before supper."

They helped me out of my dress, chattering away in German, and for once I did not reprove them. When they had stripped me to my shift, I made the discovery I had been half-expecting, yet which struck me to the heart: sometime in the afternoon my courses had begun.

"Oh, Serenissima—Barbara," Domenica said. I saw we-three exchange looks with one another, but no one said anything. "I am so sorry. I know you were hoping— You cannot go down to supper now. I will send a message to the duke."

"No, no," I said. I was close to tears. "Do not send any messages. I will go to supper, and I will tell him myself."

She clicked her tongue sympathetically. "Very well. But you must stay here quietly and rest until suppertime, and have a posset to calm you."

With that she went off for wine and spices. Meanwhile, Vittoria Beltrame fetched warm water and cloths and a fresh shift for me, clearly reveling in the portentousness of it all. When I saw the cloths, so like the ones the duke and I had discovered in Lucrezia de' Medici's coffer, I began crying in earnest. I felt like a fool, but I could not stop myself.

"Shhhh, shhhh," Katharina crooned, as she sponged me and helped me dress in a clean shift and a loose gown suitable for a private afternoon in my own chamber. "You have been married only two months—you have plenty of time. Don't cry, don't cry."

"Maria Granmammelli," I gulped. "The old witch. The duke's nursemaid. I must see her."

"Do not be a fool. Her potions are worthless."

"I do not want a potion, but I must see her. I will only ask for one of her ghastly potions to sweeten her anger toward me, after the last time."

"You will do no such thing. Look, here are Tristo and Isa, come to warm the bed for you. Play with them and think of other things. Sybille will read to you. Christine will play her lute and we will sing. Next month, it will be different, and you will be rejoicing."

No one but Katrine would have dared speak to me so. How wonderful it was to have her back and safe. "It is not what you think," I said. "I must see the old woman. Christine, please run and fetch her. I will sleep a little, perhaps, after I have spoken to her."

Christine ran off. Domenica returned and began mixing my posset. Perhaps a quarter of an hour passed, and at last Christine came back with Maria Granmammelli complaining bitterly in her wake.

"'Tis a hard thing when a poor old woman can't rest her eyes from sext to nones without fine ladies rushing in, badgering her to come running at a moment's notice. Not even a chance for a swallow of wine to open her eyes. Well, *Austriaca*? What is it? As if I don't already know."

I gestured to Christine to fetch wine. "I have learned I am not yet with child," I said stiffly and apparently superfluously. "I would like another of your potions, something to make me . . . more receptive . . . in the month to come."

"After you threw the last one on the floor for the dogs to lick?"

"I am sorry for that." I had rehearsed the words, but still they were bitter on my tongue. "No one in Ferrara, not even the duke's own physician, can make potions as powerful as yours."

"Huh," she said grudgingly. "Fine words. Very well, for the duke's sake. It'll be a different potion this time, though. More heat. You need more heat and more moisture."

It suddenly occurred to me the duke was not the only one who took it for granted he would father children—Maria Granmammelli believed it, too. So much for Nora's malevolent whispers. A fall there might have been—the scars on the duke's body testified to that—but surely his healing had been complete.

"Thank you," I said. I hoped I concealed my satisfaction that she had succumbed to my flattery. "I have another request I would make of you as well."

"What, d'you think I'm made of herbs? What now?"

"No, not another potion. I would like you to look at this."

I handed her the flask.

She took it readily enough and held it to the light, turning it and examining the jewels. I watched her closely, but there was not the slightest indication she had ever seen it before.

"What's this, *Austriaca*? Some bit of fantasy you brought from Austria? It had something in it, and it'd be prettier if you'd cleaned it properly."

"No," I said. "It is not mine. Do you think you could determine the substance it once held, from the sediment remaining?"

She stiffened instantly and looked at me with narrowed eyes. "What are you up to, *Austriaca*? I'll have naught to do with any poisonings."

"I have no desire to poison anyone, and I do not believe the substance was a poison. However, I would like to know what it was. It has been dried in the flask for almost four years, so I will understand if you cannot identify it."

That raised her hackles. "I know the tastes and smells of a thousand potions. I'll mix the dregs with a little water or aqua vitae and have your answer in no time."

"Excellent. And though you have not asked me, I will tell you the duke is one with me in this matter. You are free to show the flask to him, and tell him I gave it to you, and also what I have asked you to do."

She tossed the sinister bauble in her hand, then examined it more closely. "Mayhap I will," she said. "I may have to break the flask."

Good riddance, I thought. "You are free to do so. And the jewels are yours to keep."

Her eyes gleamed. "I'll see what I can do, then."

"Excellent. Thank you, Maria Granmammelli. And I look forward to receiving your new potion."

"Sweet-tongued as a serpent, you are, when you want something."

With that she went off, humming and muttering of ginger and cloves.

SUPPER THAT EVENING was served at the high table in the Castello's great salon. This was actually more private than it sounds. The cardinal had returned from Rome, where he had been part of the conclave that had elected the new pope, but he was supping at another Este palace called the Palazzo Schifanoia with some of his friends and most likely his pretty mistress. Crezia was keeping to her apartments, probably with her sensual-lipped Count Ercole Contrari. Nora was in the country, and if she had her way, I was sure young Tasso was reciting poetry at her feet. Thus the duke and I were alone at the high table. The talk of half-a-hundred courtiers laid a soft blanketing hum over the room, and the consort of viols wove silver threads of music through the perfumes and candle-smoke and drifting scents of rich food.

"My Austrian ladies have returned to me," I said. "Katharina Zähringen is unharmed. My lord, I am grateful for your generosity in this matter."

He held out his hands for a servitor to rinse them with rose water. "A small thing," he said.

"Nonetheless, I am grateful. I hope you will allow them to remain with me."

He took a white napkin and dried his hands. "They may remain in Ferrara for the moment."

The servitor turned to me, and I held out my hands in turn. Although the duke had brushed aside my thanks, I knew what he had done was meant as a deliberate act of consideration, and I also knew he was pleased by my gratitude. As I dried my hands I said again, "I thank you."

"And speaking of those who are to remain in Ferrara," he said, "there is something I would like to do before the first course is served. The court has been whispering, since the hunt at Belfiore, that Sandro Bellinceno is out of favor and that I mean to send him away. I was angry with him, yes, and I spoke with him privately about the matter of his disrespect to you; as far as I am concerned that was the end of it. I would like to silence the rumors tonight, with a public mark of our continuing friendship toward him."

The last time I had seen Sandro Bellinceno, he had been spurring his black Friesian horse deliberately to crowd my Tänzerin, his face twisted with anger, his voice harsh with a masculine certainty of superiority over anything feminine. I had told the duke I was willing to consider the matter forgotten, and for my ladies' sake I was; even so, I could not honestly say I would ever feel anything remotely resembling friendship for Messer Sandro.

Warily I said, "I am at your command, my lord."

He lifted one hand, and his majordomo Count Niccolò Tassoni stepped up behind him; they had a few words, and then Count Niccolò withdrew. Silence suddenly descended upon the salon. The musicians ceased to play. Every head turned toward the door.

Sandro Bellinceno and his wife stood there, just the two of

them, framed in the gilded scrollwork of the doorway as if they had been painted by Messer Leonardo da Vinci himself. He was dressed in rich russet-brown velvet; she wore green and blue, her hair braided with emeralds, blue-green Turkish stones, and pearls. The duke's largesse—and the duke's favor—was clear in every yard of new cloth and every shining stone.

They walked toward us. Whispers began to fizzle gently around the edges of the salon. The musicians took up their tune again, with only a missed note or two. When the two Bellincenos reached us at the high table, they made their reverences. Messer Sandro's fine new feathers had added no grace to his thick-bodied awkwardness; Donna Elisabetta, on the other hand, made her curtsy with her accustomed elegance.

"Sandro," the duke said. He had pitched his voice to carry. *"Mio amico."*

"Serenissimo."

There was a moment of silence. I held firmly to the thought of my Austrian ladies safely returned to my household and said through my teeth, "Messer Sandro, what a pleasure to see you about the court again."

He bowed a second time. He would not look at me. "Serenissima," he said.

"And Donna Elisabetta," I went on. It suddenly occurred to me I had the power to thwart Sandro Bellinceno's determination to keep his wife away from me, to all appearances quite innocently, in the name of assuring him of the duke's and my favor. I said, in the same carrying voice, "I am so pleased to see you as well. In point of fact, I have arranged a position in my household for you, subject to your husband's goodwill, of course."

The duke made a sound beside me, half-exasperation, half-laughter. Messer Sandro looked up at me at last, and in his expression I could clearly see dislike warring with hunger for a high place in the politics of the court.

"My goodwill is yours, Serenissima," he said.

"Excellent. I shall send for Donna Elisabetta one day soon, and we will make the arrangements."

"And you, Sandro, wait upon me tonight after the entertainment," the duke added. He put his hand on the damascened dagger at his belt. "I have a taste for some wine and some talk of the old days in France."

With that they were dismissed to one of the courtiers' tables, fairly shining with the new favor that had been heaped upon them. Servitors appeared with a salad of lettuce, caper flowers, and hazelnuts, dressed with the thick dark-colored *balsamico* vinegar that is one of the gastronomic treasures of Ferrara. Behind us at the sideboard, tasters ate from each dish and drank from each ewer of wine before it was presented.

"You did not hunt with us today," the duke said. It was a clear change of subject. "I assure you I myself have set guards to your horses and saddlery, and there is nothing to fear."

"It was not fear that kept me from the hunt, my lord," I said. "I slept far longer than I usually do, and when I awoke I did not feel fit for riding."

"Indeed." Perhaps I imagined the flash of self-satisfaction in his eyes. But then again, perhaps I did not. "Did you keep to your bed all day, then?"

"I was not quite that unfit." I let him reflect on that while I ate a piece of lettuce. The *balsamico* was delicious when mixed with salt and olive oil. "It was not long after the hunt had gone that I awoke and broke my fast and dressed. Then, as you suggested, I went to the chapel to see the work Frà Pandolf has been engaged in."

"Excellent. And what is your opinion?"

I took a sip of wine to clear my palate. "I did not expect the renovations to be so extensive. The walls themselves have been broken through to construct niches for statuary. There was a great deal of stone dust about, and bricks and sand and mortar."

The duke smiled. Conversation to do with art or architecture always pleased him, almost as much as conversation about music or sport. "It is a design of my own. I have been much pleased with the bronze figure of Neptune cast for me by Claus of Innsbruck, and always intended to commission further pieces. The renovation of the chapel offers the perfect setting for his art."

"I will look forward to the new bronzes." I said. "The work being done in the chapel reminded me, my lord, that I saw building materials at the Monastero del Corpus Domini as well. Mother Eleonora said they had been working for some time on a new cellarium—if there were workmen allowed inside the enclosure at the time the first duchess was confined there, others might have managed to slip in as well."

The carver knelt behind us with a dish of braised eels, and the duke turned his attention to it. "Allow me to serve you with an eel or two," he said. "It is an interesting question."

With the point of his knife he placed two of the choicest eels on my side of our silver dish. Then he served himself and waved the carver away. I did not care for eels, but cutting one into small bits of equal size gave me something upon which to focus my attention. "After I visited the chapel," I said, "I went to the Lions' Tower."

A pause. Perhaps it was simply because he was cutting an eel for himself.

"I see. Well, that is why I gave you the keys. Have you satisfied yourself nothing is being concealed from you?"

"I have, my lord. I looked through the four large chests and found nothing out of the ordinary. I also examined them all very closely for any evidence of secret compartments. I found nothing."

"She had another hiding place, then."

"Yes, I think she did."

He cut another eel. "And the flask?"

"I gave the flask to Maria Granmammelli. I did not tell her

where it came from, or to whom it belonged—I only asked her to attempt to identify the sediment. She claims to know the tastes and smells of a thousand potions."

"I am sure she does," the duke said, "and I also would like to know what that potion was. Well, taken as a whole, Madonna, I am not displeased by your afternoon's work."

I flushed—I actually flushed—with pleasure. I could feel the heat of the blood in my cheeks. Then immediately I felt annoyed, both at him for his condescension and at myself for responding to it. The annoyance made my next confession easier.

"There is one more thing I must tell you."

"Saint George protect me." There was an edge of irony in his voice. "I should have known there would be one more thing. Tell me, then."

"Once again, I am not with child."

He looked at me. I could have said an Ave once, twice, three times. Perhaps I should have.

"There was the fall, at the hunt," I said. "I have been afraid. We have been at odds."

Another Ave. I ran my fingers over the fabric of my skirt and folded a pleat in it. I was aware of it—since the duke had noticed my strange habit, I had been struggling to break it. But this time, in the lengthening silence, I could not stop myself.

"My father and mother spent most of their lives at odds," he said at last. "Yet she bore him five living children and mingled the blood of Valois with the blood of the Este. If a daughter of France can achieve that, Madonna, then a daughter of Austria should be able to do no less."

"I will take up your challenge. In a few days, when the time is suitable again."

"Good. I also wish to have my physician examine you. Messer Girolamo Brasavola. You know him, of course—he attended you after your fall."

"I remember him." *She came here upon Messer Girolamo Brasavola's recommendation,* Mother Eleonora had said of Lucrezia de' Medici, *and Messer Girolamo is the best of Alfonso's physicians, a doctor of our university and a great scholar.* "I will submit to an examination, if I am also permitted to ask him a few questions in return."

"You will submit to an examination because I wish it. However, you are free to ask him whatever questions you wish, so long as they are asked in my presence."

Clearly he was perfectly well aware I intended to ask Messer Girolamo about the first duchess. I smoothed the pleats out of my skirt and said, "In a few days, then?"

"In a few days. And this business of the examination is to remain private, as private as is our other—enterprise."

"Of course, my lord."

Music swirled softly through the room; the courtiers whispered and laughed. The servitors presented sweet wines and slices of *pampepato,* the dense cake rich with cinnamon, cloves, citron, and pepper. It was the same sort of cake Mother Eleonora had offered me at the Monastero del Corpus Domini. I picked my piece into small bits; it seemed too highly spiced, too cloying. Instead, I took a perfectly ripened pomegranate from an arrangement of fruit in a golden dish.

I cut it open, and its juice spilled out upon the silver dish, red as blood.

ALFONSO AND SANDRO spent most of the night drinking together.

Sandro went to his studiolo *after the supper and entertainments were over, just as Alfonso suggested, and they were there for hours. I couldn't even count the bottles of wine they drank. They talked about it all: how Alfonso galloped away from Ferrara when he was just nineteen, much to the ire of Duke Ercole. How he joined the French king Henri's war in Flanders and met Alexandre de Bellincé—Sandro—among the men under his command. The arquebus-ball in Sandro's shoulder, meant for Alfonso. The roistering and carousing they did together afterward, when Sandro'd had a chance to mend, and how Alfonso got Sandro preferment when they got back to France. The French court, where Alfonso's oldest sister was married to the Duke of Guise and Alfonso himself was much taken with his niece-in-law, the tall young Scottish queen, before she was married off to the Dauphin. Sandro gets maudlin when he drinks wine. Alfonso seems to be able to drink forever and never show a sign of it.*

Then Alfonso told the story about the fateful joust where King Henri was wounded, just like Nostradamus claims he predicted. Alfonso was one of the first gentlemen to reach the king as he lay on the ground with the splinters of a lance through his eye. Alfonso was at the king's deathbed, too. That's where he got the damascened dagger he loves so much. It was King Henri's, and the king gave it to him with his own hands, just before he died. I think it means more to Alfonso than anything his own father ever gave him.

They spoke mostly French. I couldn't understand French, other than a few words, when I was alive, but now that I'm immobila *it makes perfect sense to me. Or maybe it's because for part of the time they talked about me.*

I wish I'd never touched her, Sandro said. I wish I'd died before I touched her. I'm sorry, mon ami. Mea culpa. *Forgive me.*

Do you think I care? Alfonso said. I never wanted to marry her, and I never really thought of her as my wife. You were welcome to her.

They drank some more wine.

It's like that girl in Metz, Sandro said. We both had her. We were still friends. Like brothers.

Like brothers, Alfonso said. Of course, it's different with the new one. She is my wife. I will kill even you if you touch her.

God forbid, Sandro said. And he meant it. He doesn't like la Cavalla. Then he said, It wasn't having Lucrezia that was the worst of it. The worst of it was I was such a fool as to kill a stable boy for her sake. Killing another soldier on a battlefield's one thing. It's clean. You're face-to-face with him, and he's trying to kill you, too. Killing a filthy stable boy in the dark, lying in wait, sneaking up behind him—that'll be a stain on my soul forever.

They drank some more. Then Alfonso said, Tell me about the book, Sandro.

Merde, *Sandro said.* You know about the book?

Your wife told the duchess. The duchess told me. I wondered what had happened to it. Where is it now? The Florentines are sniffing around, and if Messer Bernardo Canigiani should find the damnable thing, I'll suffer for it. You wrote in it, so you'll suffer, too.

Don't know. She hid it, the little bitch. Taunted me with it. My damned wife talks too damned much. I think I'll beat her.

Alfonso laughed and drank more wine. Sandro's voice was getting thick and slurred, but Alfonso's was sharp-edged and precise as ever.

Do not beat your wife, he said to Sandro. I tell you truly, unexpected things happen when you beat your wife.

They both laughed. Then Sandro started to cry.

I'm sorry, mon ami, *he said again.*

I forgive you, Alfonso said. He sounded serious. Then he took out his damascened dagger and put it on the table. Here, I swear it, he said. This dagger reminds me life is short. I swear on this dagger you and I will be friends always. She meant nothing to me, nothing at all.

Nothing at all.

And Sandro isn't still suffering because of me. It's only because of what he did to Niccolò.

If I was alive, I'd want to die of shame.

Why did it matter so much to me, the sweet shudders of pleasure, the touches and kisses and bites? Why couldn't I have been more like la Cavalla, with her imperial dignity and assurance—well, her outward assurance, anyway, because she's afraid inside, and so has to struggle sometimes to show a brave front. I watch her and I think, why didn't I do that? Why was it so important to me while I was alive to have lovers, and pleasures, *and to do the opposite of whatever Alfonso wanted me to do, just to defy him?*

I wonder what la Cavalla will ask Girolamo Brasavola. I wonder what he'll find when he examines her.

He examined me, too. He's never told Alfonso. I wonder if he'll tell him now.

He examined me, too, but of course I was already dead.

CHAPTER TWENTY-THREE

$\mathcal{G}$irolamo Brasavola, physician and scholar, son of Antonio Musa Brasavola the celebrated physician, botanist, and university professor, lived in a flat-faced brick house in the new section of the city. The duke and I arrived more or less incognito, which meant we were attended by only five retainers: the duke's secretary, my ladies Christine von Hessen and Sybille von Wittelsbach, and two gentlemen-ushers.

"Welcome, Serenissimo, I am your servant, as always." Messer Girolamo bowed as we were ushered into his private study. "Good day to you, Serenissima. It is my privilege you cross my threshold. Please, seat yourselves. Pietro, bring wine."

The duke and I sat in two graceful Savonarola chairs, clearly placed with our visit in mind. He gestured for Messer Girolamo to sit as well, behind his elaborate and untidy writing-cabinet. Wine was brought. Then the servants, the gentlemen-ushers, the duke's secretary, and my ladies withdrew, leaving us alone with the physician.

"I have come for two things," the duke said. "First, I wish you to examine the duchess to determine if there is any impediment to her conceiving a child. The true purpose of this examination is to be known only to the three of us. Second, the duchess has some questions to ask you, and it is my wish you answer her with complete frankness."

Messer Girolamo raised his eyebrows. "Of course, Serenissimo. All will be done as you wish. First I shall have the duchess's horoscope cast—"

"That is not necessary." The last thing I wanted was some unknown foreigner meddling with my stars. "My stars were cast in Austria, more than once, and I have all the charts and papers in my personal library. That will provide everything you need."

The physician smiled. He was a pleasant-looking man of early middle age, everything about him plump, plain, and reassuring until you looked closely at his eyes; they were intelligent, weary, vast as the ocean with study and experience.

"Excellent," he said. "It is best when a horoscope is cast by one's own countryman. In addition, before I perform the examination I shall require exemplars of your bodily humors—your urine, your phlegm, venous and arterial blood, menstrual blood, and vaginal secretions. I will provide you with suitable containers."

Holy Virgin. The man had not yet laid a finger on me and already I was staggered with mortification. What would I do when I actually had to submit to him *touching*— But no. I would not even think about it.

"It is not so fearsome as you think, Serenissima," Messer Girolamo said gently. "You will be allowed to have your trusted ladies with you, however many you wish, and there will be draperies to preserve your dignity; all will be done quite quickly and correctly."

"I cannot imagine dignity or correctness in such a situation," I said. "But it is the duke's wish, and as such, my obligation."

"Even so." The physician picked up a pen and wrote a few

notes. "Now. You had questions you wished to ask? Remedies, perhaps, for small ailments?"

He looked at me. The duke looked at me. I took a sip of my wine—overspiced and oversweetened for my taste, but then, my taste seemed to have changed, as had so many other things—and I put the goblet down.

"No, not remedies. I wish to know, Messer Girolamo, everything you observed the morning you were called to the Monastero del Corpus Domini to attest to the death of Lucrezia de' Medici."

That clearly shocked him almost as much as his prosaic list of my bodily humors had shocked me. I could not help feeling a moment of satisfaction.

"*Per San Luca!*" he said at last. "Surely you do not—"

"Answer, please," the duke said.

Messer Girolamo sat back in his chair and looked at us both. "Very well," he said. "If you will permit me, Serenissima, I will consult my notes?"

"Of course."

He opened a drawer in his cabinet and took out a leather-bound notebook, much thumbed and scuffed. He laid it out flat on the surface of his cabinet, riffled through the pages, paused, turned over a single page or two, and stopped.

"I write my notes in cipher, of course," he said, although neither of us had asked him if that were so. "The morning you summoned me to Corpus Domini, Serenissimo, I found you, a priest, and several of the nuns gathered in one of the cells, and the body of the young duchess lying on a pallet, composed and with her eyes closed as if she had been sleeping. Her head was turned slightly to the right, one arm lay upon her breast, and the other lay straight at her side. She was dead already, and had indeed been dead for several hours, based on the coolness of her flesh and the degree of stiffening of her limbs. Publicly I supported the small fiction you described in your message to me, and I pronounced the duchess had died only moments before, after the priest gave her the holy unction."

That corresponded with what the duke had already told me. I asked, "What else did you notice, Messer Girolamo? What do you think caused her death?"

He put one finger on the page and ran it down over the written lines as he read. "There was a faint violet tinge to her lips and there were some red specks in the whites of her eyes, but no other outward sign. When I opened her body—"

"When you *what*?" The duke half-rose from his chair. Wine lurched from his goblet.

Messer Girolamo looked up, keeping his finger on the line. "She was the Duchess of Ferrara, Serenissimo," he said. "She had been ill from time to time, or so she claimed—that physician from Florence, Andrea Pasquali, was fool enough to encourage her every time he came to attend her. He returned, as you will recall, after her death, to satisfy Duke Cosimo with a final examination."

"He examined her. He did not open her body."

"Quite true. And he should have. It was out of the ordinary—a young girl found dead without explanation or any sign of distress. It was necessary to have a record, for history's sake. And in case there were ever inquiries."

Such as this one. He did not say it, of course, but the words hung in the air between us, unspoken.

I half-expected the duke to— Well, I am not sure what I half-expected the duke to do. Call his men-at-arms and have the physician arrested? Draw his own favorite damascened dagger and stab the man in the throat? As it was, the duke settled back into his chair and brushed delicately at a wine-spot on his mulberry-colored surcoat.

"Her death was out of the ordinary indeed," he said with perfect calmness. It was at that point I understood there was something unusual about the duke's relationship with this man. I doubt anyone else could have confessed such a thing and lived to tell the tale. "What did you find when you opened her body?"

Messer Girolamo looked down at his notes again. "She was with child—about three months gone," he said. "Messer Andrea missed it entirely."

"A bastard," the duke said.

"Of course. If it had been a legitimate heir, the young duchess would have been resting on silken sheets in her bedchamber at the Palazzo della Corte, and not confined to a monastery with some vague tale of disordered humors. It was female, by the way."

The duke nodded.

"Her heart and tripes were normal and healthy. There was no sign of poison's effects, and only a small amount of clear liquid in her stomach."

I looked at the duke. His face was expressionless. I looked back to Messer Girolamo and said, "Could you identify the liquid? Could it have been a potion of some kind?"

"I cannot say for certain, one way or the other," the physician said. "But whatever it was, she drank it almost immediately before she died, because there did not appear to have been any absorption."

"How then did she die?" I asked.

"I believe the young duchess was smothered, with something soft that left no mark upon her face."

"Smothered!" I cried.

"Smothered!" the duke said, at the same time.

"Yes. The violet tinge of her lips and the reddish specks in the whites of her eyes and under the skin around them were the only abnormalities of her body. I have seen those signs before. I believe she was smothered, sometime in the night."

"But that is impossible," I said. "She was alone in her cell, and it was locked. Could it have been an accident?"

"No. She could hardly have smothered herself, then rearranged the bedclothes and composed her limbs so neatly."

"So it was murder after all," the duke said. "And the holy nuns who are telling us the cell was locked are either mistaken or lying. Messer Girolamo, this is something you should have told me immediately."

The physician looked at the duke steadily. "I was under the impression, Serenissimo," he said in his inscrutable voice, "you were at the time already quite well aware of the circumstances of the young duchess's death."

At first the duke did not seem to react at all. Then I realized his fingers had tightened on the arms of his chair, and the folds of his surcoat had become disarranged, almost imperceptibly, by his Herculean effort to control himself. "I did not kill her," he said at last, stressing each individual word. "I concealed the time of her death, and I put away the flask I found beside her pallet, because I believed she had committed the sin of self-murder and I did not wish a Duchess of Ferrara to lie in unhallowed ground. But that is all. That is *all*."

Messer Girolamo's expression changed. I doubted he was often surprised, but this, now, was one of the rare occasions. "After all this time," he said slowly. "All this time, and at last I learn I have been wrong."

He said nothing more, but he did not have to. He had known the duke all his life; his father had served the duke's father. He believed him.

I think that was the moment when I truly began to believe him, too.

"Very well, then—who could have smothered her?" I asked. "She was alone in her cell, and even if the cell itself was not locked, the monastery is enclosed. No one is allowed inside but the nuns themselves."

"That is not entirely true," the duke said thoughtfully. "I myself have visited Mother Eleonora in her parlor at Corpus Domini, and my uncle Ippolito had an apartment there, before he settled at

Villa d'Este in Tivoli—such things are permitted for relatives and churchmen and patrons of the monastery, which proves exceptions are allowed."

"And there is the construction of the new cellarium," I said. "If that had already been begun at the time of—"

"It had," Messer Girolamo said. He ran his finger down his written page again, and stopped at a particular line. "I noticed the workmen and made note of them."

In my mind I went back to the day I had visited the Monastero del Corpus Domini. I had been led to Mother Eleonora's beautiful parlor, then to the infirmary, then to the choir of the church. I had seen no one but the nuns. No one—

"There are also tertiaries," I said. "I myself saw one of them in the choir of the church, the day I went to the Monastero del Corpus Domini to—to pray. She came in unhindered, and if she could do so, others could do so as well."

"Indeed," Messer Girolamo said. "Well, I have told you all I know, Serenissima. If you truly wish to find out what happened to the young duchess that night, I think you must ask your questions at Corpus Domini."

As we went out, he gave me a coffer; I heard the clink of glass inside. The suitable containers, I supposed. I shuddered at the thought of filling them all. If I was to be allowed trusted ladies with me for the examination itself, presumably I would be allowed the same trusted ladies to assist me with the collection of my humors.

Katharina, of course. And Sybille and Christine. I could not bear such intimacy with anyone but my beloved we-three.

That night I dreamed of Maria Granmammelli, the Florentine ambassador Bernardo Canigiani, and the mysterious black-clad tertiary I had glimpsed praying over Lucrezia de' Medici's grave. They were quarreling, the three of them, over a coffer full of suitable glass containers. Among them, deep at the bottom, was a beautiful, sinister little jeweled flask with silvery residue in its belly.

★　　★　　★

HE FANCIES HIMSELF *a scholar, Messer Girolamo does, and he writes everything down so five hundred years from now people will wonder at his brilliance. I'd wager he has notes in his library about Alfonso's childhood illnesses, and Luigi's French tastes, and the day and date Crezia lost her virginity to her precious Count Ercole Contrari. Soon he'll have notes about La Cavalla, too. When he said he'd have to examine her humors, I thought she'd faint away with the humiliation of it all.*

Although to be honest, I'd have hated to collect my blood and piss and spit, too.

Where was I in the tale of my death? They all agreed I was dead, and Alfonso put away my things. He then instructed the nuns to prepare my body to rest for a time before the altar of the church, until it was entombed. A few days later, after Messer Andrea the physician from Florence had come and gone, Messer Girolamo stole my body—stole it!—from the church, or at least bribed some workmen who were there to lay the foundation for the new cellarium to carry it away in a box that very night. I followed. I was still so newly immobila *I couldn't be out of sight of my poor flesh, cold and impenetrable as it was.*

Once he had it at his house, he gave the workmen money and wine and told them to wait. Then he stretched my flesh on a wooden trestle and unwound the shroud and graveclothes, and when it was naked, he looked at it for a long time. I'll wager I know what he was thinking, the pervertito*! He picked up the hands—the stiffness had long since passed off, and the arms were graceful and pliable again—and looked closely at the fingernails. Then he took out a thin knife and cut the body open, from throat to figa.*

It did not bleed. I expected it to bleed. It was as if I could feel ghosts of pain as he took out the organs, examined them, weighed them in his hands. Then he cut open my womb, and that was when I couldn't look anymore.

Later he washed his hands and made his notes, and then he had the workers return my poor stitched-together flesh to the monastery, wrapped again in its concealing graveclothes. The nuns never knew. Messer Andrea never knew. Alfonso never knew. I wonder if Messer Girolamo would ever have told him, if la Cavalla had not forced the issue with her investigations.

Blessed Baptist, I hope they keep it to themselves. I don't want my father to know the truth about me being with child. Even though I'm dead and safe from his anger, it frightens me to think what he might do—might have done, if he had known. There were those stories, after all, of how he stabbed my sister Maria when he caught her with a lover. Bearing a bastard is even worse than that.

Lies. People always tell lies about the great.

He loves me, his lost Sodona, lying at rest among the Este at the Monastero del Corpus Domini. He grieves for me. I'm sure he does.

I can't feel it, but—

I'm sure he does.

I grieve. I grieve for myself and for my daughter who was never born and who I'll never see, because she'll exist in limbo forever—please please please let her be in limbo—and I'll burn in hell.

Tomorrow they're going back to the monastery. I wonder what they'll learn there. If I were to give them a hint, I'd say: ask Sister Orsola about the key.

CHAPTER TWENTY-FOUR

The next day after dinner we went to the Monastero del Corpus Domini.

"Good day, *mio caro*," Mother Eleonora said to the duke, from the same chair in front of the window where she had been sitting when I saw her last. "I do not see you often enough. Good day to you as well, Madonna Barbara. I hope you are in better health than you were when last you visited us."

"Much better, thank you, Mother Abbess."

"Sit down. Sister Caterina will bring us wine. Have you come to make your devotions in the church? Or just as a kindness, to allay the ennui of a forgotten old woman?"

The duke smiled. "Don't be ridiculous, *mia zia*," he said. "You are no more forgotten than I am, and it would not surprise me if you know more of what goes on in the court than I do. No, we have not come to pray. We have come to speak to you of my first duchess."

Mother Eleonora's surprise was similar to Messer Girolamo's.

"God save us all! She is dead and gone, *mio caro*, and the best thing you can do is leave her in peace." She turned to me, her gaze for all the world like that of the golden-eyed lioness in the duke's menagerie. "Is it you, Madonna Barbara, who suggested this? You had a goodly number of questions when you were here last."

I smoothed my stiff brocaded skirts and looked steadily into her eyes. It was an effort. "It is a thing both the duke and I wish to speak of, Mother Abbess."

The same silent, fresh-faced novice poured our wine, placed a piled-up plate of sticky almond-sugar cakes on the table, and withdrew. "Very well then," Mother Eleonora said. "What is it about her you wish to know? We have been over this before, Alfonso."

"I would like you to tell the duchess exactly what happened that night and the next morning. Please call the infirmarian and her assistants to testify as well. I want nothing, no detail, to be left out or glossed over."

Mother Eleonora looked taken aback, and then I saw an expression I could not quite identify, a combination of arrogance, fear, and slyness. "Let me see," she said. "Sister Addolorata has been dead these two years at least. Sister Benedicta abandoned her vows and ran off with a dyer's apprentice."

"There is, of course, Sister Orsola," I said.

She smiled. She was Lucrezia Borgia's one living daughter, and I wondered if her smile was the same as her notorious mother's. Perhaps Madonna Lucrezia had smiled in just such a way, the corners of her mouth tucked in, calculating and secretive; her smile, it was whispered, had been the one weakness of Cesare Borgia, her brother. "Oh, yes, of course," Mother Eleonora said. "Sister Orsola."

"Call her," the duke said.

It was done, and before we finished our wine and cakes, the rawboned infirmarian I remembered came into the room. "*Deus vobiscum*," she said, bowing to Mother Eleonora. She paid no attention to the duke or to me.

"*Et cum spirito tuo*," Mother Eleonora replied, making a cursory sign of the cross in the air. "Come in, my daughter, and kneel beside me. The duke and duchess wish to question you about the death of Duchess Lucrezia de' Medici."

I do not believe it was my imagination that a warning passed from the abbess to the infirmarian in the tone of those words. Sister Orsola's expression went blank as an unpainted canvas as she knelt on Mother Eleonora's left.

"Yes, Mother Abbess," she said.

"I wish you to tell what you know of three things, Sister," the duke said. "First, my dealings with the duchess on the afternoon before her death. Second, what happened the night of her death. And third, what happened the morning afterward. You are to speak plainly and truthfully, and have no fear of reprisal from either the abbess or me."

Sister Orsola's eyes slewed from the duke to the abbess and back again, like a hare caught between two foxes. "Plainly and truthfully, is it?" she said. "You already know the first and the third, Serenissimo, since you were there, so maybe it's you who should be telling us. Or doesn't your fine new duchess believe your tales?"

The duke's eyes narrowed, and I wondered what he might have done to her if he had not already made his promise of no reprisals. In an even voice he said, "I wish for you to tell us what you yourself know, and at once."

A flicker of cunning passed over her face, and then it took on the blank-canvas expression again. "You came into the monastery at about an hour after nones the day before she died," she said. "I got the key to the duchess's cell from Mother Eleonora and gave it to you, and you unlocked the door and went in, and then I went on about my business."

"You could not have gone too far," I said, "or you would not have heard the shrieking you described to me. In fact, given the thickness of the walls, I cannot help but wonder if you did not keep your ear pressed hard to the door itself."

I was taking a risk to challenge her, I knew; what if she threw my ruby ring on the table and accused me of having bribed her? On the other hand, if she did that, she would have to give up the ring, and that I was fairly certain she would not do.

"Very well," she said. "I listened."

The duke sat like a statue, his face expressionless. Mother Eleonora took a deep draught from her cup of wine. After a moment I prompted, "And what did you hear?"

"*Il Serenissimo* there, he wanted her to tell him the name of the father of her brat. She swore she wasn't with child at all. He threatened her, told her he'd put her aside for her sins and shut her up in a convent for the rest of her days so he could marry again and get himself a proper heir. He could hardly swear she was still a virgin and the marriage hadn't been consummated, and no Este would ever claim consanguinity with the Medici, but making up a tale that she'd married unwillingly and always had a vocation for the church, that would've given him grounds for an annulment."

I looked at the duke. "Is this true?"

"Let her finish," he said coldly.

"Very well. Go ahead, Sister Orsola."

"She started screeching and screaming, threatening to do away with herself, swearing she'd had no lovers and wasn't with child. Said she couldn't stand being locked in, would rather die and go to hell. Proper wild, she sounded. Throwing things, too."

I thought of the broken pieces of majolica in the small coffer, the shattered mirror, and nodded. "What happened next?"

"*Il Serenissimo* came out with his face black as thunder, and I only just had time to jump back or he would have walked straight over me. He said Sister Benedicta and Sister Addolorata and I were to watch the duchess closely, night and day, and never leave her alone. Then he took himself off."

"After that, no one but you and the other sisters entered the cell until the morning?"

Again that strange shift of expression across her face, cunning followed by blankness. "No," she said. "No one else."

She was lying.

"What happened then?" I asked. "Did you stay with her?"

"Yes. No. Well, I stayed for a while, and then the bell for vespers rang."

"Who stayed with the duchess during your prayers?"

She looked down. "She wasn't left alone."

"That is not what I asked you. Who was with her?"

"Sister Addolorata was so sick with her rheumatics, she could hardly walk. Sister Benedicta was off somewhere, no one knew where. And the bell had rung. I had to go to vespers."

"Who was with her?"

The duke's voice was soft, but even so it chilled me to the bone. His eyes were fixed on the infirmarian and the monsters had leaped to the surface, teeth and claws at the ready.

"That friend of hers," Sister Orsola said sullenly. "Tommasina, she called herself. The *parruchiera*. She used to come sometimes, and she always had a trinket or two to give. What harm could she do? Better her with the duchess than one of us. By those last days, the duchess hated us all."

The duke frowned. His expression relaxed a little, and I could see him sorting back through his memories of his first wife's household, memories he had surely done his best to forget. "Tommasina," he said. "A hairdressing-woman. Yes, I remember the name. She was part of the duchess's original Florentine household, I think, and a troublemaker from the first. But she was sent home with the rest."

"You may have thought she was," Sister Orsola said, "but she made her way back into the city somehow. A small dark woman with a whispering sort of voice. Sometimes she brought the duchess cakes and sweetmeats, and they shared them with me so I wouldn't tell. I hadn't had cake since I entered here. I'm a baker's daughter,

I am, and I know cake, and what the whispering woman brought was good cake. I shared it with a duchess, I did. And that's not all I shared. I—"

She stopped suddenly.

I drew my breath to press her on what else exactly she had shared with Duchess Lucrezia, but Mother Eleonora forestalled me. It was as if she had suddenly awakened from the lull of the wine and realized something dangerous was happening.

"So for the sake of your gluttony," she said to Sister Orsola, "you allowed a secular person into the monastery, into the enclosure itself, without my permission. Go to your cell, Sister, and kneel on the bare stone floor and say one hundred Aves and one hundred Paters for your sins. I shall speak with you further this evening."

As if we ourselves are not secular persons, I thought. As if all the ladies of the court with whom you gossip are not secular persons.

Sister Orsola may have been thinking much the same thing, for she did not lower her eyes or make any move to obey. Why did I think she was actually pleased by the distraction? "The Serenissimo said I was to tell the truth," she said, "and I wouldn't be punished."

"You shall beg your bread in the refectory for a month for your insolence. Now go."

"A moment, *mia zia*." The duke's voice was pleasant but cool. I wondered if he was also curious about what else the infirmarian had shared with his young wife. "Sister Orsola is correct. I promised she would face no reprisal if she spoke frankly, and I must insist you honor my promise."

Mother Eleonora put down her wine-cup. She had an odd expression—angry, apprehensive, and at the same time weary. No, not weary, world-weary—as if she had suddenly seen one sin too many, or as if she were about to be caught in one lie too many, from which even her Este blood and her Borgia cunning could not save her.

"The results of this will be upon your head, then, Alfonso," she said. She filled her cup again, all the way to the brim. "You may continue, Sister."

"She's still here," Sister Orsola said. "Tommasina. She's a tertiary now, not a vowed sister, but one who lives nearby and—"

"The tertiary!" I burst out. "But I have seen her! When I was here before, praying in the choir, she came in and prayed at Duchess Lucrezia's tomb."

"And she visited the duchess the night of her death, after I left the monastery?" the duke demanded. I could see this was new to him; for the first time there was a spark of interest in his eyes.

"Yes," Sister Orsola said. "She was in the duchess's cell for an hour, at least, because she was there when I left for vespers, and still there when I came back. Whatever they were doing in there, they were very quiet together. Every so often they'd laugh. Then she came out and wished me good night and went away, and I didn't see her again, not for months. I hardly knew her when I saw her again, looking like an old woman and wearing a tertiary's black dress."

"I want that woman detained, the next time she comes to the monastery," the duke said to Mother Eleonora. "She may be the key to this entire matter. Very well, Sister. So this Tommasina spent at least an hour with the duchess that night. Was the duchess alive when she left?"

"Oh, yes, alive and excited. Unnatural excited. She told me all her troubles were over, and she would soon be free."

The duke and I looked at each other. The young duchess's statements could be taken to mean she meant to end her life with a flask of poison already in her possession. They could also mean the woman Tommasina had brought her the abortifacient potion at last.

"Then what did you do?" I asked.

"I locked the door and went to bed," Sister Orsola said with a touch of her old truculence. "The next morning Sister Addolorata called me to come look at her, and I saw she was dead, and that was that."

"You saw nothing out of the ordinary?"

"Just you claiming she wasn't dead when she was, tricking the priest into giving her the holy unction, and then your pet physician rushing in to pronounce her to be dead again."

The duke lifted his eyebrows slightly; it was clear he was regretting his promise to Sister Orsola that she might speak as she wished. "You may speak the truth without fear, Sister, but you had best keep a civil tongue in your head when you do," he said in a deceptively mild tone. "What you have said is essentially correct. *Mia zia?* Have you anything to add?"

Mother Eleonora blinked and put down her cup. "No," she said. "But I still cannot understand how Sister Orsola was letting the *parruchiera* in and out. I know she did not ask me for the key that night, not until after vespers."

"Yes, I did, Mother Abbess. You have just forgotten."

"I am sure you did not."

Obviously Sister Orsola could have slipped into Mother Eleonora's chamber any night, taken the key, and probably danced a *Gratiosa* stark naked on the table without the abbess being aware of it in her wine-sodden sleep. The duke seemed to be thinking the same thing.

"That is enough for now," he said. "*Mia zia*, remember I wish you to detain the tertiary the next time she comes to the monastery. Do not frighten her. Just hold her, and send for me at once."

The abbess's tawny eyes had become dulled with wine. What had it been like for her, I wondered, being shut up in the monastery like a tame kitchen-cat when she clearly had a lioness's eyes and a lioness's heart? I wondered if she'd ever actually had a vocation for the monastic life, or if she'd simply been sent to Corpus Domini at the order of her mother and father. "It shall be done, *mio caro*," she said. "May God go with you. And with you as well, of course, Madonna Barbara."

With that we made our farewells. I wondered if Mother Eleonora knew more about the mysterious Tommasina than she had given us to believe, and if she—or for that matter, Sister Orsola—could be trusted not to warn the tertiary away from the monastery. I knew Sister Orsola had been lying about some of the things she had told us, but which?

A fine mist of rain greeted us upon our short ride back to the Palazzo della Corte, and the duke's mood seemed as chill as the weather.

"I remember the hairdresser more clearly now," he said. "At least I remember her father. He is an alchemist, a favorite of Cosimo de' Medici, and it was for his sake this Tommasina received her place in Duchess Lucrezia's household."

We clopped on for a moment in the rain.

"An alchemist," I said thoughtfully. "Potions such as the one the duchess wanted are generally made by women, and in secret, for fear of the church's wrath. But if he loved his daughter, and she begged him—he could have done it, and his daughter could have given it to the duchess."

Another period of silence.

"I do not trust the infirmarian not to warn the tertiary away," the duke said. "And I do not believe everything she says. As for my aunt, she is afraid. She lives a life of comfort and idle gossip, and I think she fears she will be forced to give it up if anything untoward is proved against one of her nuns. Or even against a tertiary attached to her community."

"I agree, my lord, upon both points."

"I will set guards to watch the monastery, then, and arrest the tertiary when she appears."

"An excellent plan."

The rain worsened, and we left off further attempts at conversation. It was only after we had arrived at the Palazzo that I remembered—my surprise at learning the identity of the tertiary had led me to forget my curiosity about just what, other than cake, Sister Orsola had shared with Lucrezia de' Medici.

THEY NEVER MADE *Sister Orsola tell them about the key. That's one thing she won't confess willingly, because if she did, she'd have worse penances than Aves and Paters, even a thousand of them. She'd be stripped of her habit and veil and whipped and put out in the street in her shift, and then where'd she be? No, she's going to keep very quiet about the key.*

Mother Eleonora would faint dead away if she knew. She didn't have any idea what really went on in the monastery right under her aristocratic Este nose. Sister Benedicta, for example. She used to bring her lover into the enclosure, the dyer's apprentice she eventually ran away with, and oh, the squealing and gasping! It made me wild for a man, and if I could've seduced her lover away from her, I'd've done it in an instant.

Time, that's another thing Mother Eleonora lost track of. She'd doze off, well-pickled with wine, and forgot if it was night or morning. Say she gave Sister Orsola the key to my cell one evening, or the key to the old cellarium, or the key to the enclosure itself. She'd find the key back on her table the next morning, and tell herself it'd been returned the night before, but who knew for sure? And think of all the things that can be done with a key, over the course of a whole night.

That's how Tommasina got in to see me—she had a key of her own, copied from Mother Eleonora's. God, if you can hear anything I say, please don't let Alfonso and la Cavalla find Tommasina! She doesn't know who killed me. She wasn't even there. If they find her and question her, though, she'll probably be silenced for good when they've wrung her dry.

It's true I threw everything in the room at Alfonso when he told me he planned to set me aside and force me to take vows. I was so angry and so miserable I hardly knew what I was doing. Every time something shattered, it felt as if my own heart was shattering, with love and hate and misery and fury.

After I was dead, Alfonso gathered up the pieces and put them in that coffer, with my untouched white cloths and my giocattoli and the rock-crystal flask, whole and perfect. I wonder if la Cavalla will be clever enough to put those bits of information together and deduce I didn't have the flask yet when Alfonso and I quarreled. It's proof, right before her long imperial nose, that Tommasina brought me the flask.

Mother Eleonora's afraid, I can tell. If she finds Tommasina first, I think Tommasina will be given gold and sent far away from Ferrara. If Tommasina tells what she knows, things would have to be changed in the monastery, and that is the last thing Mother Eleonora wants.

Yes, I think she'll help Tommasina escape. Or will she just have her killed?

Even I can't believe that. She may be a Borgia whore's daughter but she's a holy nun, an abbess. She'd never commit the sin of murder. Never. Would she?

Please, please. Please let her find Tommasina first.

CHAPTER TWENTY-FIVE

$\mathcal{F}$or the rest of that day and the next I was occupied with preparations for the last week of Carnival. In Ferrara Carnival actually began on Saint Stephen's Day, the day after Christmas, but the greatest of the pageants and revels were reserved for Shrovetide, the final week before Lent. I dealt with silkmakers and jewelers, dressmakers and perfumers, all clamoring to serve the duke's new duchess. I was expected to dazzle all eyes with my costumes, particularly the white-and-silver fantasy I would wear for the nighttime revels on Shrove Thursday, the Berlingaccio.

The third day with no news from Corpus Domini dawned again cold and gray with sleet mixed with the Ferrarese fogs. I had two fires burning in my presence chamber. A silk merchant had just unrolled a magnificent bolt of silver tissue, so fine it was half-transparent, when Domenica scratched at the door and came in.

"Messer Giovanni Pigna is without, Serenissima," she said. "He says the duke requires you at once in his *studiolo*."

Had they arrested the tertiary at last?

"You must excuse me, Messer Salvestro," I said. "Apply to Donna Katharina, if you please, to arrange another audience, and do not show that silver tissue to any other lady in the court. Domenica, Christine, attend me, please."

Outside my door people clustered—talking, singing, making assignations, hoping for audiences and favors. Outside the duke's apartments it was the same. I saw the duke's sister Nora sitting in a window-bay with the poet Tasso leaning close to her, his dark curls falling over his forehead. Everything about his pose made it clear he was attending her for duty's sake, nothing more; on the other hand, Nora looked well and happy for the first time since I had arrived in Ferrara, and when I caught her eye she had the grace to look guilty. A few steps farther on, Messer Bernardo Canigiani was deep in conversation with the Venetian ambassador. He bowed with mocking precision as I passed by. I ignored him.

When I arrived at the duke's apartments, two of his gentlemen opened the doors for me with clockwork precision. I nodded to Domenica and Christine to remain in the anteroom, and I went into the *studiolo* with Messer Giovanni close behind me. The first thing I saw was a pair of—well, I did not know what to call them. They were not the well-trained, smartly turned-out men-at-arms I was accustomed to; they were hulking fellows in frieze and leather with a miasma of the dungeons about them. The taller one had a coil of coarse rope looped around his shoulder. In the shifting light of the candle-branches, the two figures might have risen straight from Messer Dante's inferno.

"Ah, there you are, Madonna," the duke said. His courtesy was unfailingly exquisite in the presence of others, but at the same time—what? Threatening? There was always that faint mocking indentation at one corner of his mouth, as if to say *I play the part of the considerate husband because it amuses me to do so, for the moment at least.* "Be seated, if you please." Then to his secretary, "Messer Giovanni, you will take down our questions and the prisoner's answers."

The tertiary stood in the center of the room, her hands clasped before her, looking straight ahead at nothing. She was just as I remembered her, a small, thin woman in a black gown and veil. Her head-covering had been pushed back and her dark hair was disarranged, but other than that, she did not appear to have been mistreated. She was younger than I had expected her to be. Now that I could see her face clearly—what was it that was so fleetingly familiar about her?

I nodded to her briefly and sat. The secretary spread out a piece of paper on the duke's gleaming rosewood-and-ebony writing-table, dipped his pen in a bottle of ink, and began to write. The scratching sound of the quill against the paper seemed unnaturally loud. Having satisfied himself we were both under his command, the duke turned his attention to his prisoner.

"You, woman. You were Serenissima Lucrezia's *parruchiera*, is that not so? What is your name?"

"Tommasina Vasari," the tertiary said. Her voice and expression were sullen. "And I was more than her *parruchiera*. I was her *amica*, her special friend."

"What made you her special friend?"

"I wrote her letters. I brought letters to her and read them for her. Private letters."

Letters from her lovers, I thought.

"Very well." The duke's voice had that dangerous gentle quality. He had deduced the same thing: this woman had secretly helped his young wife betray him. "You were first arrested on the day the duchess was taken to Corpus Domini. In the courtyard outside the kitchen gardens, is that not so? Hiding among the fruit trees covered in mud like a scullery-slut who had been digging onions."

The tertiary flushed up to her hairline. "I was not hiding."

"You were taken back to the duchess's apartments," the duke went on, as if she had not spoken, "and confined there with the rest

of her women. A few days later you were expelled from the city.
Now we find you returned in secret, ingratiated yourself at the
Monastero del Corpus Domini, and were in fact present there the
very night the young duchess died."

"I was not there that night."

"You were seen. Do you wish to contend the holy sisters are
lying?"

Mona Tommasina's eyes, like the eyes of a trapped animal,
grew huge and dark. I could see the bones of her knuckles through
the skin of her clasped hands.

"Very well, I was there. I wished to comfort Sodona, that's all."

The duke seemed to pay no attention to the pet name, although
this woman had no right to speak in such a familiar fashion of Lucrezia de' Medici, a princess of Florence, a duchess of Ferrara. He said
only, "And what did Serenissima Lucrezia say to you that night?"

"She was crying. Throwing things, breaking things. She said
you meant to force her into a convent for whoring and make her
sign papers to have your marriage annulled."

"You brought her a flask," I said. "She had spent her anger, and
everything she could break was broken. It was only then you gave
it to her."

"What is it to you—" She broke off, her eyes slanting to the
duke, full of fury and spite and fear. In a more moderate voice she
said, "Very well, yes, I gave her a flask."

"What was in it?"

"A sleeping potion."

The duke looked at her. She tried to meet his gaze, but after
a breath her eyes flickered away. She looked down at the floor and
said, "It was a woman's potion. She wanted to be rid of her bastard.
How she laughed to think she would eventually prove you wrong
about her, however right you might have been in truth."

Messer Giovanni turned over his paper and began a fresh sheet.
There was not the slightest hesitation in his note-taking.

"And so it was you who killed her," the duke said. His voice was silky and vicious. "You mixed the potion incorrectly, and by your carelessness you poisoned her—your precious Sodona."

I sat very still. Only a few days before, Messer Girolamo had assured us the young duchess had been smothered, not poisoned. Why was the duke accusing Tommasina Vasari of poisoning her mistress and friend, when he knew poison was not the cause of the young duchess's death?

"I did not mix it wrongly!" the woman cried. "May San Giacomo be my witness, the potion was already mixed and sealed when I received it from—"

She stopped suddenly.

She had said too much. And that, of course, had been the duke's intention.

"From?" he prompted with deceptive gentleness.

She had turned white as chalk. "From an old woman in the marketplace." Her voice shook. "Just an old woman, one of a hundred. I never knew her name."

The duke looked at her, his eyes black with monsters. Then he rose and stepped forward and struck her, a single cracking blow across the mouth that jolted her head around and knocked her off her feet. She sprawled to the tessellated marble floor like a disjointed poppet.

I stared at her. I stared at him. I tried to breathe and found I could not. The sudden eruption of violence in the exquisitely proportioned and furnished little room was so discordant I could not comprehend it. The duke looked at his hands for a moment; I could see a smudge, blood or spittle or both, on the back of his right glove. Quite calmly he removed both gloves—soft brown leather, embroidered with gold thread and citrines and pearls and probably worth a year's pay to either one of the guards—and tossed them fastidiously to the floor. Then he seated himself again.

"From?" he repeated.

There was blood on the woman's mouth, and her eyes glittered with hatred. She pushed herself up to her hands and knees. "An old woman," she said again. "In the marketplace."

"That is a lie, Mona Tommasina," I said. God only knows where I found the courage to intervene, but I could not bear to see him strike her again. The duke said nothing to silence me, so I took a breath and went on in my most reasonable voice.

"The flask that contained the potion was beautiful and extremely valuable. No old woman from the marketplace ever sold a potion in such a flask. You yourself could not possibly have owned such a thing. Tell us where you got it and who prepared the potion for you, and save yourself further suffering."

She would not look up at me. "I stole it," she said.

"From whom?"

"One of the ladies I attended. I don't remember which one."

Very well, I thought. Stubborn fool. Let us try another approach.

"How did you gain entry to the monastery? It is an enclosed house."

"A door was left unlocked."

"It will do you no good to lie," I said. "Mona Tommasina, I beg you, answer the questions honestly and completely, and I will speak for you. I will—"

"*Asburgo*," she hissed at me. "*Austriaca.*"

To my horror she spat at me.

I jerked back. At the periphery of my vision I saw the duke half-rise from his chair. Time stopped. Then slowly the duke seated himself again and said without expression, "Bind her. Tell one of the duchess's women to fetch water."

I started to breathe again. "It is nothing. It is no matter," I said, although I could feel my skin crawling with repulsion at the thought of the woman's spittle on my skirt. Holy Virgin. What would he do now?

The guard with the rope bound Mona Tommasina's hands before her, wrist to wrist, palm to palm, and jerked her to her knees with a few more twists of the rope about her neck. Christine came in, flushed and frightened-looking, with a vessel of water and some cloths; she knelt before me to clean the hem of my dress. I stood like a child who had dirtied her clothes. Christine finished her task, avoiding my eyes, and went out of the room.

"Now," the duke said. "The duchess has tried reason, and you have rejected it. Madonna, you will sit, if you please."

I sat. Mona Tommasina said nothing.

The duke looked to one of the guards. That was all it was, just a look—not a gesture, not a word. The man understood. He reached inside his leather jerkin and produced a mechanism consisting of two oblong steel plates about an inch wide and six or eight inches long, held together by sliding bolts at either end and a screw in the center. The end of the screw was forged into two delicately worked loops like the wings of a butterfly. The second guard dragged Mona Tommasina tautly upright upon her knees, half-choking her with the loops of rope around her neck; the first man forced her thumbs into the openings formed by shallow depressions in the top and bottom plates.

"Do you know what this device is, *parruchiera*?" the duke asked. He might have been asking her if she knew what a comb was, or a curling-rod. I shivered, although there had been no change in the temperature of the room.

"I don't remember where I got the flask," the woman whispered. "I bought the potion in the marketplace. I went into the monastery through a door that had been left unlocked."

The duke nodded to the guard.

The man turned the screw, once, twice, three times. I saw the two plates of the device move closer together around the first joints of her thumbs. Her thumbnails darkened. Her face twisted with pain. Without the slightest sign of emotion the guard turned the screw again. She made an eerie whining sound and writhed against the rope, her eyes squeezed shut, her teeth bared.

"Where did you get the flask and the potion? How did you enter the monastery?"

She had started to shudder and sob. I tried to imagine what it would be like, crushing pain and no escape, no palliation, just pain and more pain and more pain and a rope around my neck and utter helplessness. My own throat felt swollen with tears of fright and sympathy and horror.

"A key!" she cried suddenly. "I had a key! Gesù, Gesù, stop, stop!"

The duke nodded to the guard, and he loosened the screw two turns. Mona Tommasina knelt there whimpering and coughing, half-hanging against the rope around her neck.

"Very well. Where did you get it?"

"From Sister Orsola. I gave her jewelry, earrings with opals and carnelians, a bracelet—I don't remember it all. I gave her wine and fruit and cakes. She was greedy for it all."

"Jewelry, to a Clarissa? What use did she have for jewelry?"

"I don't know. She wanted it—I don't know why. There was a story she had a lover, a man from about the court."

I leaned forward a little, remembering how readily Sister Orsola had snatched up the ruby ring I had offered her. "Who was this lover?"

"I don't know. It was only a story. I don't know who it was or if it was true at all."

I remembered thinking how easy it would have been for Sister Orsola to take the abbess's keys from her luxurious chamber. Clearly she had done so, and since she had given a copy of the enclosure key to Tommasina Vasari, she could just as easily have given another copy to a lover.

"Very well," I said aloud. "At least we now know where you got the key. Let us return to the potion you gave the young duchess. Where did you get it?"

"It wasn't the potion that killed her!" She twisted against the rope. "The potion was good—it was good! I would have drunk it myself—my father is the Duke of Florence's favorite alchemist and—"

She stopped. She sucked in a shuddering breath. Her eyes were distended like the eyes of a terrified mare.

So another question was answered. The potion had come from her father in Florence.

"It wasn't the potion . . . it was her, the infirmarian, Sister Orsola . . . I saw her, I saw her put a pillow over Sodona's face and hold her down—I saw it, I swear!"

I was taken aback. Even the duke seemed surprised. Messer Giovanni's scratching paused for a moment, then began again.

"I came back to the monastery that night, much later—I wanted to make sure the potion had worked and Sodona was safe." There were tears and sweat streaking the *parruchiera*'s face. "I saw her, all in her habit and cowl, bending over Sodona's bed and pressing the pillow against her face. Why do you think I attached myself to the monastery as a tertiary? I was waiting my chance, and one day I would have had my revenge."

She broke off, coughing and shuddering. Messer Giovanni's quill scratched.

"Why did you not come forward at the time," I said, "and tell what you saw?"

"Because . . . because I was afraid . . . I would be arrested, blamed . . . no one would believe me. My father would be blamed for making the potion."

The duke sat back in his chair and looked at me. His calm self-possession both horrified me and steadied me. "What say you, Madonna?" he asked me. "Is she telling the truth?"

"I am not sure," I said. "She knows the young duchess was smothered, which is a point in her favor. On the other hand, I think she would say anything now, out of pain and fear. What reason would Sister Orsola have to kill the young duchess?"

"It appears Sister Orsola was less than strict in the practice of her vows. Perhaps the young duchess knew something about it all, or had seen something the good sister did not wish anyone else to see. Perhaps the duchess also had heard this tale of a lover connected to the court."

"Perhaps," I said thoughtfully. "But consider. Mona Tommasina admits slipping back into the monastery that night. Perhaps she herself smothered the duchess, from some reason she has not yet confessed, and is lying to save herself."

Tommasina Vasari lifted her head. The pure hatred in her eyes made me start back in fright.

"To save myself?" she hissed at me. "Do you think I don't know I'm already condemned? It was Sister Orsola who murdered my Sodona, and I only wish I'd found my chance to kill her in turn. You'd be dead, too, dead, if I'd had only one more moment of time."

"I?" I stared at her. I had dizzy, half-formed thoughts of the candied angelica and the slashed saddle-girth. "What do you mean?"

She bared her teeth at me, in what she might have meant to be a smile. Then in a husky, conspiratorial voice she whispered, *"He murdered his first duchess with his own hands, they say. She was so young, so beautiful."*

At first it did not make sense. Then in a rush I remembered the morning of my wedding day, so vividly I could smell the scent of the Po di Volano and taste the red wine and sugar and cream in the posset I had drunk, feel the weight of the silver-mounted looking-glass in my hands. The silken pavilion on the ducal barge. The snap of the wind in the imperial standard. My Austrian ladies. Strange Ferrarese ladies. Dressing me. Arranging my hair.

"You," I said. "It was you. That is why there has always been something familiar about you. On the morning of my wedding, you braided my hair with pearls."

"It was so easy." The words spilled out, hoarse, scornful, taunting. "A bribe here, a bribe there, money I had been saving one *giorgino*, one *diamante* at a time, and suddenly it was I who was to dress the hair of the new duchess and not the woman Principessa Crezia had chosen. It should have been simplicity itself—a hollow bodkin filled with venom, an accidental scratch. But I wanted you to be afraid. I wanted to be sure you knew what was to come. I waited a moment too long and lost my chance."

"Holy Virgin," I said. My voice shook so I could hardly control it. I crossed myself, and then crossed myself again. I felt the compulsion to do something over and over sink its claws into me, and I clasped my hands together hard to forestall it. "You meant to poison me that morning."

I saw her. I saw the very moment. *The court of Ferrara is like a love-apple, beautiful and rosy-red and alluring to the senses, but poisonous, so poisonous*, she had said. The braiding-bodkin had gleamed gold in her hand.

"But why? In God's name, why?"

"For her sake. Because I loved her. Because I hate him. Who is he to parade himself as the brother-in-law to the emperor, over my Sodona's grave? I will hate him until I die."

Scratch, scratch, scratch went Messer Giovanni's quill. The sound seemed to come from very far away.

She looked up at the duke again. One of the guards tightened the loops of rope around her neck, to warn her. As if in a dream I turned and looked at the duke as well, and what I saw in his face stopped my breath.

"You will die soon enough," he said to her. "So you confess you have attempted to assassinate the duchess at least once." Each word scorched the air in the elegant little room. He seemed to have forgotten the monastery keys and the potion in its jeweled flask, forgotten her accusation against Sister Orsola. "Perhaps you know something of a dish of candied angelica as well? Or a saddle-girth that was cut?"

She stared at him, her lips pressed together in defiance.

The duke nodded once. The guard turned the screw again, as casually as if he were twisting a cork into a bottle of cheap wine. I heard a cracking sound.

Tommasina Vasari shrieked and bucked against the noose of rope. Her thumbnails looked as if they would burst from the blood underneath them. I could feel myself shrinking back in my chair, huddling myself around myself, sick and speechless.

The duke waited until her screams had subsided to hoarse gasps. Then he said, "I ask you again. Did you cut the girth on the duchess's saddle, a fortnight or so ago when the court was hunting at Belfiore? Or do you know anything of anyone who might have done so?"

"No, no, no," she whispered. The thumbscrew quivered and swung from her poor broken thumbs. "No, I cut nothing. I know nothing. I am dying. A priest, I beg you."

"You are far from dying as yet." The duke gestured to the guards. "Take her to the *prigioni* under the Lions' Tower. Let her think upon her many sins, and perhaps she will have more to tell us in the morning."

The two men dragged Tommasina Vasari to her feet and removed the thumbscrew from her thumbs. I could not look at what the little machine had done. At what my own questions, my own selfish investigations, had done. I felt dizzy and sick.

"Madonna?" the duke said. The guards and the prisoner and the screams and the scratching quill seemed to have ceased to exist to him. "Come, let us collect our mantles and your little hounds and walk out on the terraces. The cold air will do us good, and we will speak of this further in the morning."

I rose unsteadily. To myself I said, *She hates you, she tried to kill you, she would try again if it were in her power,* but it did not help. I prayed I would not disgrace myself in front of them all by vomiting.

Messer Giovanni opened the door for us. The duke stood aside courteously for me to pass through first. I wanted to run, run, run. I took a step.

From behind us, Tommasina Vasari whispered, "It was a lie. I never saw the infirmarian."

I stopped. The duke stopped. No one in the room moved.

Her voice was almost gone with screaming, but there was a ghastly trace of a laugh in it. She said, "It was your fine new husband I saw, Habsburg bitch. The duke himself, pressing the pillow down over her face."

OH, TOMMASINA. OH, my poor friend.

Why don't I feel anger? Hate? Why do I feel only terrible sadness?

She shouldn't have told them she tried to kill la Cavalla. Alfonso will never forgive her now, or let her go free. La Cavalla is his possession and an imperial archduchess, and for a parruchiera to try to kill her—that's something he'll take a quick and vicious revenge for.

I think she realized that in the end. That's why she said what she said. To poison la Cavalla's mind and have that revenge, at least.

It wasn't Alfonso who smothered me, of course. Alfonso knows it's not true, because he knows he wasn't there that night. But la Cavalla doesn't know. And here she was just beginning to trust him and feel secure with him. Tommasina's no fool, and no matter what they do to her now, she's had her vengeance.

No, it wasn't Alfonso.

It wasn't Sister Orsola, either.

They're dragging Tommasina down to the dungeons under the Lions' Tower. I'm trying to stay close to her—maybe she'll sense me, maybe it'll comfort her. Her poor hands are swollen and turning black. She'll be crippled forever. Although I suppose it doesn't matter. She won't live long.

All for my sake. I never knew, I swear, I never knew it would come to this.

She was telling the truth, I think, about coming back to the monastery that night. It would've been like her, to want to make sure all was well with me. Where was she hiding? What did she really see? It couldn't have been Sister Orsola, but—

Oh.

I think I understand.

She did tell them what she saw. But it was also a lie. Let la Cavalla work it out if she can.

I wish I could help her. I wish I could hold her, I wish I could bribe the guards to arrange her escape. I wish I could cry. I wish I could scream. I wish I could feel.

Hate, yes—hate I can feel. I hate myself. I hate what I am. I hate seeing the living going on with their lives, hurting each other, loving each other, deceiving each other, while I'm nothing but a wisp of half-darkness, a flicker of half-light. Were my sins so great? Were Tommasina's sins so great?

They'll kill her. She'll disappear forever into the quicklime under the Lions' Tower. My Tommasina—she's as much my sister as Isabella was. More, really, because she stayed with me, while Isabella went off to be the Duchess of Bracciano and forgot me.

When Tommasina is dead, who will be left to pray for me?

CHAPTER TWENTY-SIX

The first thing the duke did was send a messenger to the monastery, asking Mother Eleonora to confine Sister Orsola until she could be questioned further. Then we walked in the rooftop gardens for a time in silence. Little by little my sickness and shivering passed away.

The duke said nothing to address Tommasina Vasari's accusation. It was a lie, of course, a lie calculated to strike back at him—at both of us—in the only way left to her. I knew it. We could have agreed upon it in a sentence or two and put it behind us. But for him, to speak of it would be to give it credence, and to give it credence would be beneath him. So it was left to me.

I was numb, so if he was angry it did not matter.

"It was a lie, of course," I said at last.

He said nothing.

"It was a lie," I repeated. "She wished to strike back at you, at both of us. Let us agree to that, my lord, and be done with it, so we might speak of the other things she said."

He stopped and looked carefully at a fig tree, espaliered against the wall where it was protected from the worst of the winter winds. One branch apparently did not meet his standard of perfection, because he drew the damascened dagger and cut it off.

"There is no need to dignify such an accusation with words," he said. "But if you are so trifling as to need the words—well, you have spoken them."

He dropped the branch on the ground and walked on, the dagger still glinting in his hand.

Perhaps I was not as numb as I had thought, because the word *trifling* stung. I gestured to my ladies and the little cluster of courtiers to step back, made my way to the corner of the terrace, and deliberately stepped between him and the wall so I could stand face-to-face with him.

"Yes, I need the words." It was the first time I had spoken to him with anything but courtesy or fear or both, and with all the distress I felt there was a rush of satisfaction, too. "And I do not believe it is trifling to need them. You may consider yourself above suspicion, my lord, in your Este arrogance, but others do not."

The monsters leaped to the surface of his eyes, black as candlesoot, tooth and claw a-glitter. "How dare you," he said very softly.

He still held the dagger. I thought of Tommasina Vasari on the morning of my wedding, holding the pointed braiding-bodkin.

"I dare because I am tired of being afraid to dare." I grasped two handfuls of my brocaded skirt-fabric in my fists and held them tightly to keep my fingers still. "Your first duchess may have been a pawnbroker's daughter, my lord, but I am an archduchess of Austria, and whatever mistakes I have made since I came to Ferrara, I am your wife and your equal in blood, and I will not be spoken to as if I were a simple-witted child. Half Europe believes you murdered Lucrezia de' Medici, whether you did or not—will you break my thumbs, too, for saying it?"

We stared at each other. I could hardly believe what I had just said. Where had it come from? What monsters of my own had Tommasina Vasari's screams unleashed?

"Furthermore," I said. I was shaking again. I did not know what I was going to say and did not care. "Furthermore—"

"Stop," he said. "Stop now, Madonna, before you say something unforgivable."

I sucked in my breath and pressed my lips together. For a long moment neither one of us said anything.

When I had my voice under control again, I said, "I will ask your pardon for one thing only, and that is what I said last. I know you applied the worst of the torture only after she confessed her attempt on my own life. I know such things are done, but—I have never seen it before, seen it with my own eyes, heard the screams and the breaking of bones with my own ears. Whatever her crimes, she is a woman, and helpless."

He glanced at the little knot of courtiers, desperately effacing themselves in the opposite corner of the garden. He looked at the dagger in his hand as if he had never seen it before, and slowly he slid it back into its jeweled sheath. Then without a word he took hold of my hands and unclenched my fists, one finger at a time, freeing the brocaded silk I had clutched and crumpled. His touch was perfectly gentle, in eerie contrast to the violent words that had just passed between us. I was frozen with shock at my own outburst and shame that he had once again noticed my inability to control my hands when I was distressed.

When he had my hands free, he brought his own fist up under my left hand and began to walk again, giving me little choice but to walk with him. I could not see his eyes, and I wondered how much of his restraint was due to understanding of my distress, and how much was the result of witnesses being present.

"You brought this business about yourself, Madonna, with your questions and pryings, and my original intent was to show you what you had done. The matter of her scheme against you on the day of our marriage—that was as much a shock to me as it was to you, and I will not ask your pardon for applying the question after that."

"I understand," I said. It seemed as if the world had reversed itself, because now it was I who did not wish to talk about the matter further. I felt disoriented and dizzy.

"And for every jot of my—Este arrogance—you yourself have a corresponding share of Habsburg pride."

"I cannot deny that."

He was right, of course, that I had brought it all about. If I had bowed my head in true humility before the laughter and whispers of the court, if I had never sought revenge and vindication by asking questions about the past, none of it would have happened. Paolina Tassoni would not be moldering in her untimely tomb. Tommasina Vasari would not be in the dungeons under the Lions' Tower, tortured and condemned.

"It must end, my lord," I said. "It all must end, as quickly as possible."

"I agree. And I think it will. I believe the infirmarian has the answers we seek, about my first duchess's death. Then all that is left is to find the—the missing book you mentioned, so it cannot be used against me."

That struck a spark of interest in me, despite myself. "What is it, my lord, about the book? Why is it dangerous?"

"Perhaps when we find it, I will tell you."

I said nothing more. We completed our circuit of the terrace and passed back inside the Castello, with our little clutch of courtiers following us at a wary distance.

"Go to your apartments, Madonna," the duke said. "Rest and compose yourself and have your dinner served to you privately. I have affairs of government to attend to, but tomorrow we will pursue the *parruchiera*'s accusations further."

TOMMASINA VASARI FLOATED in the air before me, her black skirts rippling in an invisible wind. She had no feet. She clutched my hand, and I could feel the broken bones in her thumbs like sharp sticks. "He murdered his first duchess with his own hands, they say," she whispered. "In the kitchen garden. Come see. Come see."

I followed her. I could not fly as high as she did because my arms were full of blossoming cherry branches and my skirts were weighed down with mud.

"Why would I be hiding when my Sodona had been taken away?" she breathed in my ear. It was as if she were screaming, but screaming so softly I could barely hear. "Covered with dirt, he said. Like a scullery-slut digging onions, he said. Fool. I was not hiding myself, but I was hiding something—"

I started awake. I was lying in my bed with the puppies pressed close, one on either side. At first I thought it was morning; but the sun in the gray winter sky outside my window was past its zenith to the west. Midafternoon, then. And earlier in the day—Holy Virgin, how could I forget, even for an instant? The questioning of Tommasina Vasari. She had given us no answers, not in so many words, at least; but the pieces had been there, and in my exhausted sleep I had put them together like one of Lucrezia de' Medici's puzzle-toys.

"She was hiding something," I said aloud. "The kitchen garden, in the Castello. The cherry tree. Everywhere I've looked, I've found cherry blossoms and cherries. That is Lucrezia de' Medici's other hiding place."

I called for Katharina and Domenica and asked them to dress me again, quickly, and to bring me my warmest hood and mantle. "I wish to go outside, into the kitchen garden of the Castello," I said. "No, I wish to go alone. Not even the puppies."

They thought I was mad. Perhaps they were right.

"Bring me a knife. No, Katrine, I wish to go alone. Find someone to show me the way to the kitchen garden."

I could not fly, as I had done in my dream. I walked, perfectly prosaically, following the servant who had been called to guide me. We went through the covered way to the Castello and around to the back where the kitchens and gardens lay. The cooks stared at me, amazed. The servant opened the gate to the kitchen garden and bowed to me. I thanked him, gave him a *quattrino*, and sent him away.

It was too early in the year for the cherry tree to be in bloom, but when I looked closely I could see new buds on the branches, shiny reddish-brown shells like minuscule chestnuts. I folded my skirts into neat pads under my knees and knelt down in the mud. The winter rains had softened the ground; Ferrara was just far enough south of Innsbruck that the ground did not freeze so hard, and the kitchen garden was protected by the Castello's walls. The knife sank in easily enough. Carefully and patiently I dug around the roots of the tree. The sun was slipping down behind the garden wall when I found it at last.

A wooden box, about the length of my forearm from finger-tips to elbow, and half that or so in width and depth. It had once been fancifully painted and gilded, although little of the decoration remained after almost four years in the ground. The cherry tree had sheltered its hiding place from the worst of the spring rains, the summer sun, and winter cold; even so, when I picked it up the joinings came apart and the lid and one side fell away. The rest of the box gaped open.

Inside I could see wrappings of stained silk. When I folded them back I found a coffer, a little smaller than the wooden box, made of silver, chased and gilded. It was black with tarnish and se-curely locked, and unlike the wooden box it held together firmly. I gathered it up—it was heavy, although I suspected most of the weight was the silver of the box itself—and went straight to the duke's chamber of government, the Camera della Stufa, on the first floor of the south wing of the Castello.

The decorated pottery stove that gave the room its name was well stocked up with wood and the room was comfortably warm.

The duke was giving audiences. The men-at-arms, the secretaries and judges and various petitioners stepped aside with shocked looks as I pushed my way forward. When had they ever seen a duchess plastered in mud and carrying a blackened silver box still half-wrapped in shreds of ruined silk? It would be a story, I thought, for them to tell their grandchildren.

"What is this, Madonna?" the duke said. His look and voice made it clear he was displeased. "I am occupied with affairs of government, and you come in unannounced and unaccompanied, covered in mud like a farmer's wife?"

"I must speak with you in private, my lord. Please."

"You could not tidy yourself first?"

"Please."

He lifted his hand, and they all went out without a word. I went up to his writing-table and placed the silver box on it. Dirt from my hands and fragments of rotted silk fell on the papers spread out before him. "Cherries," I said.

He looked at me as if I were moonstruck.

"You know I found no hidden compartments in her wedding chests. I did not find the book, either. We knew she had hidden it somewhere, so there had to be another hiding place."

His expression changed. "Have you found it?"

"I think so. This box was buried under the cherry tree in the kitchen garden. My lord, there were cherry blossoms painted in her portrait, and a basket of dried cherries among the things you collected in her cell at the monastery. She loved the flowers and fruit of the cherry, and your guardsmen found Tommasina Vasari in the kitchen garden among the fruit trees, muddied to the knees—the fruit trees. The cherry tree. Tommasina was not hiding, or at least not hiding herself—she was hiding Serenissima Lucrezia's secret treasures."

"You have an aptitude for deduction, Madonna." He examined the box with the peculiar intentness he reserved for his interest in intricate mechanical devices. "The lock is on the outside, as you can see, so although we do not have the key, we can open the box if we break the lock itself away. Stand to one side, if you please."

He picked up a heavy carved stone that weighted a stack of papers upon his writing-table and struck the lock. On the third blow the mechanism broke away from the box. He returned the stone to its place and put back the box's lid. I stepped close to the table again.

Inside, at the very top—oh yes, the book, an exquisite thing, covered in dark blue velvet only slightly damaged by the damp, richly embroidered with gold and colored silks, and studded with small pearls. The arms of Este were appliquéd in the center upon a cartouche of white satin, and the duke's personal device of the flame with its motto *Ardet Aeternum* was worked in gold and scarlet four times, one in each corner.

He opened the book gently. The figures in the first engraving leaped up at me—a woman with her back to the viewer, naked and voluptuous, her legs entwined with the legs of the man who clasped her passionately. Under the illustration was a sonnet, which began:

Fottiamci anima mia, fottiamci presto / Poiché tutti per fotter nati siamo . . .

I flamed with blushes and looked away.

"Aretino leaves little to the imagination," the duke said. "The interlineations are much more crudely written but express a similar thought."

It was the missing *I Modi*; the notes had to be Sandro Bellinceno's. Would it turn the duke against his greatest friend at last, to read the unembellished details of his wife's betrayal written in his friend's own hand? I thought of Donna Elisabetta and felt my heart break for her.

With no apparent emotion he turned the brittle, discolored pages. The bodies in the engravings writhed and strained. I tried not to read the words. One engraving was a strange one: the woman lay on her stomach with the man astride her, his muscled back to her as he gazed at her lushly rounded backside. He had a ribbon or thong in his hand, with which he might have been intending to bind her. The woman's upper body was twisted as if she were attempting to escape him—or perhaps only to gaze at his buttocks with lust of her own. She was clutching a cushion.

I wondered what tale the accompanying sonnet could possibly tell.

The duke turned two more pages. At last, to my relief, he closed the book.

"I am in debt to you, Madonna, regardless of what else comes of this business. I feared the young duchess had sent this to Florence, or to the pope himself."

"Will you tell me now," I said, "why this book is so dangerous? Embarrassing, perhaps, considering the content, but what harm could it have done to you in the hands of the Florentines?"

"When it was first printed, some forty years ago, old Pope Clement suppressed it. Messer Marcantonio Raimondi, the artist who created the engravings, was thrown into prison, and all the copies of the book itself were destroyed." He laid his hand upon the book possessively. "This one may very well be unique, the single survivor of the original printing. It has artistic value far beyond its subject matter."

"And as you hold Ferrara as a papal fief, such obvious evidence you have flouted the pope's will in this matter could damage your efforts to gain the Precedenza."

He smiled very slightly and ran his fingertips over the device worked in the corners of the book's binding. *Ardet Aeternum.* Aflame forever. He said, "Once again you surprise me, Madonna, with your grasp of political matters. That is it exactly."

"Well, if you wish to keep it, it might be wise to rebind it in a less—identifiable—covering."

"An excellent suggestion." He set the book aside; clearly he had decided what to do with it and considered the matter closed. "What else is here?"

"I do not know. I did not open the box before bringing it to you."

"Show me."

I DON'T WANT him to see what else is in the box.

I thought I did, because I knew it'd prick his monstrous Este vanity. I was happy when I realized la Cavalla had divined my secret hiding place. I laughed when she walked straight into Alfonso's presence chamber all covered with mud. I laughed even harder when I saw him break the box open so easily. Now, I thought. Now you'll learn the truth.

But now the moment has come, I wish I could keep it for myself. I'd be willing for him to have his stupid book safely back in his hands if only he'd leave the rest of the things to be my secret and mine alone.

He'll destroy them. He'll destroy them all, I know he will.

I hate him.

And yet my hate is becoming gray and thin like smoke, instead of black and blood-scarlet like it used to be. It's blowing away in shreds and tatters. I suppose what's left of my immobila self will blow away, too, so I leave nothing behind when I'm sucked down to hell.

Don't look at the rest of the things in the box, Alfonso. Don't look, la Cavalla. You have the book. Leave well enough alone. Leave something for me.

Please, please. Don't look inside the box.

CHAPTER TWENTY-SEVEN

I looked inside the box.

The young duchess's treasures were few. A small clay pot with some sort of dried color in it. Two locks of hair braided together, one red-gold and one reddish-brown. A jewel or two. A leather glove that even now, after four years, smelled of the stable. A packet of letters. And at the very bottom, a roll of linen, yellowed and stiff—a small painting. I took it out and put it on the table uncertainly.

"Unroll it," the duke said.

I found myself hesitating. The book was the duke's, a stolen thing. I felt no compunction in finding it and returning it to him. The rest of the things were different. They were hers, and she had hidden them. She had not meant for other eyes to see them.

"Unroll it," the duke said again. "Or give it to me and I will do it."

Slowly I spread the painting out on the table.

Lucrezia de' Medici smiled up at me, a languid, sated, secretive smile, her smooth cheeks flushed with delight and her golden-amber eyes glimmering like pools of fire. She lay naked amid a tangle of velvets and silks and white-pink cherry blossoms, her identity unmistakable, her skin gleaming with the sensual effort she had just expended. What beautiful sloping shoulders she had, what magnificent arms, what pert, rosy-nippled breasts, what a sweet indentation of waist and swell of hip.

She looked straight at the painter, her eyelids heavy, her lips parted and swollen. The painter's style, so detailed, so richly colored, so brilliantly discerning, was unmistakable.

Frà Pandolf.

So even the friar-painter had been her lover.

The duke gazed at it for a long time. I turned my face away. I could feel her heat radiating from the canvas, smell the musk and crushed flowers, taste the sweat gleaming on her skin, caught unerringly by her lover's brush. Peach-fleshed, heavy-eyed Lucrezia, taunting her cuckolded husband with her youth, her sensuality, her immersion in the pleasures of the flesh.

I would never look like that, never smell like that, never, not in all my life.

For an anguished moment I envied her, bitterly and hopelessly.

I heard a whisper, steel against leather, then a single indescribable sound. The writing-table lurched. I looked around. The duke had drawn his damascened dagger and driven it into the polished wood, straight through the painted canvas where the young duchess's heart might have been.

"Do you think now," he said, in a thickened voice unlike anything I had ever heard before, "I would have been wrong to kill her?"

I swallowed. "No," I whispered. "But I am glad you did not."

Methodically he began to cut the little painting to pieces. The winged pommel of the dagger glistened in the candlelight; the room itself had darkened as the sun had gone down, and the flashes of light from the damascened gold seemed to make the device of Henri II leap and play in the air. The scene caught me and held me; I counted the flashes. The cuts. Ten. Twelve. Fifteen. Finally I became aware of what I was doing, and to break the spell I forced myself to say, "My lord. The dagger. You will dull its point. Tell me about it—did it belong to your cousin the French king?"

He stopped. After a moment he brushed the pieces of canvas and broken paint to one side. There were crisscrossed slash marks on the wood of his beautiful table, but I suspected they would not matter; he would have the table itself broken up and burned and a new one put in its place.

He held the dagger out to me, and I took it. The hilt was surmounted by a pommel in the shape of two round gold medallions, each set at an angle to the grip itself so they spread apart like wings. These medallions were engraved with the capital *H* and double crescents that were the device of Henri II; the same device was etched into the damascening of the grip and the upper portion of the blade itself. The blade came to a needlelike point and had a single sharpened edge.

"I shall have to have it resharpened," the duke said. His voice had returned to its usual cool, rather distant clarity. "Yes, it belonged to Henri. It is called a *poignard d'oreilles*, an eared dagger, because of the round medallions on the pommel—some say they look like ears."

"It reminds you of your time in France."

"It reminds me of the way he died. He was injured in a joust, when a lance splintered—we were celebrating his daughter's marriage, and it was all an accident, a meaningless accident, but the splinters pierced his eye. The physicians were helpless, and he died in agony after ten days."

"I am so sorry, my lord."

"At any moment, such an accident can happen. At any moment, a lance can splinter. I loved him, yes, more than my own father, but that is not why I keep the dagger close. It is my *memento mori*—my reminder that for all my blood and wealth and possessions, I too must die."

That gave me a chill. Silently I handed the dagger back to him, and he returned it to his jeweled sheath.

"I have never told anyone of that," he said. "You, Madonna, are the first."

I bowed my head. The weight of what he had told me felt as if it would crush me. At the same time my heart lifted with pleasure that he would trust me with such a thing.

"Now, since I have told you that," he said, "I will tell you the other thing the dagger means to me. I am related by blood to kings, and I have ambition that reaches beyond Ferrara. I make no secret of it." Once again he swept his hand over the knife-scarred writing-table and scattered the last fragments of the painting of Lucrezia de' Medici to the floor. "She was a pawnbroker's daughter, fit for nothing but the stews. You, Madonna, are fit to wear a crown."

For a moment I felt as if he had struck me. Then with one great pulse my heart leaped in my breast and regained its rhythm.

You, Madonna, are fit to wear a crown.

He caught me under the arms. Our open mouths came together, hard and hot, without words. Crowns? Ambitions? Pride? I forgot them, and I think he did, too, for a few moments at least. We clawed at each other, silk, velvet, jewels, linen, then skin, hot living skin, oh, Holy Virgin, the taste and scent of it, the textures, smooth and rough. I sank my teeth into his shoulder with a groan of delight. The ruined wood of the duke's writing-table pressed against my back. I looked up at him, meeting his eyes, and in that one moment at last we were equals, two of one kind.

I sank my fingernails into his arms and said, "Alfonso."

He kissed me. It consumed everything I was thinking like a sheet of flame. I would say he took me, but the truth is we took each other. It was unlike anything we had done before. I was beyond caring, beyond shame, beyond delicacy. I felt all my muscles straining and stiffening, as if my flesh were beyond my own control, as if I were trying to fly.

The woman in the book's engraving, her face wild with ecstasy, her eyes rolled back, her arms thrown wide. Did I look like that?

Yes. I think I did.

I flew. I screamed.

Never once did he speak my name.

"ARREST THE PAINTER."

It was the duke's voice. I came to myself with a jolt, and in horror clutched for my clothing. I felt inexplicably enervated and drowsy. The duke, fully dressed and self-composed, stood at the doorway speaking to someone in the outer room. I could not make out the other voice.

"I am aware he is a Franciscan. Do you question my order?"

I struggled with my dress. The laces of the sleeves were torn.

"Good. You are dismissed."

He closed the door. I managed to get to my feet.

"I will need my women," I said. My voice sounded hoarse and my throat burned. Had I screamed so much? "I cannot dress myself alone so that I am fit to be seen."

"In a moment."

We looked at each other. I looked away first.

"You are having Frà Pandolf arrested," I said stupidly.

"Yes."

"She loved him. One can see it, in the painting."

That was a wrong thing to say. The duke's expression darkened. "Love is a chimera of poets and adulteresses," he said. "She lusted for him, nothing more."

"Whatever she felt, then." I could not bring myself to speak

Lucrezia de' Medici's name, and it was probably just as well. "If she—lusted for him, and if Sister Orsola smothered her as Tommasina Vasari says, then perhaps it was in a passion of jealousy. Perhaps that is what Sister Orsola meant when she said she shared more than a few cakes with a duchess—she shared a lover with her as well."

He looked at me sharply. "You believe Sister Orsola was also the painter's mistress?"

"Mona Tommasina did say there was a story she had a lover, a man connected with the court."

He came over to me and helped me with my torn laces. "You may be right. Even so, I am not so sure I believe the infirmarian committed the murder. The *parruchiera* lied about many things, and we may not yet have forced the full truth from her."

I could not bear the thought that he would torture her again. Not after—not after. I do not quite know where the solution came from, but it sprang from my thoughts full-fledged, like Minerva complete and armed from the brow of Jove.

I said, "The Berlingaccio Carnival revels are later this week, my lord, are they not? The night revels for which Ferrara is known?"

He looked surprised. "Yes, of course, on Shrove Thursday. Why?"

"And in those revels, anyone can ask a favor of you or me, and we are bound to grant it?"

"Yes. Although by tradition, the favors are trifles. What has this to do with the subject at hand, Madonna?"

"I would beg a favor of you. It is a few days beforetime, I know, and my favor is more than a trifle, but grant it to me now, I beg you, and I will not ask another."

He frowned. "There is a customary form for asking such a favor."

"I do not know it. Please, my lord." I looked up at his face, and for the first time since we had been married, I stared straight into the eyes of his monsters without flinching.

You, Madonna, are fit to wear a crown.

I would prove it.

"Very well," he said at last. "The prescribed request is this: 'I beg a favor of the duke, on the night of the Berlingaccio.'"

I repeated steadily, "I beg a favor of the duke, on the night of the Berlingaccio."

"Whatever you desire will be granted, in the name of Saint George and the House of Este."

Clearly, this was the prescribed reply. I said, "I ask that Tommasina Vasari be tortured no more."

His eyes narrowed. "Then we may never know the truth."

"She has lied under torture already."

He turned away. The fevered moments between us, the truth-telling, might never have happened. "As you wish," he said. "I have sworn, and the favor you ask is yours. Call your women to help you dress and compose yourself. Tomorrow I will question the *parruchiera* again, more gently."

MY POOR TOMMASINA. La Cavalla doesn't know it, but it's too late for kindness. And even if it wasn't, does she think anyone, even Alfonso's treacherous secret-grubbing university physician, can make broken thumbs whole again so they can spin gold from the hair of rich merchants' wives?

I shouldn't have kept that painting, but when I went to throw it in the fire I couldn't. It was . . . It's hard to explain. It was what I looked like, really looked like, so much more than ordinary portraits. I loved my flesh, loved washing myself and combing my hair and caressing myself. I loved being caressed. I loved seeing my flesh brought to life in paint. And that's one thing Pandolfo did, better than any other man: he made paint live.

I hid it in my silver box so I could take it out sometimes and look at it. I used to think about it at the monastery, when I was lying alone in the dark of night. How I missed the pleasures of my body, the lovely luscious tightness, the slick sweat, the sharp briny tastes and oniony-garlicky scents, the shudderings of delight. Maybe Alfonso was right about me being too soon made glad. I loved men too much, loved pleasure too much. I was too apt a pupil for my sister Isabella.

It was Pandolfo I loved. There, another secret revealed. In the beginning it was the way he looked at me and the way he made me look—like a goddess, golden, drenched in sin and pleasure. That's what I wanted to be, God help me, and that's what he made me with his paints and brushes. We were so happy at first, while he was painting me.

When he wasn't painting, it was harder for us to find ways to be together. I pretended to be sick more often, and Tommasina lied to my other ladies while I slipped out through a window in disguise. It aroused me that Pandolfo was willing to do such a forbidden thing, betray a duke, fottere *a duchess. I had loved doing forbidden things from my childhood, and it was exciting beyond anything else to find a man who was even more daring than I was.*

It was Pandolfo I wanted to run away with, Pandolfo I would've given up the world to have, Pandolfo I dosed with Maria Granmammelli's love potions, Pandolfo whose baby quickened inside me. But when I told him what I wanted, he pushed me away. I screamed at him, but it didn't move him.

There was someone he loved more than me. And it wasn't Sister Orsola.

I wonder if la Cavalla will ever find out who it is.

CHAPTER TWENTY-EIGHT

"I will accompany you to question her," I said.

The next day had come. Neither of us had eaten much of the lavish Carnival dinner set before us. We lingered at the high table, shelling almonds; the duke, I think, was waiting for me to leave first. I, on the other hand, was determined to be there when Tommasina Vasari was questioned again.

"You will not," he said, breaking open another almond-shell. "The *prigioni* are no place for a woman."

"The prisoner is a woman."

"It is not the same thing."

"Nevertheless, I wish to accompany you."

The duke picked the almond out of the fragments of shell and ate it. "You continue to surprise me," he said. "I am reminded of something I said to you on the day your wedding portrait was presented. Do you remember it?"

I remembered it very well. *I believe you have considerable depths, Madonna, that you have not shared with me.*

"How could I forget it, my lord? You said I had considerable depths."

"Indeed. I think I am beginning to glimpse some of them."

"Do you dislike them?"

"I am not certain." He paused for a moment, then took my left hand and fingered the heavy ring on my middle finger, gold with table-cut sapphires and diamonds, the blue and white of the Este.

"Considerable depths, and a designing mind," he said. "Very well, come to the dungeons if you must, but do not reproach me if you see things that disturb you."

TOMMASINA VASARI'S BODY hung against the wall of her windowless cell. Her tertiary's black veil had been twisted into a cord. One end made a noose around her neck, cutting into her flesh; the other was knotted to an iron stanchion bolted into the wall to hold a torch. Her feet hung no more than three inches from the bare stone floor, and the wooden necessary bucket was overturned beside them.

Her face was as purple-black as a ripe plum, swollen to bursting, the mouth fixed in a terrible tongue-thrusting grimace. The smell was ghastly. The light of the gaoler's torch flickered over her face, and for a moment her eyes seemed to open, her mouth to work. I started back with an involuntary cry, and dizziness overtook me.

I awoke to the duke's voice, low and cold. *You dared open the door to the duchess without making certain. . . .* Another voice, stammering, frightened, self-exculpatory. *Didn't know . . . never guessed she would . . .* The gaoler, then. I opened my eyes.

I was lying on my back in a room I had never seen before, with the taste of bile in my mouth. I could smell the sandalwood and amber I associated with the duke's clothes, and I turned my head, trying to fill my senses. It was the duke's fur-lined surcoat, spread out over some sort of pallet. Domenica and Sybille were kneeling on the floor beside me, the one with a cup of water in her hands and the other with her rosary.

"I am better." My voice felt husky, and I cleared my throat. "I am sorry to have caused such a fuss. Help me get up, please."

They helped me to my feet. Domenica handed me the cup and I drank deeply of the fresh water, rinsing the taste of horror from my mouth. Sybille held my marten-fur mantle for me. I wrapped it close; the room was cold and damp. I was still in the dungeons under the Lions' Tower, then, in a clean room with one high window, a chair and a table and the pallet; it was probably where the gaoler lived.

"I am better," I said again. I was not sure if I was trying to convince the duke, my ladies, or myself. "That was Tommasina Vasari, then? She is dead?"

"She is," the duke said. He did not say, *I warned you, you fool*, and for that I was grateful.

"Dead by her own hand?"

"So it appears. You, gaoler. Tell us everything you know at once, from the moment the *parruchiera* was placed in the cell until the moment we discovered her as she is now."

The gaoler swallowed. He was a stocky, unwashed fellow with matted hair and a spreading reddish birthmark like a wine-stain on the left side of his neck. I could not help feeling sorry for him, however derelict he might have been in his duty. "She was brought here yesterday about midday, after she'd been questioned," he stammered. "She was mostly unconscious and had to be carried. The *sergente* ordered me to lock her in a cell."

I glanced sidelong at the duke. He said nothing. "Very well," I said to the gaoler. "And then what happened?"

"Nothing, Serenissima. I put her in the cell myself and locked the door."

"And you were the only one who had the key?"

"Yes, Serenissima."

I looked at the duke again. This time he said, "You are managing perfectly well, Madonna, without assistance from me. I wonder, however, if your next question will be the same as the question I am presently pondering."

I gathered my mantle more closely around me. The sick, dizzy feeling was fading, and I found myself left with an odd combination of sorrow for Tommasina Vasari's unhappy end and resentment of the duke's disdainful tone.

"Very well," I said. "Her thumbs had been broken. The slightest movement of her hands would have been agony. As that was the case, how did she manage to twist her veil into a cord, tie it around her neck, and then reach up behind herself and tie it to the stanchion?"

"*Brava*, Madonna," the duke said softly. "We are of one mind, then."

I felt a rush of satisfaction, and then shame because I felt it. I could not seem to settle on any one emotion.

"She was mad, Serenissima," the gaoler said. His voice was high with panic. "That's the only answer. She was mad with pain and fear, and desperate to escape further agonies."

"Possibly," I said. "It is still a very singular thing. Tell me again. You locked her in the cell, and you were the only one with the key, and neither you nor anyone else entered the cell until you opened the door for the duke and me this morning?"

"I locked her up right and tight, Serenissima, I swear it, and I never went back into the cell." He stopped. Then he said suddenly, "Nor did anyone else, but for the priest, of course."

"The *priest*?"

The duke and I burst out with it at the same time.

"The Augustinian, Serenissimo, the one you sent because the prisoner had been asking for a priest. He came just as I heard the bells ringing for the first vigil of matins, and glad I was to see him, too, because she'd been crying and moaning and begging for a priest ever since she regained her wits, and it was—"

"I sent no priest, Augustinian or otherwise," the duke cut in coldly.

The guard stared at him. "But how could he have lied, Serenissimo, a priest, a man of God? He said he came directly from you."

"Of course he lied," the duke said. His voice was harsh. "I doubt he was a priest at all. What did he look like? What did he sound like? Describe him to me."

"He wore the black robe and pointed cowl," the guard said. His voice was little more than a whisper. "He was about your height, Serenissimo, and he—and he—I did not see his face. I cannot say. He spoke softly, with few words, as priests do. Oh, holy San Ippolito, forgive me."

"You will need more than San Ippolito's forgiveness," the duke said. "Did you not make sure of your prisoner's well-being, when you let this so-called priest out of the cell?"

"I did, Serenissimo, I saw her, she was lying on her pallet like she was asleep, and I thought he'd given her the holy rites and at least she'd be quiet now instead of that awful moaning."

"You are lying," I said. "I still contend she could not have hanged herself. And if she received the holy rites, she would not have taken the sin of self-murder upon her soul."

The duke looked thoughtful. "I think we should inspect the prisoner's cell again, Madonna," he said. "No"—he shook his head when he saw my expression of revulsion—"not the corpse. Just the cell. Gaoler, see to it the corpse is taken down and laid out decently in another room. I shall send my physician to examine it. Do not touch anything else in the cell."

"Yes, Serenissimo, it shall be done. Excuse me, I beg you. I'll see to it all."

He left. I was sure he felt lucky to escape with his life. We waited, and perhaps a quarter of an hour later the gaoler returned. With a fresh torch he escorted us back to the place where Tommasina Vasari had died.

I had not really looked at the cell before, other than to register that it was very small and windowless. With horrible matter-of-factness, the gaoler thrust the torch into the very stanchion from which the poor woman had been hanged and went away. I looked around. The cell was about ten paces by ten paces, constructed of rough stone, floor and walls. The smell had not been wholly eradicated. Against the wall opposite the door there was a pallet.

"There is the answer to the contradiction, Madonna," the duke said, gesturing to the pallet. "I did not see it at first. But note."

He stepped closer and prodded the mound of straw on the pallet. "The straw has been heaped here, and a blanket tucked around it. And this piece of black fabric, torn from her skirt, where a woman's head might have been. It is not a chance arrangement. It was dark, and the gaoler saw what he expected to see."

"So the Augustinian was an imposter. Worse than that. He was a murderer, and he defiled the holy habit by using it as a disguise." Automatically I crossed myself, with some thought of warding off the blasphemy of it.

"Indeed. Someone wanted the *parruchiera* silenced, and wanted it badly. Come, Madonna, let us go. Your silkmaker awaits you, does he not? I myself require some hard riding and fresh air, and so I shall hunt this afternoon."

Hard riding and fresh air. It sounded much better than an afternoon in my apartments being wrapped in silver tissue and stuck with pins.

I said, "I will join you."

"I think not. It is important that your costume for the Berlingaccio be suitably magnificent, and you have put off the silkmaker twice already. You will keep your appointment with him, if you please. Now come, let us go up."

I did not have the strength to contend with him again; I would save my protests for another time, another place. I put my hand on his and allowed him to help me up the narrow stone stairway.

"I will see you at supper," he said when we had reached the top. Either he had no idea how annoyed I was, or he knew and did not care. "Perhaps by then there will be news of the Franciscan."

MESSER SALVESTRO GREETED me with ecstasies, probably because he knew he would sell his silver tissue at last. Sybille and the uncongenial Ferrarese woman Vittoria Beltrame set about immediately to strip me to my shift. Katharina argued with Messer Salvestro's assistants over the weight and drape and sheen of the silk. Tristo and Isa frolicked about, reveling in the scents of so many new people and pouncing on stray ribbons. Domenica Guarini and my dear Christine sat in the window embrasure, singing together to entertain me. Domenica had written the lyric for the song and Christine the music, and I wished I were in a proper frame of mind to appreciate their efforts.

I stood in the midst of the clamor, holding my arms out from my sides, feeling the same sense of not-being-present I had felt on the afternoon Frà Pandolf had presented my portrait to the duke. *The Duchess of Ferrara, being dressed for the Berlingaccio, the famous night revels of Shrove Thursday*: I might have been a piece of statuary instead of living flesh. All that mattered was that the duchess's costume was rich enough and the accompanying jewels and headdress suitably magnificent.

At least it turned my thoughts from Tommasina Vasari's awful death.

When it was over, I sent them all away and lay down with the puppies. I did not go to supper. Vespers had long been rung and compline was drawing on when he sent for me, and as it was a direct order, I could not refuse. Domenica and Katharina helped me into a night-gown and brushed out my hair; I instructed them to scent it liberally with apricot perfume and then made my way to the duke's apartments. I found him alone in his *studiolo*, seated at his ebony writing-table. Several letters were lying on the table before him. He was looking at one, and his expression was unreadable.

"Good evening, my lord." The writing-table made me think of another such table, in the duke's presence chamber in the Castello. I averted my eyes and made the briefest of curtsies.

"Good evening." He put the letter down and looked up at me. "You were not at supper."

"No."

"Has the work commenced upon your costume for the Berlingaccio?"

"It has."

"Excellent. It is important you make the correct impression. Now, I thought you would be interested in these papers. They were part of the packet of letters in Lucrezia de' Medici's silver coffer."

He was taking possession of the whole business, as he took possession of everything and everyone around him. I felt—what? Relief, yes. But at the same time, anger and resentment. I would have to take care with what I said.

"Has there been news of Frà Pandolf?"

"No. I have, however, had a message from Mother Eleonora— Sister Orsola fled Corpus Domini before my aunt received my message to confine her. The Carnival processions are making the search more difficult, as so many folk are masked and wearing dress they might not ordinarily wear."

"Has your aunt any idea why Sister Orsola ran away?"

"No. Only that she disappeared shortly after the *parruchiera* was arrested. I suspect my aunt is actually glad the woman is gone—she has written her off as a runaway and intends to make no effort to find her."

"Does she have a family in Ferrara? Anyone who could be giving her shelter?"

"She is from a family of bakers in Copparo. I have already had them questioned—they have not seen or spoken to her for years, and they know nothing of where she might have gone."

He put down the letter he was holding and picked up another. Clearly he had nothing more to say about Sister Orsola.

"Do the letters provide any useful information, my lord?"

"A great deal. They are letters—although hardly letters, more scrawled notes on scraps of accounts and sketches—from the Franciscan. Clearly responses to letters she sent to him. He was hardly more literate than she was, but he managed to make several things clear."

I waited.

"First, she was infatuated with him and he cooled rapidly toward her. Second, she wished to run away with him and he did not wish to go. Third, he was the father of her child."

"Holy Virgin."

"Indeed.

"I wonder why he disappeared when he did," I said. "He could not have known we had seen the painting in the silver coffer."

"Sister Orsola may have fled to him when she left Corpus Domini. He may have taken fright as well."

"Particularly if she confessed to him she killed Serenissima Lucrezia for his sake."

He gathered the letters into a packet again and put them aside.

"I have had the gaoler taken into custody," he said. "I wish to question him further."

"Perhaps he will remember some detail that will help us identify the false Augustinian."

"Perhaps." He sounded noncommittal.

"Poor Mona Tommasina. I know she wanted to kill me—but what a ghastly way to die. We are agreed she obtained the abortifacient potion from her father?"

"We are. The flask is Florentine work, that much is certain."

"Florentine work," I said slowly, allowing my thoughts to run freely. "And her father a favorite of Duke Cosimo. The fact the potion was an abortifacient—perhaps, my lord, Duke Cosimo himself wished you to be proven wrong in imprisoning Serenissima Lucrezia, and even wished to force you to accept her again as your wife. I do not think the mortal sin of providing such a potion to his daughter would concern him."

I felt the duke's start of surprise. Clearly he had not considered this possibility.

"And when the scheme to restore his daughter failed," I went on, "Duke Cosimo turned his attention to a second design: undermining your standing with the pope and the world by encouraging the rumors you were responsible for the young duchess's death."

"Have you read Messer Niccolò Machiavelli's book?" the duke said unexpectedly. "It describes some of the exploits of Duke Cesare Borgia, who was, of course, my great-uncle."

"No, my lord, I have not read it. It was not considered suitable for ladies in Innsbruck."

"I shall commission a copy for you. Your mind appears to work with much of the same subtlety as that of Messer Niccolò's prince."

It was not at all clear if he meant that as a compliment or not. I said nothing.

"Very well. Let us test this new assumption," he said. "Tommasina Vasari asks her father for the abortifacient. He is a favorite of Duke Cosimo's—perhaps he thinks he can curry additional favor by telling the duke of his daughter's predicament. They conspire together—Vasari makes up the potion, and the duke provides the flask."

I nodded. "It falls into place quite neatly."

"Mona Tommasina gives the flask to the young duchess that night, after I have left the monastery. The young duchess takes the potion and arranges everything she will need when it begins its work."

I nodded again. He went on. "However, before it can take its effect, Sister Orsola smothers the young duchess in her bed, presumably out of jealousy, or for some other unknown motive."

"Or possibly," I said thoughtfully, "just possibly—to thwart the Medici conspiracy. She was greedy for jewels and luxuries, perhaps to make herself more attractive to her lover. Who knows what she might have been paid to do, and by whom?"

"I myself," the duke said in a dry voice, "would have been the person most interested in thwarting any such conspiracy. If I had known of its existence. I believe—"

The door to his bedchamber swung open with a crash and a tiny black-clad figure appeared, framed in the doorway like a demon from hell in a *marionetta* morality play. The duke broke off midsentence, and I stepped back in surprise.

"By the lance of Saint George," he said, sounding both exasperated and—if such a thing could be—affectionate. "One day you will go too far, *mia nonna*. Well, come in. What do you want?"

It was, of course, Maria Granmammelli. I was coming to understand she prided herself on these sudden appearances and disappearances.

"Good evening to you, *caro Serenissimo*. I have some news for the *Austriaca*, and since she said you knew of the commission she gave me, I mean to tell her now, before your eyes, and catch her out if what she said was a lie."

"Do not be ridiculous," I said. "Of course it was not a lie."

At the same time, the duke said, "You will speak to the duchess with proper respect."

"Oho, so that's how the wind blows," the old woman said. "Very well, Serenissimo, proper respect it will be, for your sake and the love I bear you. Do you want to know what I found in your crystal flask, or not?"

"The duchess and I believe we have pieced together the truth. The substance in the flask was an abortifacient, was it not? An expensive and efficacious one?"

Maria Granmammelli came to the duke's writing-table and stepped up on a footstool so as to put her face at a level with mine. It was surprisingly eerie to look her straight in the eyes.

"That it was not, Serenissimo," she said. "You and your lady have the wrong dog by the ear entirely. The powder in that flask was the dregs of poison. Deadly poison."

WHAT?

Poison?

Has the old witch gone feeble? There was nothing poisonous about that potion—Tommasina gave me the sealed flask with her own hands and smiled as she watched me drink it. She promised me it would rid me of my child and set me free of my prison, and she would never have lied to me. It's Maria Big-Breasts who's either moon-mad or lying.

And it can't possibly be true that Tommasina's father told my father about the potion. She swore him to secrecy, and he would have kept his oath. He loved her and wanted her to come home, and she always wrote back to say she was staying here in Ferrara for love of me. He pleaded and begged with her, and I was always pleased she loved me more. She would have made sure her father kept my secret, and he would have done it for love of her.

My poor dead Tommasina.

The way she died, it wasn't exactly how Alfonso and la Cavalla imagined it. Tommasina was unconscious when they locked her in the cell, and for a long time afterward. She was dying, I think, from shock and fear, because I could see her soul almost but not quite separated from her flesh. Then she awoke, and the soul sank back into her, and she started to cry for a priest, just like the gaoler described.

She didn't get one. It was the gaoler himself who came into her cell again, deep in the night. He never said a word. He just grabbed her neck with his bare hands and twisted, quick and cool as a farm-wife might kill a chicken, then tied her veil around her neck, and hung her up on the wall.

He thought she was dead, but she wasn't. Her soul was still coupled to her flesh. She hung there, her heels twitching and kicking against the wall, and saw him placing the necessary bucket so it would look like she'd stood on it and hanged herself. He didn't arrange the straw on the pallet then. He only did that later, when he was sent away to remove her body, so it would support his tale of a mysterious priest.

He left her hanging there, and after a few more minutes she died. She didn't become immobila. *She just—died.*

My poor Tommasina.

She prayed over my tomb every day, and after my mother died she was the only person left who prayed for me. Now she's gone.

The old witch is wrong. Alfonso and la Cavalla are wrong. They're wrong about Pandolfo and that cow-eyed Sister Orsola, too. Why would he have had anything to do with her, when he had me? When I was ready to give up everything and run away with him? He hadn't cooled to me, he hadn't! Well, maybe a little. I thought the baby would make him more willing to run away with me, but it turned out to be the opposite.

The potion was just what Tommasina said it was, and it would've worked if I'd lived to see the morning. Tommasina never lied to me.

She told Alfonso and la Cavalla the truth, too, about what she saw that night. But she saw what she saw and no more, and what she saw was a figure in monastic robes, in the dark.

Who could it have been but Sister Orsola?

CHAPTER TWENTY-NINE

"$\mathcal{S}$he could be mistaken," I said. "The residue in the flask was almost four years old. And Messer Girolamo determined the young duchess was smothered, not poisoned."

Maria Granmammelli had departed, satisfied with the sensation she had created. The duke had gathered up Lucrezia de' Medici's letters and papers and put them in a box of his own, made of plain iron and with its locking mechanism on the inside rather than on the outside. He locked the box with an iron key and put the key in his pouch.

"I would be more likely to believe Girolamo Brasavola was mistaken," he said. "Doctor of the university or no. In matters of herbalism and potions, Maria Granmammelli's knowledge is without peer."

I could not help but think that so far her potions had done me little good. But of course I did not say so.

"The simplest explanation," he went on, "is that they are both correct. There was an amount of liquid in her stomach. She drank the poison, but before it had a chance to take its effect, she was smothered."

"But Tommasina Vasari loved her. She would never have given her poison, and she confessed to giving her the flask."

"The flask, yes. Perhaps she was mistaken, or deliberately mis-led, as to its contents."

"Misled," I repeated thoughtfully. Suddenly a new and com-plex maze of possibilities sprang into existence. "By her father? What reason could he have had to wish the young duchess dead?"

"The *parruchiera* told us she stayed here in Ferrara, a fugitive, for the young duchess's sake," the duke said. "Perhaps her father was angry with his daughter for her disobedience, or feared for her, or had arranged a marriage for her and wished her to be free of the entanglement. Perhaps he simply hated the duchess as a rival for his daughter's affections, and seized an opportunity to be rid of her."

"If so, it had the opposite effect. Tommasina Vasari blamed you, and she became all the more determined to stay and take her vengeance."

The duke's expression darkened. "There is one way to know for sure. Bring the alchemist here to Ferrara and confront him with the flask, or what remains of it after Maria Granmammelli's experiments."

"He will never leave Florence willingly. And in any case, even if he agrees to come to Ferrara, surely the Medici will prevent him."

I knew, the moment the words were out of my mouth, it was a wrong thing to have said. Being told his desires would be thwarted by the Medici was not something the duke would ever take plea-sure in hearing.

"I can send agents in secret to persuade him. To abduct him, if necessary. I will get to the bottom of this matter, Madonna, one way or another." He stood up, just as he did when he was dismiss-ing ambassadors. "Now, I tire of this, and so I will wish you a good night. Tomorrow is the Berlingaccio, and I will be occupied all day with preparations. See you make your preparations as well. Perhaps once Carnival is over, I will have sufficient leisure to take up this matter again."

And you will not pursue it independently. He did not say it, but he did not have to. *Remember the vow you swore to me in the Garden of the Seasons at Belfiore.*

There was nothing else I could do, and so I sank into a curtsy. "I wish you a good night as well, my lord."

He was not quite finished with me. "Messer Girolamo tells me you have not yet presented yourself for his examination."

"There has been little time, my lord, what with our investigation, and my preparations for the Carnival."

"You will see him on the Thursday after Ash Wednesday, if you please."

"Yes, my lord."

He turned away from me without acknowledging my response. I waited for a moment, finding rather to my mortification that I wished to stay with him. He ignored me. At last I went silently out of his bedchamber, with my loose hair and apricot perfume all for naught.

THE NEXT MORNING was indeed Shrove Thursday, the Berlingaccio, the beginning of the feverish final week of Carnival. In Ferrara it was celebrated with double nighttime revels famous all over Europe—the Notte del Duca and the Notte della Duchessa.

The gentlemen and the ladies were strictly separated for these celebrations, with even the entertainers and servants being all men and all women respectively. The Castello gates were thrown open and the townspeople were welcomed in over the drawbridges; it was a great tradition that any favor asked of the duke or duchess on Berlingaccio night must be granted. Domenica assured me no one ever asked

for anything but a sweetmeat or a paste jewel or some equally in-
consequential trifle, which would then be treasured and passed down
from mother to daughter as a mark of good fortune. I would be well-
provided with such favors, she told me, in overflowing gilded baskets
traditionally made to look like the cornucopia of Amalthea.

The separation of the gentlemen and the ladies did not go so
far as to require the festivities to be mounted in different palaces;
that would spoil the revelers' pleasures in the connecting rooms
and shadowy corridors. The Notte del Duca was held in the great
central courtyard of the Castello, and the Notte della Duchessa in a
smaller courtyard near the foot of the Saint Catherine Tower. Under
the flaring torches and amid the largesse and wine and dreamlike
costumes, even the commonest soldier or shoemaker might speak
to the duke, and sewing-women and pie-makers might touch the
hand of their duchess.

By further custom both the duke and duchess wore white at
the Notte revels and were the only ones to go unmasked. So when
I mounted my fanciful Carnival throne in the Saint Catherine
courtyard, just at nightfall, I wore a costume of white satin and
Messer Salvestro's silver tissue, sewn with hundreds of jeweled medallions, Berlingaccio sun-faces, and roses of crystals and pearls.
My hair was caught up in a net of silver threads knotted with more
pearls, each one the size of a hazelnut. Over my brow I wore a circlet of diamonds that Eleonora of Naples had brought to Ferrara as
part of her dowry, three generations before.

All in all, it was heavy, tight, prickly, and in every way uncomfortable, but surely it was magnificent enough to please even the
duke. Would he ever see it? I had sent him no messages, received
none from him, and remained in my apartments all day for my
preparations as he had instructed me to do. What had happened to
the passionate accord we had experienced in his presence chamber?
Or had I alone experienced it, and for the duke was it indeed nothing but a chimera fit only for poets and adulteresses?

My taste for Carnival gambolings was also dampened by the ghastly death of Tommasina Vasari, which was still vivid in my dreams. I concealed my distress as best I could and engaged myself earnestly in the pleasures of my ladies and of the court. They, after all, had not seen the *parruchiera*'s thumbs broken. They had not seen her hanging in her cell.

Of course, I could conceal nothing from Katharina.

"You look troubled, Bärbel," she whispered as she crouched in front of me, arranging the gilded baskets so they would be easy for me to reach and fussing with my glittering skirts and train. I never could sit in such a way that the fall of my skirts pleased her. "All will be well. Rest here on the dais and watch the dancing, and I will fetch you some wine."

I looked out over the courtyard and tried to imagine what this night would have been like if I had never disobeyed the duke, never suffered his displeasure, never heard Nora's laughter or listened to Messer Bernardo's insinuations in the cold, bare chapel. Would I feel queenly and serene, like the luminous Duchess Elisabetta Gonzaga in *Il Libro del Cortegiano*, after whom I had so longed to model my life? Would I offer my gifts to the court and the people with a light heart and a confident spirit?

It was too late. My first Berlingaccio was corrupted by my own hand.

"Your wine, Bärbel."

I took the cup. "Katrine, do you ever wish you could go back and do something over again?"

"Of course I do. What is this, melancholy on Shrove Thursday? For shame. You must smile and be joyous for your people's sake—you are the duchess and they look to you."

I could not help but smile. Only Katrine would dare say such a thing to me. "You are right. Let the petitioners approach. Crezia first, as she has the right of precedence."

I sipped wine as the crowd of women sorted themselves out

by rank. Then Crezia stepped forward, sumptuously dressed in the blue and white of the Este, wearing only a narrow ribbon of silver and a few feathers as a mask so there was no question who she really was. She swept a regal curtsy.

"I beg a favor of the duchess, on the night of the Berlingaccio."

She pronounced each word clearly and impeccably, and I realized she wanted this first gift-giving to be perfect so as to instill me with confidence. From that moment, for all her pride and peculiarities, I truly loved her as a sister.

I answered with the prescribed response: "Whatever you desire will be granted, by Saint George and the House of Este."

"I desire a red lacquer casket." She had pitched her voice to carry, and the women's side of the courtyard had gone suddenly silent. "Painted with white unicorns and blue flowers, and filled with sweet chestnut cakes soaked in honey and rolled in cinnamon."

I looked at the basket on my right. At the very top there was just such a casket, and I had every faith that when it was opened, it would indeed reveal honey-soaked, cinnamon-covered chestnut cakes. I reached over and picked it up, flicked the latch, and put back the lid with a flourish. I had been right about the cakes. I offered the casket to her.

"What you ask is yours," I said.

She took the casket and curtsied again. As she straightened, she flashed me a conspiratorial smile.

"I thank you on this Berlingaccio, and forever swear my loyalty to the House of Este."

"So be it. Go in peace."

She turned and held out the casket for all the women to see. Someone cheered. The others joined in. The hum of talk became excited and good-natured, as it should have been from the beginning. Katrine handed me another goblet of wine.

Perhaps, I thought, my first Berlingaccio would not be so terrible after all.

★   ★   ★

THE REVELS CONTINUED, and little by little the basket emptied—feathers, paste jewels, bits of lace and embroidery, poppets dressed with tinsel and spangles, gloves, filigree fans, carved figures brightly painted. Elisabetta Bellinceno was there—I knew her by the green-and-blue dress and Turkish stones she wore, despite her naiad's mask. She begged her favor with her customary exquisite grace and correctness, and when I handed it to her—a tiny gilded loaf of Ferrara's famous *pampepato* cake—I clasped her hands for a moment and smiled encouragingly into her eyes.

Half-a-dozen women in Carnival costumes played lutes and dulcimers, and court ladies danced with washerwomen, becoming more and more boisterous as the evening wore on. Although it was only the middle of February, the courtyard soon grew hot with what must have been a hundred torches and twice as many women, and my costume grew heavier and more stifling with each favor I granted.

Katrine and Domenica brought me wine, again and again. Even the wine was warm, and sweet, too sweet. I would have to ask them, I thought, to mix water with it, or even stop bringing it altogether.

"I beg a favor of the duchess, on the night of the Berlingaccio."

I knew her voice from her very first word. She had not been in the courtyard to take her rightful place after Crezia, and I had hoped against hope she had chosen not to attend the revels at all. Had she waited deliberately, to call more attention to herself?

It was, of course, my enemy, my nemesis, the duke's younger sister Nora.

She was magnificently dressed, all in red, the worst possible color for her unhealthy complexion. Her dress was a mass of blazing flame-scarlet skirts; its low, square bodice was sewn with rubies and pearls. Unlike Crezia, she wore a real mask, a fanciful golden creation with slanting eyes like a faun's and a cockscomb of crimson feathers.

She was the duke's sister, and I had no choice but to answer her. "Whatever you desire will be granted, by Saint George and the House of Este."

Domenica handed me a bracelet of twisted and braided silver wires with tiny sparkling crystals caught inside the whorls. I held it up, so she might know what she was to ask for.

"I want you to tell Alfonso," she said loudly, paying no attention to my gesture, "to withdraw his patronage from Tasso, so he is not forever writing, writing, writing, and paying no attention to me."

A few of the women laughed, then pressed their hands over their mouths. Nora paid them no attention. To my own surprise, it outraged me that she was not following the correct form—I had denied myself even a few private words with Elisabetta Bellinceno because they would have broken the tradition.

"Nora, not so loudly," I said. "We cannot talk now, and you know I cannot do as you ask. In the first place, Tasso is in the cardinal's household, not the duke's. And in the second place, he is a genius. Other courts are vying for his presence. He will hardly be allowed to leave Ferrara, or asked to stop writing."

"You have to do what I ask. That is the rule."

She sounded as if she were about to weep openly, and that was unthinkable. I did not know what to do. I looked around for Crezia.

"You hate me because of what I told you," Nora cried. "But it is only the truth, and you should not blame me that Alfonso is—"

"Nora, no!"

I cut her off just in time. Holy Virgin, did she intend to shout her lies aloud in the Saint Catherine courtyard with a hundred women of the town looking on and hanging on every word?

"Nora, listen," I gabbled on, desperate to distract her. "I will ask him, I promise it. Here, look, I have this bracelet for you. See, it has crystals—"

She struck it out of my hand with a cry. "I do not want your bracelet! I want Tasso to love me. I want him to give up his scribbling for me. He says he lives for his art, not for me. He says he will kill me before he gives up his art for me. Is that not enough for Alfonso to send him away? A threat to kill me? Is that not enough?"

She did start to cry. What could I do? She was the duke's sister, after all, and the townswomen were watching. I stood up and gathered her into my arms to quiet her.

He says he will kill me before he gives up his art for me.

Tasso, poor boy, had probably never said any such thing; it would be the grossest of lèse-majesté. The threat almost certainly existed only in Nora's fevered imagination.

But. But . . .

I groped for something, some connection I could not quite fit together.

Give up his art.

He says he will kill me before he gives up his art for me.

Lucrezia de' Medici had been Frà Pandolf's lover. She had been carrying his child. Had she, too, demanded her genius give up his art for her sake?

"Promise, promise, promise," Nora was sobbing. "Promise you will make him love me."

Crezia came up to the dais at last, with her ladies and three or four of Nora's own women. "She has had too much wine, that is all. We will take her to bed. Come, *mia sorellina*, it is sleep you need. You will feel better in the morning."

I stood there like a statue, transfixed by my thoughts.

"Barbara. *Barbara.* You must finish it. Everyone is watching, and you must make it look as ordinary as possible."

I came back to the present. Finish it. The ritual, of course. The ritual was important. Everyone was watching me.

"What you ask is yours," I said. I picked up the bracelet and slipped it onto Nora's wrist. She had stopped crying and had fallen into a drunken swoon. "Go in peace, my sister."

They took her away.

AFTER THAT, I went down into the courtyard. I had to think, and I could bear no more heart-wrenching pleas. I could hear the city's bells ringing the first vigil of matins. The first array of torches had burned out, and servants were replacing them with fresh ones, the flames rippling and flapping in the air like burning pennants. The smoke was black as the night and smelled like the outer reaches of hell. My costume would be ruined, but opulent as it was, it had never been intended for anything but this single Berlingaccio.

Frà Pandolf was her lover. He was the father of her child. Would he give up his art for cozy domesticity, even with—

"Serenissima, Serenissima!"

There were masked women everywhere, calling me, pulling at my skirts. The scents of smoke and sweat and spilled wine were overwhelming. Dancers jostled me, and I lost one of my shoes. Nicoletta went back to search for it. I could not see Katrine at all. A hulking townswoman in a gray linen dress, with a white wimple and coif caught up and pinned to mask her face, thrust a sheaf of flowers into my arms. Gratefully I bent my head and breathed in their sweet fragrance.

"Thank you," I said. "A favor—I will give you a favor—"

I felt dizzy. I tried to finish the sentence, but my lips and tongue were suddenly numb.

I went to my knees, I think. I cannot remember. I tried to call my ladies but I could not remember their names, and the crowd was pressing in, swirling, dancing, laughing. I heard a high, shrill voice shrieking, "There she is! The duchess! She is over there, in her white dress!"

Which could not be, of course, because I was here, on my knees in the dust.

I dropped the flowers. And then I thought, *The flowers*. On my wedding day, Tommasina Vasari had warned me: *any piece of fruit, any flower you are offered, might be poisoned.*

But Tommasina Vasari was dead.

I tried to push myself to my feet, and fell, and fell, and fell.

THE FLOWER-WOMAN CAUGHT her as she fell, and rolled her up quick in a gray mantle. Nobody noticed—all the women in the courtyard were gawking and pointing and rushing off after a woman in a white dress running away from the courtyard. Obviously that was part of the game.

How fast it happened! One moment, there was la Cavalla enthroned like a queen, shining in the torchlight with her silver tissue and crystals and diamond tiara. Then she left her throne and went down into the courtyard where the people were, and they greeted her happily. She was popular with the people, la Cavalla, because she always gave alms. It didn't seem strange at all when a woman came up to her and gave her flowers.

A woman. Well, dressed like a woman. That was one of the most popular tricks of the Berlingaccio, for men to dress up like women and slip into the women's revels. I would've liked to dress in men's clothes and join the men's revels; there were stories that once or twice reckless ladies did just that. Anyway, the person who gave la Cavalla the flowers may have been wearing a dress, with a woman's coif for a mask, but I knew who it was instantly.

Pandolfo.

He'd put a powder on the flowers. Maybe he wanted to kill her outright and it didn't quite work, or maybe he just wanted to make her unconscious so he could spirit her away. The other part of the plan was obviously for a second person to distract the attention of the crowd from the real duchess to another woman in a white dress, who ran away from the courtyard and somehow got out of the Castello to run along the drawbridge. The guards were probably drunk or enjoying a little Berlingaccio revelry of their own. Everyone ran after her, but she disappeared into the town.

Who was she?

Sister Orsola, of course.

La Cavalla was so far unconscious, she might as well have been dead. Pandolfo dragged her into the Castello, up the spiral stairs beside the Tower of the Lions to the chapel where he'd been working on the frescoes and the niches for the new statues. Everything was strewn around, bricks and mortar, buckets of plaster and paint, scaffolding along one wall. I couldn't imagine what he was planning to do with her. What he did was just leave her lying on the floor while he lit a torch and began to mix up a batch of fresh mortar.

It didn't make any sense at all.

After a while, who came panting in but Sister Orsola. She'd taken off the white dress and put on her nun's habit again, everything but the wimple and veil. She must've slipped back into the Castello in the midst of all the screaming and running and everyone blaming everyone else.

It worked, she said.

Good, he said. He kept mixing the mortar.

Is she dead?

When she said that, I decided I'd just call her Orsola, because obviously she wasn't a holy nun anymore.

Pandolfo laughed. No, he said, she's not dead. Do you know how much that damned apothecary wanted for a powder that would've actually killed her? The sleeping-powder was one-tenth the price, and it doesn't matter when she dies. She has to disappear, that's all, so the duke has a new mystery to think about. He'll spend no more time meddling in what happened to his first duchess, when his second duchess vanishes before his eyes.

What does it matter? Orsola said. We'll be far away.

No. We won't. I won't give up the duke's patronage. These frescoes—

He gestured, a huge flamboyant gesture, at Saint Elizabeth and Saint Anne and the Holy Virgin as a child, flickering in and out in the light of the one torch.

—will make my name forever. I'm staying here. So I have to give the duke another mystery to worry at, so he won't keep picking at old sores.

He didn't know la Cavalla had found the secret painting! He didn't know no matter what he did, the duke was going to find him and rip his coglioni *off. He could make la Cavalla disappear a thousand times, and it wouldn't do him any good.*

But he didn't know.

What about me? Orsola said. You said we would go away together.

If I thought I hated him before, I hated him a hundred times more when she said that.

Pandolfo stood up. He picked up a mallet.

I did say that, didn't I? he said, all sly and foxy-looking. Well, four years ago I needed your help to make me a key to Corpus Domini. After that I needed to keep you quiet. Then I needed you to help me again, so I could carry off this duchess, this Barbara. But now I don't need you anymore.

He swung his arm around and smashed her in the face with the mallet, so fast she never made a sound. She just fell down.

Then la Cavalla woke up.

CHAPTER THIRTY

$\mathcal{I}$ was a child again, seven or eight years old, in the austere old imperial nursery in Innsbruck. My nurse was making *milchreis*, rice pudding, my favorite supper. Thump-thump-thump went the wooden spoon in the pan as she stirred it and stirred it. Each stroke made a thick wet swishing sound. Milk and rice and eggs and sugar, and then the reddish-brown dusting of cinnamon. When it was finished we would share it, Margareta and Ursula and Helena and I, because we were all too young to eat supper anywhere but in the nursery.

I loved the cinnamon. Cinnamon—

—*charmingly childlike freckles like a dusting of cinnamon over her nose and forehead*—

A face that didn't belong in the nursery. Didn't belong in the dream at all.

Radiant. Smiling. Wrong, so wrong.

I opened my eyes.

Flickering darkness. One torch. Women's faces, appearing to

move in smoky ripples of light. The sound. Stirring, squelching. Not *milchreis*, then. Not the nursery in Innsbruck.

Where? What?

Holy Virgin, my head hurt. My mouth was as dry and bitter as bone.

I pushed myself up on my hands and looked around. A patterned marble floor, under a film of white dust. Familiar. Why was I lying on the floor in the ducal chapel? The women's faces—they were not women at all, but Frà Pandolf's frescoes, Saint Elizabeth and Saint Anne and the Virgin as a child. There was a woman, though, a real one, over by the niches where the statues were to be placed—

I have been much pleased with the bronze figure of Neptune cast for me by Claus of Innsbruck, and always intended to commission further pieces—

My mind kept slipping away from me. I recollected myself. There was a woman, tall and thick-bodied, over by the niches. She was mixing something in a bucket.

"You," I said. My voice was hoarse, and the effort to speak hurt my throat. "Woman. I do not know how I came to be here, but I am not well. Water, I beg you, and then find my own ladies. I am the duchess, and I promise you will not be the poorer for it."

She straightened and turned around.

I knew her.

But—

Reddish-brown hair and a bristling beard, black eyes, a foxy pointed nose, a self-satisfied smile.

Not a woman at all.

Frà Pandolf in his Franciscan habit. Not so much different, really, from a townswoman's dress.

The Berlingaccio revels, the flap and flare of torches in the cold night air. Women in one courtyard, men in another. Crezia and Elisabetta Bellinceno, both punctiliously correct. Nora wine-flown and sobbing, not correct at all. Townswomen pressing in, demanding the favors due them. Smells and noise and confusion. A woman handing me an armful of flowers, and me breathing deep, desperately grateful for the fresh sweetness.

Tommasina Vasari's voice, whispering from the other side of death: *any piece of fruit, any flower you are offered might be poisoned.* . . .

He had worn a woman's dress, so he could mingle with the other women. Probably over his habit, so it could be easily pulled off and discarded. He had wrapped a woman's coif over his face and beard. He had given me flowers.

"You poisoned the flowers," I said.

He laughed. "Not I, Serenissima. You're still alive, aren't you? A sleeping-powder, no more—the apothecary wanted too much gold for the real poison."

What did he want? Why had he brought me here?

"I will give you money," I said. "You can go away, change your name—"

"She said the same. 'Come away, we will have money, we will change our names.' Can't you duchesses understand I don't want to go away, and I don't want to change my name? My name—that's what I value above all else."

He says he will kill me before he gives up his art for me. Nora joined the mad gabbling in my head. For Tasso, it had been only words, only theatrics. For Frà Pandolf, it had been deadly serious.

I saw her, all in her habit and cowl, bending over Sodona's bed and pressing the pillow against her face. Tommasina Vasari had seen exactly what she had described, a figure in a monastic habit smothering her mistress. What difference would there be, in a nighttime silhouette, between thickset, rawboned Sister Orsola and Frà Pandolf?

I struggled to throw off the effects of the soporific powder. "I will say nothing. Let me go now and no one will ever know."

He picked up a mallet and tossed it from one hand to the other as if testing its weight. "Don't be a fool," he said. "There's not a woman in the world who can keep a secret."

"Surely there is something you want."

"What I want is for the court to be like it was before you arrived and began poking your long Habsburg nose where it didn't belong. I want you and your questions to disappear, and the duke to have a new mystery to consume him. Then I'll finish the chapel and increase my renown, and the name of Frà Pandolf will live forever."

"It is you who are a fool." I pushed myself to my feet, staggered, and fell to my knees again. I was still dizzy, and my elaborate Berlingaccio costume impeded me. The diamonds of Eleonora of Naples felt like a circlet of thorns around my forehead. I tried again to get up, and this time I succeeded. "It will make no difference if I disappear. The duke already—"

The shock of the blow snapped my head around. The floor came up and cracked into my hands and knees. There was a moment of nothing but shock and then it hurt, Holy Virgin, it hurt like nothing I had ever felt before. The whole side of my face pounded with agony. I think I vomited. Or perhaps it was blood dripping down from my nose and lips.

"Be silent," the Franciscan said, as if from far away. "I could kill you now if I wanted another mortal sin on my soul, but I've got enough of those already. I'll be ready for you in a moment."

He went back to his stirring. Swish-thump, swish-thump, swish-thump.

Think. Do not tell him the duke has already seen the secret portrait of Lucrezia de' Medici, the duke's men are already searching for him, and this plan of his, whatever it is, is hopeless. If he knows that, he will kill you quickly. Let him believe he is still in the duke's favor, and look about for a way to escape.

I lifted my head carefully. How far to the doorway? Could I manage it without being struck down again? And what was that heap of clothing? Was it the woman's dress he had used to insinuate himself into the women's revels?

A low groan. For a dizzy moment I thought Frà Pandolf himself had been taken ill, and I would have my chance to escape after all. Then I realized the heap of clothing was not just clothing but another woman in a gown and tunic. There was blood like a dark red mantle wrapped around her head and flung out over the floor. My first thought was that it was one of my ladies, Katharina or Domenica or Nicoletta. But none of them would wear such rough clothes.

Then I saw my own ruby ring on the woman's finger.

Sister Orsola.

Of course. I had been right. Frà Pandolf was her lover from about the court. Frà Pandolf was the second thing she had shared with Lucrezia de' Medici.

But if they were lovers, why was she lying on the floor groaning?

"All right, Orsolina." It was the Franciscan. "You first."

He grasped her by the shoulders and heaved her up, and I saw her face. It was indeed Sister Orsola, although I might not have known her if I had not recognized the ring. Her face was a mask of blood, her nose sickeningly misshapen, her left cheekbone crushed. I retched again and put my face down against the cold marble of the floor.

He dragged her to one of the niches along the side wall, where statues cast by Claus of Innsbruck were intended to stand. There was a low wall of brick built up before the niche, of a height to reach to a man's knees. Why would he do that? How would the bronze be settled in the niche, if there was mortared brick blocking the way?

He dropped Sister Orsola into the niche, behind the wall. I heard her gasp and sob.

"Now you, Serenissima. Up you go."

I screamed when he lifted me, screamed as loudly as I could. It was like trying to scream in a dream—no matter how frantic my gasps for breath, no matter how violently I forced the air out, little sound was made. I screamed again and again. He laughed.

I kicked and scratched and bit like a child, but he did not care. He stuffed me down behind the wall, next to Sister Orsola. My jeweled skirts filled up so much of the space it was hard to move.

To my horror, he stroked my cheek softly.

"You do have pretty hair," he said. "Take comfort, *mia cara*. My painting of you will live through the ages—the duchess who vanished into thin air—the duchess who ran away—who knows what they will say? They will look at the painting and tell a hundred stories, a thousand, and always they will say, 'It was Frà Pandolf, the magnificent Franciscan, who made her live.'"

"Get your hand away from me," I said through clenched teeth. "The duke will find you and tear you to pieces."

"He'll never know. This is your own fault—if you hadn't tried to rake the midden of Duchess Lucrezia's death, I'd have no quarrel with you."

Rather than dignify that with an answer, I grasped the top of the wall and tried to drag myself out of the niche. He picked up a mallet—blood on it, thick, dark blood . . . oh Holy Virgin, that was what he had used then, her face, my face—swung it hard and smashed my fingers.

WHEN I CAME to myself again, he had built the wall high enough that I could just see over the top. The mortar—that was what he had been stirring. I cradled my left hand against my breast and watched him as he fitted a brick into the half-finished top row. The mortar oozed out like clotted cream. I could smell it—like wet dust, with a cold bite of quicklime.

"Frà Pandolf." I was amazed my voice sounded anything like I remembered it. "This is madness. You are a holy brother, and already you have mortal sins upon your conscience—you yourself confessed it. If you finish that wall and leave me here, I will surely die. Sister Orsola will die also. Even if you escape the duke, you will be held accountable before God for our deaths."

"It was God who made me a great artist," he said. He placed another brick. "He won't blame me for the deaths of a few chattering women. And anyway, I'm not killing you. You're both still alive."

"You are mad."

He shrugged and pressed the brick down. I could hear the trowel scraping against the brick on the outside of the wall as he trimmed away the excess mortar. I pushed one foot against the bricks at the bottom of the wall but found them immovable. Either the mortar was already hardening, or the weight of the bricks themselves was holding the wall in place. Probably both.

"I can give you a fortune in gold and jewels. I can give you this diamond tiara—you can break it up, sell the stones one by one."

"Keep your diamonds, Serenissima. I have no need for riches, and they will make a pretty sparkle when your body has turned to dust."

"They will see the blood." I struggled to keep desperation out of my voice. "When they come searching for me, they will know something terrible happened here."

He laughed. "I've already thought of that. A little water, a little fresh sand—there will be no trace left."

I have to make some mark, I thought. Leave something outside the wall so when the searchers come they will know we are here. Something small, so he will not notice—yet something that will be seen and identified as mine.

There were the hundreds of medallions sewn on my skirts, the Berlingaccio sun-faces and roses. With my right hand I scrabbled at them, trying to tear one free, damning the skills of Messer Salvestro's needlewomen. I dug my nails into the fragile silver tissue itself, and finally I felt it tear and one of the medallions come away.

"Frà Pandolf!" I called. He had bent down to pick up another brick. "You are a priest. Confess me—do not leave me here to die in my sins."

I braced myself against the wall behind me and managed to straighten a bit. My whole body was shaking in terror of that ghastly mallet, but with my eyes squeezed shut I grasped the top of the wall again. The pain in my left hand was like fire. Sister Orsola groaned as I moved.

"Confess me," I said again.

His face appeared in the remaining empty space. "Don't be stupid. I'm a friar, not a priest. Don't ask me to absolve you of your sins."

"Then there is no priest here at all." As I spoke, I edged the little rosette of crystals over the top of the wall. To cover the sound of its fall, I wailed as if in the greatest anguish of soul. "Saint Augustine himself has said it—if a priest be wanting, even a layman may hear confessions."

"The more fool you, Serenissima, to think I care about your sins." He troweled down more mortar, and I pulled my hands away just in time. Streaks of blood remained on the brick. Would anyone see? Would anyone guess? "Try confessing to Sister Orsola there— she's a nun, and for all her sins probably holier than I am."

I sank back into the niche. Sister Orsola stirred. Holy Virgin, I prayed, Saint Barbara, Saint Monica, Saint George great patron of Ferrara, please do not let him find it. I promise a hundred novenas, a thousand. Please, please, please.

The Franciscan continued to build his wall. I found myself counting the bricks as he placed them. My hands were shaking with the terrible compulsion to do something, to straighten my skirt, pleat the fabric—but the left hand was too painful to move and the right one was now pinned by Sister Orsola's weight.

He placed the last brick but one. There was only a crack of light left at the top, and already the niche felt hot and airless. Sister Orsola was crying quietly, although I did not think she knew where she was or what had happened to us.

"What's this?" Frà Pandolf's voice said. It sounded faint and far away. "A bit of crystal frippery? Was it here before? I don't think so."

His hand thrust through the little patch of light. His fingers moved. There was a soft chinking sound as the rosette of crystals fell back inside the niche.

"The duke will find you," I said. My voice shook with fury and terror.

"I will see the duke every day. He will stand in this very room and tell me my frescoes are magnificent. How I'll laugh to know your bones are moldering behind the wall, while he loads me with more commissions."

"That he will not. He will—"

I stopped myself. If I told the Franciscan the duke had seen the painting, he would flee. At least I could do that much. I could keep it a secret and send Frà Pandolf unwitting to his own destruction.

There was a slap of mortar and a scrape of brick, and the last light was gone.

Sister Orsola sobbed and wrapped her arms around me.

I stared into black darkness. There were more sounds, much muffled. Most likely he was plastering over the fresh brickwork. He would throw dust against the plaster to make it look dry, and probably place scaffolding over that. We had all become accustomed to seeing the chapel in disarray, with bricks and wet frescoes and half-made niches. Would anyone realize one of the niches had disappeared? Would he make another niche, perhaps, so the number would match the number of bronzes ordered from Innsbruck?

"Where are we?" It was Sister Orsola, her voice thick through the ruin of her nose and face. "Strike a light. Fetch water, I am thirsty."

"There is no light," I said. "There is no water."

"Who are you?"

"My name is—" What use were fine families and titles, here in the dark? "My name is Barbara."

My whole body shook. I needed to move my hands but I could not. I could not see to count the bricks. I felt a scream welling up in my throat.

"Are you another of his women?" Sister Orsola said. "I've always known he had other women, from the day he was the duchess's lover. Did you know he was the duchess's lover? The first one, I mean. The other duchess, the new one, her name is Barbara, too."

I could not start screaming. I would go mad.

Did it matter now?

"I know," I said to Sister Orsola. "He was the first duchess's lover."

"Please, light a light. It's dark."

"There are no lights."

"Are we in hell?"

I choked back tears. "No," I said. "This is not hell. Not yet."

"It should be. I'm going to hell."

I found I could just move the fingertips of my right hand, the one pinned under Sister Orsola's body. I could touch the tip of each finger to the tip of my thumb. I could count. *One, two, three, four . . .* It calmed me a little.

Aloud I said, "Why are you going to hell?"

"I broke my vows. I had a man. I lied to Mother Abbess and took the keys and gave them to him. That's how he came in and killed the young duchess—he had them copied, he had his own key. He came to bed with me that night and I told him the *parruchiera* had brought her a potion. He got angry. He said if she got out of the monastery, she'd only be whining again for him to give up his place and run away with her."

She said it so simply, as if it were nothing important. Yet Lucrezia de' Medici was dead.

One, two, three, four . . .

I said, "Did he give her poison?"

"No. He put a pillow over her face. It was quick, he told me. She was asleep."

That was what Tommasina Vasari saw, then—a figure in a Franciscan habit. Of course she would assume it was Sister Orsola. Who else but a nun would be there in the Monastero? She knew Sister Orsola had a lover, but not that he was a Franciscan or that he had his own clandestine keys.

I was beginning to feel light-headed. It was difficult to breathe. "She had a flask," I said. "A potion. The woman Tommasina gave her a potion. If it was not poison, what was it?"

"It was to rid her of the babe. For the love of Saint Clare, give me a drink."

So Maria Granmammelli had been wrong. She might know the tastes and smells of a thousand potions, and the duke might trust her knowledge beyond that of Girolamo Brasavola, but in this one case she had been wrong.

"I have no water," I said.

. . . two, three, four . . . one . . .

She put her head down on my breast. "I'm going to hell," she said again. "Call a priest."

"There is no priest."

She began to cry, choking and hiccupping. It sounded as if she were about to choke on her own blood. "A priest," she said again. "I beg you."

"You have told me your sins," I said. "Tell me you repent. That is all that matters."

"I'm sorry. I'm so sorry for it all."

I managed to lift my broken left hand and trace a cross on her forehead with the thumb. I could not move the fingers at all. Was it a sacrilege? I could not help but think God would forgive me for giving her some last shred of peace. I said, "May God forgive you your sins by the grace of the Holy Spirit. Amen."

She let out her breath with a sigh.

I wanted to ask her more questions about the flask, the potion, but she was slipping away, and who was I to disturb her last moments on Earth with selfish questions? I held her, as best I could. I prayed for her and hoped she could hear me. I counted on my fingers and felt Juana la Loca's hot breath on my own cheek.

After a little while, she died.

I was alone in the dark. The air was becoming hotter and more stifling. For a while, I confess, I gave in to despair and wept. I counted my four fingers over and over and talked to my long-dead mad grandmother. Then somehow—did she help me?—I found my resolve again. My hands stopped shaking. Despair was a deadly sin, and there was no one here, priest or lay, to absolve me. I was a Habsburg by blood and an Este by marriage—titles that demanded an outward show, at least, of courage.

Even if there was no one but a dead woman to see.

So I said the Miserere, and with more steadiness I began to count a rosary instead of meaningless numbers on the fingers of my right hand. And beyond that, there was nothing left for me to do but wait a little while, and stare into the dark, and die in my turn.

IT'S TRUE.

It was Pandolfo who killed me. He smothered me with a pillow, and then he arranged my body so it would look as if I was sleeping peacefully. He caressed me as he did it, just like he petted la Cavalla's cheek.

He did love me. He never loved me. The one person he loved? It was himself.

Isn't it strange that he will have killed both of us, la Cavalla and me? I wonder if she'll become immobila. *She should probably go straight to purgatory, unless she remains here with her spirit imprisoned in the chapel just like her flesh. At least she knows the truth now, that the potion in the flask was not poison. Tommasina would never have given me poison.*

And Pandolfo will pay. I'm not much more than a wisp anymore, but I'll cling on as hard as I can just to see the moment when Pandolfo meets Alfonso next, thinking he'll continue in Alfonso's favor. In the meantime, I'll tell the tale of what happened in the courtyard after Pandolfo abducted la Cavalla, and Sister Orsola went running off down the drawbridge in her white dress, acting the part of the duchess.

The Austrian woman, Katharina, started screeching Bärbel, Bärbel! That got the rest of them started, and they all went pelting across the drawbridge shrieking, Austrian and Ferrarese alike. They must have thought la Cavalla'd gone mad. The rest of the women just drank some more and danced some more and stole all the rest of the favors.

Finally someone had the sense to send a message to Alfonso, who was lording it over the men's revels in the main courtyard. Such swearing! Even I'd never heard Alfonso swear so foully. He went to the Saint Catherine courtyard with Sandro Bellinceno and Luigi and all his gentlemen and a contingent of men-at-arms, and of course all the women told him different stories. Finally he sent them all away to the duchess's apartments and started a proper search, down the street where the woman in the white dress had run and into the old town.

They searched all night. Morning came and went, and it was noon before they found the dress cast aside in the gutter. When Alfonso looked at it, he knew it wasn't la Cavalla's—it was just a plain white dress of the cheapest doppi silk—no satin, no silver tissue, no jewels and crystals and diamond tiaras. So the question then was, where was la Cavalla in her real costume? She might as well have vanished into the smoky night air of the Saint Catherine courtyard.

Alfonso was no fool. She'd vanished in the courtyard, and if she hadn't run off down the drawbridge, well, she was probably still inside the Castello somewhere. He questioned the guards at the other gates, but none of them would admit to seeing anything suspicious. By then it was suppertime, and no one had eaten a bite all day, and he called all his men together and sent them off to search. Sandro Bellinceno was ordered to search the Saint Catherine Tower, and for Alfonso's sake he set to work with a will—after their drunken carouse together, he knows this duchess matters to Alfonso more than I ever did. Luigi and his gentlemen went off to the Great Gallery on the first floor with torches, because it was already dark again. You'd think he'd be praying, but Luigi was always more prince than priest. He admires la Cavalla, I think—he flirted with me, but he's much more respectful to her.

While everyone was searching, Alfonso went to question la Cavalla's ladies again. He found them in her apartments, crying. Half of them were crying out of love for la Cavalla and the other half were crying for fear for their own skins. He had each one come forward and repeat what she knew, and precious little it was. Meanwhile those beneamato puppies were barking and running about, and the servants were rushing back and forth with cups of wine, and all through the Castello the men-at-arms were standing in the different rooms and looking around at emptiness and trembling with their own fears for their places.

Domenica Guarini was the only one who kept her head. I wish she'd been one of my ladies when I was alive, because maybe she would've loved me like she loved la Cavalla. Instead of just wailing uselessly, she put the red leather leashes on the two hound puppies and took them to the duke, and what did she say?

Serenissimo, do you remember that day in the Lions' Tower? When her little dogs ran in and disturbed you, because they had been following her scent from one room to the next?

Alfonso looked at her as if she'd gone moon-mad.

Domenica said, Set her dogs to find her.

CHAPTER THIRTY-ONE

*D*ark.

    Hot.

Pain everywhere, focused in my face and my left hand, beating with my heart.

I could not move my fingers anymore. It did not matter, because for the first time I could remember, I was free of the compelling need to count and arrange. If Juana la Loca had bequeathed it to me, in the prison of the wall she had taken it back to herself.

Sister Orsola's corpse was heavy against my breast. She smelled unwashed. Or perhaps her flesh was beginning to mortify. It was so hot. There was no air. How long had I been here?

I no longer had the strength to move.

Thirst. Holy Virgin, such thirst.

The duke and I had parted in anger. He had never seen my white costume. He would never find Eleonora of Naples' diamonds. He would never know love was, indeed, more than a chimera of poets and adulteresses.

I could not breathe. I could not think. I could not remember the words of the prayers.

I closed my eyes.

A BLOW FROM outside made the wall shudder. The sound in the silent, airless niche jolted me awake. It hurt my head. I did not believe it was real, and I turned my face away.

Another blow. And another.

LIGHT.

Dazzling.

I fainted.

HANDS UNDER MY arms, hard, insistent, pulling me up. What had happened to Sister Orsola? She was gone. What had happened to the brickwork? It was gone. The light hurt my eyes and the air hurt my skin. I felt arms wrap around me, cradling me like a child. I did not have the strength to hold on in return. I was so thirsty. I heard dogs barking and barking.

"*Barbara.*"

The duke's voice. The duke's arms.

"Barbara. I have you. You are safe now."

I fainted again.

"IT WAS THOSE little hounds Elizabeth Tudor sent you," the duke said. "We searched through the night and the next day, and then about suppertime Guarini's sister suggested the dogs. I took them to the Saint Catherine courtyard, and once they found your scent, they followed it directly to the chapel. I did not understand at first—the chapel was empty and I thought they were mistaken. But they would not leave the spot in front of that plasterwork. The little one, the female, sat and keened as if she would never be consoled. The male lay down at the base of the wall and refused to be moved."

I was in my own bed. I had been given water, a little at a time, and then wine, and then fine white bread sopped in meat broth. My bruised face had been tended—both by Messer Girolamo, with calves' kidneys and leeches, and by Maria Granmammelli, with a much more agreeable lotion made of sweet almond oil and milk—and the fingers of my left hand had been straightened and splinted. Only one was actually broken. My heavy wedding ring had taken the brunt of the blow; the duke had ordered it cut from my swollen finger and sent off to be mended.

Had I dreamed the moment when he pulled me from the wall and enfolded me in his arms and said, *Barbara*? Perhaps I had. He seemed no different. At the same time, Katharina told me he had not left my side until both the physician and the herb-woman had assured him I would recover completely.

Barbara.

He had refused to leave me. He was telling me so coolly of Tristo and Isa refusing to leave the wall in the chapel, but he himself—

I could not think about it. All I could comprehend was that I was alive. I was clean. I had fresh air to breathe. I could have as much water and wine as I wanted. The room was cool and full of sunlight. I was not sure what day it was, but I did not care. Blessed, blessed sunlight.

I would never take light or air or water for granted again.

"There was blood on the floor," I said. "My nose and mouth bled when he struck me. He said he would clean it away, but I suppose even if it could not be seen, the hounds could smell it."

"They did."

"And I dropped a jewel from my dress, hoping he would not see it. He picked it up again, but still—it might have left a scent."

"Indeed."

Tristo and Isa were curled up on the bed next to me, sound asleep and stuffed with every possible delicacy. I stroked their russet-velvet heads with my bandaged hand. "My saviors," I said to them. My throat tightened, and I had to swallow back tears. "Both of you. My little saviors."

Then to the duke I said, "What day is it?"

"The Thursday after Ash Wednesday. It has been a week. The public tale is that you were taken ill in the midst of the Berlingaccio revels, and suffered a fall—that accounts for your injuries, as well as your absence from the rest of the Carnival and the Mass at the cathedral yesterday."

I felt tears start again. I had been crying at the smallest things—it was not like me at all, and it made me angry at myself. "I am sorry," I said. "It is over now, though, is it not? I only want it to be over, and done, and—" The tears spilled over. I was not sure if I was crying from remorse or unhappiness or exasperation that I could not stop crying. "I want to go back. I want to begin again. I want to be a fine and beloved duchess, like Elisabetta Gonzaga."

Holy Virgin. I sounded like a puling child. I almost said, *I want you to love me*, but at least I managed to spare myself that humiliation.

"I will remind you, Madonna," the duke said in a bracing voice, "you are an imperial archduchess by birth, and as my wife you bear a nine-hundred-years-old name. The Gonzaga are upstarts in comparison. If you continue overexalting them, perhaps I should remove *Il Libro del Cortigiano* from your library and replace it with something more suitable to your station."

"No, no," I said. Suddenly I was laughing, and I do not think he meant to make me laugh. If I were to be a fine and beloved duchess with a nine-hundred-years-old name, I had to stop laughing and crying from moment to moment.

The duke put his own hand over my right hand where it lay on the coverlet. "You are overwrought," he said more gently. "And understandably so. The odd thing, Madonna, is that as agitated as you have been since I pulled you out of the wall, your hands have been still as a nun's. That is new—I had come to depend upon your hands as a sign of when you were disturbed."

I felt the color flooding up into my face. "I knew you had noticed it. I tried to prevent myself from doing it. I was afraid it was a sign I was going mad."

His hand remained on mine. "Mad? Why?"

"Because—because of her. My grandmother Johanna of Castile. Juana la Loca. I am sure you have heard her story."

He smiled. "Yes, I have heard her story. I myself am a distant cousin of hers, I believe, through that same Eleonora of Naples whose diamonds you wore for the Berlingaccio. I assure you, Madonna, you are the least likely person I know to go mad, now or ever."

"I am not so sure. I felt her with me, when I was in the wall."

"You were badly injured. You had no water and very little air, and the dead body of Sister Orsola pressed up against you. I would be more surprised if you had not seen and heard strange things."

"Perhaps," I said. "In any case, I think you shall have to find another way to determine whether or not I am disturbed. It is a great relief to me."

"It is a great relief to me that you are safe, whatever the state of your hands."

I waited, hoping he would say more. He did not, and after a moment I asked, "What have you done with Frà Pandolf?"

"He was arrested shortly after I took you out of the wall. He did not know we had found you and had made no attempt to flee."

"Nor did he know you had seen the secret painting of Serenissima Lucrezia. He thought he would continue in your patronage, and my disappearance would be such a mystery, it would distract you from any further inquiries into your first duchess's death."

"The more fool he. Luigi will manage the business of having him degraded from his orders. In the meantime he is in the dungeons, and when I am satisfied he has told all he knows, he will be executed there."

"He deserves no better. Have you questioned him about the deaths of Paolina Tassoni and Tommasina Vasari? About my slashed girth?"

"He confessed to suborning a kitchen servant, the night of the Festival delle Stelle—he had been painting her, it seems, and he gave her a few coppers to take the prepared angelica to the sign of Taurus."

"How did he even know I had begun to ask questions about— But of course, Sister Orsola would have told him. It was that very afternoon I first questioned her."

"So he said. He cut your girth as well. Your groom withdrew for a moment, as you remember, and that was all it took."

Poor Conradt. At least he had reached Prague safely and found a place with Ferdinand.

"And Tommasina Vasari?"

"That he denied, no matter how strongly the question was applied. About that, at least, I believe he was telling the truth."

"So you have discovered the identity of the false Augustinian?"

"There was no false Augustinian."

"I do not understand."

"Rest now," the duke said. "Tomorrow it will all be made clear to you."

"Tell me now."

"You must rest. I will tell you this—the alchemist Vasari is in Ferrara, of his own free will. And the gaoler has a tale to tell as well."

TOMMASINA'S FATHER? HERE in Ferrara? Well, at least he'll tell Alfonso the potion was an abortifacient and my father never knew I was with child.

The gaoler, I suppose, is going to confess he's the one who killed Tomma-sina. The only other thing he could tell them is who paid him to do it.

I don't want to know. I'm trying not to hate anyone anymore.

How Pandolfo screamed when they broke his fingers and tore his shoul-ders apart with the strappado. Alfonso didn't tell la Cavalla he watched, and directed the torturers, and asked the questions himself. In the end, even Messer Giovanni Pigna was sick and had to leave, but Alfonso remained, cold as ice. I'm not sure if Pandolfo was suffering more for cuckolding Al-fonso with me, or for trying to murder la Cavalla. Alfonso certainly didn't care that Sandro Bellinceno had had me. So I suppose that answers that question.

They're keeping him alive for now. Alfonso said he had more questions. I think he wants Pandolfo to suffer more and more and more, before he does away with what's left of him.

After hearing him scream, I don't hate him anymore. Even I wouldn't have wished such an end on him.

I'm glad the puppies found la Cavalla. I haven't hated her for a while now. How could I hate her after what Pandolfo did to her?

Alfonso? Can I truly say I don't hate him anymore?

No. Not yet. He loves her now, whether he ever actually says the words to her or not.

And he never loved me.

How can I ever stop hating him for that?

CHAPTER THIRTY-TWO

"Chess is generally considered a game of war," the duke said. "But it is a game of politics as well. Do you play, Madonna?"

Several more days had passed. I was much recovered from my ordeal and had returned to court life, repeating the tale the duke had fabricated about a spell of sickness and a fall on the night of the Berlingaccio. Naturally everyone assumed I was with child. I could only pray that tidbit of gossip would soon be made into fact.

"No, my lord, I never learned to play chess. My father also considered it a game of war and politics, and as such not suitable for women."

He smiled. "You are an unusual woman," he said. "Messer Bernardo Canigiani is to join us shortly, but before he does, I wish to give you a sketch of the situation so you do not expect too much."

We had settled ourselves in the Appartamento della Pazienza in the Saint Catherine Tower; the duke had directed our two heavy carved chairs to be placed on either side of a table made of mahogany, marble, and horn, its top inlaid with alternating squares in translucent white and black marble. Behind us was a magnificent painting by Messer Battista Dossi called *Justice*. I had hoped for justice rather than politics in the matter of Messer Bernardo Canigiani and his master, but perhaps I was indeed expecting too much.

"Please continue, my lord."

The chess pieces were stored in a drawer under the table. He took out two pieces, one white, one black, made of carved and polished wood. They were about four inches in height and amazingly detailed, representing richly dressed gentlemen on horseback, spurred and crowned, bearing not weapons but scepters symbolizing worldly power.

"These are the most important pieces in the game," he said. "The two kings." He placed the kings on the board, the white one on a white square, the black one on a black square on the opposite side. "Let us say they represent Cosimo de' Medici and me."

I wondered whether he intended himself to be the white king or the black king.

"Then there is the queen." He drew another piece out of the drawer. It was a little smaller than the kings and depicted a lady on horseback with a falcon on her wrist. Her saddle was an uncanny duplicate of the chairlike saddle I had been obliged to use on the ride back from Belfiore. She was a white piece. He placed her next to the white king.

"Only one queen?" I asked.

"She is you, Madonna, and there is not another like her." I could not tell if he meant it as a compliment or a reproach, but at least now I knew which color was which. "In this game, Cosimo de' Medici has no queen. But he does have Bernardo Canigiani."

He placed another piece on the board. The figure was riding a mule rather than a horse, without a saddle, and wearing the *cappello*, the broad-brimmed Roman hat of a churchman. He was one of the black pieces.

"This fellow is usually called a bishop, but for the moment we shall designate him as an ambassador." He placed the figure diagonally in front of the black king, directly across from the white queen. I looked at the unobstructed path between the two figures and felt a chill of fear.

"There are also two pawns in this game," he went on. He took out two smaller white pieces representing foot-soldiers carrying spears. "One is the alchemist Tommaso Vasari. The other you shall meet shortly."

"I wish to know one thing only, my lord," I said. "How does the game end?"

"Unfortunately, not with a checkmate. Our two pawns are not strong enough. But"—he placed the two pawns together in the black square immediately in front of the white queen—"they are strong enough to protect you, Madonna, from any further machinations on the part of Messer Bernardo or his master. That is the best I can promise."

"I pray it is so," I said. I reached out and picked up the white king. His bearded chin jutted arrogantly, much like the duke's; there was even a tiny carved dagger at his belt. His horse was caparisoned as if for war, or jousting.

Jousting.

But I could not ask him now. Messer Bernardo Canigiani would arrive shortly. The duke would put our two pawns in play. We would find out what the end of the game would be.

I put the white king back on the board. My questions about the tournament at Blois would have to wait.

"IT IS ALWAYS my greatest delight, Serenissimo, to be called into your presence. And of course the presence of the Serenissima."

Messer Bernardo Canigiani swept one of his ostentatious bows, the feather of his hat skimming the marble floor.

"It is our pleasure as well," the duke said. "You will note I have dismissed my secretaries and the rest of the court. The duchess and I wish to speak with you quite privately."

Bernardo Canigiani continued to smile. "I am entirely at your service, Serenissimo. I see you and your charming duchess have been enjoying a game of chess."

"Not in any conventional manner. In fact, the board is laid out to represent your audience with us, at this moment. You will see the duchess and me on the one side, and you yourself, with of course your master, Duke Cosimo, figuratively present behind you, on the other."

He looked at the board. "A clever conceit," he said. "What, then, do the two pawns represent? It is highly irregular to place two pawns upon one square."

"Perhaps. They also represent real people. I shall call them in one at a time, and we will see if they are as one in their purpose."

The duke lifted his hand, and Tommaso Vasari stepped into the room from the adjoining terrace garden.

"What is this?" Messer Bernardo's smile froze upon his face, and for the first time since I had come to Ferrara, I saw him discomfited. "What is this man doing here?"

"You know him, then," the duke said in a silky voice.

"Of course I know him. He is a Florentine alchemist in the employ of Duke Cosimo. Serenissimo, I demand to know what he is doing here in Ferrara and—"

"You may demand nothing." Messer Bernardo started back at the sudden harshness in the duke's voice, and I must confess I did the same. "Messer Tommaso, tell the ambassador what you have told me, if you please."

The alchemist came forward. He was a short, thin fellow with hollow eyes like his daughter's, dark and burning. His graying hair was combed straight back, and although he had tried to grow the long luxuriant beard that was an alchemist's badge of office, he had produced only a few thin strings. His skin was mushroom-white, as if he never set foot in sunlight.

"Serenissimo," he said. He bowed to the duke. Then he turned to Messer Bernardo. "Ambasciatore," he said. His voice was soft and perfectly respectful. Which made it all the more astonishing when he sprang at Messer Bernardo with a knife suddenly glittering in his hand.

"Ho, guards!" the duke shouted. Messer Bernardo flailed at his attacker, screaming like a woman, his cape and the feathered hat in his hand taking the worst of the knife-cuts. I suddenly heard Tommasina Vasari's voice—*a hollow bodkin, an accidental scratch*—and I cried, "Take care, the knife may be poisoned!"

One of the men-at-arms struck the alchemist from behind, and he went to his knees; the knife skidded across the polished floor. Messer Bernardo, sweating and shaking, cast his slashed cape and hat away from him with terror and disgust.

"Serenissimo, I protest!" he gasped. "I am a *patrizio* of Florence and Duke Cosimo's accredited ambassador. I will not be treated in this manner. What have I to do with this alchemist, that you so much as bring him into the room with me?"

"What you have to do with him," the duke said, "is that you arranged the murder of his daughter."

There was a moment of absolute silence.

Tommaso Vasari sobbed. It sounded like a piece of paper being torn in half. "She did not know," he said. "She was innocent. Her only sin was to love the young duchess more than she loved her father and her home. She knew nothing about the substitution of the poison for the abortifacient potion."

"What are you talking about, fellow?" Messer Bernardo demanded. "Poison? Potion? I know nothing of any poisons or potions."

"Perhaps our second pawn will make the matter clearer." The duke gestured for the guards to leave, and when they had gone, another man came into the room. I did not know him at first. It was only when he turned his head and I saw the purple birthmark on his neck that I recognized him: it was the gaoler who had been given charge of Tommasina Vasari, and under whose oversight she had been killed. He had been bathed, barbered, and dressed in the livery of the duke's house servants.

"Tell your story," the duke said.

"My name is Matteo Fabbri." The man was pale but resolute, and I could not help thinking he showed more courage than Messer Bernardo did. "'Twas I who killed her, Serenissimo, Serenissima, and I've not had a night's sleep since. There was no Augustinian. That was a tale I made up when the Serenissima pointed out the poor lady couldn't have hanged herself, not with her thumbs all broken and crushed."

Tommaso Vasari sobbed again.

"He paid me." Matteo Fabbri pointed at Messer Bernardo. "Two gold florins. He said she would die anyway, and he was right, poor lady—she was crying and begging for a priest, and I don't think she could have lived much longer. Just a quick twist, and she was gone."

"I have never seen you before in my life," Messer Bernardo said. "You are mistaken, gaoler."

I sucked in my breath.

The duke said very softly, "And how did you know this man's occupation, Messer Bernardo? He is dressed in ordinary livery, and nothing has been said of prisons or gaolers."

Once again that deadly silence.

"A fortuitous guess." Messer Bernardo straightened his doublet and made an effort to look unconcerned. "It was in your prison that the woman hanged herself, is that not so, Serenissimo? Who else but a gaoler would have access to a prisoner? Surely you cannot expect to accuse me of murder based upon the word of this fellow."

He was babbling. He knew he had been trapped.

"I do," the duke said. He reached out and flicked one finger against the figure on the chessboard representing the ambassador. It fell over with a single tick of wood against polished black marble. "And I also intend to accuse your master."

"Duke Cosimo? That is ridiculous."

"I think not. Messer Tommaso, I will ask you again to tell your tale. No knives this time, if you please."

The alchemist lifted his head. Tears streaked his face. "When I received the letter from my daughter," he said, "I was angry. She had refused, time and again, to come home—and she was even willing to take mortal sin upon herself by purveying a forbidden potion, all for the sake of Lucrezia de' Medici. I thought to revenge myself upon them both by showing Duke Cosimo the letter, showing him his daughter's dishonor. He fell into a rage, as he is well-known for doing, and swore he would see his daughter dead before she shamed him."

Messer Bernardo stood absolutely white and still, as if he had been turned to salt.

"He gave me a rich flask covered with jewels, which he said Tommasina could keep for herself—she could have sold it for ten times the amount she would have needed to return safely home. At his instruction I made up the poison and sealed it into the flask, and sent it off to Tommasina with a letter assuring her it was the safest and most efficacious of abortifacients."

I spoke for the first time. "Messer Tommaso, did he have no sorrow, no regret for his daughter?"

"None, Serenissima. He said she would be served as she justly merited—if she was not with child, she would not drink the potion, and thus she would not die; but if she drank the potion so as to kill a bastard she had conceived in sin, well, then, she would die, and rightly so."

"God forgive him," I said softly. I looked at the black king on the chessboard. He was a mirror image of the white king. Surely the duke and Cosimo de' Medici were not so similar. Surely the duke would never—

"There was no longer any advantage to be gained from a marriage between Ferrara and Florence," the duke said. "Half her dowry would be returned if she died childless, and that was better than nothing. The scandal would become the scandal of her death, attached to me, rather than the scandal of her bearing a bastard, blackening the name of the Medici."

Messer Tommaso bowed his head. "Just so," he said. "And so it happened, Serenissimo, just as you say. But Tommasina did not come home. The rest of the young duchess's household returned, but not my Tommasina. I made inquiries—and was told to make no more, if I wished to retain my position and Duke Cosimo's favor. I think he ultimately convinced himself the tale he put about was true—that you, Serenissimo, had poisoned his daughter in secret."

"I will not stand by and allow this low fellow to blacken Duke Cosimo's name," Messer Bernardo said in a harsh and shaky voice. "He lies, and I demand he be returned to Florence to be tried and punished for this betrayal."

"I think not," the duke said again. "Continue, Messer Tommaso."

"I heard nothing more of Tommasina until your man came to me, Serenissimo, and told me she had been murdered in Ferrara after being questioned in the matter of Lucrezia de' Medici's death. I knew immediately it was Duke Cosimo's hand, stretching out from Florence, that had silenced her."

"And so it was," the duke said. "However much Messer Bernardo may deny it."

"You would not dare make this tale public," Messer Bernardo said. He might have aged ten years in the past ten minutes. I looked at the fallen figure of the black ambassador's piece on the chessboard, and the two pawns in the square in front of the white queen, and in that moment the duke's design became wholly clear to me.

The duke touched the black king, but did not tip the figure over. Duke Cosimo could not be openly accused of murder, any more than the Duke of Ferrara himself. "Madonna, I see you have divined my purpose in bringing forward our two pawns. Perhaps you would care to explain it to Messer Bernardo."

I thought of Messer Bernardo whispering to me in the chapel. I thought of the dead, one image after another as if I were running through a gallery of paintings—the glowing young duchess with her branch of cherry blossoms in her hand, the painter-friar with his magnificent genius and fatal hubris, the rawboned infirmarian with her pathetic greed for jewels and pleasures, the vengeful *parruchiera* whispering madness to me on my wedding morning, then screaming and screaming as her thumbs cracked in the thumbscrew.

"I would be delighted to explain it to Messer Bernardo," I said.

"Surely there is some way—" the ambassador began.

"Be silent." It was my Habsburg blood speaking, and it did not fail me. "Shall I tell it to you in the form of a tale by Boccaccio? No? Then I will say it to you plainly. Messer Tommaso and Matteo Fabbri are to be conveyed to a safe place, where even Duke Cosimo's hand cannot reach. I suspect they will write their confessions before priests, and sign them, and swear to their veracity on holy relics. Their persons and their confessions may not be revealed in public, but they will remain in Duke Alfonso's possession, a weapon known only to him and Duke Cosimo. Perhaps one day Duke Alfonso will choose to use his weapon in secret, with the emperor, with the pope, if the circumstances warrant."

Messer Bernardo said nothing. He stood white and trembling. There was no answer he could give.

The duke picked up the two pawns and held them in his fist. Every monster I had ever seen in his eyes leaped out, and I half-expected Bernardo Canigiani to fall down dead on the marble floor, just as the chess piece that represented him lay on its side on the board.

"I will use them," the duke said in the soft, vicious voice I had learned to fear, "if you ever threaten or attempt to suborn the duchess again. If she ever reports to me that you have so much as spoken a word to her in private again. You are not above the law, nor are you above your master's own poisons if he should think you have become a liability to him. Do you understand?"

"I understand," the ambassador said. His voice was so faint and hoarse, I could barely hear him.

"Now, you are dismissed. You may consider yourself free to leave for Florence. I will not expect you in Ferrara again until after Easter."

Messer Bernardo made a short bow like a stick broken in half at its center—what a difference!—and left the Appartamento della Pazienza without a word.

I wondered if we would ever see him again.

The men-at-arms returned and took Messer Tommaso and Matteo Fabbri away—them, I knew I would not see again. I felt light and empty and a little sick. The duke began to put the chess pieces away.

"Whether you know it or not, Madonna," he said, "you are far more a student of Machiavelli than you are of Castiglione."

I'D RATHER BE in hell than hear this.

My father knew everything? He knew about the baby? He knew about the abortifacient? Oh, God, and he hated me so much for it all that he sent me poison in its place, and it was only by chance Pandolfo pressed the pillow down over my face before the poison took me?

I remember how bitter it was.

My father hated me.

My father wanted to kill me, even if it was just for a day, in one of his rages.

I'm slipping down into hell and I don't care anymore. I haven't given up my hatred for Alfonso and I wanted to, I wanted to— No! I'm not ready! Oh, God, I do care, I do, I do! Forgive me, help me, pray for me—

CHAPTER THIRTY-THREE

"And what," I said to the duke, "does Machiavelli say of justice?"

A few more days had passed, and we were in the third week of Lent. I had become tired of resting, and the sick, empty feeling had lessened. The bruises on my face had faded, with the help of more lotions and the most disgusting leeches one could possibly imagine. My hand was also better, although the first finger, the one that had been broken, would always be crooked. My compulsion to count and pleat and arrange things had not come back. The ghastly hours—days?—of imprisonment in the wall seemed to have burned it out of me forever.

I was ready—as ready as I could be—for the end game. Cosimo de' Medici might escape direct retribution by reason of his position, and Bernardo Canigiani might shelter under his master's hand in everything but his threats to me here in Ferrara, but Frà Pandolf had played his part as well, and at least he could feel the full weight of justice for his crimes.

"Messer Niccolò had little use for justice," the duke said. "In fact, he writes that lovers of justice often come to sad ends."

"I will come to a sad end, then. Frà Pandolf must pay for what he did."

"He has."

"Tell me."

"Are you sure you wish to hear?"

"I am sure."

"Very well. He suffered the question, as you know. When I was satisfied he had confessed everything, he was entombed alive under the floor of an oubliette beneath the Marchesana Tower. I myself observed the paving-stones set into place over him, down to the last one, and I ground my heel in the dust above him. Then I left him to experience the death he designed for you."

A fortnight ago the duke's dispassionate description of the Franciscan's end would have horrified me. Today it did not. I crossed myself. "May God have mercy upon his soul."

We walked on a little, our ladies and gentlemen and a little gaggle of whispering courtiers following at a discreet distance. March had come, and with it the first stirrings of spring—the air was softer and the all-embracing fog no longer seemed chilled with fine crystals of ice. I could smell the beginning of new green in the marshes and fields outside the city. As we passed through the gardens, the duke seemed to have a destination in mind, and I was willing to follow him.

"He was a magnificent artist, I will give him that," the duke said after a moment. "Because of that, there is a further punishment I intend to impose."

"Such a terrible death is not enough?"

"No. He dishonored me. He murdered a duchess of Ferrara and a sinless unborn child. He murdered a Clarissa, his sister in God. He murdered your waiting-woman and came close to murdering you. Not only will he die, but his art with him."

"I do not understand."

"I will destroy it. Every painting, every fresco, every sketch. I will expunge his name from the records of Ferrara. He will exist no longer, as a man, a Franciscan, or an artist. He did it all for the sake of glory, and glory is what I will deny him."

"You would destroy art? You?"

He laughed. I was reminded how cruel he could be when he chose. "I would. Come into this courtyard with me, Madonna, and I will show you."

I went in with him. A bonfire had been constructed in the center and was already crackling and snapping in the afternoon breeze; two chairs had been placed against the courtyard's western wall and a cloth of state erected over them. Our entourage was barred from entering by halbardiers. The duke allowed Domenica and Christine to see I was comfortably seated, to fetch orange-water and wine, and then he ordered them away as well.

"This entire business is not something I wish to be generally known," he said. "There will be tittle-tattle, of course—there always is when misfortune befalls the great."

Only Alfonso d'Este could say such a thing without the slightest hint of irony.

"So you will not make it publicly known that Serenissima Lucrezia was murdered?"

"I have said many times she died of an imbalance of humors, and I cannot tell a different tale now. The difference is that now Cosimo de' Medici will tell the same tale."

"So we hope."

"So we hope. You will attest to the tale as well if anyone dares speak to you of the matter, just as you have attested to the public explanation of your own injuries."

"Yes, my lord," I said gravely.

"As for the rest—Sister Orsola's body was returned to Corpus

Domini and interred there. She was of no consequence, and no one will ask what became of her, or care."

I crossed myself. "She was of consequence to God."

"God shall deal with her. Now, I wish you to see the Franciscan's work destroyed. You began this business, Madonna, with your questions. Here, at last, will be the end of it."

Four men-at-arms of the rougher sort entered the courtyard from a low inner gate, pushing handcarts. Two were jammed with books and paints, palettes and brushes and rags, rolls of canvas and half-painted sketches. The other two contained finished paintings, some still in their ornate frames and some showing raw edges where they had been cut free.

"The paint shall cause the fire to burn merrily," the duke said. He gestured to the men. "Proceed."

They began to cast it all into the fire. I saw the cardinal's face, smiling indulgently through the flames—then blackening and curling. Crezia followed, and Nora, and Anna the Duchess of Guise in France, the duke's widowed older sister whom I had never met. Pots of paint and turpentine exploded like fireworks. Sketchbooks fell to ash.

I drank orange-water and the duke drank wine, and we watched the flames. I thought of the duke's device. *Ardet Aeternum.* Aflame for eternity. I felt inexplicably close to him. Perhaps it was nothing but the knowledge we had hunted down the truth together. Perhaps it was more than that.

Dusk fell, and the fire burned on.

"The frescoes in the chapel have been scraped away," he said. "Painting over them would not be sufficient destruction. I have engaged another artist to paint the walls and ceiling. There will be no niches and no statuary."

"There are small paintings, Stations of the Cross, at the Monastero del Corpus Domini."

"They have been removed and burned already."

My own portrait was next to the last. Looking at it, I was reminded of the afternoon I sat for it, the way the light had spilled over the floor in squares. Frà Pandolf had leaned over my shoulder, close enough that I could feel the heat of his breath against my cheek and smell the scents of paint and turpentine on his habit. He had said, *It is you, Serenissima*—

My red silk wedding dress. Hair smoothly combed back, shimmering apricot-gold. Eyes the color of cloves, clear and steady and full of secrets.

I turned away. I felt the heat of the fire blaze up, and I knew the portrait was gone.

"This is the last, Serenissimo."

It was, of course, the long-hidden portrait of Lucrezia de' Medici. There were others, by other artists. They would remain. This one would not.

The duke and I both looked at it for a moment. I thought— how beautiful she was, how young, how like those cherry blossoms she loved to be painted with—beautiful and transitory. She had known only two springs in Ferrara. I wondered how often she had gone to the cherry tree and broken off a branch, to revel in the glory and fragrance of the flowers. To eat the ripe sweet fruit. To ride on her white mule, round and round in the dizzying fragrance. She loved it so much she chose it as a hiding place for her most secret treasures.

"Alfonso," I said. I remembered how strange the word had sounded in the dusty tower room where Lucrezia de' Medici's wedding chests had been stored. "Why did you hide this painting? There are others of Lucrezia de' Medici in the main gallery. Why did you hide this particular one?

He looked at the painting for a long time. The bonfire whipped and crackled, hungry for the wood and paint and canvas. "I do not think I myself could have told you," he said at last, "until I saw the other, the one in her hidden box. That one revealed her as she truly was, and now I can see that this one does as well—she was a creature entirely of the flesh. She did not belong among the Este."

"Why did you not destroy it, then?"

He smiled a little. "Because it is a beautiful piece of art," he said. "Surely you see that. I would look at it sometimes—when I could put the identity of the woman out of my mind, it gave me . . . great pleasure to look at it. However many pieces of art I may commission, however many paintings I may own, until the day I die I will never own one more exquisitely beautiful."

"Paolina Tassoni once hinted to me that you displayed it upon occasion. Not just to Ferdinand—to other people, strangers. Used it as a means of disparaging the young duchess's character, and exculpating yourself in the rumors about her death."

"And do you believe such whispers, after all that has happened?" His voice was perfectly even and calm.

I had expected an angry reply. I had expected to feel guarded and anxious. How much we had both changed. "No," I said. "I do not believe it. You would never stoop to such familiarity with strangers."

He nodded to the man-at-arms. The portrait went into the flames. It seemed to flare up more brightly than the others.

And that was the end of it. Frà Pandolf was gone, and now his art as well was gone as if it had never been. The men-at-arms took the empty handcarts away, and the duke and I were left alone in the courtyard with the dying fire.

"The tales will never completely be silenced," the duke said. "And Cosimo de' Medici and I will continue to strive for the Precedenza. But Bernardo Canigiani will whisper to you no more. And you, Madonna, have found the truth you sought."

"Yes," I said. "Although the cost was high. I would not have done it, if I had known."

"I do not believe you. You are disquisitive and difficult, after all."

"And require firm handling." Someday I would make my

brother Ferdinand pay for his masquerade as the envoy of the Count of Tyrol, and his lighthearted words describing me that the duke apparently would never forget.

The duke smiled. "No," he said. "In that your brother was wrong, and it was my misjudgment that I listened to him. You require reason and—honor for your position. From now on you shall have them."

Again I felt that new, indefinable closeness between us. I felt as if I could say anything to him. I remembered the white king from his chess set, crowned and spurred on his caparisoned horse, off to war. Or to a joust.

"Alfonso," I said again. It still did not feel natural. That would come, I hoped. "I would ask a question of you."

"Ask."

"What happened at the tournament at Blois?"

"Blois?" He sounded genuinely puzzled for a moment. Then he said, "Ah, yes. Blois. Someone has been whispering ugly tales to you."

"Yes." I did not tell him who had said it, and he did not ask.

"I was unhorsed. You have seen the scar. The animal fell on me with its whole weight. Even so, however painful and embarrassing it might have been, I suffered no lasting injury."

I said nothing.

"It is my desire to beget heirs for Ferrara with you, Madonna, and I am fully confident my desire will come to pass. I cannot be any more forthright than that."

"In that we are as one." I looked down at my hands, which rested peacefully on the carved arms of my chair. I saw my poor broken finger, still splinted and bandaged with linen strips. My wedding ring had protected the others. When the splints and bandages were no longer needed, I would wear the ring again.

He put his own hand over mine. "We are," he said.

"And the chimera of poets and adulteresses?"

That did not puzzle him; he knew at once what I was referring to. He smiled. "I still contend that is true, on the whole. Perhaps there are exceptions."

We sat for a while in silence, alone in the courtyard, our hands joined. It was so rare for either of us to be unattended. It was as if we said more to each other, much more, without words.

"I will buy Masses for their souls, the three of them," the duke said aloud, at last. "My aunt will arrange it, I am sure, at Corpus Domini."

"I will pray for them privately. And there are four, not three."

"Four? The Tassoni girl, the *parruchiera*, and the nun. Surely you do not intend to pray for the Franciscan."

"No. The fourth is your first duchess."

A dark shadow of monsters flickered up under the surface of his eyes. They would always be there. I would always have to take care when I saw them. "Why would you pray for her? She brought her end upon herself."

"Not such an end as she suffered. You will not pray for her, for charity's sake?"

"No. And I do not wish to speak of the matter again. Come, let us go in. It is almost time for supper."

He rose. I rose as well and put my hand upon his. Everything had changed between us, but that was something for us alone to know. The world would see only the duke and his duchess, grave and courteous as always, their sport and their entertainments, their art and their music, their patronage and their court.

I was content with that.

"Very well, I will not speak of it again," I said. "But here and now I make a vow before God and the Holy Virgin, and before you too, my lord—I will pray for her, all the rest of my life."

I FEEL FLAME, but I don't think I'm in hell.

I was Lucrezia de' Medici, a princess of Florence, a duchess of Ferrara.

Will I remember that? I'm not sure. I've already forgotten a lot. I want to forget more.

Who is she, this woman who's vowing to pray for me? I had a scornful name for her but I don't remember it now. Her name is Barbara, and she's the Duchess of Ferrara, too. She wanted a life she read about in a book. She got Alfonso instead. Did I hate him once? I can't remember. I may have hated Barbara, too. Someone tried to kill her, and her puppies saved her. I've forgotten so much, but I remember the puppies.

Be happy, pretty puppies. Be happy, book-reading Barbara. Think of me when you eat cherries in the spring, and live a long sweet life as the second Duchess of Ferrara.

MY LAST DUCHESS
by Robert Browning

FERRARA

That's my last Duchess painted on the wall,
Looking as if she were alive. I call
That piece a wonder, now: Frà Pandolf's hands
Worked busily a day, and there she stands.
Will't please you sit and look at her? I said
"Frà Pandolf" by design, for never read
Strangers like you that pictured countenance,
The depth and passion of its earnest glance,
But to myself they turned (since none puts by
The curtain I have drawn for you, but I)
And seemed as they would ask me, if they durst,
How such a glance came there; so, not the first
Are you to turn and ask thus. Sir, 'twas not
Her husband's presence only, called that spot
Of joy into the Duchess' cheek: perhaps
Frà Pandolf chanced to say "Her mantle laps
Over my lady's wrist too much," or "Paint
Must never hope to reproduce the faint
Half-flush that dies along her throat"; such stuff
Was courtesy, she thought, and cause enough
For calling up that spot of joy. She had
A heart—how shall I say—too soon made glad,
Too easily impressed; she liked whate'er
She looked on, and her looks went everywhere.

Sir, 'twas all one! My favour at her breast,
The dropping of the daylight in the West,
The bough of cherries some officious fool
Broke in the orchard for her, the white mule
She rode with round the terrace—all and each
Would draw from her alike the approving speech,
Or blush, at least. She thanked men—good! but thanked
Somehow—I know not how—as if she ranked
My gift of a nine-hundred-years-old name
With anybody's gift. Who'd stoop to blame
This sort of trifling? Even had you skill
In speech (which I have not) to make your will
Quite clear to such an one, and say, "Just this
Or that in you disgusts me; here you miss,
Or there exceed the mark"—and if she let
Herself be lessoned so, nor plainly set
Her wits to yours, forsooth, and made excuse,
—E'en that would be some stooping; and I choose
Never to stoop. Oh sir, she smiled, no doubt,
Whene'er I passed her; but who passed without
Much the same smile? This grew; I gave commands;
Then all smiles stopped together. There she stands
As if alive. Will't please you rise? We'll meet
The company below, then. I repeat,
The Count your master's known munificence
Is ample warrant that no just pretence
Of mine for dowry will be disallowed;
Though his fair daughter's self, as I avowed
At starting, is my object. Nay, we'll go
Together down, sir. Notice Neptune, though,
Taming a sea-horse, thought a rarity,
Which Claus of Innsbruck cast in bronze for me!

First published as "Italy" in 1842 in *Dramatic Lyrics*, the second volume in a series of self-published books entitled *Bells and Pomegranates* by Robert Browning. In 1845 it was given the title "My Last Duchess" in the seventh volume of the series, entitled *Dramatic Romances and Lyrics*.

AUTHOR'S NOTE

*T*he wonderful thing about good poetry is the way it lends itself to multiple—and often contradictory—interpretations. My vision of "My Last Duchess" is not wholly the traditional one of the duke as a monster and a madman who murdered his innocent young wife out of sheer pride and possessiveness. Browning wrote with the sensibility of the Victorian age, and today we read his nineteenth-century take with twenty-first-century eyes; I have tried to put the duke back in the sixteenth century, where he belongs. Pride and possessiveness were not, after all, unappreciated traits in a Renaissance prince.

As I WROTE the novel, I read and reread the poem, and I simultaneously read both primary and secondary historical sources. I tried to work Browning's dramatic fictionalizations into the historical world of the real Alfonso II d'Este, Lucrezia de' Medici, and Barbara of Austria.

Refictionalizing the material that Browning himself had fictionalized in his poem sometimes gave me an eerie feeling. Browning's art is such that he makes his version seem so real—more real, sometimes, than the historical record—and yet the real personages behind the figures frozen in the luminous amber of the poem cried out to be heard.

ALFONSO II D'ESTE was a soldier, a sportsman, a musician. He fought in the French army with his cousin Henri II and his brother-in-law Duc François de Guise; he was a world-class tennis player (the first written book of rules for tennis was dedicated to him); he was a great patron of the art and literature of the day and the inventor and supporter of the first professional female singing group in Europe, the Consort of Ladies. So although he was indeed vain, arrogant, and vengeful, in his context these qualities did not make him a monster. After all, Cesare Borgia, of whom *The Prince* was written, was Alfonso's great-uncle.

Alfonso's device of the flame and the motto *Ardet Aeternum* are historical, although some sources contend they were adopted only later in his life.

LUCREZIA DE' MEDICI, the "Last Duchess" of the poem's title, is generally characterized as a charming innocent, a victim of the duke's jealousy and madness. Even Browning, however, drops a hint this is not entirely true: ". . . and if she let / Herself be lessoned so, nor plainly set / Her wits to yours, forsooth, and made excuse . . ." I collected one or two hints from the historical record that she was not entirely meek and sweet-tempered, spiced it with the much better-known lives of her sisters and sisters-in-law, imagined myself in her place—and found a very different Lucrezia.

AFTER A FLURRY of contemporary whispers about poisoning and strangulation, history settled down and decided that Lucrezia de'

Medici had died a natural death, probably of tuberculosis. Perhaps she did. Then again, perhaps she did not. On his first trip to Italy in 1838, Robert Browning clearly came across some of the old rumors about Lucrezia's death, and so fictionalized her relationship with Alfonso in "My Last Duchess." As my stepping-off point for my story was Browning's poem, I have followed his fictionalization and woven it together with my own research into the historical record.

Am I maligning Cosimo de' Medici by suggesting he might have poisoned his own daughter? Possibly. But he was known to have had a violent temper, and even during his own life there were accusations that he stabbed his elder daughter, Maria (who was originally to have married Alfonso), to death for taking a lover. Other rumors hinted that he murdered his son Garzia after Garzia supposedly murdered another of his sons, Giovanni. (This was ultimately disproven by modern-day exhumations and forensic science, which showed the two boys and their mother, Eleonora of Toledo, died together from malaria in 1562.) The fact remains that there were whispers; and what is considered evil today was unexceptional for a great prince in sixteenth-century Italy. Cosimo is certainly known to have ordered the assassination of his relative Lorenzino de' Medici, his last rival within the Medici family.

COSIMO IS ALSO known to have had a passionate interest in alchemy.

THE DEVICE OF creating a poison and disguising it as an abortifacient, leaving the choice of swallowing it in the victim's own hands—and the decision taken only because she had disgraced the Medici name by the standards of the time—was very typical of the elaborate contrivances of the day.

AS FOR MESSER Bernardo Canigiani, he was indeed Cosimo de' Medici's ambassador to Ferrara. He was a successful diplomat for many years (he did indeed return to Ferrara, but that is another story) and a man of the world, and I believe he would have had few qualms about carrying out his master's wishes, whatever they might have been.

BARBARA OF AUSTRIA, my wonderful heroine and the historical second duchess of Alfonso II, has little recorded about her as a personality. She received a deeply religious upbringing with her sisters, at least two of whom became nuns; at the same time she embraced her worldly position as Duchess of Ferrara with every apparent evidence of satisfaction. I have made that dichotomy one of the keys to the character of my own Barbara. She is recorded in more than one document as being—well, there's no way to soften it—ugly. But in her portrait in the Kunsthistorisches Museum in Vienna, her hair does glow apricot-gold under her jaunty little cap.

IN PORTRAYING THESE characters and the magnificent Renaissance court and city of Ferrara, I have tried to be as accurate as possible. I've imagined and interpreted, of course, but always done my best to keep within the realm of known fact and sixteenth-century possibility. The Neptune banquet in chapter three, for example, is historical in all its detail. The Festival delle Stelle and the dual night revels of the Berlingaccio are fictional—although they are entirely in the style of the court of Ferrara of the time. Many books, articles, and papers have provided details; generous historians have given their time and expertise to help me. Whatever errors have made their way into the narrative are mine alone.

ACKNOWLEDGMENTS

First of all, thanks are due to Mr. Robert Browning for writing "My Last Duchess."

Here in the modern world, I'd like to thank my brilliant agent, Diana Fox of Fox Literary, for picking me out of her slush. Also Betty Anne Crawford and the rest of the team at Books Crossing Borders.

Thanks as well to everyone at NAL, including my thoughtful and meticulous editor, Ellen Edwards; the design team who created this book's beautiful cover art; the copy editor who saved me from multiple howlers; and everyone else who has contributed to this extraordinary experience.

To Jim, the Broadcasting Legend™, who supported and encouraged me from the first spark of inspiration to the final copyedits, and to the rest of my family. I am particularly grateful for the endless support of my dear mother, who now will never hold this book in her hands but who knew it was coming and never ceased to take pleasure in talking about it.

To fellow writers and friends for camaraderie and moral support throughout the crazy process of writing and publishing a book, including Dana Fredsti, Lisa Brackmann, Bryn Greenwood, Maire Donivan, Maureen Zogg, Les Berkley and Paula Horvath, Lesia Valentine, Melanie Morris, Cheryl Barton, and Vanessa Davisson.

To the tireless and patient librarians who fulfilled my many (and sometimes odd) requests for inter-library loans and document deliveries.

To Dr. Charles Rosenberg for kindly providing me with detailed information regarding coins struck in Ferrara during the reign of Alfonso II.

To producer Mark Smalley and presenter Peggy Reynolds for the delightful experience of being interviewed for the BBC's *Adventures in Poetry:* "My Last Duchess."

To Don Huff, for his beautiful diagram of the city of Ferrara; also to Mark Oristano for coaxing me through the agonizing process of having my picture taken.

And last but not least, to the beagles for their silky ears (so soothing in any time of stress) and lucky crossed paws: Raffles, who was my faithful shadow for eleven years and who lives on in the story as brave little Tristo; and our present companions, Cressie and Boudin.

THE SECOND DUCHESS

ELIZABETH LOUPAS

A DISCUSSION WITH ELIZABETH LOUPAS

Q. *Robert Browning's poem "My Last Duchess" was your original inspiration for this novel, but what about the story kept you fascinated? When did the characters take on a life of their own?*

A. What fascinated me from the beginning about the poem's story was the unseen character of the duke's second wife. Would she be given a choice as to whether or not she wanted to be married to the duke? Probably not. What would she think when she arrived in Ferrara and heard the whispers—because of course there would be whispers—of the fate of the duke's first duchess?

The characters took on a life of their own when I began to research the historical personages upon whom Robert Browning based his story. All of a sudden it wasn't just a story anymore—these were real people. The poem's truth was not necessarily history's truth. The greatest fascination was in somehow connecting the two truths.

Q. *Did you know much about sixteenth-century Italy before you began to write* The Second Duchess? *What kind of research did you do?*

A. I was interested in the sixteenth century in general, but my reading had been mostly centered on England and France. (I'm a first cousin thirteen times removed of Bessie Blount, Henry VIII's mistress.) When I thought of Lucrezia Borgia and the Medici, I thought mostly of poison rings and worldly popes.

I've since read books, academic papers, and journal articles in English, Italian, and German. I've visited libraries and archives in Ferrara and Florence via the magic of the Internet. I've talked to people who live in Ferrara and collected thousands of images—fortunately, most of the sixteenth-century buildings in Ferrara have been saved or restored. I've listened to music in the style of the Renaissance and tried out the dances (much to the amusement of my family). I've cooked and baked from recipes in actual period cookbooks. (They cooked and ate the most extraordinary things!) Research into historical periods is never-ending and endlessly fascinating.

Q. In The Second Duchess, *you portray Barbara of Austria as having been strongly influenced by her childhood reading of Baldassare Castiglione's* Il Libro del Cortegiano (Book of the Courtier). *Can you tell us more about this book?*

A. Il Libro del Cortegiano, originally published in 1528, was a "bestseller" of its time—it was translated into English, French, Spanish, and German, and more than a hundred different editions were published between 1528 and 1616. It was one of the original self-help books—it provided a model of looks, intellectual and physical achievements, fashion, and manners for the "courtier," the ideal aristocratic man of the day. And of course there was a section on the ideal female courtier as well. It could be called the *What Not to Wear* of its day, with Emily Post and your favorite fitness guru adding notes.

Barbara would have been taught Italian at an early age, as several Italian marriages were considered for her. It seemed possible that she would have been given a copy of this book to help her learn not only the language, but also the etiquette of the courts she might one day live in.

Q. *How much of your portrait of Alfonso and Barbara is based on the historical record, and when did you depart from what is known?*

A. I have based them on the historical record as closely as possible, in both appearance and personality although of course I have extrapolated and fictionalized "behind the scenes" where there is no historical record. However, I've tried not to attribute to any of my historical characters anything that goes against known facts.

Q. *What happened to Alfonso and Barbara, and some of the other characters, after the events of the novel?*

A. Alfonso and Barbara were happy together, surprisingly so, considering that it was an arranged marriage of state. Barbara was admired and even loved as duchess, maintaining a correspondence with Alfonso's mother, Renée of France, despite their religious differences, and using her own income to build an orphanage for girls in Ferrara.

Lucrezia d'Este (my "Crezia"—I gave her a nickname to differentiate her from all the other "Lucrezias" in the story) was eventually married to Francesco Maria II della Rovere, who was—ironically, considering Barbara's attachment to the *Book of the Courtier*—the heir to the Duke of Urbino. She was thirty-five; her young groom was twenty. The marriage was very unhappy for both of them, and they were soon separated. She returned to Ferrara and resumed her affair with Ercole Contrari, with disastrous consequences.

Nora never married. Her supposed passion for Torquato Tasso has been celebrated through the centuries, but no one really knows the whole truth of the matter. Tasso himself descended into madness (probably what we today would call schizophrenia), was confined to a madhouse in Ferrara for some years, and later died on the eve of being crowned poet laureate in Rome.

Q. *I've never heard of ghostlike presences called* immobili. *Are they based in history as well?*

A. No, I made them up completely! I wanted Lucrezia to be able to watch the living and comment on their actions, but I did not want her to be visible or audible or even a patch of cold like all the other ghosts and presences seemed to be. So I made up the *immobili.* It means "still ones." It partly describes how Lucrezia is caught between the world of the living and the world of the afterlife—immobile or still—and partly refers to her stillness or inability to communicate with the living.

Q. *The two beagle puppies, Tristo and Isa, bring more than just "the cute" to the story. You're a beagle owner and beagle lover—did beagles as we know them today actually exist in the sixteenth century?*

A. There were certainly dogs called "beagles," and paintings show parti-colored hounds somewhat similar to the standardized breeds of beagles and foxhounds of today. Dogs were widely used for hunting, and miniature lapdogs were extremely popular among court ladies all over Europe. Queen Elizabeth I did indeed have a pack of small beaglelike dogs she called her "pocket beagles" or "singing beagles," so Tristo and Isa, unlike the *immobili,* are firmly based in real history.

Q. *Browning wrote his poem in 1842, during England's Victorian era, when there was revived interest in the Renaissance era. What prevailing attitudes of that time might have influenced Browning to see Alfonso as a madman and a murderer?*

A. A man like Duke Alfonso, a typically ruthless and vainglorious Renaissance prince, would have compared poorly with the Victorian ideal of the aristocratic male, the gentlemanly and relatively self-effacing figure of the queen's husband, Prince Albert. Thus, from the beginning the duke was seen as the villain of the piece. Part of my object in writing the book was to rescue him from this undeserved opprobrium.

Browning's style was considered experimental in his day, and he didn't really become a major commercial success until twenty-five years or so after he published "My Last Duchess." Today he's considered one of the foremost Victorian poets.

In 1846 he married Elizabeth Barrett, who was already one of the most popular writers of the day. Her *Sonnets from the Portuguese*—including #43, the famous "How do I love thee? Let me count the ways . . ."—was written during her romance with Robert Browning and published at his urging.

Q. *The written word is obviously a great spark to your imagination. Were there books you read in childhood, or in the years afterward, that greatly impacted your life? What stands out for you in your current reading?*

A. I began to read adult books long before I really understood what I was reading—it's fun to go back today and read them again as an adult. Writers who influenced me include Elizabeth Goudge (particularly *The White Witch*), Mary Stewart, and the incomparable Dorothy Dunnett. Currently I'm reading more nonfiction than fiction, but (not surprisingly) I love historical fiction and historical mysteries.

Q. *What novels by you might we hope to see in the future?*

A. I am presently working on another historical novel with the working title *The Silver Casket*, featuring Mary Queen of Scots, some secret quatrains of Nostradamus, a lost relic called the Black Rood of Scotland (a real object, which did indeed disappear mysteriously), and a girl who can read the future in flowers. After that, I'm planning a historical-but-not-quite book (or maybe books) set in sixteenth-century England. And I'd love to write more adventures of Barbara and Alfonso, in Ferrara and the other cities that were part of their world.

QUESTIONS FOR DISCUSSION

1. How does *The Second Duchess* compare to other novels about Renaissance Italy that you might have read? Did you enjoy the strong mystery element?

2. Barbara is portrayed as a woman of her time, who must submit to her powerful husband. Nevertheless, she sometimes defies him, and she manages to retain a sense of her own identity and ultimately forges a satisfying marriage with Alfonso. How do you think she manages to do this? How risky are her choices?

3. How do you see Alfonso—as the Renaissance ideal of a prince and a man; as a megalomaniac and murderer; or perhaps as a modern man of power, wealth, and position (a head of state, corporate CEO, mega-star actor, or major athlete)? Do you find him attractive or repellent?

4. Did you enjoy the sections from Lucrezia de' Medici's point of view? Did you sympathize with her or think she got what she deserved? Do you think Lucrezia has good reasons—or at least understandable motivation—for her anger and vengefulness?

5. Lucrezia de' Medici's personality is strongly influenced by Isabella, her older sister. How might this compare with the sexualization of very young girls today?

6. Which character do you find the most interesting and why? Is there anyone whose life you'd most like to live?

7. Were you familiar with Robert Browning's "My Last Duchess" before reading this novel? How is it similar to the novel? How has the novel reinterpreted the poem?

8. Barbara is portrayed as having been inspired by Baldassare Castiglione's *Book of the Courtier*. Were you strongly influenced and shaped by a book you read while growing up? What book, and what ideas and assumptions in it became part of you?

9. At the end of the novel, Alfonso destroys every drawing and painting by Frà Pandolf, despite the great esteem in which Alfonso holds brilliant artists and their work. Would you have done the same thing? Or does the worth of great art transcend the behavior, moral or immoral, of its human creator?

10. In Italy during the sixteenth century, the Catholic Church was highly corrupt. Did anything about its portrayal here particularly surprise you?

11. The clothes described in the book are dazzling, luxurious, and complicated. Did any outfit stand out for you? Would you enjoy wearing Barbara's clothes?

12. What do you think of the pageantry, formality, and extravagance of the d'Este court?

13. What do you think you'll take away from this novel? What aspect will leave the strongest impression on you?

SUGGESTIONS FOR FURTHER READING

Murder of a Medici Princess, by Caroline P. Murphy. Nonfiction as riveting as any novel. The true story of Isabella de' Medici, Lucrezia's older sister.

The Splendid Table: Recipes from Emilia-Romagna, the Heartland of Northern Italian Food, by Lynne Rossetto Kasper. A sumptuous cookbook with many traditional Ferrarese recipes. Also packed with fascinating tidbits of history.

I Modi: the Sixteen Pleasures: an Erotic Album of the Italian Renaissance, by Guilio Romano, Marcantonio Raimondi, Pietro Aretino, and Count Jean-Frederic-Maximilien de Waldeck, edited, translated from the Italian, and with a commentary by Lynne Lawner. Beautiful and sometimes shocking. Wonderful commentary.

Sacred Hearts, by Sarah Dunant. This is a wonderful novel also set in sixteenth-century Ferrara. All of Dunant's books are excellent.

For a complete bibliography, and further ideas on book club meetings, ranging from simplified modern recipes for Ferrarese-style tidbits to details on arranging a telephone or video chat with Elizabeth as part of your book club's discussion, visit www.elizabethloupas.com.

Elizabeth Loupas has worked as a writer, producer, and executive in the broadcasting industry; in other times and other places she has been a librarian, a magazine editor, a teacher, and a marketing consultant. She holds degrees in literary studies and library/information science.

She lives on the Elm Fork of the Trinity River, halfway between Dallas and Fort Worth, with her husband and two beagles. Please visit her at elizabethloupas.com.